Who is Jack Reacher?

Have you read them all?

Other Jack Reacher thrillers by Lee Child listed in the order in which they first appeared:

KILLING FLOOR

Introducing Jack Reacher: in a small town
in Georgia, the former military policeman
gets off a bus and is thrown into the county jail.
For a murder he didn't commit.

DIE TRYING

Reacher is locked in a stifling van with
a kidnapped woman claiming to be FBI. And driven
right across America. Into a brand new country.

TRIPWIRE

Reacher is digging swimming pools when
a detective comes round asking questions.
Then Reacher finds the guy dead, with his
fingertips sliced off. Was Reacher to blame?

THE VISITOR

Two women found at home, naked,
in a bath filled with paint. Both dead.
Both victims of a man just like Reacher.

ECHO BURNING

Texas. A pretty young woman.
Her husband's in jail.
When he comes out, he will kill her.
Can Reacher say no to a lady in distress?

WITHOUT FAIL

A Washington woman asks Reacher for help.
Her job? Protecting the Vice President.
Her problem? Someone wants him dead.

PERSUADER

Boston. As usual, Reacher takes the law
into his own hands. But a cop dies.
Has Reacher lost his sense of right and wrong?

THE ENEMY

Takes Reacher back to his army days.
A two-star general is found dead on Reacher's
watch. And then he finds another corpse:
the general's wife. Is this the start of Reacher's
disenchantment with the service?

ONE SHOT

A heartland city. A lone psychopath has shot
five people dead. But the accused guy says they
have the wrong man. And asks for Reacher.

THE HARD WAY

What starts on a busy New York street explodes
three thousand miles away in the English countryside.
With Reacher striding alone in the shadows.
Armed and dangerous.

For an exclusive preview
from the **NEW Jack Reacher** thriller

BAD LUCK
AND TROUBLE

turn to the back of this book

Jack Reacher: CV

Name:
Jack Reacher
(no middle name)

Nationality:
USA

Born:
29 October 1960

Vital statistics:
6 foot 5 inches;
220-250 lbs,
50-inch chest

Clothes:
3XLT coat,
95cm inside leg

Education:
US Army base schools
in Europe and the
Far East; West Point
Military Academy

Service:
13 years in US
Military Police;
demoted from
Major to Captain
in 1990, mustered
out with rank of
Major in 1997

Service awards:
Top row:
Silver Star, Defense
Superior Service Medal,
Legion of Merit
Middle row:
Soldier's Medal,
Bronze Star, Purple Heart
Bottom row:
'Junk awards'

Mother:
Josephine Moutier Reacher,
b.1930 in France, d.1990

Father:
Career US Marine,
served in Korea
and Vietnam

Brother:
Joe, b.1958, d. 1997;
5 years in US Military
Intelligence;
Treasury Dept.

Last known address:
Unknown

What he doesn't have:
Driver's licence; Federal
benefits; tax returns;
dependents

THE HARD WAY

Lee Child

BANTAM BOOKS

LONDON · TORONTO · SYDNEY · AUCKLAND · JOHANNESBURG

TRANSWORLD PUBLISHERS
61–63 Uxbridge Road, London W5 5SA
a division of The Random House Group Ltd
www.booksattransworld.co.uk

THE HARD WAY
A BANTAM BOOK : 9780553815870

First published in Great Britain
in 2006 by Bantam Press
a division of Transworld Publishers
Bantam edition published 2007

Addresses for Random House Group Ltd companies outside
the UK can be found at: www.randomhouse.co.uk
The Random House Group Ltd Reg. No. 954009

The Random House Group Ltd makes every effort to ensure that the
papers used in its books are made from trees that have been legally
sourced from well-managed and credibly certified forests.
Our paper procurement policy can be found at:
www.randomhouse co.uk/paper.htm

Typeset in 11/12pt Times by Kestrel Data, Exeter, Devon.
Printed and bound in Germany by
GGP Media GmbH, Pössneck.

2 4 6 8 10 9 7 5 3 1

For Katie and Jess:
two sweet sisters

ONE

Jack Reacher ordered espresso, double, no peel, no cube, foam cup, no china, and before it arrived at his table he saw a man's life change forever. Not that the waiter was slow. Just that the move was slick. So slick, Reacher had no idea what he was watching. It was just an urban scene, repeated everywhere in the world a billion times a day: a guy unlocked a car and got in and drove away. That was all.

But that was enough.

The espresso had been close to perfect, so Reacher went back to the same café exactly twenty-four hours later. Two nights in the same place was unusual for Reacher, but he figured great coffee was worth a change in his routine. The café was on the west side of Sixth Avenue in New York City, in the middle of the block between Bleecker and Houston. It occupied the ground floor of an undistinguished four-storey building. The upper storeys looked like anonymous rental apartments. The café itself looked like a transplant from a back street in Rome. Inside it had low light and scarred wooden walls and a dented chrome machine as hot and long as a locomotive, and a counter. Outside there was a single line of metal tables on the sidewalk behind a low canvas screen. Reacher took the same end table he had used the night before and chose the same seat. He stretched out and got comfortable and tipped his chair up on two legs. That put his back against the café's outside wall and left him looking east, across the sidewalk and the width of the avenue. He liked to sit outside in the summer, in New York City. Especially at night. He liked the electric darkness and the hot dirty air and the blasts of noise and traffic and the manic barking sirens and the crush of people. It helped a lonely man feel connected and isolated both at the same time.

He was served by the same waiter as the night before and ordered the same drink, double espresso in a foam cup, no sugar, no spoon. He paid for it as soon as it arrived and left his change on the table. That way he could leave exactly when he wanted to without insulting the waiter or bilking the owner or stealing the china. Reacher always arranged the smallest details in his life so he could move on at a split second's notice. It was an obsessive habit. He owned nothing and carried nothing. Physically he was a big man, but he cast a small shadow and left very little in his wake.

He drank his coffee slowly and felt the night heat come up off the sidewalk. He watched cars and people. Watched taxis flow north and garbage trucks pause at the kerbs. Saw knots of strange young people heading for clubs. Watched girls who had once been boys totter south. Saw a blue German sedan park on the block. Watched a compact man in a grey suit get out and walk north. Watched him thread between two sidewalk tables and head inside to where the café staff was clustered in back. Watched him ask them questions.

The guy was medium height, not young, not old, too solid to be called wiry, too slight to be called heavy. His hair was grey at the temples and cut short and neat. He kept himself balanced on the balls of his feet. His mouth didn't move much as he talked. But his eyes did. They flicked left and right tirelessly. The guy was about forty, Reacher guessed, and furthermore Reacher guessed he had gotten to be about forty by staying relentlessly aware of everything that was happening around him. Reacher had seen the same look in elite infantry veterans who had survived long jungle tours.

Then Reacher's waiter turned suddenly and pointed straight at him. The compact man in the grey suit stared over. Reacher stared back, over his shoulder, through the window. Eye contact was made. Without breaking it the man in the suit mouthed *thank you* to the waiter and started back out the way he had entered. He stepped through the door and made a right inside the low canvas screen and threaded his way down to Reacher's table. Reacher let him stand there mute for a moment while he made up his mind. Then he said 'Yes' to him, like an answer, not a question.

'Yes what?' the guy said back.

'Yes whatever,' Reacher said. 'Yes I'm having a pleasant evening, yes you can join me, yes you can ask me whatever it is you want to ask me.'

The guy scraped a chair out and sat down, his back to the river of traffic, blocking Reacher's view.

'Actually I do have a question,' he said.

'I know,' Reacher said. 'About last night.'

'How did you know that?' The guy's voice was low and quiet and his accent was flat and clipped and British.

'The waiter pointed me out,' Reacher said. 'And the only thing that distinguishes me from his other customers is that I was here last night and they weren't.'

'You're certain about that?'

'Turn your head away,' Reacher said. 'Watch the traffic.'

The guy turned his head away. Watched the traffic.

'Now tell me what I'm wearing,' Reacher said.

'Green shirt,' the British guy said. 'Cotton, baggy, cheap, doesn't look new, sleeves rolled to the elbow, over a green T-shirt, also cheap and not new, a little tight, untucked over flat-front khaki chinos, no socks, English shoes, pebbled leather, brown, not new, but not very old either, probably expensive. Frayed laces, like you pull on them too hard when you tie them. Maybe indicative of a self-discipline obsession.'

'OK,' Reacher said.

'OK what?'

'You notice things,' Reacher said. 'And I notice things. We're two of a kind. We're peas in a pod.

14

I'm the only customer here now who was also here last night. I'm certain of that. And that's what you asked the staff. Had to be. That's the only reason the waiter would have pointed me out.'

The guy turned back.

'Did you see a car last night?' he asked.

'I saw plenty of cars last night,' Reacher said. 'This is Sixth Avenue.'

'A Mercedes Benz. Parked over there.' The guy twisted again and pointed on a slight diagonal at a length of empty kerb by a fire hydrant on the other side of the street.

Reacher said, 'Silver, four-door sedan, an S-420, New York vanity plates starting OSC, a lot of city miles on it. Dirty paint, scuffed tyres, dinged rims, dents and scrapes on both bumpers.'

The guy turned back again.

'You saw it,' he said.

'It was right there,' Reacher said. 'Obviously I saw it.'

'Did you see it leave?'

Reacher nodded. 'Just before eleven forty-five a guy got in and drove it away.'

'You're not wearing a watch.'

'I always know what time it is.'

'It must have been closer to midnight.'

'Maybe,' Reacher said. 'Whatever.'

'Did you get a look at the driver?'

'I told you, I saw him get in and drive away.'

The guy stood up.

'I need you to come with me,' he said. Then he put his hand in his pocket. 'I'll buy your coffee.'

'I already paid for it.'

'So let's go.'

'Where?'

'To see my boss.'

'Who's your boss?'

'A man called Lane.'

'You're not a cop,' Reacher said. 'That's my guess. Based on observation.'

'Of what?'

'Your accent. You're not American. You're British. The NYPD isn't that desperate.'

'Most of us are Americans,' the British guy said. 'But you're right, we're not cops. We're private citizens.'

'What kind?'

'The kind that will make it worth your while if you give them a description of the individual who drove that car away.'

'Worth my while how?'

'Financially,' the guy said. 'Is there any other way?'

'Lots of other ways,' Reacher said. 'I think I'll stay right here.'

'This is very serious.'

'How?'

The guy in the suit sat down again.

'I can't tell you that,' he said.

'Goodbye,' Reacher said.

'Not my choice,' the guy said. 'Mr Lane made it mission-critical that nobody knows. For very good reasons.'

Reacher tilted his cup and checked the contents. Nearly gone.

'You got a name?' he asked.

'Do you?'

16

'You first.'

In response the guy stuck a thumb into the breast pocket of his suit coat and slid out a black leather business card holder. He opened it up and used the same thumb to slide out a single card. He passed it across the table. It was a handsome item. Heavy linen stock, raised lettering, ink that still looked wet. At the top it said: *Operational Security Consultants*.

'OSC,' Reacher said. 'Like the licence plate.'

The British guy said nothing.

Reacher smiled. 'You're security consultants and you got your car stolen? I can see how that could be embarrassing.'

The guy said, 'It's not the car we're worried about.'

Lower down on the business card was a name: *John Gregory*. Under the name was a subscript: *British Army, Retired*. Then a job title: *Executive Vice President*.

'How long have you been out?' Reacher asked.

'Of the British army?' the guy called Gregory said. 'Seven years.'

'Unit?'

'SAS.'

'You've still got the look.'

'You too,' Gregory said. 'How long have you been out?'

'Seven years,' Reacher said.

'Unit?'

'US Army CID, mostly.'

Gregory looked up. Interested. 'Investigator?'

'Mostly.'

'Rank?'

'I don't remember,' Reacher said. 'I've been a civilian seven years.'

'Don't be shy,' Gregory said. 'You were probably a lieutenant colonel at least.'

'Major,' Reacher said. 'That's as far as I got.'

'Career problems?'

'I had my share.'

'You got a name?'

'Most people do.'

'What is it?'

'Reacher.'

'What are you doing now?'

'I'm trying to get a quiet cup of coffee.'

'You need work?'

'No,' Reacher said. 'I don't.'

'I was a sergeant,' Gregory said.

Reacher nodded. 'I figured. SAS guys usually are. And you've got the look.'

'So will you come with me and talk to Mr Lane?'

'I told you what I saw. You can pass it on.'

'Mr Lane will want to hear it direct.'

Reacher checked his cup again. 'Where is he?'

'Not far. Ten minutes.'

'I don't know,' Reacher said. 'I'm enjoying my espresso.'

'Bring it with you. It's in a foam cup.'

'I prefer peace and quiet.'

'All I want is ten minutes.'

'Seems like a lot of fuss over a stolen car, even if it was a Mercedes Benz.'

'This is not about the car.'

'So what is it about?'

'Life and death,' Gregory said. 'Right now more likely death than life.'

Reacher checked his cup again. There was less than a lukewarm eighth-inch left, thick and scummy with espresso mud. That was all. He put the cup down.

'OK,' he said. 'So let's go.'

TWO

The blue German Sedan turned out to be a new BMW 7-series with OSC vanity plates on it. Gregory unlocked it from ten feet away with a key fob remote and Reacher got in the front passenger seat sideways and found the switch and moved the seat back for leg room. Gregory pulled out a small silver cell phone and dialled a number.

'Incoming with a witness,' he said, clipped and British. Then he closed the phone and fired up the engine and moved out into the midnight traffic.

The ten minutes turned out to be twenty. Gregory drove north on Sixth Avenue all the way through Midtown to 57th Street and then two blocks west. He turned north on Eighth, through Columbus Circle, onto Central Park West, and into 72nd Street. He stopped outside the Dakota Building.

'Nice digs,' Reacher said.

'Only the best for Mr Lane,' Gregory said, nothing in his voice.

They got out together and stood on the sidewalk

and another compact man in a grey suit stepped out of the shadows and into the car and drove it away. Gregory led Reacher into the building and up in the elevator. The lobbies and the hallways were as dark and baronial as the exterior.

'You ever seen Yoko?' Reacher asked.

'No,' Gregory said.

They got out on five and Gregory led the way around a corner and an apartment door opened for them. The lobby staff must have called ahead. The door that opened was heavy oak the colour of honey and the warm light that spilled out into the corridor was the colour of honey too. The apartment was a tall solid space. There was a small square foyer open to a big square living room. The living room had cool air and yellow walls and low table lights and comfortable chairs and sofas all covered in printed fabric. It was full of six men. None of them was sitting down. They were all standing up, silent. Three wore grey suits similar to Gregory's and three were in black jeans and black nylon warm-up jackets. Reacher knew immediately they were all ex-military. Just like Gregory. They all had the look. The apartment itself had the desperate quiet feel of a command bunker far from some distant point where a battle was right then turning to shit.

All six men turned and glanced at Reacher as he stepped inside. None of them spoke. But five men then glanced at the sixth, which Reacher guessed identified the sixth man as Mr Lane. The boss. He was half a generation older than his men. He was in a grey suit. He had grey hair, buzzed close to his scalp. He was maybe an inch above average height, and slender. His face was pale and full of worry. He was standing absolutely straight, racked with tension, with his fingertips spread and touching the top of a table that held an old-fashioned telephone and a framed photograph of a pretty woman.

'This is the witness,' Gregory said.

No reply.

'He saw the driver,' Gregory said.

The man at the table glanced down at the phone and then moved away from it, towards Reacher, looking him up and down, assessing, evaluating. He stopped a yard away and offered his hand.

'Edward Lane,' he said. 'I'm very pleased to meet you, sir.' His accent was American, originally from some hardscrabble place far from the Upper West Side of Manhattan. Arkansas, maybe, or rural Tennessee, but in either case overlaid by long exposure to the neutral tones of the military. Reacher said his own name and shook Lane's hand. It was dry, not warm, not cold.

'Tell me what you saw,' Lane said.

'I saw a guy get in a car,' Reacher said. 'He drove it away.'

'I need detail,' Lane said.

'Reacher is ex-US Army CID,' Gregory said. 'He described the Benz to perfection.'

'So describe the driver,' Lane said.

'I saw more of the car than the driver,' Reacher said.

'Where were you?'

'In a café. The car was a little north and east of me, across the width of Sixth Avenue. Maybe a twenty degree angle, maybe ninety feet away.'

'Why were you looking at it?'

'It was badly parked. It looked out of place. I guessed it was on a fireplug.'

'It was,' Lane said. 'Then what?'

'Then a guy crossed the street towards it. Not at a crosswalk. Through gaps in the traffic, at an angle. The angle was more or less the same as my line of sight, maybe twenty degrees. So most of what I saw was his back, all the way.'

'Then what?'

'He stuck the key in the door and got inside. Took off.'

'Going north, obviously, this being Sixth Avenue. Did he turn?'

'Not that I saw.'

'Can you describe him?'

'Blue jeans, blue shirt, blue baseball cap, white sneakers. The clothing was old and comfortable. The guy was average height, average weight.'

'Age?'

'I didn't see his face. Most of what I saw was his back. But he didn't move like a kid. He was at least in his thirties. Maybe forty.'

'How exactly did he move?'

'He was focused. He headed straight for the car. Not fast, but there was no doubt where he was going. The way he held his head, I think he was looking directly at the car the whole way. Like a definite destination. Like a target. And the way he held his shoulder, I think he might have had the key out in front of him, horizontally. Like

23

a tiny lance. Focused, and intent. And urgent. That's how he moved.'

'Where did he come from?'

'From behind my shoulder, more or less. He could have been walking north, and then stepped off the sidewalk at the café, north and east through the traffic.'

'Would you recognize him again?'

'Maybe,' Reacher said. 'But only by his clothes and his walk and his posture. Nothing that would convince anyone.'

'If he crossed through the traffic he must have glanced south to see what was coming at him. At least once. So you should have seen the right side of his face. Then when he was behind the wheel, you should have seen the left side.'

'Narrow angles,' Reacher said. 'And the light wasn't great.'

'There must have been headlight beams on him.'

'He was white,' Reacher said. 'No facial hair. That's all I saw.'

'White male,' Lane said. 'Thirty-five to forty-five. I guess that eliminates about eighty per cent of the population, maybe more, but it's not good enough.'

'Didn't you have insurance?' Reacher asked.

'This is not about the car,' Lane said.

'It was empty,' Reacher said.

'It wasn't empty,' Lane said.

'So what was in it?'

'Thank you, Mr Reacher,' Lane said. 'You've been very helpful.'

He turned and walked back to where he had

24

started, next to the table with the phone and the photograph. He stood erect beside it and spread his fingers again and laid the tips lightly on the polished wood, right next to the telephone, like his touch might detect an incoming call before the electronic pulse started the bell.

'You need help,' Reacher said. 'Don't you?'

'Why would you care?' Lane asked.

'Habit,' Reacher said. 'Reflex. Professional curiosity.'

'I've got help,' Lane said. He gestured with his free hand around the room. 'Navy SEALS, Delta Force, Recon Marines, Green Berets, SAS from Britain. The best in the world.'

'You need a different kind of help. The guy who took your car, these folks can start a war against him, that's for sure. But first you need to find him.'

No reply.

'What was in the car?' Reacher asked.

'Tell me about your career,' Lane said.

'It's been over a long time. That's its main feature.'

'Final rank?'

'Major.'

'Army CID?'

'Thirteen years.'

'Investigator?'

'Basically.'

'A good one?'

'Good enough.'

'110th Special Unit?'

'Some of the time. You?'

'Rangers and Delta. Started in Vietnam, ended

in the Gulf the first time around. Started a second lieutenant, finished a full colonel.'

'What was in the car?'

Lane looked away. Held still and quiet for a long, long time. Then he looked back, like a decision had been made.

'You need to give me your word about something,' he said.

'Like what?'

'No cops. That's going to be your first piece of advice, go to the cops. But I'll refuse to do it, and I need your word that you won't go behind my back.'

Reacher shrugged.

'OK,' he said.

'Say it.'

'No cops.'

'Say it again.'

'No cops,' Reacher said again.

'You got an ethical problem with that?'

'No,' Reacher said.

'No FBI, no nobody,' Lane said. 'We handle this ourselves. Understand? You break your word, I'll put your eyes out. I'll have you blinded.'

'You've got a funny way of making friends.'

'I'm looking for help here, not friends.'

'My word is good,' Reacher said.

'Say you understand what I'll do if you break it.'

Reacher looked around the room. Took it all in. A quiet desperate atmosphere and six Special Forces veterans, all full of subdued menace, all as hard as nails, all looking right back at him, all full of unit loyalty and hostile suspicion of the outsider.

'You'll have me blinded,' Reacher said.

'You better believe it,' Lane said.

'What was in the car?'

Lane moved his hand away from the phone. He picked up the framed photograph. He held it two-handed, flat against his chest, high up, so that Reacher felt he had two people staring back at him. Above, Lane's pale and worried features. Below, under glass, a woman of breathtaking classical beauty. Dark hair, green eyes, high cheekbones, a bud of a mouth, photographed with passion and expertise and printed by a master.

'This is my wife,' Lane said.

Reacher nodded. Said nothing.

'Her name is Kate,' Lane said.

Nobody spoke.

'Kate disappeared late yesterday morning,' Lane said. 'I got a call in the afternoon. From her kidnappers. They wanted money. That's what was in the car. You watched one of my wife's kidnappers collect their ransom.'

Silence.

'They promised to release her,' Lane said. 'And it's been twenty-four hours. And they haven't called back.'

27

THREE

Edward Lane held the framed photograph like
an offering and Reacher stepped forward to
take it. He tilted it to catch the light. Kate Lane
was beautiful, no question about it. She was
hypnotic. She was younger than her husband by
maybe twenty years, which put her in her early
thirties. Old enough to be all woman, young
enough to be flawless. In the picture she was
gazing at something just beyond the edge of
the print. Her eyes blazed with love. Her mouth
seemed ready to burst into a wide smile. The
photographer had frozen the first tiny hint of it
so that the pose seemed dynamic. It was a still
picture, but it looked like it was about to move.
The focus and the grain and the detail were
immaculate. Reacher didn't know much about
photography, but he knew he was holding a high-
end product. The frame alone might have cost
what he used to make in a month, back in the
army.

'My Mona Lisa,' Lane said. 'That's how I think
of that picture.'

Reacher passed it back. 'Is it recent?'

Lane propped it upright again, next to the telephone.

'Less than a year old,' he said.

'Why no cops?'

'There are reasons.'

'This kind of a thing, they usually do a good job.'

'No cops,' Lane said.

Nobody spoke.

'You were a cop,' Lane said. 'You can do what they do.'

'I can't,' Reacher said.

'You were a military cop. Therefore all things being equal you can do better than them.'

'All things aren't equal. I don't have their resources.'

'You can make a start.'

The room went very quiet. Reacher glanced at the phone, and the photograph.

'How much money did they want?' he asked.

'One million dollars in cash,' Lane answered.

'And that was in the car? A million bucks?'

'In the trunk. In a leather bag.'

'OK,' Reacher said. 'Let's all sit down.'

'I don't feel like sitting down.'

'Relax,' Reacher said. 'They're going to call back. Probably very soon. I can pretty much guarantee that.'

'How?'

'Sit down. Start at the beginning. Tell me about yesterday.'

So Lane sat down, in the armchair next to the telephone table, and started to talk about the previous day. Reacher sat at one end of a sofa.

Gregory sat next to him. The other five guys distributed themselves around the room, two sitting, two squatting on chair arms, one leaning against the wall.

'Kate went out at ten o'clock in the morning,' Lane said. 'She was heading for Bloomingdale's, I think.'

'You think?'

'I allow her some freedom of action. She doesn't necessarily supply me with a detailed itinerary. Not every day.'

'Was she alone?'

'Her daughter was with her.'

'*Her* daughter?'

'She has an eight-year-old by her first marriage. Her name is Jade.'

'She lives with you here?'

Lane nodded.

'So where is Jade now?'

'Missing, obviously,' Lane said.

'So this is a *double* kidnapping?' Reacher said.

Lane nodded again. 'Triple, in a way. Their driver didn't come back either.'

'You didn't think to mention this before?'

'Does it make a difference? One person or three?'

'Who was the driver?'

'A guy called Taylor. British, ex-SAS. A good man. One of us.'

'What happened to the car?'

'It's missing.'

'Does Kate go to Bloomingdale's often?'

Lane shook his head. 'Only occasionally. And never on a predictable pattern. We do nothing regular or predictable. I vary her drivers, vary her routes, sometimes we stay out of the city altogether.'

'Because? You got a lot of enemies?'

'My fair share. My line of work attracts enemies.'

'You're going to have to explain your line of work to me. You're going to have to tell me who your enemies are.'

'Why are you sure they're going to call?'

'I'll get to that,' Reacher said. 'Tell me about the first conversation. Word for word.'

'They called at four o'clock in the afternoon. It went pretty much how you would expect. You know, we have your wife, we have your daughter.'

'Voice?'

'Altered. One of those electronic squawk boxes. Very metallic, like a robot in a movie. Loud and deep, but that doesn't mean anything. They can alter the pitch and the volume.'

'What did you say to them?'

'I asked them what they wanted. They said a million bucks. I asked them to put Kate on the line. They did, after a short pause.' Lane closed his eyes. 'She said, you know, help me, help me.' He opened his eyes. 'Then the guy with the squawk box came back on and I agreed to the money. No hesitation. The guy said he would call back in an hour with instructions.'

'And did he?'

Lane nodded. 'At five o'clock. I was told to wait six hours and put the money in the trunk of the Mercedes you saw and have it driven down to the Village and parked in that spot at eleven forty exactly. The driver was to lock it up and walk

31

away and put the keys through a mail slot in the front door of a certain building on the southwest corner of Spring Street and West Broadway. Then he was to walk away and keep on walking away, south on West Broadway. Someone would move in behind him and enter the building and collect the keys. If my driver stopped or turned around or even looked back, Kate would die. Likewise if there was a tracking device on the car.'

'That was it, word for word?'

Lane nodded.

'Nothing else?'

Lane shook his head.

'Who drove the car down?' Reacher asked.

'Gregory,' Lane said.

'I followed the instructions,' Gregory said. 'To the letter. I couldn't risk anything else.'

'How far of a walk was it?' Reacher asked him.

'Six blocks.'

'What was the building with the mail slot?'

'Abandoned,' Gregory said. 'Or awaiting renovations. One or the other. It was empty, anyway. I went back there tonight, before I came to the café. No sign of habitation.'

'How good was this guy Taylor? Did you know him in Britain?'

Gregory nodded. 'SAS is a big family. And Taylor was very good indeed.'

'OK,' Reacher said.

'OK what?' Lane said.

'There are some obvious early conclusions,' Reacher said.

FOUR

Reacher said, 'The first conclusion is that Taylor is already dead. These guys clearly know you to some extent, and therefore we should assume they knew who and what Taylor was. Therefore they wouldn't keep him alive. No reason for it. Too dangerous.'

Lane asked, 'Why do you think they know me?'

'They asked for a specific car,' Reacher said. 'And they suspected you might have a million dollars in cash lying around. They asked for it after the banks were closed and told you to deliver it before the banks reopened. Not everyone could comply with those conditions. Usually even very rich people take a little time to get a million bucks in cash together. They get temporary loans, wire transfers, they use stock as collateral, stuff like that. But these guys seemed to know that you could just cough it up instantly.'

'How do they know me?'

'You tell me.'

Nobody spoke.

'And there are three of them,' Reacher said. 'One to guard Kate and Jade wherever they took them. One to watch Gregory's back while he walked south on West Broadway, on a cell phone to a third who was waiting to move in and pick up the keys as soon as it was safe.'

Nobody spoke.

'And they're based a minimum two hundred miles upstate,' Reacher said. 'Let's assume the initial action went down before about eleven o'clock yesterday morning. But they didn't call for more than five hours. Because they were driving. Then they issued instructions at five o'clock for a ransom drop more than six hours later. Because they needed the six hours because two of them had to drive all the way back. Five, six hours, that's two hundred miles, maybe two fifty, maybe more.'

'Why upstate?' Lane said. 'They could be anywhere.'

'Not south or west,' Reacher said. 'Or they would have asked for the ransom car south of Canal, so they could head straight for the Holland Tunnel. Not east on Long Island, or they would have wanted to be near the Midtown Tunnel. No, north on Sixth was what they wanted. That implies they were happy to head up towards the George Washington Bridge, or the Henry Hudson and the Saw Mill, or the Triborough and the Major Deegan. Eventually they hit the Thruway, probably. They could be in the Catskills or anywhere. A farm, probably. Certainly somewhere with a big garage block or a barn.'

'Why?'

'They just inherited your Mercedes Benz. Right after hijacking whatever Taylor drove to

Bloomingdale's yesterday. They need a place to hide them.'

'Taylor was driving a Jaguar.'

'There you go. Their place must look like a luxury car lot by now.'

'Why are you so sure they're going to call back?'

'Because of human nature. Right now they're mad as hell. They're kicking themselves. They know you, but maybe not all that well. They took a chance and asked for a million dollars in cash, and you bagged it up without a moment's hesitation. You shouldn't have done that. You should have gambled and stalled. Because now they're saying, damn it, we should have asked for more. They're saying, we should have tested the limits. So they're going to get back on the phone and hit you up for another chunk. They're going to feel out exactly how much cash you've got lying around. They're going to bleed you dry.'

'Why wait so long?'

'Because it's a significant change in strategy,' Reacher said. 'Therefore they're arguing about it. They've been arguing about it all day. That's human nature, too. Three guys always argue, pro and con, stick to the plan or improvise, play it safe or take the risk.'

Nobody spoke.

'How much *have* you got in cash?' Reacher asked.

'I'm not going to tell you,' Lane said.

'Five million,' Reacher said. 'That's what they'll ask for next. The phone is going to ring and they're going to ask for another five million dollars.'

Seven pairs of eyes turned towards the phone. It didn't ring.

'In another car,' Reacher said. 'They must have a big barn.'

'Is Kate safe?' Lane asked.

'Right now, she's as safe as houses,' Reacher said. 'She's their meal ticket. And you did the right thing, asking to hear her voice the first time. That set up a good pattern. They'll have to repeat it. The problem will come after they've had the last payment. That's the toughest part of any kidnap. Giving the money away is easy. Getting the person back is hard.'

The phone stayed silent.

'So should I stall?' Lane asked.

'I would,' Reacher said. 'Parcel it out. Keep it going. Buy some time.'

The phone didn't ring. No sound in the room except the hiss of cooled air and men breathing low. Reacher glanced around. Everyone was waiting patiently. Special Forces soldiers were good at waiting. For all the occasional spectacular action they saw, they spent a lot more time waiting, standing by, passing the time in readiness. And then nine times out of ten they were stood down, action cancelled.

The phone didn't ring.

'Good conclusions,' Lane said, to nobody in particular, through the silence. 'Three guys, far away. Upstate. On a farm.'

*   *   *

But Reacher was completely wrong. Just four miles away through the electric city darkness, right there on the island of Manhattan, a lone man pushed open a door to a small, hot room. Then he stepped back. Kate Lane and her daughter Jade passed in front of him without meeting his eyes. They stepped inside the room and saw two beds. The beds looked hard and narrow. The room felt damp and unused. The window was draped with black cloth. The cloth was duct-taped to the walls, across the top, across the bottom, down both sides.

The lone man closed the door and walked away.

FIVE

The phone rang at exactly one o'clock in the morning. Lane snatched it out of the cradle and said, 'Yes?' Reacher heard a faint voice from the earpiece, distorted twice, first by a machine and then again by a bad connection. Lane said, 'What?' and there was a reply. Lane said, 'Put Kate on the phone. You've got to do that first.' Then there was a pause, and then there was a different voice. A woman's voice, distorted, panicked, breathy. It said just one word, possibly Lane's name, and then it exploded in a scream. The scream died into silence and Lane screwed his eyes shut and the electronic robot voice came back and barked six short syllables. Lane said, 'OK, OK, OK,' and Reacher heard the line go dead.

Lane sat in silence, his eyes clamped shut, his breathing fast and ragged. Then his eyes opened and moved from face to face and stopped on Reacher's.

'Five million dollars,' he said. 'You were right. How did you know?'

'It was the obvious next step,' Reacher

said. 'One, five, ten, twenty. That's how people think.'

'You've got a crystal ball. You can see the future. I'm putting you on the payroll. Twenty-five grand a month, like all these guys.'

'This isn't going to last a month,' Reacher said. 'It can't. It's going to be all over in a couple of days.'

'I agreed to the money,' Lane said. 'I couldn't stall. They were hurting her.'

Reacher nodded. Said nothing.

Gregory asked, 'Instructions later?'

'In an hour,' Lane said.

The room went quiet again. More waiting. All around the room men checked their watches and settled back imperceptibly. Lane put the silent handset back in the cradle and stared off into space. But Reacher leaned forward and tapped him on the knee.

'We need to talk,' he said quietly.

'About what?'

'Background. We should try to figure out who these guys are.'

'OK,' Lane said vaguely. 'We'll go to the office.'

He stood up slowly and led Reacher out of the living room and through a kitchen to a maid's room in back. It was small and plain and square and had been fixed up as an office. Desk, computer, fax machine, phones, file cabinets, shelves.

'Tell me about Operational Security Consultants,' Reacher said.

Lane sat down in the desk chair and turned it to face the room.

'Not much to tell,' he said. 'We're just a bunch of ex-military trying to keep busy.'

'Doing what?'

'Whatever people need. Bodyguarding, mostly. Corporate security. Like that.'

There were two framed photographs on the desk. One was a smaller reprint of Kate's stunning picture from the living room. A seven-by-five instead of a fourteen-by-eleven, in a similar expensive gold frame. The other was of another woman, about the same age, blonde where Kate was dark, blue eyes instead of green. But just as beautiful, and photographed just as masterfully.

'Bodyguarding?' Reacher said.

'Mostly.'

'You're not convincing me, Mr Lane. Bodyguards don't make twenty-five grand a month. Bodyguards are big dumb lumps lucky to make a tenth of that. And if you had guys trained for close personal protection you'd have sent one of them out with Kate and Jade yesterday morning. Taylor driving, maybe Gregory riding shotgun. But you didn't, which suggests that bodyguarding isn't exactly the business you're in.'

'My business is confidential,' Lane said.

'Not any more. Not if you want your wife and daughter back.'

No reply.

'A Jaguar, a Mercedes, and a BMW,' Reacher said. 'Plus more where they came from, I'm sure. Plus a co-op in the Dakota. Plus lots of cash lying around. Plus half a dozen guys on twenty-five grand a month. Altogether big bucks.'

'All legal.'

'Except you don't want the cops involved.'

Involuntarily Lane glanced at the photograph of the blonde woman.

'No connection,' he said. 'That's not the reason.'

Reacher followed Lane's gaze.

'Who is she?' he asked.

'Was,' Lane said.

'Was what?'

'Anne,' Lane said. 'She was my first wife.'

'And?'

Silence for a long moment.

'You see, I've been through this before,' Lane said. 'Five years ago. Anne was taken from me. In just the same way. But back then I followed procedure. I called the cops, even though the men on the phone had been very clear that I shouldn't. The cops called the FBI.'

'And what happened?'

'The FBI screwed up somehow,' Lane said. 'They must have been spotted at the ransom drop. Anne died. They found her body a month later in New Jersey.'

Reacher said nothing.

'That's why there's no cops this time,' Lane said.

SIX

Reacher and Lane sat in silence for a long time. Then Reacher said, 'Fifty-five minutes. You should be ready for the next call.'

'You're not wearing a watch,' Lane said.

'I always know what time it is.'

Reacher followed him back to the living room. Lane stood by the table again, with his fingers spread on the surface. Reacher guessed he wanted to take the call with his men all around him. Maybe he needed the comfort. Or the support.

The phone rang right on time, at two o'clock in the morning exactly. Lane picked it up and listened. Reacher heard faint robot squawks from the earpiece. Lane said, 'Put Kate on,' but his request must have been refused, because then he said, 'Please don't hurt her.' He listened for another minute and said, 'OK.' Then he hung up.

'Five hours from now,' he said. 'Seven o'clock in the morning. Same place, same routine. The blue BMW. One person only.'

'I'll do it,' Gregory said.

The other men in the room stirred with

frustration. 'We should all be there,' one of them said. He was a small dark American who looked like an accountant, except for his eyes, which were as flat and dead as a hammerhead shark's. 'Ten minutes later we would know where she is. I can promise you that.'

'One man,' Lane said. 'That was the instruction.'

'This is New York City,' the guy with the shark's eyes said. 'There are always people around. They can't be expecting deserted streets.'

'Apparently they know us,' Lane said. 'They would recognize you.'

'I could go,' Reacher said. 'They wouldn't recognize me.'

'You came in with Gregory. They might be watching the building.'

'Conceivable,' Reacher said. 'But unlikely.'

Lane said nothing.

'Your call,' Reacher said.

'I'll think about it,' Lane said.

'Think fast. Better if I leave here well in advance.'

'Decision in one hour,' Lane said. He moved away from the phone and headed back towards the office. *Gone to count out the money*, Reacher thought. He wondered briefly what five million dollars looked like. *The same as one million*, he guessed. *But with hundreds instead of twenties*.

'How much money has he got?' Reacher asked.

'A lot,' Gregory said.

'He's down six million in two days.'

The guy with the shark's eyes smiled.

'We'll get it back,' he said. 'You can count on

43

that. As soon as Kate's home safe we'll make our move. Then we'll see who's down and who's up. Someone poked a stick in the wrong hornets' nest this time, that's for damn sure. And they wasted Taylor. He was one of us. They'll be sorry they were ever born.'

Reacher glanced into the guy's empty eyes and believed every word he said. Then the guy stuck out his hand, abruptly. And a little warily. 'I'm Carter Groom,' he said. 'I'm pleased to meet you. I think. I mean, as much as I can be, given the circumstances.'

The four other men introduced themselves with a quiet cascade of names and handshakes. Each man was polite, nothing more. Each was full of reserve in front of a stranger. Reacher tried to tie the names to faces. Gregory he already knew. A guy with a big scar over his eye was called Addison. The shortest guy among them was a Latino called Perez. The tallest was called Kowalski. There was a black guy called Burke.

'Lane told me you do bodyguarding and corporate security,' Reacher said.

Sudden silence. No reply.

'Don't worry,' Reacher said. 'I wasn't convinced anyway. My guess is you guys were all operational noncoms. Fighting men. So I think your Mr Lane is into something else entirely.'

'Like what?' Gregory asked.

'I think he's pimping mercenaries,' Reacher said.

The guy called Groom shook his head. 'Wrong choice of words, pal.'

'What would be the right choice?'

'We're a private military corporation,' Groom said. 'You got a problem with that?'

'I don't really have an opinion.'

'Well, you better get one, and it better be a good one. We're legal. We work for the Pentagon, just like we always did, and just like you did, back in the day.'

'Privatization,' Burke said. 'The Pentagon loves it. It's more efficient. The era of big government is over.'

'How many guys have you got?' Reacher asked. 'Just what's here?'

Groom shook his head again. 'We're the A-team. Like senior NCOs. Then there's a Rolodex full of B-team squad members. We took a hundred guys to Iraq.'

'Is that where you've been? Iraq?'

'And Colombia and Panama and Afghanistan. We go anywhere Uncle Sam needs us.'

'What about where Uncle Sam doesn't need you?'

Nobody spoke.

'My guess is the Pentagon pays by cheque,' Reacher said. 'But there seems to be an awful lot of cash around here, too.'

No response.

'Africa?' Reacher said.

No response.

'Whatever,' Reacher said. 'Not my business where you've been. All I need to know is where Mrs Lane has been. For the last couple of weeks.'

'What difference does that make?' Kowalski asked.

'There was some surveillance,' Reacher said.

45

'Don't you think? I don't suppose the bad guys were just hanging out at Bloomingdale's every day on the off-chance.'

'Mrs Lane was in the Hamptons,' Gregory said. 'With Jade, most of the summer. They only came back three days ago.'

'Who drove them back?'

'Taylor.'

'And then they were based here?'

'Correct.'

'Anything happen out in the Hamptons?'

'Like what?' Groom asked.

'Like anything unusual,' Reacher said. 'Anything out of the ordinary.'

'Not really,' Groom said.

'A woman showed up at the door one day,' Gregory said.

'What kind of a woman?'

'Just a woman. She was fat.'

'Fat?'

'Kind of heavyset. About forty. Long hair, centre part. Mrs Lane took her walking on the beach. Then the woman left. I figured it was a friend on a visit.'

'Ever saw her before?'

Gregory shook his head. 'Maybe an old friend. From the past.'

'What did Mrs Lane and Jade do after they got back here to the city?'

'I don't think they did anything yet.'

'No, she went out once,' Groom said. 'Mrs Lane, I mean. Not Jade. On her own, shopping. I drove her.'

'Where?' Reacher asked.

'Staples.'

'The office supply store?' Reacher had seen them all over. A big chain, red and white décor, huge places full of stuff he had no need of. 'What did she buy?'

'Nothing,' Groom said. 'I waited twenty minutes on the kerb, and she didn't bring anything out.'

'Maybe she arranged a delivery,' Gregory said.

'She could have done that on-line. No need to drag me out in the car.'

'So maybe she was just browsing,' Gregory said.

'Weird place to browse,' Reacher said. 'Who does that?'

'School is back soon,' Groom said. 'Maybe Jade needed stuff.'

'In which case she'd have gone along,' Reacher said. 'Don't you think? And she'd have bought something.'

'Did she take something in?' Gregory asked. 'Maybe she was returning something.'

'She had her tote,' Groom said. 'It's possible.' Then he looked up, beyond Reacher's shoulder. Edward Lane was back in the room. He was carrying a large leather duffel, and struggling with its bulk. *Five million dollars*, Reacher thought. *So that's what it looks like*. Lane dropped the bag on the floor at the entrance to the foyer. It thumped down on the hardwood and settled like the carcass of a small fat animal.

'I need to see a picture of Jade,' Reacher said.

'Why?' Lane asked.

'Because you want me to pretend I'm a cop. And pictures are the first things cops want to see.'

47

'Bedroom,' Lane said.

So Reacher fell in behind him and followed him to a bedroom. It was another tall square space, painted a chalky off-white, as serene as a monastery and as quiet as a tomb. There was a cherrywood king-size bed with pencil posts at the corners. Matching tables at each side. A matching armoire that might have held a television set. A matching desk, with a chair standing in front of it and a framed photograph sitting on it. The photograph was a ten-by-eight, rectangular, set horizontal, not vertical, on the axis that photographers call landscape, not portrait. But it was a portrait. That was for sure. It was a portrait of two people. On the right was Kate Lane. It was the same shot as in the living-room print. The same pose, the same eyes, the same developing smile. But the living-room print had been cropped to exclude the object of her affection, which was her daughter Jade. Jade was on the left of the bedroom picture. Her pose was a mirror image of her mother's. They were about to look at each other, love in their eyes, smiles about to break out on their faces like they were sharing a private joke. In the picture Jade was maybe seven years old. She had long dark hair, slightly wavy, as fine as silk. She had green eyes and porcelain skin. She was a beautiful kid. It was a beautiful photograph.

'May I?' Reacher asked.

Lane nodded. Said nothing. Reacher picked the picture up and looked closer. The photographer had caught the bond between mother and child perfectly and completely. Quite apart from the similarity in appearance there was no doubt about their relationship. No doubt at all. They were mother and daughter. But they were also friends. They looked like they shared a lot. It was a great picture.

'Who took this?' Reacher asked.

'I found a guy downtown,' Lane said. 'Quite famous. Very expensive.'

Reacher nodded. Whoever the guy was, he was worth his fee. Although the print quality wasn't quite as good as the living-room copy. The colours were a little less subtle and the contours of the faces were slightly plastic. Maybe it was a machine print. Maybe Lane's budget hadn't run to a custom hand-print where his stepdaughter was concerned.

'Very nice,' Reacher said. He put the photograph back on the desk, quietly. The room was totally silent. Reacher had once read that the Dakota was the most soundproof building in New York City. It had been built at the same time as Central Park was landscaped. The builder had packed three feet of excavated Central Park clay and mud between the floors and the ceilings. The walls were thick, too. All that mass made the building feel like it was carved from solid rock. *Which must have been a good thing*, Reacher figured, *back when John Lennon lived here*.

'OK?' Lane said. 'Seen enough?'

'You mind if I check the desk?'

'Why?'

'It's Kate's, right?'

'Yes, it is.'

'So it's what the cops would do.'

Lane shrugged and Reacher started with the bottom drawers. The left-hand drawer held boxes of stationery and notepaper and cards engraved simply with the name *Kate Lane*. The right-hand drawer was fitted with file hangers and the contents related exclusively to Jade's education. She was enrolled at a private school nine blocks north of the apartment. It was an expensive school, judging by the bills and the cancelled cheques. The cheques were all drawn on Kate Lane's personal account. The upper drawers held pens and pencils, envelopes, stamps, self-stick return address labels, a chequebook. And credit card receipts. But nothing very significant. Nothing recent. Nothing from Staples, for instance.

The centre drawer at the top held nothing but two American passports, one for Kate and one for Jade.

'Who is Jade's father?' Reacher asked.

'Does it matter?'

'It might. If this was a straightforward abduction, we'd definitely have to look at him. Estranged parents are who usually snatch kids.'

'But this is a kidnap for ransom. And it's Kate they're talking about. Jade was just there by chance.'

'Abductions can be disguised. And her father would need to clothe and feed her. And send her to school. He might want money.'

'He's dead,' Lane said. 'He died of stomach cancer when Jade was three.'

'Who was he?'

'He owned a jewellery store. Kate ran it for a

year, afterwards. Not very well. She had been a model. But that's where I met her. In the store. I was buying a watch.'

'Any other relatives? Possessive grandparents, aunts, uncles?'

'Nobody that I ever met. Therefore nobody that saw Jade in the last several years. Therefore nobody you could really describe as possessive.'

Reacher closed the centre drawer. Straightened the photograph and turned around.

'Closet?' he said.

Lane pointed at one of a pair of narrow white doors. Behind it was a closet, large for a New York City apartment, small for anywhere else. It had a pull chain for a light. Inside were racks of women's clothes and shoes. Fragrance in the air. There was a jacket neatly folded on the floor. Ready for the dry cleaner, Reacher thought. He picked it up. There was a Bloomingdale's label in it. He checked the pockets. Nothing in them.

'What was she wearing when she went out?' he asked.

'I'm not sure,' Lane said.

'Who would know?'

'We all left before her,' Lane said. 'I don't think anyone was still here. Except Taylor.'

Reacher closed the closet door and stepped away to the armoire. It had double doors at the top and drawers below. One of the drawers held jewellery. One was full of miscellaneous junk like paper packets of spare buttons from new garments and discarded pocket change. One was full of lacy underwear. Bras, pants, all of them either white or black.

'May I see Jade's room?' Reacher asked.

Lane led him through a short interior hallway. Jade's room was all pale pastels and kid stuff. Furry bears, china dolls, toys, games. A low bed. Pyjamas folded on the pillow. A nightlight still burning. A low desk covered in drawings done with wax crayons on butcher paper. A small chair, neatly tucked in.

Nothing that meant anything to a military cop.

'I'm done,' Reacher said. 'I'm very sorry to intrude.'

He followed Lane back to the living room. The leather bag was still there on the floor, near the foyer. Gregory and the five other soldiers were still in their places, still quiet and pensive.

'Decision time,' Lane said. 'Do we assume Reacher was observed entering the building tonight? Or not?'

'I didn't see anyone,' Gregory said. 'And I think it's very unlikely. Round-the-clock surveillance would eat manpower. So I would say not.'

'I agree,' Lane said. 'I think Reacher is still Joe Public to them. So he should be on the street at seven o'clock. We should try a little surveillance of our own.'

There was no objection. Reacher nodded.

'I'll watch the front of the Spring Street building,' he said. 'That way I'll see one of them at least. Maybe two of them.'

'Don't show yourself,' Lane said. 'You understand my concern, right?'

'Completely,' Reacher said. 'They won't make me.'

'Surveillance only. Absolutely no intervention.'

'Don't worry.'

'They'll be there early,' Lane said. 'So you be in position earlier.'

'Don't worry,' Reacher said again. 'I'll leave right now.'

'Don't you want to know which building you're supposed to be watching?'

'I don't need to know,' Reacher said. 'I'll see Gregory leave the keys.'

Then he let himself out of the apartment and rode down in the elevator. Nodded to the doorman and walked out to the street. Headed for the subway at 72nd and Broadway.

The woman who was watching the building saw him go. She had seen him arrive with Gregory, and now he was leaving alone. She checked her watch and made a note of the time. She craned her head and tracked his progress west. Then she lost sight of him and moved back deep in the shadows.

SEVEN

First in was a 9 train. Reacher used the Metrocard he had bought the day before and rode eleven stops south to Houston Street. Then he came up from under the ground and walked south on Varick. It was past three o'clock in the morning, and very quiet. In Reacher's experience the city that doesn't sleep sometimes did, at least for an hour or two, on some nights of the week. There was sometimes a short intermission after the late folk had rolled home and before the early people had gotten up. Then the city went silent and took a breath and shiny darkness owned the streets. That was Reacher's time. He liked to picture the sleeping people stacked twelve, thirty, fifty storeys high, often head to head with perfect strangers on opposite sides of thin apartment walls, deep in slumber, unaware of the tall quiet man striding beneath them in the shadows.

He made a left on Charlton Street, and crossed Sixth Avenue, and Charlton became Prince. Three blocks later he was on West Broadway, in the heart of Soho, a block north of Spring Street, three hours and forty minutes ahead of schedule.

He walked south, with the leisurely gait of a man with a place to go but in no hurry to get there. West Broadway was wider than the cross streets, so as he ambled past Spring he had a good view of the southwest corner. There was a narrow iron-fronted building with a dull red door set high. Three steps up to it. The building's façade was covered with graffiti low down and laced with a complex fire escape high up. The upper storey windows were filthy and backed with some kind of a dark fabric. On the ground floor there was a single window, pasted over with faded building permits. There was a mail slot in the door, a narrow rectangle with a flap. Maybe once it had been shiny brass, but now it was dull with tarnish and pitted by corrosion.

That's the one, Reacher thought. *Got to be.*

He turned east a block later on Broome and then backtracked north on Greene Street, past shuttered boutiques that sold sweaters that cost more than first-class airplane tickets and household furniture that cost more than domestic automobiles. He turned west on Prince and completed his circuit around the block. Walked south on West Broadway again and found a doorway on the east sidewalk. It had a stoop a foot and a half high. He kicked garbage out of his way and lay down on his back, his head cradled on his folded arms, his head canted sideways like a somnolent drunk, but with his eyes half open and focused on the dull red door seventy feet away.

Kate Lane had been told not to move and to make absolutely no noise at all, but she decided to take a risk. She couldn't sleep, obviously. Neither could Jade. How could anyone sleep, under circumstances like theirs? So Kate crept out of her bed and grasped the rail at the end and inched the whole bed sideways.

'Mom, don't,' Jade whispered. 'You're making a noise.'

Kate didn't answer. Just crept to the head of the bed and inched it sideways. After three more cautious back-and-forth movements she had her mattress butted up hard against Jade's. Then she got back under the sheet and took her daughter in her arms. Held her tight. If they had to be awake, at least they could be awake together.

The clock in Reacher's head crept around to six in the morning. Down in the brick and iron canyons of Soho it was still dark, but the sky above was already brightening. The night had been warm. Reacher hadn't been uncomfortable. He had been in worse spots. Many times. Often for much longer. So far he had seen no activity at the dull red door. But the early people were already out and about all around him. Cars and trucks were moving on the streets. People were passing by on both sidewalks. But nobody was looking at him. He was just a guy in a doorway.

He rolled onto his back and looked around. The door he was blocking was a plain grey metal thing. No exterior handle. Maybe a fire exit, maybe a loading dock. With a little luck he wouldn't be disturbed before seven. He rolled on his side and gazed south and west again. Arched his back like he was relieving a cramp, then glanced north. He figured whoever was coming would be in position soon. They clearly weren't fools. They would aim for a careful stake-out. They would check rooftops and windows and parked cars for watching cops. Maybe they would check doorways, too. But Reacher had never been mistaken for a cop. There was always something phoney about a cop who dresses down. Reacher was the real thing.

Cops, he thought.

The word snagged in his mind the way a twig on a current catches on a riverbank. It hung up just briefly before spinning clear and floating away. Then he saw a real-life cop, in a car, coming north, going slow. Reacher squirmed upright and propped his back against the grey door. Rested his head against the cold hard metal. Sleeping horizontally in public seemed to be against the city's vagrancy laws. But there appeared to be some kind of a constitutional right to sit down. New York cops see a guy lying down in a door-way or on a bench, they blip their siren and yell through their loudhailer. They see a guy sleeping upright, they give him a hard stare and move on.

The prowl car moved on.

Reacher lay down again. Folded his arms behind his head and kept his eyes half open.

Four miles north, Edward Lane and John Gregory rode down in the Dakota's elevator. Lane was carrying the bulging leather duffel. Outside in the grey dawn light the blue BMW waited at the kerb. The man who had ferried it back from the garage got out and handed the keys to

Gregory. Gregory used the remote to open the trunk and Lane dumped the bag inside. He looked at it for a second and then he slammed the lid on it.

'No heroics,' he said. 'Just leave the car, leave the keys, and walk away.'

'Understood,' Gregory said. He walked around the hood and slid into the driver's seat. Started the motor and took off west. Then he turned south on Ninth Avenue. This early in the morning, he figured the traffic would be OK.

At that same moment four miles south a man turned off Houston Street and started down West Broadway. He was on foot. He was forty-two years old, white, five feet eleven inches tall, one hundred and ninety pounds. He was wearing a denim jacket over a hooded sweatshirt. He crossed to the west sidewalk and headed for Prince. He kept his eyes moving. Left, right, near, far. *Reconnaissance.* He was justifiably proud of his technique. He didn't miss much. He never had missed much. He imagined his gaze to be twin moving searchlights, penetrating the gloom, revealing everything.

Revealing: forty-five degrees ahead and to the left, a man sprawled in a doorway. A big man, but inert. His limbs were relaxed in sleep. His head was cradled on his arms and canted sideways at a characteristic angle.

Drunk? Passed out?

Who was he?

The man in the hooded sweatshirt paused at the Prince Street crosswalk. Waited for the light, even though there was no traffic. Used the time to complete his inspection. The big guy's clothes were garbage, but his shoes were good. Leather, heavy, solid, proper stitched welts. Probably English. Probably three hundred dollars a pair. Maybe three-fifty. Each shoe on its own was worth twice the price of everything else the guy was wearing.

So who was he?

A bum who had stolen a pair of fancy shoes? Or not?

Not, thought the man in the hooded sweatshirt.

He turned ninety degrees and crossed West Broadway against the light. Headed straight for the doorway.

Gregory blew past a small traffic snarl at 42nd Street and caught green lights all the way to the back of the post office at 31st. Then the lights and his luck changed. He had to stop the BMW behind a garbage truck. He waited. Checked his watch. He had plenty of time.

The man in the hooded sweatshirt stopped one quiet pace north of the doorway. Held his breath. The guy at his feet slept on. He didn't smell. His skin was good. His hair was clean. He wasn't malnourished.

Not a bum with a pair of stolen shoes.

The man in the hooded sweatshirt smiled to himself. This was some asshole from some million-dollar Soho loft, been out for some fun, had a little too much, couldn't make it home.

A prime target.

He shuffled half a pace forward. Breathed out, breathed in. Levelled the twin searchlights on the chino pockets. Scoped them out.

There it was.

The left-hand front pocket. The familiar delicious bulge. Exactly two and five-eighths inches wide, half an inch thick, three and a quarter inches long.

Folding money.

The man in the hooded sweatshirt had plenty of experience. He could call it sight unseen. There would be a bunch of crisp new twenties from an ATM, a couple of leathery old fives and tens from taxi change, a wrapping of crumpled ones. Total: *A hundred and seventy-three dollars.* That was his prediction. And his predictions were usually pretty good. He doubted that he would be disappointed. But he was prepared to be pleasantly surprised.

He bent at the waist and extended his arm.

He used his fingertips to lift the top seam of the pocket. To make a little tunnel. Then he flattened his hand, palm down, and slid his index and middle fingers inside, light, like feathers. He crossed them, like scissors, or a promise. His index finger went under the cash, all the way to the first knuckle. His middle finger went over the cash. Over the fold. Like a pincer. He used light pressure. Used the pad of his middle finger to press down through the wad to the nail of his index finger. Used a brief subtle tug to break the fibre-on-fibre bond between money and pocket. Started the slow, smooth extraction.

Then his wrist broke.

Two giant hands seized it and snapped it like a rotten twig. One shattering sudden explosion of motion. A blur. At first there was no pain. Then it kicked in like a tidal wave. But by then it was too late to scream. One of the giant hands was clamped over his mouth. It was like being hit hard in the face with a first baseman's mitt.

'I've got three questions,' the big guy said quietly. 'Tell me the truth and I'll let you go. Tell me a lie and I'll break your other wrist. We clear on that?'

The big guy had hardly moved. Just his hands, once, twice, three times, fast, efficient, and lethal. He wasn't even breathing hard. The man in the hooded sweatshirt couldn't breathe at all. He nodded desperately.

'OK, first question: what exactly are you doing?' The big guy took his hand away, to enable the answer.

'Your money,' the man in the hooded sweatshirt said. His voice wouldn't work properly. It was all strangled up with pain and panic.

'Not your first time,' the big guy said. His eyes were half open, clear blue, expressionless. Hypnotic. The man in the sweatshirt couldn't lie.

'I call it the dawn patrol,' he said. 'There's sometimes two or three guys like you.'

'Not exactly like me,' the big guy said.

'No.'

'Bad choice.'

'I'm sorry.'

'Second question: are you alone?'

'Yes, I am.'

'Third question: do you want to walk away now?'

'Yes, I do.'

'So do it. Slow and natural. Go north. Turn right on Prince. Don't run. Don't look back. Just disappear. Right now.'

Gregory was a block and a half from the fireplug and about eight minutes early. He figured he would pull in at the kerb before he got there. He figured he should try to time it exactly.

Reacher's heart rate was back to normal within about fifteen seconds. He jammed his cash deeper in his pocket and put his arms back behind his head. Let his head fall sideways and let his eyes half close. He saw nobody near the red door. Saw nobody even glance at it.

The man in the hooded sweatshirt cradled his broken wrist and made it as far as Prince. Then he abandoned the slow and natural walk and just ran east as fast as he could. Stopped two blocks away and threw up in the gutter. Stayed there for a spell, bent at the waist, panting, his good hand on his knee, his bad hand tucked in the sweatshirt pocket like a sling.

Reacher had no watch but he figured when he saw Gregory it must have been between eight and nine minutes after seven o'clock. Below Houston the north–south blocks are long. Eight or nine minutes was about right for the walk down from the fireplug on Sixth. So Gregory was right on time. He came in on Spring from the west. He was walking briskly. His hand was in the pocket of his suit coat. He stopped on the sidewalk outside the dull red door and turned with military precision and walked up the three short steps, light and easy, balanced on the balls of his feet. Then his hand came out of his pocket and Reacher saw the flash of metal and black plastic. Saw Gregory lift the mail slot's flap with his left hand and shovel the keys through with his right. Saw him drop the flap back into place and turn and walk away. Saw him make the right onto West Broadway. He didn't look back. He just kept on walking, playing his part, trying to keep Kate Lane alive.

Reacher kept his eyes on the red door. Waited. Three minutes, he figured. Five million bucks was a lot of money. There would be a certain degree of impatience. As soon as the one guy confirmed that Gregory was safely distant, the other guy would be in through the door. And they would figure one long block plus a crosswalk was safely distant. So as soon as Gregory was south of Broome, the call would come.

One minute.

Two minutes.

Three minutes.

Nothing happened.

Reacher lay back, stayed relaxed, stayed casual. No outward sign of his interest. Or his concern.

Four minutes. Nothing happened.

Reacher kept his eyes half closed but stared at the door so hard that its details etched themselves in his mind. Scars, nicks, streaks of dirt and rust, graffiti overspray. He felt that fifty years in the future he would be able to draw a picture as accurate as a Polaroid.

Six minutes. Eight. Nine.

Nothing happened.

There were all kinds of people on the sidewalks now but none of them went anywhere near the red door. There was traffic and there were trucks unloading and there were bodegas and bakeries open for business. There were people with news-papers and closed cups of coffee heading for the subway.

Nobody stepped up to the red door.

Twelve minutes. Fifteen.

Reacher asked himself: did they see me? He answered himself: of course they did. Close to a certainty. The mugger saw me. That was for damn sure. And these other guys are smarter than any mugger. They're the type who see everything. Guys good enough to take down an SAS veteran outside a department store were going to check the street pretty carefully. Then he asked him-self: but were they worried? Answered himself: no, they weren't. The mugger saw a professional opportunity. That was all. To these other guys, people in doorways were like trash cans or mail boxes or fire hydrants or cruising taxis. Street furniture. You see them, you see the city. And he was alone. Cops or FBI would have come in a group. Mob-handed. There would have been a whole bunch of unexplained people hanging around looking shifty and awkward with walkie-talkies in brown paper bags made up to look like pints of liquor.

So they saw me, but they didn't scare.
So what the hell was happening?
Eighteen minutes.
Fire hydrants, Reacher thought.

The BMW was parked on a fire hydrant. Rush hour was building. NYPD tow trucks were firing up and leaving their garages and starting their day. They all had quotas to make. How long could a sane person leave five million bucks inside an illegally parked car in New York City?

Nineteen minutes.

Reacher gave it up after twenty. Just rolled out of the doorway and stood up. Stretched once and hustled north, and then west on Prince all the way to Sixth Avenue, and then north again across Houston to the kerb with the fireplug.

It was empty. No BMW.

EIGHT

Reacher headed south again, all the way back to Spring Street. Six blocks, moving fast, seven minutes. He found Gregory on the sidewalk outside the dull red door.

'Well?' Gregory said.

Reacher shook his head.

'Nothing,' he said. 'Not a damn thing. Nobody showed up. It all turned to rat shit. Isn't that what you SAS guys call it?'

'When we're feeling polite,' Gregory said.

'The car is gone.'

'How is that possible?'

'There's a back door,' Reacher said. 'That's my best guess right now.'

'Shit.'

Reacher nodded. 'Like I said, rat shit.'

'We should check it out. Mr Lane is going to want the whole story.'

They found an alley entrance two buildings west. It was gated and the gates were chained. The chains were secured with a padlock the size of a frying pan. Unbreakable. But reasonably new. Oiled, and frequently used. Above the gates was a single iron screen covering the whole width of the alley and extending twenty feet in the air.

No way in.

Reacher stepped back and looked left and right. The target building's right-hand neighbour was a chocolate shop. A security screen was down over the window but Reacher could see confections the size of babies' fists displayed behind it. *Fakes*, he guessed. Otherwise they would melt or go white. There was a light on in back of the store. He cupped his hands against the glass and peered inside. Saw a small shadowy figure moving about. He banged on the door, loud, with the flat of his hand. The small figure stopped moving and turned around. Pointed at something waist-high to Reacher's right. There was a neatly engraved card taped to the door glass: *Opening hours, 10 a.m.–10 p.m.* Reacher shook his head and beckoned the small figure closer. It gave a little universal shrug of exasperation and headed his way. It was a woman. Short, dark, young, tired. She turned numerous complicated locks and opened the door against a thick steel chain.

'We're closed,' she said, through the narrow gap.

'Department of Health,' Reacher said.

'You don't look like it,' the woman said. And she was right. Reacher had looked convincing as a bum in a doorway. He didn't look convincing as a city bureaucrat. So he nodded at Gregory, in his neat grey suit.

'He's with the city,' he said. 'I'm with him.'

'I was just inspected,' the woman said.

'This is about the building next door,' Reacher said.

'What about it?'

Reacher glanced behind her. *A confectionery store full of luxury items that nobody really needs. Therefore, a fragile client base. Therefore, an insecure proprietor.*

'Rats,' he said. 'I'm the exterminator. We've had reports.'

The woman went quiet.

'You got a key for the alley gate?' Gregory asked her.

The woman nodded. 'But you can use my back door if you want. That would be quicker.'

She took the door off the chain. Led them inside through air intense with the smell of cocoa. The front of the store was dressed up for retail, and there was a working kitchen in back. Ovens, just now warming up. Dozens of shiny trays. Milk, butter, sugar. Vats of melting chocolate. Steel work surfaces. A rear door, at the end of a short tiled hallway. The woman let them out through it and Reacher and Gregory found themselves in a brick alley about wide enough for the kind of carts and trucks they had in 1900. The alley ran east to west across the block with a single gated exit on Thompson Street at one end and a right-angle dogleg to the gate they had already seen on Spring at the other. The target building looked just as bad from the back as it had from the front. Or maybe even worse. Less graffiti, more decay. Ice damage on the brickwork, moss from spilling gutters.

One ground floor window. And a back door.

It was the same dull red colour as the front door, but it looked even more decrepit. It looked like a wooden core sheeted over with steel and last painted by some GI looking for work after Korea. Or after World War Two. Or World War One. But it had a modern lock, just one, a good solid deadbolt. The handle was an old-fashioned brass ball, black and pitted with age. Impossible to tell whether it had been touched within the last hour. Reacher grabbed it and pushed. The door gave an eighth-inch and then stopped dead against the lock's steel tongue.

No way in.

Reacher turned back and headed for the chocolatier's kitchen. She was squeezing molten chocolate out of a heavy linen bag through a silver nozzle, dotting a baking sheet with one squeeze every two inches.

'Want to lick the spoon?' she asked, watching him watching her.

'You ever seen anyone next door?' he asked back.

'Nobody,' she said.

'Not even coming and going?'

'Never,' she said. 'It's a vacant building.'

'Are you here every day?'

'From seven thirty in the morning. I fire up the ovens first thing, and I turn them off at ten in the evening. Then I clean up and I'm out of here by eleven thirty. Sixteen-hour days. I'm regular as clockwork.'

'Seven days a week?'

'Small business. We never rest.'

'Hard life.'

'For you too.'

'Me?'

'With the rats in this town.'

Reacher nodded. 'Who's the owner next door?'

'Don't you know?' the woman asked. 'You're with the city.'

'You could save me some time,' Reacher said. 'The records are a mess.'

'I've got no idea,' the woman said.

'OK,' Reacher said. 'Have a great day.'

'Check the building permits on the front window. They have a bunch of phone numbers on them. The owner's probably listed. You should have seen the shit I had to list to get this place done.'

'Thanks,' Reacher said.

'Want a chocolate?'

'Not on duty,' he said.

He followed Gregory out of the front of the store and they turned right and checked the target building's front window. It was backed with dark curtains. There were a dozen permits pasted to the glass. The glass was filthy with soot and the permits were dry and curled. All of them were long expired. But they still had phone numbers handwritten with a black marker pen, one number for each of the participants in the abandoned project. Architect, contractor, owner. Gregory didn't write them down. Just took out his small silver cell phone and took a picture with it. Then he used it again, this time to make a call to the Dakota.

'Incoming,' he said.

He and Reacher walked west to Sixth Avenue

and rode the C train eight stops north to 72nd Street. They came up into the daylight right next to Strawberry Fields. Walked into the Dakota's lobby at eight thirty exactly.

The woman who was watching the building saw them enter and made a note of the time.

NINE

The bad news put Edward Lane on a knife edge. Reacher watched him carefully and saw him struggling for control. He paced back and forth across the living room floor and curled his hands compulsively and scratched at his palms with his nails.

'Conclusions?' he asked. Like a demand. Like an entitlement.

'I'm revising my conclusions,' Reacher said. 'Maybe there aren't three guys. Maybe there are only two. One stays with Kate and Jade, the other comes down to the city alone. He doesn't really need to watch Gregory walk away down West Broadway because he's planning on using the back door anyway. He's already in the alley, out of sight.'

'Risky. Safer to be loose on the street.'

Reacher shook his head. 'They did their homework. The neighbour is in her building from seven thirty in the morning until eleven thirty at night. Which explains the times they chose. Seven o'clock this morning, before she arrived. Eleven forty the first night, after she left. Eleven forty is a weirdly precise choice of time, don't you think? There had to be some reason for it.'

Edward Lane said nothing.

Reacher said, 'Or maybe there's only one guy. On his own. It's possible. If Kate and Jade are secured upstate, he could have come down alone.'

'Secured?'

'Locked up somewhere. Maybe bound and gagged.'

'For twelve hours at a time? There and back?'

'This is a kidnap. They're not at a health spa.'

'Just one guy?'

'It's possible,' Reacher said again. 'And maybe he wasn't in the alley at all. Maybe he was actually inside the building, waiting and ready. Maybe right behind the front door. Maybe Gregory dropped the keys right in his hand.'

'Will they call again?' Lane asked. 'Will he?'

'Four hours from now that same argument will start all over again.'

'And?'

'What would you do?'

Lane didn't answer directly. 'If there's only one guy, how can he argue?'

'With himself,' Reacher said. 'And that's the toughest kind of argument to have.'

Lane paced. But his hands stopped moving. It was like he had been hit with a new consideration. Reacher had been expecting it. *Here it comes*, he thought.

'Maybe you're right,' Lane said. 'Maybe it isn't three guys.'

Reacher waited.

'Maybe it's *four* guys,' Lane said. 'And maybe

73

you're the fourth guy. Maybe that's why you were in that coffee shop the first night. You were watching your buddy's back. Making sure he got away OK.'

Reacher said nothing.

'It was you who elected to watch the front door this morning,' Lane said. 'Because you knew nothing would happen there. You should have watched the car. You should have been on Sixth Avenue, not Spring Street. And you knew they were going to ask for five million more. You're one of them, aren't you?'

Silence in the room.

'Two questions,' Reacher said. 'Why would I have gone back to the coffee shop the second night? Nothing was happening the second night. And if I was a bad guy why would I have told Gregory I had seen anything at all?'

'Because you wanted to worm your way inside where you could steer us wrong. You knew I would send someone out to look for witnesses. That was obvious. And you were right there, like a spider waiting for a fly.'

Lane glanced around the room. Reacher followed his gaze. A quiet desperate atmosphere, subdued menace, six Special Forces veterans, all looking back at him, all as hard as nails, all full of hostility towards the stranger and all full of any fighting soldier's suspicion of an MP. He checked their faces, one through six. Then he looked down at Kate Lane's photograph.

'Pity,' he said. 'Your wife is a beautiful woman, Mr Lane. And your daughter is a lovely kid. And if you want to get them back, then I'm all you've got. Because like I said, these guys here can start a war, but they're not investigators. They can't find what you're looking for. I know guys like these. Guys like these, they couldn't find their own assholes if I gave them a mirror on a stick.'

Nobody spoke.

'You know where I live?' Reacher asked.

'I could find out,' Lane said.

'You couldn't,' Reacher said. 'Because I don't really live anywhere. I move around. Here, there, and everywhere. So if I choose to walk out of here today, you'll never see me again, the whole rest of your life. You can count on that.'

Lane didn't answer.

'And therefore Kate,' Reacher said. 'You'll never see her again either. You can count on that, too.'

'You wouldn't get out of here alive,' Lane said. 'Not unless I chose to let you.'

Reacher shook his head. 'You won't use firearms in here. Not inside the Dakota Building. I'm sure that would break the terms of your co-op lease. And I'm not worried about hand-to-hand combat. Not against little guys like these. You remember how it was back in the service, don't you? Your guys stepped out of line, who did you call? The 110th Special Unit, that's who. Hard men need harder cops. I was one of those cops. And I'm willing to be one again. Against all of you at once, if you like.'

Nobody spoke.

'I'm not here to steer you wrong,' Reacher said. 'If I wanted to steer you wrong, I'd have given you descriptions of two fantasy guys this morning. Short, tall, fat, thin, whatever. Eskimos in fur hats. Africans in full tribal dress. I'd have had you chasing shadows all over the place. But I didn't. I came back here and told you I'm sorry that actually I'm not steering you anyplace yet. Because I am sorry about that. Really. I'm sorry about the whole damn thing.'

Nobody spoke.

'But you need to hang with it,' Reacher said. 'We all do. Things like this are never easy.'

The room stayed quiet. Then Lane exhaled. He nodded.

'I apologize,' he said. 'Most sincerely. Please forgive me. It's the stress.'

Reacher said, 'No offence taken.'

Lane said, 'One million dollars to find my wife.'

'For me?' Reacher said.

'As a fee.'

'That's some raise. It was twenty-five grand a few hours ago.'

'The situation is more serious now than it was a few hours ago.'

Reacher said nothing.

'Will you accept?' Lane asked.

'We'll talk about a fee afterwards,' Reacher said. 'If I succeed.'

'If?'

'I'm way behind the curve here. Success depends on how much longer we can keep this thing going.'

'Will they call back again?'

'Yes, I think they will.'

'Why did you mention Africans?'

'When?'

'Just now. You said Africans in full tribal dress. As an example of a fantasy description.'

'It was an example. Like you said.'

'What do you know about Africa?'

'It's a large continent south of Europe. I've never been there.'

'What do we do next?'

'We think,' Reacher said.

Lane went to his office and five men went out for breakfast. Reacher stayed in the living room. Gregory stayed in there with him. They sat across from each other on a pair of low sofas. Between the sofas was a coffee table. The coffee table was topped with French-polished mahogany. The sofas were covered with flowery chintz. There were velvet throw pillows. The whole room seemed ludicrously over-decorated and over-styled and over-civilized, given the issues at hand. And it was totally dominated by the portrait of Kate Lane. Her eyes were everywhere.

'Can you get her back?' Gregory asked.

'I don't know,' Reacher said. 'Usually this kind of a thing doesn't end happily. Kidnapping is a brutal business. Usually it's the exact same thing as homicide, just delayed a little.'

'That's pretty defeatist.'

'No, it's realistic.'

'Any chance at all?'

'Maybe some, if we're only halfway through. Probably none, if we're near the end. I don't have any traction yet. And any kidnap, the end game is always the hardest part.'

'You think they were really in the building when I dropped the keys?'

'It's possible. And it would make sense. Why wait outside when they could wait inside?'

'OK,' Gregory said. 'So how about this: that's their base. That's where they *are*. Not upstate.'

'Where are the cars?'

'In parking garages all around the city.'

'Why the five-hour delays?'

'To create a false impression.'

'It would be one hell of a double-bluff,' Reacher said. 'They led us right there. Gave us the exact address.'

'But it's conceivable.'

Reacher shrugged. 'Not very. But stranger things have happened, I guess. So go call those numbers. Find out what you can. If possible, aim to have someone meet us with a key. But not right there. On the corner of Thompson. Out of sight. Just in case.'

'When?'

'Now. We need to be back here before the next ransom demand.'

Reacher left Gregory working with his cell phone on the sofa and wandered back through the kitchen to Lane's office. Lane was at his desk, but he wasn't doing anything productive. Just swinging his chair back and forth through a tiny arc and staring at the twin photographs in front of him. His two wives. One lost. Maybe both lost.

'Did the FBI find the guys?' Reacher asked. 'The first time, with Anne?'

Lane shook his head.

78

'But you knew who they were.'

'Not at the time,' Lane said.

'But you found out later.'

'Did I?'

'Tell me how.'

'It became a threshold question,' Lane said. 'Who would do such a thing? At first I couldn't imagine anyone doing it. But clearly someone had, so I revised the threshold of possibilities downward. But then everyone in the world seemed to be a possibility. It was beyond my understanding.'

'You surprise me. You move in a world where hostage-taking and abduction aren't exactly unknown.'

'Do I?'

'Foreign conflicts,' Reacher said. 'Irregular forces.'

'But this was domestic,' Lane said. 'This was right here in New York City. And it was my wife, not me or one of my men.'

'But you did find the guys.'

'Did I?'

Reacher nodded. 'You're not asking me if I think it could be the same people all over again. You're not speculating. It's like you know for sure it isn't.'

Lane said nothing.

'How did you find them?' Reacher asked.

'Someone who knew someone heard some talk. Arms dealers, up and down their network.'

'And?'

'There was a story about four guys who had heard about a deal I had done and concluded that I had money.'

79

'What happened to the four guys?'

'What would you have done?'

'I would have made sure they couldn't do it all over again.'

Lane nodded. 'Let's just say I'm completely confident that this isn't the same people doing it again.'

'Have you heard any new talk?' Reacher asked.

'Not a word.'

'A rival in this business?'

'I don't have rivals in this business. I have inferiors and junior partners. And even if I did have rivals, they wouldn't do something like this. It would be suicide. They would know that sooner or later our paths would cross. Would you risk antagonizing a bunch of armed men you're likely to stumble across under the radar somewhere in the back of beyond?'

Reacher didn't reply.

'Will they call again?' Lane asked.

'I think they will.'

'What will they ask for?'

'Ten,' Reacher said. 'That's the next step. One, five, ten, twenty.'

Lane sighed, distracted.

'That's two bags,' he said. 'Can't get ten million dollars in one bag.'

He showed no other outward reaction. Reacher thought: *One plus five already gone, plus one promised to me, plus ten more. That's seventeen million dollars. This guy is right now looking at a running total of seventeen million dollars, and he hasn't even blinked yet.*

'When will they call?' Lane asked.

80

'Drive time plus argument time,' Reacher said. 'Late afternoon, early evening. Not before.'

Lane kept on swinging his chair through its tiny arc. He lapsed into silence. Then there was a quiet knock at the door and Gregory stuck his head in the room.

'I got what we need,' he said, to Reacher, not to Lane. 'The building on Spring Street? The owner is a bankrupt developer. One of his lawyer's people is meeting us there in a hour. I said we were interested in buying the place.'

'Good work,' Reacher said.

'So maybe you should revise what you said about a mirror on a stick.'

'Maybe I should. Maybe I will one day.'

'So let's go.'

They were met at the 72nd Street kerb by another new BMW 7-series sedan. This one was black. This time the driver stayed behind the wheel and Gregory and Reacher climbed in the back. The woman who was watching the building saw them go, and she noted the time.

TEN

The guy from the bankrupt developer's lawyer's office was a reedy paralegal of about thirty. His suit pockets were bagged out from all the keys he carried. Clearly his firm specialized in distressed real estate. Gregory gave him an OSC business card and introduced Reacher as a contractor whose opinion he valued.

'Is the building habitable?' Gregory asked. 'I mean, as of right now?'

'You worried about squatters being in there?' the reedy guy asked back.

'Or tenants,' Gregory said. 'Or anybody.'

'There's nobody in there,' the guy said. 'I can assure you of that fact. No water, no power, no gas, capped sewer. Also, if I'm thinking of the right building, there's another feature that makes it highly unlikely.'

He juggled his keys and unlocked the Thompson Street alley gate. The three men walked east together, behind the chocolate shop, to the target building's red rear door.

'Wait,' Gregory said. Then he turned to Reacher and whispered, 'If they're in there, we need to think about how we do this. We could get them both killed right here.'

'It's unlikely they're in there,' Reacher said.

'Plan for the worst,' Gregory said.

Reacher nodded. Stepped back and looked up and checked the windows. They were black with filth and dusty black drapes were drawn tight behind them. Street noise was loud, even in the alley. Therefore, their approach thus far was still undetected.

'Decision?' Gregory asked.

Reacher looked around, pensive. Stepped up next to the lawyer's guy.

'What makes you so sure there's nobody in there?' he asked.

'I'll show you,' the guy said. He shoved the key in the lock and pushed open the door. Then he raised his arm to stop Gregory and Reacher from crowding in too closely behind him. Because the feature that made current habitation of the building unlikely was that it had no floors.

The back door was hanging open over a yawning ten-foot pit. At the bottom of the pit was the original basement floor. It was knee-deep in trash. Above it was nothing at all. Just fifty feet of dark void, all the way up to the underside of the roof slab. The building was like a giant empty shoe box set on its end. Stumps of floor joists were faintly visible in the gloom. They had been cut off flush with the walls. The remains of individual rooms were still clearly delineated by patches of different wallpapers and vertical scars where interior partitions had been ripped out. Bizarrely, all the windows still had their drapes.

83

'See?' the lawyer's guy said. 'Not exactly habitable, is it?'

There was a ladder set next to the rear door. It was a tall old wooden thing. A nimble person could grasp the door frame and swing sideways and get on it and climb down into the basement trash. Then that person could pick his way forward to the front of the building and root through the garbage with a flashlight and collect anything that had fallen the thirteen feet from the letter slot above.

Or, a nimble person could be already waiting down there and could catch whatever came through the slot like a pop-up in the infield.

'Was that ladder always there?' Reacher asked.

'I don't recall,' the guy said.

'Who else has keys to this place?' Reacher asked.

'Everyone and his uncle, probably,' the guy said. 'It's been vacant nearly twenty years. The last owner alone tried half a dozen separate schemes. That's half a dozen architects and contractors and God knows who else. Before that, who knows what went on? The first thing you'll need to do is change the locks.'

'We don't want it,' Gregory said. 'We were looking for something ready to move into. You know, maybe a little paint. But this is off the charts.'

'We could be flexible on price,' the guy said.

'A dollar,' Gregory said. 'That's all I'd pay for a dump like this.'

'You're wasting my time,' the guy said.

He leaned in over the yawning void and pulled the door closed. Then he relocked it and walked back up the alley without another word. Reacher and Gregory followed him out to Thompson Street. The guy relocked the gate and walked away south. Reacher and Gregory stayed where they were, on the sidewalk.

'Not their base, then,' Gregory said, clipped and British.

'Mirror on a stick,' Reacher said.

'Just a dead drop for the car keys. They must be up and down that ladder like trained monkeys.'

'I guess they must.'

'So next time we should watch the alley.'

'I guess we should.'

'If there is a next time.'

'There will be,' Reacher said.

'But they've already had six million dollars. Surely there's going to come a point where they decide they've got enough.'

Reacher recalled the feel of the mugger's hand in his pocket.

'Look south,' he said. 'That's Wall Street down there. Or take a stroll on Greene Street and look in the store windows. There's no such thing as enough.'

'There would be for me.'

'For me too,' Reacher said.

'That's my point. They could be just like us.'

'Not exactly like us. I never abducted anyone. Did you?'

Gregory didn't answer that. Thirty-six minutes later the two men were back in the Dakota, and the woman who was watching the building had made another entry in her log.

ELEVEN

Reacher had a late breakfast delivered from a gourmet deli on Edward Lane's tab and he ate it alone in the kitchen. Then he lay down on a sofa and thought until he was too tired to think any more. Then he closed his eyes and dozed, and waited for the phone to ring.

Kate and Jade were sleeping too. It was nature's way. They had been unable to sleep at night, so exhaustion had overtaken them midway through the day. They were on their narrow beds, close together, deep in slumber. The lone man opened their door quietly and saw them. Paused a moment, just looking. Then he backed out of the room and left them alone. *No hurry*, he thought. In a way he was enjoying this particular phase of the operation. He was addicted to risk. He always had been. No point in denying it. It made him who he was.

Reacher woke up and found himself all alone in the living room except for Carter Groom. The guy with the shark's eyes. He was sitting in an armchair, doing nothing.

'You pulled guard duty?' Reacher asked.

'You're not exactly a prisoner,' Groom said. 'You're in line to get a million bucks.'

'Does that bother you?'

'Not really. You find her, you'll have earned it. The workman is worthy of his hire. Says so in the Bible.'

'Did you drive her often?'

'My fair share.'

'When Jade was with her, how did they ride?'

'Mrs Lane always rode in the front. She was basically embarrassed about the whole chauffeur thing. The kid in the back, obviously.'

'What were you, back in the day?'

'Recon Marine,' Groom said. 'First Sergeant.'

'How would you have handled the takedown at Bloomingdale's?'

'Good guy or bad guy?'

'Bad guy,' Reacher said.

'How many with me?'

'Does it matter?'

Groom thought for less than a second and shook his head. 'Lead guy is the important guy. Lead guy could be the only guy.'

'So how would it have gone down?'

'Only one way to do it clean,' Groom said. 'You'd have to keep all the action inside the car, before they even got out. Bloomie's is on the east side of Lexington Avenue. Lex runs downtown. So Taylor would pull over on the left and stop opposite the main entrance. Double parked, just temporarily. Whereupon our guy would grab the rear door and slide in right next to the kid. She's belted in behind her mother. Our guy puts a

87

gun straight to the kid's head and grabs her hair with his free hand and holds on tight. That's game over right there. Nobody on the street is worried. For them, it's a pick-up, not a drop-off. And Taylor would do what he's told from that point on. What choice does he have? He's got Mrs Lane screaming in the seat next to him. And what can he do anyway? He can't flip the lever and shove the seat off its runners back on the guy, because the Jaguar's got electric seats. He can't turn around and fight, because the gun is to the kid's head. He can't use violent evasive driving manoeuvres because he's in slow traffic and the guy has hold of the kid's hair and won't get thrown loose anyway. Game over, right there.'

'And then what?'

'Then our guy makes Taylor drive somewhere quiet. Maybe in town, more likely out of town. Then he shoots him, spine shot through the seat, so he doesn't bust the windshield. He makes Mrs Lane dump him out. Then he makes her drive the rest of the way. He wants to stay in the back with the kid.'

Reacher nodded. 'That's how I see it.'

'Tough on Taylor,' Groom said. 'You know, that final moment, the guy tells him to pull over, put the transmission in park, sit tight. Taylor will have known what was coming.'

Reacher said nothing.

'They haven't found his body yet,' Groom said.

'You optimistic?'

Groom shook his head. 'It's not somewhere populated, that's all it means. It's a balance. You want rid of the guy early, but you keep him alive until the location is safe. He's most likely in the countryside somewhere with the coyotes gnawing on him. Race against time whether someone finds him before he's all eaten up.'

'How long was he with you?'

'Three years.'

'Did you like him?'

'He was OK.'

'Was he good?'

'You already asked Gregory.'

'Gregory might be biased. They were from the same unit. They were Brits together overseas. What did you think?'

'He was good,' Groom said. 'SAS is a good outfit. Better than Delta, maybe. Brits are usually more ruthless. It's in their genes. They ruled the world for a long time, and they didn't do it by being nice. An SAS veteran would be second only to a Recon Marine veteran, that would be my opinion. So yes, Gregory was right. Taylor was good.'

'What was he like as a person?'

'Off duty he was gentle. He was good with the kid. Mrs Lane seemed to like him. There's two types of people here. Like an inner circle and an outer circle. Taylor was inner circle. I'm outer circle. I'm all business. I'm kind of stunted, in a social situation. I can admit it. I'm nothing, away from the action. Some of the others can be both.'

'Were you here five years ago?'

'For Anne? No, I came just after. But there can't be a connection.'

'So I heard,' Reacher said.

* * *

The clock in Reacher's head ticked around to four thirty in the afternoon. For Kate and Jade, the third day. Probably fifty-four hours since the snatch. Fifty-four hours was an incredibly long time for a kidnap to sustain itself. Most were over in less than twenty-four, one way or the other, good result or bad. Most law enforcement people gave up after thirty-six. Each passing minute made the likely outcome more and more dire.

Around a quarter to five in the afternoon Lane came back into the room and people started drifting in after him. Gregory, Addison, Burke, Kowalski. Perez came in. The vigil around the telephone started up again unannounced. Lane stood next to the table. The others grouped themselves around the room, all facing the same way, inward. There was no doubt about the centre of their attention.

But the phone didn't ring.

'Has that thing got a speaker?' Reacher asked.

'No,' Lane said.

'What about in the office?'

'I can't do it,' Lane said. 'It would be a change. It would unsettle them.'

The phone didn't ring.

'Hang in there,' Reacher said.

In her apartment across the street the woman who had been watching the building picked up her phone and dialled.

TWELVE

The woman across the street was called Patricia Joseph, Patti to her few remaining friends, and she was dialling an NYPD detective named Brewer. She had his home number. He answered on the second ring.

'I've got some activity to report,' Patti said.

Brewer didn't ask who his caller was. He didn't need to. He knew Patti Joseph's voice about as well as he knew anybody's.

'Go ahead,' he said.

'There's a new character on the scene.'

'Who?'

'I don't have a name for him yet.'

'Description?'

'Very tall, heavily built, like a real brawler. He's in his late thirties or early forties. Short fair hair, blue eyes. He showed up late last night.'

'One of them?' Brewer asked.

'He doesn't dress like them. And he's much bigger than the rest. But he acts like them.'

'Acts? What have you seen him do?'

'The way he walks. The way he moves. The way he holds himself.'

'So you think he's ex-military too?'

'Almost certainly.'

'OK,' Brewer said. 'Good work. Anything else?'

'One thing,' Patti Joseph said. 'I haven't seen the wife or the daughter in a couple of days.'

Inside the Dakota living room the phone rang at what Reacher figured was five o'clock exactly. Lane snatched the receiver out of the cradle and clamped it to his ear. Reacher heard the drone and squawk of the electronic machine, faint and muffled. Lane said, 'Put Kate on,' and there was a long, long pause. Then a woman's voice, loud and clear. But not calm. Lane closed his eyes. Then the electronic squawk came back and Lane opened his eyes again. The squawk droned on for a whole minute. Lane listened, his face working, his eyes moving. Then the call ended. Just cut off before Lane had a chance to say anything more.

He put the receiver back in the cradle. His face was half filled with hope, half filled with despair.

'They want more money,' he said. 'Instructions in an hour.'

'Maybe I should get down there right now,' Reacher said. 'Maybe they'll throw us a curveball by changing the time interval.'

But Lane was already shaking his head. 'They already threw us a different kind of curveball. They said they're changing the whole procedure. It's not going to be the same as before.'

Silence in the room.

'Is Mrs Lane OK?' Gregory asked.

Lane said, 'There was a lot of fear in her voice.'

'What about the guy's voice?' Reacher asked. 'Anything?'

'It was disguised. Same as always.'

'But beyond the sound. Think about this call and all the other calls. Word choice, word order, cadence, rhythm, flow. Is it an American or a foreigner?'

'Why would it be a foreigner?'

'Your line of work, if you've got enemies, some of them might be foreign.'

'It's an American,' Lane said. 'I think.' He closed his eyes again and concentrated. His lips moved like he was replaying conversations in his head. 'Yes, American. Certainly a native speaker. No stumbles. Never any weird or unusual words. Just normal, like you would hear all the time.'

'Same guy every time?'

'I think so.'

'What about this time? Anything different? Mood? Tension? Is he still in control or is he losing it?'

'He sounded OK,' Lane said. 'Relieved, even.' Then he paused. 'Like this whole thing was nearly over. Like this might be the final instalment.'

'It's too soon,' Reacher said. 'We're not even close yet.'

'They're calling the shots,' Lane said.

Nobody spoke.

'So what do we do now?' Gregory asked.

'We wait,' Reacher said. 'Fifty-six minutes.'

'I'm sick of waiting,' Groom said.

'It's all we can do,' Lane said. 'We wait for instructions and we obey them.'

'How much money?' Reacher asked. 'Ten?'

93

Lane looked right at him. 'Guess again.'

'More?'

'Four and a half,' Lane said. 'That's what they want. Four million five hundred thousand US dollars. In a bag.'

THIRTEEN

Reacher spent the remaining fifty-five minutes puzzling over the choice of amount. It was a bizarre figure. A bizarre progression. One, five, four and a half. Altogether ten and a half million dollars. It felt like a destination figure. Like the end of a road. But it was a bizarre total. Why stop there? It made no kind of sense at all. Or did it?

'They know you,' he said to Lane. 'But maybe not all that well. As it happens you could afford more, but maybe they don't fully appreciate that. So was there a time when ten and half million was all the cash you had?'

But Lane just said, 'No.'

'Could someone out there have that impression?'

'No,' Lane said again. 'I've had less and I've had more.'

'But you've never had exactly ten and a half?'

'No,' Lane said for the third time. 'There's absolutely no reason for anyone to believe that they're cleaning me out at ten and a half.'

So Reacher gave it up and just waited for the phone to ring.

*　　*　　*

It rang right on time, at six in the evening. Lane picked it up and listened. He didn't speak. He didn't ask for Kate. Reacher figured he had learned that the privilege of hearing his wife's voice was reserved for the first call in any given sequence. The demand call. Not the instruction call.

This instruction call lasted less than two minutes. Then the electronic squawk cut off abruptly and Lane put the receiver back in the cradle and gave a bitter little half-smile, like he was reluctantly admiring a hated opponent's skill.

'This is the final instalment,' he said. 'After this, it's over. They promise I get her back.'

Too soon, Reacher thought. *Ain't going to happen.*

Gregory asked, 'What do we do?'

'One hour from now,' Lane said. 'One man leaves here alone with the money in the black BMW and cruises anywhere he wants. He'll be carrying my cell phone and he'll get a call anywhere between one and twenty minutes into the ride. He'll be given a destination. He's to keep the line open from that point on so they know he's not conversing with anyone else in the car or on any other phones or on any kind of a radio net. He'll drive to the destination he's been given. He'll find the Jaguar parked on the street there. The car that Taylor drove Kate in, the first morning. It'll be unlocked. He's to put the money on the back seat and drive away and not look back. Any chase cars, any co-ordination with anyone else, any tricks at all, and Kate dies.'

'They've got your cell phone number?' Reacher asked.

'Kate will have given it to them.'

'I'll be the driver,' Gregory said. 'If you want.'

'No,' Lane said. 'I want you here.'

'I'll do it,' Burke said. The black guy.

Lane nodded. 'Thank you.'

'Then what?' Reacher asked. 'How do we get her back?'

Lane said, 'After they've counted the money, there'll be another call.'

'On the cell or here?'

'Here,' Lane said. 'It will take some time. Counting large sums is an arduous process. Not for me at this end. The money is already bricked and banded and labelled. But they won't trust that. They'll break the bands and examine the bills and count them by hand.'

Reacher nodded. It was a problem he had never really considered before. If the money was in hundreds, that would give them forty-five thousand bills. If they could count to a hundred every sixty seconds, that would take them four hundred and fifty minutes, which was seven and a half hours. Maybe six hours drive time, and seven and half counting time. *A long night ahead*, he thought. *For them and for us*.

Lane said, 'Why are they using the Jaguar?'

'It's a taunt,' Reacher said. 'It's to remind you.'

Lane nodded.

'Office,' he said. 'Burke and Reacher.'

In the office Lane took a small silver Samsung phone out of a charging cradle and handed it to

Burke. Then he disappeared, to his bedroom, maybe.

'Gone to get the money,' Burke said.

Reacher nodded. Gazed at the twin portraits on the desk. Two beautiful women, both equally stunning, roughly the same age, but with no real similarities. Anne Lane had been blonde and blue, somehow a child of the Sixties even though she must have been born well after that decade was over. She had long straight hair parted in the middle, like a singer or a model or an actress. She had clear guileless eyes and an innocent smile. A flower child, even though house or hip hop or acid jazz would have been the thing when she got her first record player. Kate Lane was more a child of the Eighties or Nineties. More subtle, more worldly, more accomplished.

'No kids with Anne, right?' Reacher asked.

'No,' Burke said. 'Thank God.'

So maybe motherhood accounted for the difference. There was a weight to Kate, a gravity, a heft, not physical, but somewhere deep inside her. Choose one to spend the night with, you might well pick Anne. To spend the week with, you might want Kate.

Lane came back awkwardly with a bulging leather bag. He dropped the bag on the floor and sat down at his desk.

'How long?' he asked.

'Forty minutes,' Reacher said.

Burke checked his watch.

'Yes,' he said. 'Forty minutes.'

'Go wait in the other room,' Lane said. 'Leave me alone.'

Burke went for the bag but Reacher picked it up for him. It was heavy and wide, and easier for a big guy to manage. He carried it to the foyer and dropped it near the door where its predecessor had waited twelve hours before. It flopped and settled like the same dead animal. Reacher took a seat and started counting off the minutes. Burke paced. Carter Groom drummed his fingers on the arm of a chair, frustrated. The Recon Marine, beached. *I'm all business*, he had said. *I'm nothing, away from the action*. Next to him Gregory sat quiet, all British reserve. Next to him was Perez, the Latino, tiny. Next to him was Addison, with the scarred face. *A knife, probably*, Reacher thought. Then Kowalski, taller than the others but still small next to Reacher himself. Special Forces guys were usually small. They were usually lean, fast, and whippy. Built for endurance and stamina and full of smarts and cunning. Like foxes, not like bears.

Nobody talked. There was nothing to talk about, except the fact that the end of a kidnap was always the period of greatest risk. What was there that compelled kidnappers to keep their word? Honour? A sense of business ethics? Why risk a complex transfer when a shallow grave and a bullet in the victim's head were a whole lot safer and simpler? Humanity? Decency? Reacher glanced at Kate Lane's picture next to the phone and went a little cold. She was closer to dead now than at any point in the last three days, and he knew it. He guessed they all knew it.

'Time,' Burke said. 'I'm going.'

'I'll carry the bag for you,' Reacher said. 'You know, down to the car.'

They rode down in the elevator. In the ground floor lobby a small dark woman in a long black coat swept past surrounded by tall men in suits, like staff or assistants or bodyguards.

'Was that Yoko?' Reacher said.

But Burke didn't answer. He just walked past the doorman and out to the kerb. The black BMW was waiting there. Burke opened the rear door.

'Stick the bag on the back seat,' he said. 'Easier for me that way, for a seat-to-seat transfer.'

'I'm coming with you,' Reacher said.

'That's stupid, man.'

'I'll be on the floor in back. It'll be safe enough.'

'What's the point?'

'We have to do something. You know as well as I do there's not going to be any cute little Checkpoint Charlie scene in this story. She's not going to come tottering towards us through the mist and the fog, smiling bravely, with Jade holding her hand. That's not going to happen. So we're going to have to get proactive at some point.'

'What are you planning to do?'

'After you've switched the bag I'll get out around the next corner. I'll double back and see what I can see.'

'Who says you'll see anything?'

'They'll have four and a half million bucks sitting in an unlocked car. My guess is they won't leave it there very long. So I'll see something.'

'Will it help us?'

'A lot more than sitting upstairs doing nothing will help us.'

'Lane will kill me.'

'He doesn't have to know anything about it. I'll be back well after you. You'll say you have no idea what happened to me. I'll say I went for a walk.'

'Lane will kill you if you screw it up.'

'I'll kill myself if I screw it up.'

'I'm serious. He'll kill you.'

'My risk.'

'Kate's risk.'

'You still banking on the Checkpoint Charlie scenario?'

Burke paused. Ten seconds. Fifteen.

'Get in,' he said.

FOURTEEN

Burke stuck Lane's cell phone in a hands-free cradle mounted on the BMW's dash and Reacher crawled into the rear footwell on his hands and knees. There was grit on the carpet. It was a rear-drive car and the transmission hump made it an uncomfortable location. Burke started up and waited for a hole in the traffic and then U-turned and headed south on Central Park West. Reacher squirmed around until the transmission tunnel was wedged above his hips and below his ribs.

'Don't hit any big bumps,' he said.

'We're not supposed to talk,' Burke said.

'Only after they call.'

'Believe it,' Burke said. 'You see this?'

Reacher struggled a little more upright and saw Burke pointing at a small black bud on the driver's-side A-pillar up near the sun visor.

'Microphone,' Burke said. 'For the cell. Real sensitive. You sneeze back there, they'll hear you.'

'Will I hear them? On a speaker?'

'On ten speakers,' Burke said. 'The phone is

102

wired through the audio system. It cuts in automatically.'

Reacher lay down and Burke drove on, slowly. Then he made a tight right turn.

'Where are we now?' Reacher asked.

'Fifty-seventh Street,' Burke said. 'Traffic is murder. I'm going to get on the West Side Highway and head south. My guess is they'll want us downtown somewhere. That's where they've got to be. Street parking for the Jaguar would be impossible anyplace else right now. I can come back north on the East River Drive if they don't call before we get to the Battery.'

Reacher felt the car stop and start, stop and start. Above him the money bag rolled one way and then the other.

'You serious that this could be just one guy?' Burke asked.

'Minimum of one,' Reacher said.

'Everything's a minimum of one.'

'Therefore it's possible.'

'Therefore we should take him down. Make him talk. Solve the whole problem right there.'

'But suppose it's not just one guy.'

'Maybe we should gamble.'

'What were you?' Reacher asked. 'Back in the day?'

'Delta,' Burke said.

'Did you know Lane in the service?'

'I've known him forever.'

'How would you have done the thing outside Bloomingdale's?'

'Quick and dirty inside the car. As soon as Taylor stopped.'

103

'That's what Groom said.'

'Groom's a smart guy, for a jarhead. You disagree with him?'

'No.'

'It would be the only way. This isn't Mexico City or Bogotá or Rio de Janeiro. This is New York. You couldn't survive a fuss on the sidewalk. You've got eight beat cops right there, two on each corner, armed and dangerous, worried about terrorists. No, quick and dirty inside the car would be the only way at Bloomingdale's.'

'But why would you have been at Bloomingdale's at all?'

'It's the obvious place. It's Mrs Lane's favourite store. She gets all her stuff there. She loves that big brown bag.'

'But who would have known that?'

Burke was quiet for a spell.

'That's a very good question,' he said.

Then the phone rang.

FIFTEEN

The ring tone sounded weird, coming in over ten high-quality automobile speakers. It filled the whole car. It sounded very loud and rich and full and precise. The cellular network's harsh electronic edge was taken right off it. It purred.

'Shut up now,' Burke said.

He leaned to his right and hit a button on the Samsung.

'Hello?' he said.

'Good evening,' a voice said back, so slowly and carefully and mechanically that it made four separate words out of two. Like: *Good-Eve-Ven-Ing.*

It was a hell of a voice. It was completely amazing. It was so heavily processed that there would be no chance of recognizing it again without the electronic machine. The machines were commercial items sold in spy stores. Reacher had seen them. They clamped over the telephone mouthpiece. On one side was a microphone, which was backed by circuit boards, and then came a small crude loudspeaker. Battery powered. There were rotary dials that shaped the sound. Zero to ten, for various different parameters. The dials on this machine must have been cranked all the way to eleven. The high frequencies were entirely missing. The low tones had been scooped out and turned around and reconstituted. They boomed and thumped like an irregular heartbeat. There was a phase effect that hissed and roared on every drawn breath and made the voice sound like it was hurtling through outer space. There was a metallic pulse that came and went. It sounded like a sheet of heavy steel being hit with a hammer. The volume was set very high. Over the BMW's ten speakers the voice sounded huge and alien. Gigantic. Like a direct connection to a nightmare.

'Who am I speaking with?' it asked, slowly.

'The driver,' Burke said. 'The guy with the money.'

'I want your name,' the voice said.

Burke said, 'My name is Burke.'

The nightmare voice asked, 'Who's that in the car with you?'

'There's nobody in the car with me,' Burke said. 'I'm all alone.'

'Are you lying?'

'No, I'm not lying,' Burke said.

Reacher figured there might be a lie-detector hooked up to the other end of the phone. Probably a simple device sold in the same kind of spy stores as the distortion machines. Plastic boxes, green lights and red lights. They were supposed to be able to detect the kind of voice stress that comes with lying. Reacher replayed Burke's answers in his head and figured they would pass muster. It would be a crude machine and Delta soldiers were taught to beat better tests than a person could buy retail on Madison Avenue. And after a second it was clear that the box had indeed lit up green because the nightmare voice just went ahead calmly and asked, 'Where are you now, Mr Burke?'

'Fifty-seventh Street,' Burke said. 'I'm heading west. I'm about to get on the West Side Highway.'

'You're a long way from where I want you.'

'Who are you?'

'You know who I am.'

'Where do you want me?'

'Take the highway, if that's what you prefer. Go south.'

'Give me time,' Burke said. 'Traffic is real bad.'

'Worried?'

'How would you feel?'

'Stay on the line,' the voice said.

The sound of distorted breathing filled the car. It was slow and deep. *Unworried*, Reacher thought. *A patient person, in control, in command, safe somewhere.* He felt the car sprint and hook left. *Onto the highway through a yellow light*, he thought. *Take care, Burke. A traffic stop could be real awkward tonight.*

'I'm on the highway now,' Burke said. 'Heading south.'

'Keep going,' the voice said. Then it lapsed back to breathing. There was an audio compressor somewhere in the chain. Either in the voice machine itself or in the BMW's stereo. The breathing started out quiet and then ramped up

107

slowly until it was roaring in Reacher's ears. The whole car was filled with it. It felt like being inside a lung.

Then the breathing stopped and the voice asked, 'How's the traffic?'

'Lots of red lights,' Burke said.

'Keep going.'

Reacher tried to follow the route in his head. He knew there were plenty of lights between 57th Street and 34th Street. The Passenger Ship Terminal, the Intrepid, the Lincoln Tunnel approaches.

'I'm at 42nd Street now,' Burke said.

Reacher thought: *Are you talking to me? Or the voice?*

'Keep going,' the voice said.

'Is Mrs Lane OK?' Burke asked.

'She's fine.'

'Can I talk to her?'

'No.'

'Is Jade OK too?'

'Don't worry about either one of them. Just keep on driving.'

American, Reacher thought. *For sure*. Behind the wall of distortion he could hear the inflections of a native speaker. Reacher had heard more than his share of foreign accents, but this wasn't one of them.

'I'm at the Javits now,' Burke said.

'Just keep going,' the voice said back.

Young, Reacher thought. *Or at least not old*. All the dirt and grit in the voice came from the electronic circuitry, not from the effects of age. *Not a big guy*, Reacher thought. The booming bass was artificial. There was a speed and a lightness there. No big chest cavity. *Or, maybe a fat guy.* Maybe one of those fat guys who have high-pitched voices.

'How much further?' Burke asked.

'You low on gas?' the voice asked.

'No.'

'So what do you care?'

The breathing came back, slow and steady. *Not close yet*, Reacher thought.

'Coming up on 24th Street,' Burke said.

'Keep going.'

The Village, Reacher thought. *We're going back to Greenwich Village.* The car was moving faster now. Most of the left turns into the West Village were blocked off, so there were fewer lights. And most of the traffic would be going north, not south. A clear run, relatively speaking. Reacher craned his neck and got an angle through the rear side window. He could see buildings with the evening sun reflected in their windows. They flashed past in a dizzy kaleidoscope.

The voice asked, 'Where are you now?'

'Perry,' Burke said.

'Keep going. But stand by now.'

Getting close, Reacher thought. *Houston? Are we going to take Houston Street?* Then he thought: *Stand by now? That's a military term. But is it exclusively military? Is this guy ex-military too? Or not? Is he a civilian? A wannabe?*

'Morton Street,' Burke said.

'Left turn in three blocks,' the voice said. 'On Houston.'

He knows New York City, Reacher thought. *He*

knows that Houston is three blocks south of Morton and he knows you say it House-ton, not like the place in Texas.

'OK,' Burke said.

Reacher felt the car slow. It stopped. It waited and inched forward. Then it sprinted to catch the light. Reacher rolled heavily against the rear seat.

'East on Houston now,' Burke said.

'Keep going,' the voice said.

The traffic on Houston was slow. Cobblestones, stop signs, potholes, lights. Reacher paced it out in his head. Washington Street, Greenwich Street, Hudson Street. Then Varick, where he had come up out of the subway for his fruitless morning vigil. The car bounced over patches of frost heave and thumped into dips.

'Sixth Avenue next,' Burke said.

The voice said, 'Take it.'

Burke turned left. Reacher craned his neck again and saw the apartments above his new favourite café.

The voice said, 'Get in the right-hand lane. Now.'

Burke dabbed the brake hard and Reacher jolted forward and hit the front seat. He heard the turn signal click. Then the car jumped right. And slowed.

The voice said, 'You'll see your target on the right. The green Jaguar. From the first morning. Exactly halfway up the block. On the right.'

'I already see it,' Burke said.

Reacher thought: *The same place? It's right there on the same damn fireplug?*

The voice said, 'Stop and make the transfer.'

Reacher felt the transmission slam into park and he heard the click of the hazard lights start up. Then Burke's door opened and noise blew in. The suspension rocked as Burke climbed out. There was honking on the street behind. An instant traffic jam. Ten seconds later the door next to Reacher's head opened wide. Burke didn't look down. Just leaned in and grabbed the bag. Reacher craned his neck the other way and looked at the Jaguar upside down. Saw a flash of dark green paint. Then the door shut in his face. He heard the Jaguar's door open. Then he heard it shut again. He heard a faint hydraulic *thunk* from somewhere outside. Ten seconds after that Burke was back in his seat. He was a little out of breath.

'The transfer is done,' he said. 'The money is in the Jaguar.'

The nightmare voice said, 'Goodbye.'

The phone clicked off. The car filled with silence. Profound and absolute.

'Go now,' Reacher said. 'Turn right on Bleecker.'

Burke took off with the hazard warning still clicking. He caught the light and barged through the crosswalk. Accelerated for twenty yards and then jammed the brakes on hard. Reacher fumbled horizontally above his head and found the door handle. Pulled it and butted the door open and scrambled out. He stood up and slammed the door and paused for a second and tugged his shirt down. Then he hustled back to the corner.

SIXTEEN

Reacher stopped while he was still on Bleecker and jammed his hands in his pockets and then restarted at a more appropriate pace. He turned left onto Sixth like a man walking home. Maybe after a busy day at work, maybe planning a stop in a bar, maybe with grocery shopping on his mind. Just blending in, which he was surprisingly good at, given that he was always a head taller than anyone else around him. The height advantage was a mixed blessing for surveillance. It made him theoretically conspicuous. But it meant he could see farther than the average guy. Simple trigonometry. He stayed in the middle of the sidewalk and looked straight ahead and put the green Jaguar firmly in his peripheral vision. Checked left. Nothing. Checked right, over the Jaguar's roof.

And saw a guy six feet from the driver's door.

It was the same guy he had seen the very first night. He was absolutely sure of that. Same stature, same posture, same movements, same clothes. White, a little sunburned, lean, chiselled, clean-shaven, jaw clamped, not smiling, maybe forty years old. Calm, focused, intent. Neat and quick, dodging traffic, just into his final two strides before reaching the car. Fluid, economical movements. The guy pulled the door and slid into the seat and started the engine and clipped his belt and took a long glance back over his shoulder at the traffic. Then he pulled out neatly into a gap and took off north. Reacher kept on walking south but turned his head to watch him go. The guy flashed past, out of sight.

Six seconds, beginning to end. Maybe less.

And for what?

Just a white guy, average height, average weight, dressed like every other off-duty white guy in the city. Jeans, shirt, sneakers, ball cap. Maybe forty. Unremarkable in every way. Description? Nothing to say, except: just a guy.

Reacher glanced south at the river of traffic. There were no free cabs coming. None at all. So he turned again and jogged back to the corner of Bleecker to see if Burke had waited for him. But Burke hadn't. So Reacher set out walking. He was too frustrated to take the subway. He needed to walk it off. He charged north on Sixth, fast and furious, and people moved out of his way like he was radioactive.

Twenty minutes and twenty blocks later he saw a Staples store on the opposite sidewalk. Red and white signs. Windows full of office supply bargains. He dodged cars and crossed over to check it out. It was a big place. He didn't know which branch Carter Groom had taken Kate Lane to, but he figured chains carried the same stuff everywhere. He went inside and passed a corral made from inch-thick chrome bars where shopping trolleys were racked together. Beyond that on the left were the checkout registers. Beyond the trolleys on the right was a print shop full of industrial-strength photocopiers. In front of him were about twenty narrow aisles with shelves that reached the ceiling. They were piled high with an intimidating array of stuff. He started at the left front corner and zigzagged all the way through the store to the rear of the last aisle on the right. The biggest thing he saw was a desk. The smallest, either a thumbtack or a paperclip, depending on whether he judged by size or weight. He saw paper, computers, printers, toner cartridges, pens, pencils, envelopes, file boxes, plastic crates, parcel tape. He saw things he had never seen before. Software for designing houses and filing taxes. Label printers. Cell phones that took video pictures and sent e-mail.

He walked back to the front of the store with absolutely no idea at all of what Kate Lane might have been looking for.

He stood in a daze and watched a photocopier at work. It was a machine as big as a launderette dryer and it was spitting copies out so hard and so fast that it was rocking back and forth on its feet. And costing some customer a fortune. That was clear. A sign overhead said that photocopying cost between four cents and two dollars a sheet, depending on the quality of the paper and the choice between black and white and colour. A lot of money, potentially. Opposite the print shop corral was a display of inkjet cartridges. They were expensive, too. Reacher had no idea what they were for. Or what they did. Or why they cost so much. He pushed past a line of people at a checkout desk and headed for the street.

Another twenty minutes and twenty blocks later he was at Bryant Park, eating a hot dog from a street vendor. Twenty minutes and twenty blocks after that he was in Central Park, drinking a bottle of still water from another street vendor. Twelve more blocks north he was still in Central Park, directly opposite the Dakota Building, under a tree, stopped dead, face to face with Anne Lane, Edward Lane's first wife.

SEVENTEEN

The first thing Anne Lane did was tell Reacher he was wrong.

'You saw Lane's photograph of her,' she said.

He nodded.

'We were very alike,' she said.

He nodded again.

'Anne was my sister,' she said.

'I'm sorry,' he said. 'I'm sorry for staring. And I'm sorry for your loss.'

'Thank you,' the woman said.

'Were you twins?'

'I'm six years younger,' the woman said. 'Which means right now I'm the same age as Anne was, in that photograph. Like a virtual twin, maybe.'

'You look exactly like her.'

'I try to,' the woman said.

'It's uncanny.'

'I try very hard.'

'Why?'

'Because it feels like I'm keeping her alive. Because I couldn't, back when it mattered.'

'How could you have kept her alive?'

'We should talk,' the woman said. 'My name is Patti Joseph.'

'Jack Reacher.'

'Come with me,' the woman said. 'We have to double back. We can't go too near the Dakota.'

She led him south through the park, to the exit at 66th Street. Across to the far sidewalk. Then north again, and into the lobby of a building at 115 Central Park West.

'Welcome to the Majestic,' Patti Joseph said. 'Best place I ever lived. And just wait until you see where my apartment is.'

Reacher saw where it was five minutes later, after a walk down a corridor, an elevator ride, and another walk down another corridor. Patti Joseph's apartment was on the Majestic's seventh floor, north side. Its living room window looked out over 72nd Street, directly at the Dakota's entrance. There was a dining chair placed in front of the sill, as if the sill was a desk. On the sill was a notebook. And a pen. And a Nikon camera with a long lens, and a pair of Leica 10×42 binoculars.

'What do you do here?' Reacher asked.

'First tell me what you do there,' Patti said.

'I'm not sure I can.'

'Do you work for Lane?'

'No, I don't.'

Patti Joseph smiled.

'I didn't think you did,' she said. 'I told Brewer, you're not one of them. You're not like them. You weren't Special Forces, were you?'

'How did you know?'

'You're too big. You wouldn't have made it through the endurance hazing. Big men never do.'

'I was an MP.'

'Did you know Lane in the service?'

'No, I didn't.'

Patti Joseph smiled again.

'I thought not,' she said. 'Otherwise you wouldn't be there.'

'Who is Brewer?'

'NYPD.' She pointed at the notebook and the pen and the camera and the binoculars. A big, sweeping gesture. 'I do all this for him.'

'You're watching Lane and his guys? For the cops?'

'For myself, mostly. But I check in.'

'Why?'

'Because hope springs eternal.'

'Hope of what?'

'That he'll slip up, and I'll get something on him.'

Reacher stepped closer to the window and glanced at the notebook. The handwriting was neat. The last entry read: *2014 hrs. Burke returns alone, no bag, in black BMW OSC 23, enters TDA.*

'TDA?' Reacher asked.

'The Dakota Apartments,' Patti said. 'It's the building's official name.'

'You ever see Yoko?'

'All the time.'

'You know Burke by name?'

'Burke was around when Anne was there.'

The last-but-one entry read: *1859 hrs. Burke and Venti leave TDA in black BMW OSC 23, with bag, Venti concealed in rear.*

'Venti?' Reacher asked.

'That's what I've been calling you. Like a code name.'

'Why?'

'Venti is the largest cup that Starbucks sells. Bigger than the others.'

'I like coffee,' Reacher said.

'I could make some.'

Reacher turned away from the window. The apartment was a small one-bedroom. Plain, neat, painted. Probably worth the best part of a million bucks.

'Why are you showing me all this?' he asked.

'A recent decision,' she said. 'I decided to watch for new guys, and waylay them, and warn them.'

'About what?'

'About what Lane is really like. About what he did.'

'What did he do?'

'I'll make coffee,' Patti said.

There was no stopping her. She ducked into a small pass-through kitchen and started fiddling with a machine. Pretty soon Reacher could smell coffee. He wasn't thirsty. He had just drunk a whole bottle of water. But he liked coffee. He figured he could stay for a cup.

Patti called out, 'No cream, no sugar, right?'

'How did you know that?'

'I trust my instincts,' she said.

And I trust mine, Reacher thought, although he

wasn't entirely sure what they were telling him right then.

'I need you to get to the point,' he said.

'OK,' Patti Joseph said. 'I will.' And then she said: 'Anne wasn't kidnapped five years ago. That was just a cover story. Lane murdered her.'

EIGHTEEN

Patti Joseph brought Jack Reacher black coffee in a huge white Wedgwood mug. Twenty ounce. *Venti*. She set it on an oversize coaster and turned her back on him and sat on the dining chair at the window. Picked up the pen in her right hand and the binoculars in her left. They looked heavy. She held them the way a shot putter holds the big iron ball, balanced on her open palm, close to her neck.

'Edward Lane is a cold man,' she said. 'He demands loyalty and respect and obedience. He *needs* those things, like a junkie needs a fix. That's what this whole mercenary venture is about, really. He couldn't bear losing his command position, when he left the military. So he decided to recreate it all over again. He needs to give orders and have them obeyed. Like you or I need to breathe. He's borderline mentally ill, I think. Psychotic.'

'And?' Reacher said.

'He ignores his stepdaughter. Have you noticed that?'

Reacher said nothing. *He didn't mention Jade*

121

had been taken until later, he thought. *He had her cropped out of the picture in the living room.*

'My sister Anne wasn't very obedient,' Patti said. 'Nothing outrageous. Nothing unreasonable. But Edward Lane ran the marriage like a military operation. Anne couldn't handle it. And the more she chafed, the more Lane demanded discipline. It became his fetish.'

'What did she see in him in the first place?'

'He can be charismatic. He's strong and silent. And intelligent, in a narrow way.'

'What was she before?'

'A model.'

Reacher said nothing.

'Yes,' Patti said. 'Just like the next one.'

'What happened?'

'Between them they drove the marriage on the rocks. It was inevitable, I guess. One day she told me she wanted a divorce. I was all in favour of that, of course. It was the best thing for her. But she tried to do the whole drag-out knock-down thing. Alimony, division of assets, the whole nine yards. Which was the worst possible thing she could have done. I knew it was a mistake. I told her just to get the hell out while she still could. But she had brought money to the relationship. Lane had used it for part of his initial stake. Anne wanted her share back. But Lane couldn't even handle the insubordination of his wife wanting out of the marriage. To be made to give her money as well was out of the question for him. And it would have been a public humiliation, because he would have had to go out and find another investor. So he went completely postal. He faked a kidnapping and had her killed.'

Silence for a moment.

'The police were involved,' Reacher said. 'The FBI, too. There must have been a certain level of scrutiny.'

Patti turned around to face the room. Smiled, sadly.

'Here we go,' she said. 'We've reached the point where the little sister is sounding a little crazy and obsessed. But obviously Lane planned it well. He made it seem very real.'

'How?'

'His men. He employs a bunch of killers. They're all used to obeying orders. And they're all smart. They all know how to do stuff like this. And they aren't virgins. Every single one of them has been out on covert operations. And probably every single one of them has killed before, up close and personal.'

Reacher nodded. *No question about it. Every one of them has. Many times.*

'You got any particular suspects in mind?' he asked.

'None of the guys you've seen,' Patti said. 'Nobody who's still in the A-team. I don't think the dynamic would permit that. Not as time went by. I don't think it would be sustainable, psychologically. But I don't think he would have used B-teamers. He would have needed people he could trust completely.'

'So who?'

'A-team guys who aren't around any more.'

'Who would be in that category?'

'There were two,' Patti said. 'A guy called Hobart and a guy called Knight.'

'Why aren't they around any more? Why would two trusted A-teamers just up and leave?'

'Shortly after Anne died there was an operation overseas somewhere. Apparently it went bad. Two men didn't come back. Those two.'

'That would be a coincidence,' Reacher said. 'Wouldn't it? The two guilty men were the two who didn't come back?'

'I think Lane made sure they didn't come back. He wanted to tidy things up.'

Reacher said nothing.

'I know,' Patti said. 'The little sister is crazy, right?'

Reacher gazed at her. She didn't look crazy. A little spacey, maybe. In a Sixties way, like her sister. She had a curtain of long blond hair, straight, parted in the middle, just the same as Anne in the photograph. Big blue eyes, a button nose, a dusting of freckles, pale skin. She was wearing a white peasant blouse and faded blue jeans. She was barefoot and braless. You could have taken her picture and put it straight on the cover of a compilation CD. *The Summer of Love*. The Mamas and the Papas, Jefferson Airplane, Big Brother and the Holding Company. Reacher liked music like that. He had been seven during the summer of love, and he wished he had been seventeen.

'How do you think it went down?' he asked.

'Knight drove Anne that day,' Patti said. 'That's an established fact. He took her shopping.

124

Waited at the kerb. But she never came out of the store. Next thing anyone knew was a phone call four hours later. The usual thing. No cops, a ransom demand.'

'Voice?'

'Disguised.'

'How?'

'Like the guy was talking through a handkerchief or something.'

'How much was the ransom?'

'A hundred grand.'

'But Lane did call the cops.'

Patti nodded. 'But only to cover his ass. It was like he wanted independent witnesses. Very important to retain his credibility with the other guys that weren't in on the scheme.'

'Then what?'

'Like you see in the movies. The FBI tapped the phones and moved in on the ransom drop. Lane's story is that they were seen. But the whole thing was phoney. They waited, nobody showed up, because nobody was ever going to show up. So they brought the money home again. It was all a performance. A charade. Lane acted it all out and came home and gave the word that he was in the clear, that the cops had bought the story, that the FBI was convinced, and then Anne was killed. I'm sure of that.'

'Where was the other guy during all of this? Hobart?'

'Nobody knows for sure. He was off duty. He said he was in Philadelphia. But obviously he had been in the store, just waiting for Anne to show. He was the other half of the equation.'

'Did you go to the cops at the time?'

'They ignored me,' Patti said. 'Remember, this all was five years ago, not long after the Twin Towers. Everyone was preoccupied. And the military was suddenly back in fashion. You know, everyone was looking for their daddy, so people like Lane were the flavour of the month. Ex-Special Forces soldiers were pretty cool back then. I was fighting an uphill battle.'

'What about this cop Brewer? Now?'

'He tolerates me. What else can he do? I'm a taxpayer. But I don't suppose he's doing anything about it. I'm realistic.'

'You got any evidence against Lane at all?'

'No,' Patti said. 'None at all. All I've got is context and feeling and intuition. That's all I can share.'

'Context?'

'Do you know what a private military corporation is really for? Fundamentally?'

'Fundamentally its purpose is to allow the Pentagon to escape Congressional oversight.'

'Exactly,' Patti said. 'They're not necessarily better fighters than people currently enlisted. Often they're worse, and they're certainly more expensive. They're there to break the rules. Simple as that. If the Geneva Conventions get in the way, it doesn't matter to them, because nobody can call them on it. The government is insulated.'

'You've studied hard,' Reacher said.

'So what kind of a man is Lane to participate?'

'You tell me.'

'He's a sordid egomaniac weasel.'

'What do you wish you had done? To keep Anne alive?'

'I should have convinced her. I should have just gotten her out of there, penniless but alive.'

'Not easy,' Reacher said. 'You were the kid sister.'

'But I knew.'

'When did you move here?'

'About a year after Anne died. I couldn't let it rest.'

'Does Lane know you're here?'

She shook her head. 'I'm very careful. And this city is incredibly anonymous. You can go years without ever laying eyes on your neighbour.'

'What do you want me to do?'

'Do?'

'You brought me here for a purpose. And you took a hell of a risk doing it.'

'I think it's time for me to take risks.'

'What do you want me to do?'

'I want you to just walk away from him. For your own sake. Don't dirty your hands with his business. No possible good can come of it.'

Silence for a moment.

'And he's dangerous,' Patti said. 'More dangerous than you can know. It's not smart to be anywhere near him.'

'I'll be careful,' Reacher said.

'They're all dangerous.'

'I'll be careful,' Reacher said again. 'I always am. But I'm going back there now. I'll walk away on my own schedule.'

Patti Joseph said nothing.

'But I'd like to meet with this guy Brewer,' Reacher said.

'Why? Because you want to trade guy jokes about the nutty little sister?'

'No,' Reacher said. 'Because if he's any kind of a cop at all he'll have checked with the original detectives and the FBI agents. He might have a clearer picture.'

'Clearer which way?'

'Whichever way,' Reacher said. 'I'd like to know.'

'He might be here later.'

'Here?'

'He usually comes over after I phone in a report.'

'You said he wasn't doing anything.'

'I think he just comes for the company. I think he's lonely. He drops by, at the end of his shift, on his way home.'

'Where does he live?'

'Staten Island.'

'Where does he work?'

'Midtown.'

'So this isn't exactly on his way home.'

Patti Joseph said nothing.

'When does his shift end?' Reacher asked.

'Midnight.'

'He visits you at midnight? Way out of his way?'

'I'm not involved with him or anything,' Patti said. 'He's lonely. I'm lonely. That's all.'

Reacher said nothing.

'Make an excuse to get out,' Patti said. 'Check my window. If Brewer's here, the light will be on. If he isn't, it won't be.'

128

NINETEEN

Patti Joseph went back to her lonely vigil at the window and Reacher let himself out and left her there. He walked clockwise around her block for caution's sake and came up on the Dakota from the west. It was a quarter to ten in the evening. It was warm. There was music somewhere in the park. Music and people, far away. It was a perfect late-summer night. Probably baseball up in the Bronx or out at Shea, a thousand bars and clubs just warming up, eight million people looking back on the day or looking forward to the next.

Reacher stepped inside the building.

The lobby staff called up to the apartment and let him go ahead to the elevator. He got out and turned the corner and found Gregory in the corridor, waiting for him.

'We thought you'd quit on us,' Gregory said.

'Went for a walk,' Reacher said. 'Any news?'

'Too early.'

Reacher followed him into the apartment. It smelled sour. Chinese food, sweat, worry. Edward Lane was in the armchair next to the phone. He was staring up at the ceiling. His face was composed. Next to him at the end of a sofa was an empty place. A dented cushion. Recently occupied by Gregory, Reacher guessed. Then came Burke, sitting still. And Addison, and Perez, and Kowalski. Carter Groom was leaning on the wall, facing the door, vigilant. Like a sentry. *I'm all business*, he had said.

'When will they call?' Lane asked.

Good question, Reacher thought. *Will they call at all? Or will you call them? And give them the OK to pull the triggers?*

But he said: 'They won't call before eight in the morning. Drive time and counting time, it won't be any faster than that.'

Lane glanced at his watch.

'Ten hours from now,' he said.

'Yes,' Reacher said.

Somebody will call somebody ten hours from now.

The first of the ten hours passed in silence. The phone didn't ring. Nobody said a word. Reacher sat still and felt the chance of a happy outcome receding fast. He pictured the bedroom photograph in his mind and felt Kate and Jade moving away from him. Like a comet that had come close enough to Earth to be faintly visible but had then flung itself into a new orbit and was hurtling away into the frozen wastes of space and dwindling to a faint speck of light that would surely soon vanish forever.

'I did everything they asked,' Lane said, to nobody except himself.

Nobody replied.

*   *   *

The lone man surprised his temporary guests by moving towards the window, not the door. Then he surprised them more by using his fingernails to pick at the duct tape seam that held the cloth over the glass. He peeled the tape away from the wall until he was able to fold back a narrow rectangle of fabric and reveal a tall slim sliver of New York City at night. The famous view. A hundred thousand lit windows glittering against the darkness like tiny diamonds on a field of black velvet. Like nowhere else in the world.

He said, 'I know you love it.'

Then he said, 'But say goodbye to it.'

Then he said, 'Because you're never going to see it again.'

Halfway through the second hour Lane looked at Reacher and said, 'There's food in the kitchen, if you want some.' Then he smiled a thin humourless smile and said, 'Or to be technically accurate there's food in the kitchen whether you want some or not.'

Reacher didn't want food. He wasn't hungry. He had eaten a hot dog not long before. But he wanted to get the hell out of the living room. That was for sure. The atmosphere was like eight men sitting around a deathbed. He stood up.

'Thanks,' he said.

He walked quietly into the kitchen. Nobody followed him. There were dirty plates and a dozen open containers of Chinese food on the countertop. Half eaten and cold and pungent and congealed. He left them alone and sat on a stool. Glanced to his right at the open office door. He could see the photographs on the desk. Anne Lane, identical to her sister Patti. Kate Lane, gazing fondly at the child that had been cut out of the picture.

He listened hard. No sound from the living room. Nobody coming. He got off the stool and stepped inside the office. Stood still for a moment. *Desk, computer, fax machine, phones, file cabinets, shelves.*

He started with the shelves.

There were maybe eighteen linear feet of them. There were phone books on them, and manuals for firearms, and a one-volume history of Argentina, and a book called *Glock: The New Wave in Combat Handguns*, and an alarm clock, and mugs full of pens and pencils, and an atlas of the world. The atlas was old. The Soviet Union was still in it. And Yugoslavia. Some of the African countries still had their former colonial identities. Next to the atlas there was a fat Rolodex full of five hundred index cards with names and phone numbers and MOS codes on them. *Military Occupational Specialties.* Most of them were 11-Bravo. Infantry. Combat arms. At random Reacher flipped to *G* and looked for Carter Groom. Not there. Then *B* for Burke. Not there either. So clearly this was the B-team candidate pool. Some names had black lines through them with KIA or MIA notations written on the corners of the cards. *Killed in Action, Missing in Action.* But the rest of the names were still in the game. Nearly five hundred guys, and maybe some women, ready and available and looking for work.

Reacher put the Rolodex back and touched the computer mouse. The hard drive started up and a dialog box on the screen asked for a password. Reacher glanced at the open door and tried *Kate*. Access was denied. He tried *O5LaneE* for Colonel Edward Lane. Same result. Access denied. He shrugged and gave it up. The password was probably the guy's birthday or his old service number or the name of his high school football team. No way of knowing, without further research.

He moved on to the file cabinets.

There were four of them, standard store-bought items made of painted steel. Maybe thirty inches high. Two drawers in each of them. Eight drawers total. Unlabelled. Unlocked. He stood still and listened again and then slid the first drawer open. It moved quietly on ball bearing runners. It had twin hanging rails with six file dividers made of thin yellow cardboard slung between them. All six were full of paperwork. Reacher used his thumb and riffled through. Glanced down, obliquely. Financial records. Money moving in and out. No amount bigger than six figures and none smaller than four. Otherwise, incomprehensible. He closed the drawer.

He opened the bottom drawer on the left. Same hanging rails. Same yellow dividers. But they were bulky with the kind of big plastic wallets that come in the glove boxes of new cars. Instruction books, warranty certificates, service records. Titles. Insurance invoices. BMW, Mercedes Benz, BMW, Jaguar, Mercedes Benz, Land Rover. Some had valet keys in see-through plastic envelopes. Some had spare keys and remote fobs on the kind of promotional key rings that dealers give away. There were EZ-Pass toll records. Receipts from gas stations. Business cards from salesmen and service managers.

Reacher closed the drawer. Glanced back at the door. Saw Burke standing there, silent, just watching him.

TWENTY

Burke didn't speak for a long moment. Then he said, 'I'm going for a walk.'

'OK,' Reacher said.

Burke said nothing back.

'You want company?' Reacher asked.

Burke glanced at the computer screen. Then down at the file drawers.

'I'll keep you company,' Reacher said.

Burke just shrugged. Reacher followed him out through the kitchen. Through the foyer. Lane glanced at them from the living room, briefly, preoccupied with his thoughts. He didn't say anything. Reacher followed Burke out to the corridor. They rode down in the elevator in silence. Stepped out to the street and turned east towards Central Park. Reacher looked up at Patti Joseph's window. It was dark. The room behind it was unlit. Therefore she was alone. He pictured her in the chair behind the sill, in the gloom. Pictured her pen scratching on her pad of paper. *2327 hrs. Burke and Venti leave TDA on foot, head east towards Central Park.* Or *CP*. A person who wrote *TDA* for the Dakota would write *CP*

135

for Central Park, surely. And maybe she had dropped *Venti* and was using his real name now. He had told her what it was. Maybe she had written *Burke and Reacher leave TDA*.

Or maybe she was asleep. She had to sleep sometime.

'That question you asked,' Burke said.

'What question?' Reacher said.

'Who knew Mrs Lane loved Bloomingdale's?'

'What about it?'

'It was a good question,' Burke said.

'What's the answer?'

'There's another question,' Burke said.

'Which is?'

'Who knew she was heading there that particular morning?'

'I'm assuming you all knew,' Reacher said.

'Yes, I guess we all did, more or less.'

'Therefore it's not much of a question.'

'I think there's inside involvement,' Burke said. 'Somebody tipped somebody else off.'

'Was it you?'

'No.'

Reacher stopped at the crosswalk on Central Park West. Burke stopped beside him. He was as black as coal, a small man, about the size and shape of an old-fashioned Major League second baseman. A Hall of Famer. Like Joe Morgan. He had the same physical self-confidence in the way he held himself.

The light changed. The upright red hand blinked out and the forward-leaning white man came on. Reacher had always regretted the switch from the words WALK and DONT WALK.

Given the choice, he preferred words to pictograms. And as a kid he had been scandalized by the bad punctuation. Ten thousand missing apostrophes in every city in America. It had been a secret thrill, to know better.

He stepped off the kerb.

'What happened after Anne?' he asked.

'With the four guys who took her?' Burke said. 'Better that you don't know.'

'I'm guessing that you helped out with that.'

'No comment.'

'Did they admit it?'

'No,' Burke said. 'They claimed it was nothing to do with them.'

'But you didn't believe them.'

'What else were they going to say?'

They reached the far sidewalk. The park loomed ahead of them, dark and empty. The music had finished.

'Where are we going?' Reacher asked.

'Doesn't matter,' Burke said. 'I just wanted to talk.'

'About the insider involvement?'

'Yes.'

They turned south together and headed for Columbus Circle. There were lights and traffic down there. Crowds on the sidewalks.

'Who do you think it was?' Reacher asked.

'I have no idea,' Burke said.

'Then that's a pretty short conversation,' Reacher said. 'Isn't it? You wanted to talk, but you don't have much to talk about.'

Burke said nothing.

'But who got tipped off?' Reacher asked. 'Not

who did the tipping. I think that would be the more important answer. And I think that's what you want to tell me.'

Burke walked on in silence.

'You as good as dragged me out here,' Reacher said. 'Not because you're worried if I'm getting enough fresh air and exercise.'

Burke stayed quiet.

'You going to make me play Twenty Questions?' Reacher said.

'That might be the best way to do it,' Burke said.

'You think this is about the money?'

'No,' Burke said.

'So the money is a smokescreen?'

'Half the equation at best. Maybe a parallel aim.'

'The other half of the equation being punishment?'

'You got it.'

'You think there's someone out there with a grudge against Lane?'

'Yes.'

'One person?'

'No.'

'How many?'

'Theoretically there might be hundreds,' Burke said. 'Or thousands. Whole nations, maybe. We've messed with a lot of people, here and there.'

'Realistically?'

'More than one person,' Burke said.

'Two?'

'Yes.'

'What kind of a grudge?'

'What's the worst thing one man can do to another?'

'Depends who you are,' Reacher said.

'Exactly,' Burke said. 'So who are we?'

Reacher thought: *Navy SEALS, Delta Force, Recon Marines, Green Berets, SAS from Britain. The best in the world.*

'Special Forces soldiers,' he said.

'Exactly,' Burke said again. 'So what don't we do?'

'You don't leave bodies behind on the battle-field.'

Burke said nothing.

'But Lane did,' Reacher said. 'He left two bodies behind.'

Burke stopped on the north curve of Columbus Circle. Traffic roared all around. Headlight beams swept wild tangents. To the right, the tall silvery bulk of a brand-new building. A wide base blocking 59th Street and twin towers rising above.

'So what are you saying?' Reacher asked. 'They had brothers or sons? Someone's come out of the woodwork looking for revenge? Finally? On their behalf?'

'Doesn't necessarily take brothers or sons,' Burke said.

'Buddies?'

'Doesn't necessarily take buddies either.'

'So who?'

Burke didn't answer. Reacher stared at him.

'Christ,' he said. 'You left two guys behind *alive*?'

'Not me,' Burke said. 'Not us. It was Lane.'

139

'And you think they finally made it home?'

'I'm sure they would have tried hard.'

'Hobart and Knight,' Reacher said.

'You know their names.'

'Evidently.'

'How? Who have you been talking to? There's nothing about them in those file cabinets you were looking through. Or in the computer. They've been erased. Like they never existed. Like they're dirty little secrets. Which they are.'

'What happened with them?'

'They were wounded. According to Lane. We never saw them. They were in forward observation posts and we heard small arms fire. Lane went up the line and came back and said they were hit bad and couldn't possibly make it. He said we couldn't bring them in. He said we'd lose too many guys trying. He flat ordered us to pull out. We left them there.'

'And what do you suppose happened to them?'

'We assumed they'd be taken prisoner. In which case we assumed their life expectancy would be about a minute and a half.'

I think Lane made sure they didn't come back.

'Where was this?' Reacher asked.

'I can't tell you,' Burke said. 'I'd go to jail.'

'Why did you stick around afterwards? All this time?'

'Why wouldn't I?'

'Sounds like you're unhappy with how things went down.'

'I obey orders. And I let officers decide things. That's how it always was and that's how it always will be.'

140

'Does he know they're back? Lane?'

'You're not listening,' Burke said. 'Nobody *knows* they're back. Nobody even knows if they're alive. I'm just guessing, is all. Based on how big of a deal this all is.'

'Would they do it? Hobart and Knight? Hurt a woman and a child to put a scare into Lane?'

'You mean, is it justified? Of course it isn't. But would they do it? Hell yes, they would do it. Pragmatic people do what works. Especially after what Lane did to them.'

Reacher nodded. 'Who would be talking to them? From the inside?'

'I don't know.'

'What were they?'

'Jarheads.'

'Like Carter Groom.'

'Yes,' Burke said. 'Like Carter Groom.'

Reacher said nothing.

'Marines hate that,' Burke said. 'Especially Recon Marines. They hate leaving guys behind. More than anyone. It's their code.'

'So why does *he* stick around?'

'Same reason I do. Ours is not to reason why. That's also a code.'

'Maybe in the service,' Reacher said. 'Not necessarily in some half-assed private company.'

'I don't see a difference.'

'Well, you ought to, soldier.'

'Watch your mouth, pal. I'm helping you out here. I'm earning you a million bucks. You find Hobart and Knight, you find Kate and Jade, too.'

'You think?'

'Dollars to doughnuts. A *million* dollars to doughnuts. So watch your mouth.'

'I don't need to watch my mouth,' Reacher said. 'If you've still got a code, then I'm still an officer. I can say what I like and you can stand there and take it and salute.'

Burke turned away from the swirling river of traffic in front of him and headed back north. Reacher let him get five yards away and then caught up and fell in beside him. Nothing more was said. Ten minutes later they turned into 72nd Street. Reacher glanced up and to his left. Patti Joseph's window was blazing with light.

TWENTY-ONE

Reacher said, 'You go on ahead. I'm going to walk some more.'

'Why?' Burke asked.

'You gave me things to think about.'

'You can't think unless you're walking?'

'No point looking for Hobart and Knight inside the apartment.'

'That's for sure. They were erased.'

'One more thing,' Reacher said. 'When did Lane and Kate get together?'

'Soon after Anne died. Lane doesn't like to be alone.'

'Do they get along OK?'

'They're still married,' Burke said.

'What does that mean?'

'It means they get along OK.'

'How well?'

'Well enough.'

'As well as he got along with Anne? The first time around?'

Burke nodded. 'About the same.'

'I'll see you later,' Reacher said.

* * *

Reacher watched Burke disappear inside the Dakota and then moved on west, away from Patti Joseph's place. Routine caution, which paid off big time when he glanced back and saw Burke coming after him. Clearly Burke had turned around inside the Dakota's lobby and was trying a pretty poor imitation of a clandestine tail. He was sneaking along in the shadows, his black skin and his black clothes mostly invisible but lit up like a superstar every time he passed under a street light.

He doesn't trust me, Reacher thought.

A Delta noncom doesn't trust an MP.

Well, there's a big surprise.

Reacher walked to the end of the block and took the stairs down to the subway. To the northbound platform. Used his Metrocard at the turnstile. He figured Burke wouldn't have a Metrocard. Lane's people drove everywhere. In which case Burke would be hung up at the machine, swiping his credit card or feeding creased bills into the slot. In which case the tail would fail at the first hurdle. If a train came soon.

Which it didn't.

It was midnight, and the trains were well into their off-peak schedules. Average wait time was probably fifteen or twenty minutes. Reacher was ready to get lucky, but he didn't. He turned and saw Burke collect a brand new card from the machine and hang back, just waiting.

Reacher thought: *He doesn't want to be on the platform with me. He's going to come through the turnstile at the last possible minute.*

Reacher waited. There were twelve people

144

waiting with him. A knot of three, a knot of two, seven people on their own. Mostly they were well dressed. They were folks going home after movies or restaurant meals, heading back to cheaper rents in the hundreds or all the way up in Hudson Heights.

The tunnel stayed quiet. The air was warm. Reacher leaned on a pillar and waited. Then he heard the rails start their strange metallic keening. A train, half a mile away. He saw a faint light in the darkness and felt the push of hot air. Then the noise built and the twelve people on the platform shuffled forward.

Reacher shuffled backward.

He pressed himself into a maintenance recess the size of a phone booth. Stood still. A train rolled in, fast, long, loud, hissing and squealing. A 1 train, local. Shiny aluminium, bright windows. It stopped. People got off, people got on. Then Burke came through the turnstile and made it through the doors just before they closed. The train moved away, left to right, and Reacher saw Burke through the windows. He was walking forward, eyes front, hunting his quarry, car by car.

He would be all the way up in the Bronx, 242nd Street, Van Cortlandt Park, before he realized his quarry wasn't on the train at all.

Reacher came out of the recess and brushed dirt off the shoulders of his shirt. Headed for the exit and up to the street. He was down two bucks, but he was alone, which was what he wanted to be.

* * *

The doorman at the Majestic called upstairs and pointed Reacher towards the elevator. Three minutes later he was shaking hands with Brewer, the cop. Patti Joseph was in the kitchen, making coffee. She had changed her clothes. Now she was wearing a dark trouser suit, prim and proper. She had shoes on. She came out of the kitchen with two mugs, the same huge Wedgwood items she had used before. She gave one to Brewer and one to Reacher and said, 'I'll leave you guys to talk. Maybe easier if I'm not here. I'll go for a walk. Night-time is about the only time it's safe for me to be out.'

Reacher said, 'Burke will be coming out of the subway in about an hour.'

Patti said, 'He won't see me.'

Then she left, with a nervous glance back, as if her future was at stake. Reacher watched the door close behind her and turned and took a better look at Brewer. He was everything anyone would expect a New York City detective to be, except magnified a little. A little taller, a little heavier, longer hair, more unkempt, more energetic. He was about fifty. Or forty-something and prematurely grey.

'What's your interest here?' he asked.

'I crossed paths with Edward Lane,' Reacher said. 'And I heard Patti's story. So I want to know what I'm getting into. That's all.'

'Crossed paths how?'

'He wants to hire me for something.'

'What's your line of work?'

'I was in the army,' Reacher said.

'It's a free country,' Brewer said. 'You can work for whoever you want.'

146

Then he sat down on Patti Joseph's sofa like he owned it. Reacher stayed away from the window. The light was on and he would be visible from the street. He leaned on the wall near the lobby and sipped his coffee.

'I was a cop once myself,' he said. 'Military police.'

'Is that supposed to impress me?'

'Plenty of your guys came from the same place as me. Do they impress you?'

Brewer shrugged.

'I guess I can give you five minutes,' he said.

'Bottom line,' Reacher said. 'What happened five years ago?'

'I can't tell you that,' Brewer said. 'Nobody in the NYPD can tell you that. If it was a kidnap, that's FBI business, because kidnapping is a federal crime. If it was a straightforward homicide, then that's New Jersey business, because the body was found on the other side of the George Washington Bridge, and it hadn't been moved postmortem. Therefore it was never really our case. Therefore we never really developed an opinion.'

'So why are you here?'

'Community relations. The kid is hurting, and she needs an ear. Plus she's cute and she makes good coffee. Why wouldn't I be here?'

'Your people must have gotten copied in on the paperwork.'

Brewer nodded.

'There's a file,' he said.

'What's in it?'

'Cobwebs and dust, mostly. The only thing anyone knows for sure is that Anne Lane died

147

five years ago in New Jersey. She was a month decomposed when they found her. Not a pretty sight, apparently. But there was a definitive dental identification. It was her.'

'Where was this?'

'A vacant lot near the Turnpike.'

'Cause of death?'

'Fatal GSW to the back of her head. Large-calibre handgun, probably a nine, but impossible to be precise. She was out in the open. Rodents had been in and out the bullet hole. And rodents aren't dumb. They figure they're going to get fat on the good stuff inside, so they widen the hole before they go in. The bone was gnawed. But it was probably a nine, probably jacketed.'

'I hope you didn't tell Patti all of that.'

'What are you? Her big brother? Of course I didn't tell her all of that.'

'Anything else at the scene?'

'There was a playing card. The three of clubs. Shoved down the neck of her shirt, from the back. No forensics worth a damn, nobody knew what it meant.'

'Was it like a signature?'

'Or a tease. You know, some random crap to make everyone go blind trying to figure it out.'

'So what do you think?' Reacher said. 'Kidnap or murder?'

Brewer yawned. 'No reason to look for complications. You hear hoofbeats, you look for horses, not zebras. A guy calls in that his wife has been kidnapped, you assume it's true. You don't start assuming it's a complex plot to do away with

148

her. And it was all plausible. There were real phone calls, there was real cash money in a bag.'

'But?'

Brewer went quiet for a moment. Took a long pull on his mug of coffee, swallowed, exhaled, rested his head back on the sofa.

'Patti kinds of sucks you in,' he said. 'You know? Sooner or later you have to admit it's just as plausible the other way around.'

'Gut feeling?'

'I just don't know,' Brewer said. 'Which is a weird feeling in itself, for me. I mean, sometimes I'm wrong, but I always *know*.'

'So what are you doing about it?'

'Nothing,' Brewer said. 'It's an ice-cold case outside of our jurisdiction. Hell will freeze over before the NYPD voluntarily books another un-solved homicide.'

'But you keep on showing up here.'

'Like I said, the kid needs an ear. Grief is a long and complicated process.'

'You do this for all the relatives?'

'Only the ones that look like they belong in *Playboy* magazine.'

Reacher said nothing.

'What's your interest here?' Brewer asked again.

'Like I said.'

'Bullshit. Lane was a combat soldier. Now he's a mercenary. You're not worried about whether he offed someone he shouldn't have five years ago. Find me a guy like Lane who didn't.'

Reacher said nothing.

'Something's on your mind,' Brewer said.

149

Silence for a moment.

'One thing Patti told me,' Brewer said. 'She hasn't seen the new Mrs Lane for a couple of days. Or the kid.'

Reacher said nothing.

Brewer said, 'Maybe she's missing and you're looking for parallels in the past.'

Reacher stayed quiet.

Brewer said, 'You were a cop, not a combat soldier. So now I'm wondering what kind of thing Edward Lane would want to hire you for.'

Reacher said nothing.

Brewer said, 'Anything you want to tell me?'

'I'm asking,' Reacher said. 'Not telling.'

More silence. A long hard look, cop to cop.

'As you wish,' Brewer said. 'It's a free country.'

Reacher finished his coffee and stepped into the kitchen. Rinsed his mug under the tap and left it in the sink. Then he leaned his elbows on the counter and stared straight ahead. The living room in front of him was framed by the pass-through. The high-backed chair was at the window. On the sill was the neat surveillance array. The notebook, the pen, the camera, the binoculars.

'So what do you do with the stuff she calls in? Just bury it?'

Brewer shook his head.

'I pass it on,' he said. 'Outside the department. To someone with an interest.'

'Who?'

'A private detective, downtown. A woman. She's cute too. Older, but hey.'

'NYPD is working with private detectives now?'

'This one is in an unusual position. She's retired FBI.'

'They're all retired something.'

'This one was the lead agent on the Anne Lane case.'

Reacher said nothing.

Brewer smiled. 'So like I said, this one has an interest.'

Reacher said, 'Does Patti know?'

Brewer shook his head. 'Better that Patti doesn't. Better that Patti never finds out. It would make for a bad combination.'

'What's this woman's name?'

'I thought you'd never ask,' Brewer said.

TWENTY-TWO

Reacher left Patti Joseph's apartment with two business cards. One was Brewer's official NYPD issue and the other was an elegant item with *Lauren Pauling* engraved at the top and *Private Investigator* under the name. Then: *Ex-Special Agent, Federal Bureau of Investigation*. At the bottom was a downtown address, with 212 and 917 phone numbers for landline and cell, and e-mail, and a website URL. It was a busy card. But the whole thing looked crisp and expensive, professional and efficient. Better than Brewer's NYPD card, and better even than Gregory's OSC card.

Reacher tossed Brewer's card in a Central Park West trash can and put Lauren Pauling's in his shoe. Then he took a circuitous route back towards the Dakota. It was close to one o'clock in the morning. He circled the block and saw a cop car on Columbus Avenue. *Cops*, he thought. The word hung up in his mind the same way it had down in Soho. The way a twig on a swirling current catches on a riverbank. He stopped walking and closed his eyes and tried to catch it.

But it spun away again. He gave it up and turned into 72nd Street. Turned into the Dakota's lobby. The night crew doorman was a dignified old guy. He called upstairs and inclined his head like an invitation to proceed. On five Gregory was out in the corridor with the door open and ready. Reacher followed him inside and Gregory said, 'Nothing yet. But we've got seven more hours.'

The apartment was dead-of-night quiet and still smelled of Chinese food. Everyone was still in the living room. Except Burke. Burke wasn't back yet. Gregory looked full of energy and Lane was upright in a chair but the others were slumped in various tired poses. The lights were low and yellow and the drapes were drawn and the air was hot.

'Wait with us,' Lane said.

'I need to sleep,' Reacher said. 'Three or four hours.'

'Use Jade's room,' Lane said.

Reacher nodded and headed off through the interior hallways to Jade's room. The nightlight was still burning. The room smelled faintly of baby powder and clean skin. The bed was way too small for a guy Reacher's size. Too small for any guy, really. It was some kind of a half-size piece, probably from a specialist children's boutique. There was an attached bathroom carved out of another maid's room. A sink, a toilet, a tub with a shower over it. The shower head was on a sliding pole. It was set about three feet above the drain hole. The shower curtain was clear plastic with yellow ducks on it.

Reacher slid the head all the way to the top and stripped and took a fast shower, with a cake of pink soap shaped like a strawberry, and baby shampoo. *No tears*, the bottle said. *I wish*, he thought. Then he dried himself on a small pink towel and put the tiny fragrant pyjamas on a chair and took the pillow and the sheet and the comforter off the bed and made himself a bivouac on the floor. He cleared bears and dolls out of his way. The bears were all plush and new and the dolls looked untouched. He moved the desk a foot to one side to make room and all the papers fell off it. Drawings, in crayon on cheap paper. Trees, like bright green lollipops on brown sticks, with a big grey building beyond. The Dakota, from Central Park, maybe. There was another of three stick figures, one much smaller than the others. The family, maybe. Mother, daughter, stepfather. Mother and daughter were smiling but Lane was drawn with black holes in his mouth like someone had punched half his teeth out. There was a picture of an airplane low in the sky. Green earth below, a stripe of blue above, a yellow ball for the sun. The plane's fuselage was shaped like a sausage and had three portholes with faces in them. The wings were drawn as if from above. Like the plane was in a panic turn. The last picture was of the family again, but twice over. Two Lanes close together and side by side, two Kates, two Jades. It was like looking at the second picture again with double vision.

Reacher restacked the papers neatly and switched out the nightlight. Burrowed into the bedclothes. They covered him from his chest to his knees. He could smell baby shampoo. From his own hair, or from Jade's pillow. He wasn't sure. He set the alarm in his head for five in the morning. He closed his eyes, breathed once, breathed twice, and fell asleep, on a floor made hard and dense and solid by three feet of Central Park clay.

Reacher woke as planned at five o'clock in the morning, uncomfortable, still tired, and cold. He could smell coffee. He found Carter Groom in the kitchen, next to a big Krups drip machine.

'Three hours to go,' Groom said. 'Think they're going to call?'

'I don't know,' Reacher said. 'Do you think they will?'

Groom didn't reply. Just drummed his fingers on the counter as he waited for the machine to finish. Reacher waited with him. Then Burke came in. He looked like he hadn't slept. He didn't say anything. Nothing pleasant, nothing hostile. He just acted like the previous evening had never existed. Groom filled three mugs with coffee. Took one, and left the room. Burke took one and followed him. Reacher drank his sitting on the counter. The clock on the wall oven said five-ten. He figured it was a little slow. He felt it was closer to a quarter past.

Time for ex-Special Agent Lauren Pauling's wake-up call.

He stopped in the living room on his way out. Lane was still in the same chair. Immobile.

155

Still upright. Still composed. Still stoic. Real or phoney, either way, it was one hell of a display of endurance. Gregory and Perez and Kowalski were asleep on sofas. Addison was awake but inert. Groom and Burke were drinking their coffee.

'I'm going out,' Reacher said.

'Another walk?' Burke asked, sourly.

'Breakfast,' Reacher said.

The old guy in the lobby was still on duty. Reacher nodded to him and turned right on 72nd and headed for Broadway. Nobody came after him. He found a pay phone and used a quarter from his pocket and the card from his shoe and dialled Pauling's cell. He figured she would keep it switched on, top of her nightstand, near her pillow.

She answered on the third ring.

'Hello?' she said.

Rusty voice, not sleepy, just not yet used today. Maybe she lived alone.

Reacher asked, 'You heard the name Reacher recently?'

'Should I have?' Pauling asked back.

'It will save us a lot of time if you just say yes. From Anne Lane's sister Patti, through a cop called Brewer, am I right?'

'Yes,' Pauling said. 'Late yesterday.'

'I need an early appointment,' Reacher said.

'You're Reacher?'

'Yes, I am. Half an hour, at your office?'

'You know where it is?'

'Brewer gave me your card.'

'Half an hour,' Pauling said.

And so half an hour later Reacher was standing on a West 4th Street sidewalk, with a cup of coffee in one hand and a doughnut in the other, watching Lauren Pauling walk towards him.

TWENTY-THREE

Reacher knew it was Lauren Pauling walking towards him because of the way her eyes were fixed on his face. Clearly Patti Joseph had passed on his physical description as well as his name. So Pauling was looking for a tall, wide, blond, untidy man waiting near her office door, and Reacher was the only possibility that morning on West 4th Street.

Pauling herself was an elegant woman of about fifty. Or maybe a little more, in which case she was carrying it well. Brewer had said *she's cute too* and he had been right. She was about an inch taller than average, dressed in a black pencil skirt that fell to her knees. Black stockings, black shoes with heels. An emerald green blouse that could have been silk. A rope of big fake pearls at her neck. Hair frosted gold and blond. It fell in big waves to her shoulders. Green eyes that smiled. A look on her face that said: *I'm very pleased to meet you but let's get straight to the good stuff.* Reacher could imagine the kind of team meetings she must have run for the Bureau.

'Jack Reacher, I presume,' she said.

Reacher shoved his doughnut between his teeth and wiped his fingers on his chinos and shook her hand. Then he waited at her shoulder as she unlocked her street door. Watched as she deactivated an alarm with a keypad in the lobby. The keypad was a standard three-by-three cluster with the zero alone at the bottom. She was right-handed. She used her middle finger, index finger, ring finger, index finger, without moving her hand much. Brisk, decisive motion. Like typing. *Probably 8461*, Reacher thought. *Dumb or distracted to let me see. Distracted, probably. She can't be dumb.* But it was the building's alarm. Not her personal choice of numbers. So she hadn't given away her home system or her ATM card.

'Follow me,' she said.

Reacher followed her up a narrow staircase to the second floor. He finished his doughnut on the way. She unlocked a door and led him into an office. It was a two-room suite. Waiting room first, and then a back room for her desk and two visitor chairs. Very compact, but the décor was good. Good taste, careful application. Full of the kind of expensive stuff a solo professional leases to create an impression of confidence in a client. A little bigger, it could have been a lawyer's place, or a cosmetic surgeon's.

'I spoke to Brewer,' she said. 'I called him at home after you called me. I woke him up. He wasn't very happy about that.'

'I can imagine,' Reacher said.

'He's curious about your motives.'

Lauren Pauling's voice was low and husky,

like she had been recovering from laryngitis for the last thirty years. Reacher could have sat and listened to it all day long.

'Therefore I'm curious too,' she said.

She pointed at a leather client chair. Reacher sat down in it. She squeezed sideways around the end of her desk. She was slender and she moved well. She turned her chair to face him. Sat down.

'I'm just looking for information,' Reacher said.

'But why?'

'Let's see if it leads me to where I need to tell you.'

'Brewer said you were a military cop.'

'Once upon a time.'

'A good one?'

'Is there any other kind?'

Pauling smiled, a little sadly, a little wistfully.

'Then you know you shouldn't be talking to me,' she said.

'Why not?'

'Because I'm not a reliable witness. I'm hopelessly biased.'

'Why?'

'Think about it,' she said. 'Isn't it obvious? If Edward Lane didn't kill his wife, then who the hell did? Well, *I* did, that's who. Through my own carelessness.'

160

TWENTY-FOUR

Reacher moved in his chair and said, 'Nobody scores a hundred per cent. Not in the real world. Not me, not you, not anybody. So get over it.'

'That's your response?' Pauling said.

'I probably got more people killed than you ever met. I don't beat myself up over them. Shit happens.'

Pauling nodded. 'It's the sister. She's up there in that weird little eyrie all the time. She's like my conscience.'

'I met her,' Reacher said.

'She weighs on my mind.'

'Tell me about the three of clubs,' Reacher said.

Pauling paused, like a gear change.

'We concluded it was meaningless,' she said. 'There had been a book or a movie or something where assassins left calling cards. So we tended to get a lot of that at the time. But usually they were picture cards. Mostly aces, mostly spades. There was nothing in the databases about threes. Not much about clubs, either. Then we thought maybe this was one of three connected things, you know, but there was never anything else similar to put with it. We studied symbolism and number theory. We checked with UCLA, talked to the people who study gang culture. Nothing there. We talked to semiotics people at Harvard and Yale and the Smithsonian. We talked to Wesleyan in Connecticut, got some linguistics person working on it. Nothing there. We had a grad student at Columbia working on it. We had people with brains the size of planets working on it. Nothing anywhere. So the three of clubs meant nothing. It was designed to make us chase our tails. Which in itself was a meaningless conclusion. Because what we needed to know was who would *want* us to chase our tails.'

'Did you look at Lane back then? Even before you heard Patti's theories?'

Pauling nodded. 'We looked at him very carefully, and all his guys. More from the point of view of threat assessment, back then. Like, who knew him? Who knew he had money? Who even knew he had a wife?'

'And?'

'He's not a very pleasant man. He's borderline mentally ill. He has a psychotic need to command.'

'Patti Joseph says the same things.'

'She's right.'

'And you know what?' Reacher said. 'His men are mostly a couple of sandwiches short of a picnic, too. They've got a psychotic need to be commanded. I've talked to some of them. They're civilians, but they're holding fast to their old military codes. Like security blankets. Even when they don't really enjoy the results.'

'They're a weird bunch. All Special Forces and black ops, so naturally the Pentagon wasn't very forthcoming. But we noticed two things. Most of them had been around the block many, many times, but there were far fewer medals among them than you would normally expect to see. And most of them got general discharges. Not honourable discharges. Including Lane himself. What do you think all of that means?'

'I suspect you know exactly what it means.'

'I'd like to hear it from your professional perspective.'

'It means they were bad guys. Either low-level and irritating, or bigger deals but with charges not proven.'

'What about the lack of medals?'

'Messy campaigns,' Reacher said. 'Gratuitous collateral damage, looting, prisoner abuse. Maybe prisoners got shot. Maybe buildings got burned.'

'And Lane himself?'

'Ordered abuse or failed to prevent it. Or maybe participated in it. He told me he quit after the Gulf the first time around. I was there. There were pockets of bad behaviour.'

'Stuff like that can't be proved?'

'Special Forces operate on their own miles from anywhere. It's a clandestine world. There would have been rumours, that's all. Maybe a whistleblower or two. But no hard evidence.'

Pauling nodded again. 'Those were our conclusions. Internally generated. We employed a lot of ex-military in the Bureau.'

'You employed the good ones,' Reacher said.

'The ones with honourable discharges and medals and recommendations.'

'Is that what you got?'

'All of the above. But I had a couple of promotion hiccups, because I'm not a very co-operative guy. Gregory asked me about that. The first one of them I spoke to. The first conversation we had. He asked if I'd had career problems. He seemed happy that I had.'

'Puts you in the same boat.'

Reacher nodded. 'And it kind of explains why they're sticking with Lane. Where else are they going to get twenty-five grand a month with their records?'

'Is that what they get? That's three hundred thousand a year.'

'It was back when I learned math.'

'Is that what Lane offered you? Three hundred grand?'

Reacher said nothing.

'What is he hiring you for?'

Reacher said nothing.

'What's on your mind?'

'We're not done with the information yet.'

'Anne Lane died, five years ago, in a vacant lot near the New Jersey Turnpike. That's all the hard data we'll ever have.'

'Gut feeling?'

'What's yours?'

Reacher shrugged. 'Brewer said something to me. He said he just didn't know, which was weird for him, he said, because whereas he was some-times wrong, he always *knew*. And I'm exactly the same. I always know. Except this time I don't know. So what's on my mind right now is that I have nothing on my mind.'

'I think it was a genuine kidnap,' Pauling said. 'I think I blew it.'

'Do you?'

She paused a beat. Shook her head.

'Not really,' she said. 'Truthfully, I just don't know. God knows I *want* Lane to have done it. Obviously. And maybe he did. But for the sake of my sanity I have to acknowledge that's mostly wishful thinking, to excuse myself. And I have to file the whole thing somewhere, mentally. So I tend to come down on the side of avoiding self-indulgence and cheap consolation. And usually the simple option is the right option anyway. So it was a simple kidnap, not an elaborate charade. And I blew it.'

'How did you blow it?'

'I don't know. I've lain awake a hundred nights going over it. I don't see how I made a mistake.'

'So maybe you didn't blow it. Maybe it *was* an elaborate charade.'

'What's on your mind, Reacher?'

He looked at her.

'Whatever it was, it's happening again,' he said.

TWENTY-FIVE

Lauren Pauling sat forward in her chair and said, 'Tell me.' So Reacher told her, everything, from the first night in the café, the first double espresso in its foam cup, the badly parked Mercedes Benz, the anonymous driver threading through the Sixth Avenue traffic on foot and then driving the Benz away. The second day, with Gregory scouting witnesses. The third day, with the unopened red door and the blue BMW. And then the nightmare electronic voice, guiding the black BMW back to the exact same fireplug.

'If that's a charade it's unbelievably elaborate,' Pauling said.

'My feeling exactly,' Reacher said.

'And insanely expensive.'

'Maybe not,' Reacher said.

'You mean because the money comes around in a big circle?'

'I haven't actually seen any money. All I've seen are zippered bags.'

'Cut up newspaper?'

'Maybe,' Reacher said. 'If it's a charade.'

'What if it isn't?'

'Exactly.'

'It feels real.'

'And if it isn't real, I can't imagine who's doing it. He would need people he trusts, which means A-teamers, but there's nobody AWOL.'

'Were they getting along? Man and wife?'

'Nobody says otherwise.'

'So it's real.'

Reacher nodded. 'There's an internal consistency to it. The initial takedown must have depended on an inside tip, as to where Kate and Jade were going to be, and when. And we can prove that inside involvement two ways. First, these people know something about Lane's operation. They know exactly what cars he's got, for instance.'

'And second?'

'Something that was nagging at me. Something about cops. I asked Lane to repeat what was said during the first phone call. And he did, word for word. And the bad guys never said *no cops*. That's kind of standard, isn't it? Like, *don't go to the cops*. But that was never said. Which suggests these people knew the story from five years ago. They knew Lane wouldn't go to the cops anyway. So it didn't need saying.'

'That would suggest that five years ago was for real.'

'Not necessarily. It might only reflect what Lane put out there for public consumption.'

'If it's real this time, does that make it more likely it was real last time?'

'Maybe, maybe not. But whatever, give yourself a break.'

'This is like a hall of fun house mirrors.'

Reacher nodded. 'But there's one thing I can't make fit under any scenario. Which is the initial takedown itself. The only viable method would have been quick and dirty inside the car, as soon as it stopped. Everyone agrees on that. I asked a couple of Lane's guys, theoretically, in case there was something I hadn't thought of. But there wasn't. And the problem is, Bloomingdale's is a whole block long. How could anyone have predicted exactly what yard of Lexington Avenue Taylor's Jaguar was going to stop on? And if they didn't predict it exactly right, then the whole thing would have fallen apart immediately, there and then. Either Kate and Jade would have been out on the sidewalk already, or Taylor would have seen the takedown guy running up, in which case he would have reacted and taken off. Or at least hit the door locks.'

'So what are you saying?'

'I'm saying real or fake there's something wrong with this whole thing. I'm saying I can't get a handle on what happened. I can't get traction. I'm saying for the first time in my life I just don't know. Like Brewer said, I've been wrong plenty of times, but I've always known before.'

'You should talk to Brewer, officially.'

'No point. NYPD can't do anything without a complaint from Lane. Or at least a missing person report from someone with an interest.'

'So what are you going to do?'

'I'm going to have to do it the hard way,' Reacher said.

'What way is that?'

'It's what we called it in the service when we didn't catch a break. When we actually had to work for a living. You know, start over at square one, re-examine everything, sweat the details, work the clues.'

'Kate and Jade are probably already dead.'

'Then I'll make someone pay.'

'Can I help?'

'I need to know about two guys called Hobart and Knight.'

Pauling nodded. 'Knight was the driver the day Anne was taken and Hobart was in Philadelphia. Now Patti Joseph talks about them. They died overseas.'

'Maybe they didn't die overseas. They were abandoned wounded but alive. I need to know where, when, how, and what's likely to have happened to them.'

'You think they're alive? You think they're back?'

'I don't know what to think. But at least one of Lane's guys wasn't sleeping too well last night.'

'I met Hobart and Knight, you know. Five years ago. During the investigation.'

'Did either of them look like the guy I saw?'

'Medium-sized and ordinary-looking? Both of them, exactly.'

'That helps.'

'What are you going to do now?'

'I'm going back to the Dakota. Maybe we'll get a call and this whole thing will be over. But more likely we won't, and it's just beginning.'

'Give me three hours,' Pauling said. 'Then call my cell.'

TWENTY-SIX

By the time Reacher got back to the Dakota it was seven o'clock and dawn had given way to full morning. The sky was a pale hard blue. No cloud. Just a beautiful late summer day in the capital of the world. But inside the fifth floor apartment the air was foul and hot and the drapes were still drawn. Reacher didn't need to ask whether the phone had rung. Clearly it hadn't. The tableau was the same as it had been nine hours earlier. Lane upright in his chair. Then Gregory, Groom, Burke, Perez, Addison, Kowalski, all silent, all morose, all arrayed here and there, eyes closed, eyes open, staring into space, breathing low.

Medals not approved.

General discharges.

Bad guys.

Lane turned his head slowly and looked straight at Reacher and asked, 'Where the hell have you been?'

'Breakfast,' Reacher said.

'Long breakfast. What was it, five courses at the Four Seasons?'

'A diner,' Reacher said. 'Bad choice. Slow service.'

'I pay you to work. I don't pay you to be out stuffing your face.'

'You don't pay me at all,' Reacher said. 'I haven't seen dime one yet.'

Lane kept his body facing forward and his head turned ninety degrees to the side. Like a querulous sea bird. His eyes were dark and wet and glittering.

'Is *that* your problem?' he asked. 'Money?'

Reacher said nothing.

'That's easily solved,' Lane said.

He kept his eyes on Reacher's face and put his hands on the chair arms, palms down, pale parchment skin ridged with tendons and veins ghostly in the yellow light. He levered himself upright, with an effort, like it was the first time he had moved in nine hours, which it probably was. He stood unsteadily and walked towards the lobby, stiffly, shuffling like he was old and infirm.

'Come,' he said. Like a command. Like the colonel he had been. Reacher followed him to the master bedroom suite. The pencil post bed, the armoire, the desk. The silence. The photograph. Lane opened his closet. The narrower of the two doors. Inside was a shallow recess, and then another door. To the left of the inner door was a security keypad. It was the same type of three-by-three-plus-zero matrix as Lauren Pauling had used at her office. Lane used his left hand. Index finger, curled. Ring finger, straight. Middle finger, straight. Middle finger, curled. *3785*, Reacher thought. *Dumb or distracted to let me see*. The keypad beeped and Lane opened the inner door. Reached inside and pulled a chain. A light came on and showed a chamber maybe six feet by three. It was stacked with cube-shaped bales of something wrapped tight in heavy heat-shrunk plastic. Dust and foreign printing on the plastic. At first Reacher didn't know what he was looking at.

Then he realized: The printing was French, and it said *Banque Centrale*.

Central Bank.

Money.

US dollars, bricked and banded and stacked and wrapped. Some cubes were neat and intact. One was torn open and spilling bricks. The floor was littered with empty plastic wrap. It was the kind of thick plastic that would take real effort to tear. You would have to jam a thumbnail through and hook your fingers in the hole and really strain. It would stretch. It would part reluctantly.

Lane bent at the waist and dragged the open bale out into the bedroom. Then he lifted it and swung it through a small arc and let it fall on the floor near Reacher's feet. It skidded on the shiny hardwood and two slim bricks of cash fell out.

'There you go,' Lane said. 'Dime one.'

Reacher said nothing.

'Pick it up,' Lane said. 'It's yours.'

Reacher said nothing. Just moved away to the door.

'Take it,' Lane said.

Reacher stood still.

Lane bent down again and picked up a spilled

172

brick. He hefted it in his hand. Ten thousand dollars. A hundred hundreds.

'Take it,' he said again.

Reacher said, 'We'll talk about a fee if I get a result.'

'*Take it!*' Lane screamed. Then he hurled the brick straight at Reacher's chest. It struck above the breastbone, dense, surprisingly heavy. It bounced off and hit the floor. Lane picked up the other loose brick and threw it. It hit the same spot.

'*Take it!*' he screamed.

Then he bent down and plunged his hands into the plastic and started hauling out one brick after another. He threw them wildly, without pausing, without straightening, without looking, without aiming. They hit Reacher in the legs, in the stomach, in the chest, in the head. Wild random salvos, ten thousand dollars at a time. A torrent. Real agony in the force of the throws. Then there were tears streaming down Lane's face and he was screaming uncontrollably, panting, sobbing, gasping, punctuating each wild throw with: *Take it! Take it!* Then: *Get her back! Get her back! Get her back!* Then: *Please! Please!* There was rage and pain and hurt and fear and anger and loss in every desperate yelp.

Reacher stood there smarting slightly from the multiple impacts, with hundreds of thousands of dollars littered at his feet, and he thought: *Nobody's that good of an actor.*

He thought: *This time it's real.*

TWENTY-SEVEN

Reacher waited in the inner hallway and listened to Lane calm down. He heard the sink running in the bathroom. *Washing his face*, he thought. *Cold water*. He heard the scrape of paper on hardwood and the quiet crackle of plastic as the bale of cash was reassembled. He heard Lane drag the bale back into the inner closet. He heard the door close, and he heard the keypad beep to confirm it was locked. Then he walked back to the living room. Lane followed a minute later and sat down in his chair, quietly, calmly, like nothing at all had happened, and stared at the silent phone.

It rang just before seven forty-five. Lane snatched it out of the cradle and said 'Yes?' in a voice that was a shout strangled almost to nothing by sheer tension. Then his face went blank and he shook his head in impatience and irritation. *Wrong caller*. He listened for ten seconds more and hung up.

'Who was it?' Gregory asked.

'Just a friend,' Lane said. 'A guy I reached out to earlier. He's had his ear to the ground for me.

Cops found a body in the Hudson River this morning. A floater. At the 79th Street boat basin. Unidentified white male, maybe forty years old. Shot once.'

'Taylor?'

'Has to be,' Lane said. 'The river is quiet up there. And it's an easy detour off the West Side Highway, at the boat basin. Ideal for someone heading north.'

Gregory asked: 'So what do we do?'

'Now?' Lane said. 'Nothing. We wait here. We wait for the right phone call. The one we want.'

It never came. Ten long hours of anticipation ended at eight o'clock in the morning and the phone did not ring. It did not ring at eight fifteen, or eight thirty, or eight forty-five. It did not ring at nine o'clock. It was like waiting for a stay of execution from the Governor's mansion that never came. Reacher thought that a defence team with an innocent client must run through the same range of emotions: puzzlement, anxiety, shock, disbelief, disappointment, hurt, anger, outrage.

Then despair.

The phone did not ring at nine thirty.

Lane closed his eyes and said, 'Not good.'

Nobody replied.

By a quarter to ten in the morning all the resolve had leaked out of Lane's body like he had accepted something inevitable. He sank into the chair cushion and laid his head back and opened his eyes and stared up at the ceiling.

'It's over,' he said. 'She's gone.'

Nobody spoke.

'She's gone,' Lane said again. 'Isn't she?'

Nobody answered. The room was totally silent. Like a wake, or the bloodstained site of a fatal and tragic accident, or a funeral, or a service of remembrance, or an ER trauma room after a failed operation. Like a heart monitor that had been beeping bravely and resolutely against impossible odds had just abruptly gone quiet.

Flatline.

At ten o'clock in the morning Lane raised his head off the back of the chair and said, 'OK.' Then he said it again: 'OK.' Then he said, 'Now we move on. We do what we have to do. We seek and destroy. As long as it takes. But justice will be done. Our kind of justice. No cops, no lawyers, no trials. No appeals. No process, no prison, no painless lethal injections.'

Nobody spoke.

'For Kate,' Lane said. 'And for Taylor.'

Gregory said, 'I'm in.'

'All the way,' Groom said.

'Like always,' Burke said.

Perez nodded. 'To the death.'

'I'm there,' Addison said.

'I'll make them wish they had never been born,' Kowalski said.

Reacher checked their faces. Six men, fewer than a rifle company, but with a whole army's worth of lethal determination.

'Thank you,' Lane said.

Then he sat forward, newly energized. He

176

turned to face Reacher directly. 'Almost the first thing you ever said in this room was that these guys of mine could start a war against them, but first we had to find them. Do you remember that?'

Reacher nodded.

'So find them,' Lane said.

Reacher detoured via the master bedroom and picked up the framed photograph from the desk. The inferior print. The one with Jade in it. He held it carefully so as not to smudge the glass. Looked at it, long and hard. *For you*, he thought. *For both of you. Not for him*. Then he put the photograph back and walked quietly out of the apartment.

Seek and destroy.

He started at the same pay phone he had used before. Took the card out of his shoe and dialled Lauren Pauling's cell. Said, 'It's real this time and they're not coming back.'

She said, 'Can you be at the United Nations in half an hour?'

TWENTY-EIGHT

Reacher couldn't get close to the UN building's entrance because of security, but he saw Lauren Pauling waiting for him in the middle of the First Avenue sidewalk. Clearly she had the same problem. No pass, no clearance, no magic words. She had a printed scarf around her shoulders. She looked good. She was ten years older than him, but he liked what he saw. He started towards her and then she saw him and they met in the middle.

'I called in a favour,' she said. 'We're meeting with an army officer from the Pentagon who liaises with one of the UN committees.'

'On what subject?'

'Mercenaries,' Pauling said. 'We're supposed to be against them. We signed all kinds of treaties.'

'The Pentagon loves mercenaries. It employs them all the time.'

'But it likes them to go where it sends them. It doesn't like them to fill their down time with unauthorized sideshows.'

'Is that where they lost Knight and Hobart? On a sideshow?'

'Somewhere in Africa,' Pauling said.

'Does this guy have the details?'

'Some of them. He's reasonably senior, but he's new. He's not going to tell you his name, and you're not allowed to ask. Deal?'

'Does he know my name?'

'I didn't tell him.'

'OK, that sounds fair.'

Then her cell phone chimed. She answered it and listened and looked around.

'He's in the plaza,' she said. 'He can see us but he doesn't want to walk right up to us. We have to go to a coffee shop on Second. He'll follow.'

The coffee shop was one of those mostly brown places that survive on equal parts counter trade, booth trade, and to-go coffee in cardboard cups with Greek decoration on them. Pauling led Reacher to a booth all the way in back and sat so she could watch the door. Reacher slid in next to her. He never sat any other way than with his back to a wall. Long habit, even in a place with plenty of mirrors, which the coffee shop had. They were tinted bronze and made the narrow unit look wide. Made everyone look tan, like they were just back from the beach. Pauling waved to the waitress and mouthed *coffee* and held up three fingers. The waitress came over and dumped three heavy brown mugs on the table and filled them from a Bunn flask.

Reacher took a sip. Hot, strong, and generic.

He made the Pentagon guy before he was even in through the door. There was no doubt about what he was. Army, but not necessarily a fighting man. Maybe just a bureaucrat. Dull. Not old, not young, corn-coloured buzz cut, cheap blue wool suit, white broadcloth button-down shirt, striped tie, good shoes polished to a mirror shine. A different kind of uniform. It was the kind of outfit a captain or a major would wear to his sister-in-law's second wedding. Maybe this guy had bought it for that very purpose, long before a spell of résumé-building temporary detached duty in New York City appeared in his future.

The guy paused inside the door and looked around. *Not looking for us*, Reacher thought. *Looking for anyone else who knows him. If he sees somebody, he'll fake a phone call and turn around and leave. Doesn't want any awkward questions later. He's not so dumb after all.*

Then he thought: *Pauling's not so dumb, either. She knows people who can get in trouble just by being seen with the wrong folks.*

But the guy evidently saw nothing to worry about. He walked on back and slid in opposite Pauling and Reacher and after a brief glance at each of their faces he centred his gaze between their heads and kept his eyes on the mirror. Up close Reacher saw that he was wearing a black subdued-order crossed-pistols lapel pin and that he had mild scarring on one side of his face. Maybe grenade or IED shrapnel at maximum range. Maybe he had been a fighting man. Or maybe it was a childhood shotgun accident.

'I don't have much for you,' the guy said. 'Private-enterprise Americans fighting overseas are rightly considered to be very bad news, especially when they go fight in Africa. So this stuff is very compartmentalized and need-to-know and

180

it was before my time, so I simply don't know very much about it. So all I can give you is what you can probably guess anyway.'

'Where was it?' Reacher asked.

'I'm not even sure of that. Burkina Faso or Mali, I think. One of those small West African places. Frankly there are so many of them in trouble it's hard to keep track. It was the usual deal. Civil war. A scared government, a bunch of rebels ready to come out of the jungle. An unreliable military. So the government pays through the nose and buys what protection it can on the international market.'

'Does one of those countries speak French?'

'As their official language? Both of them. Why?'

'I saw some of the money. In plastic wrap printed in French. *Banque Centrale*, central bank.'

'How much?'

'More than you or I would earn in two lifetimes.'

'US dollars?'

Reacher nodded. 'Lots of them.'

'Sometimes it works, sometimes it doesn't.'

'Did it work this time?'

'No,' the guy said. 'The story that did the rounds was that Edward Lane took the money and ran. Can't blame him for running, I guess. They were hopelessly outnumbered and strategically weak.'

'But not everyone got out.'

The guy nodded. 'It seemed that way. But getting information out of those places is like trying to get a radio signal from the dark side of the moon. It's mostly silence and static. And

181

when it isn't, it's faint and garbled. So usually we rely on the Red Cross or Doctors Without Frontiers. And eventually we got a solid report that two Americans had been captured. A year later we got names. It was Knight and Hobart. Recon Marines back in the day, mixed records.'

'It surprises me that they stayed alive.'

'The rebels won. They became the new government. They emptied the jails, because the jails were full of their buddies. But a government needs full jails, to keep the population scared. So the old good guys became the new bad guys. Anyone who had worked for the old regime was suddenly in big trouble. And a couple of Americans were like trophies. So they were kept alive. But they suffered very cruelly. The Doctors Without Frontiers report was horrific. Appalling. Mutilation for sport was a fact of life.'

'Details?'

'I guess there are lots of bad things a man can do with a knife.'

'You didn't think about a rescue attempt?'

'You're not listening,' the guy said. 'The State Department can't admit that there are bunches of renegade American mercenaries running wild in Africa. And like I told you, the rebels became the new government. They're in charge now. We have to be nice to them. Because all those places have got stuff that we want. There's oil, and diamonds, and uranium. Alcoa needs tin and bauxite and copper. Halliburton wants to get in there and make a buck. Corporations from Texas want to get in there and run those same damn jails.'

'Anything about what happened in the end?'

'It's sketchy, but you can join the dots. One died in captivity, but the other one got out, according to the Red Cross. Some kind of humanitarian gesture that the Red Cross pushed for, to celebrate the fifth anniversary of the coup. They let out a whole bunch. End of story. That's all the news there is from Africa. One died and one got out, relatively recently. But then, if you do some detective work and jump to the INS, you find a lone individual entering the US from Africa shortly afterward on Red Cross documentation. And then, if you jump to the Veterans Administration, there's a report of someone just back from Africa getting the kind of remedial outpatient care that might be consistent with tropical diseases and some of the mutilations that DWF reported on.'

Reacher asked, 'Which one got out?'

'I don't know,' the guy said. 'All I've heard is that one got out and the other didn't.'

'I need more than that.'

'I told you, the initial event was before my time. I'm not specifically in the loop. All I've got is water-cooler stuff.'

'I need his name,' Reacher said. 'And I need his address, from the VA.'

'That's a tall order,' the guy said. 'I would have to go way beyond my remit. And I would need a very good reason to do that.'

'Look at me,' Reacher said.

The guy took his eyes off the mirror and glanced at Reacher.

Reacher said, 'Ten-sixty-two.'

No reaction.

Reacher said, 'So don't be an asshole. Pony up, OK?'

The guy looked at the mirror again. Nothing in his face.

'I'll call Ms Pauling's cell,' he said. 'When, I don't know. I just can't say. It could be days. But I'll get what I can as soon as I can.'

Then he slid out of the booth and walked straight to the door. Opened it and made a right turn and was lost to sight. Lauren Pauling breathed out.

'You pushed him,' she said. 'You were a little rude there.'

'But he's going to help.'

'Why? What was that ten-sixty-two thing?'

'He was wearing a military police lapel pin. The crossed pistols. MP is his day job. Ten-sixty-two is MP radio code for *fellow officer in trouble, requests urgent assistance*. So he'll help. He has to. Because if one MP won't help another, who the hell will?'

'Then that's a lucky break. Maybe you won't have to do it all the hard way.'

'Maybe. But he's going to be slow. He seemed a little timid. Me, I'd have busted straight into somebody's file cabinet. But he's going to go through channels and ask nicely.'

'Maybe that's why he's getting promoted and you didn't.'

'A timid guy like that won't get promoted. He's probably terminal at major.'

'He's already a Brigadier General,' Pauling said. 'Actually.'

'That guy?' Reacher stared at the door, as if it might have retained an after-image. 'He was kind of young, wasn't he?'

'No, you're kind of old,' Pauling said. 'Everything is comparative. But putting a Brigadier General on it shows how seriously the US is taking this mercenary stuff.'

'It shows how seriously we're whitewashing it.'

Silence for a moment.

'Mutilation for sport,' Pauling said. 'Sounds horrible.'

'Sure does.'

Silence again. The waitress came over and offered refills of coffee. Pauling declined, Reacher accepted. Said, 'NYPD found an unexplained body in the river this morning. White male, about forty. Up near the boat basin. Shot once. Lane got a call.'

'Taylor?'

'Almost certainly.'

'So what next?'

'We work with what we've got,' Reacher said. 'We adopt the theory that Knight or Hobart came home with a grudge.'

'How do we proceed?'

'With hard work,' Reacher said. 'I'm not going to hold my breath on getting anything from the Pentagon. However many scars and stars he's got, that guy's a bureaucrat at heart.'

'Want to talk it through? I was an investigator once. A good one, too. I thought so, anyway. Until, you know, what happened.'

'Talking won't help. I need to think.'

'So think out loud. What doesn't fit? What's

out of place? What surprised you in any way at all?'

'The initial takedown. That doesn't work at all.'

'What else?'

'Everything. What surprises me is that I can't get anywhere with anything. There's either something wrong with me, or there's something wrong with this whole situation.'

'That's too big,' Pauling said. 'Start small. Name one thing that surprised you.'

'Is this what you did? In the FBI? In your brainstorming sessions?'

'Absolutely. Didn't you?'

'I was an MP. I was lucky to find anyone with a brain to storm.'

'Seriously. Name one thing that surprised you.'

Reacher sipped his coffee. *She's right*, he thought. *There's always something out of context even before you know what the context ought to be.*

'Just one thing,' Pauling said again. 'At random.'

Reacher said, 'I got out of the black BMW after Burke had switched the bag into the Jaguar and I was surprised how fast the guy was into the driver's seat. I figured I would have time to stroll around the corner and set up a position. But he was right there, practically on top of me. A few seconds, maximum. I barely got a glimpse of him.'

'So what does that mean?'

'That he was waiting right there on the street.'

'But he wouldn't risk that. If he was Knight or

Hobart, Burke would have recognized him in a heartbeat.'

'Maybe he was in a doorway.'

'Three times running? He used that same fireplug on three separate occasions. At three different times of day. Late night, early morning, rush hour. And he might be memorable, depending on the mutilation.'

'The guy I saw wasn't memorable at all. He was just a guy.'

'Whatever, it was still hard to find appropriate cover each time. I've done that job. Many times. Including one special night five years ago.'

Reacher said, 'Give yourself a break.'

But he was thinking: *Appropriate cover.*

He remembered bouncing around in the back of the car listening to the nightmare voice. Remembered thinking: *It's right there on the same damn fireplug?*

The same damn fireplug.

Appropriate cover.

He put his coffee cup down, gently, slowly, carefully, and then he picked up Pauling's left hand with his right. Brought it to his lips and kissed it tenderly. Her fingers were cool and slim and fragrant. He liked them.

'Thank you,' he said. 'Thank you very much.'

'For what?'

'He used a fireplug three times running. Why? Because a fireplug almost always guarantees a stretch of empty kerb, that's why. Because of the parking prohibition. No parking next to a hydrant. Everyone knows that. But he used the *same* fireplug each time. Why? There are plenty

187

to choose from. There's at least one on every block. So why that one? Because he liked that one, that's why. But why did he like that one? What makes a person like one fireplug more than another?'

'What?'

'Nothing,' Reacher said. 'They're all the same. They're mass-produced. They're identical. What this guy had was a *vantage point* that he liked. The vantage point came first, and the fireplug was merely the nearest one to it. The one most visible from it. As you so correctly pointed out, he needed cover that was reliable and unobtrusive, late night, early morning, and rush hour. And potentially he might have needed to be there for extended periods. As it happened Gregory was punctual both times, but he could have hit traffic. And who knew where Burke was going to be when he got the call on the car phone? Who knew how long he might take to get down there? So wherever this guy was waiting, he was comfortable doing it.'

'But does this help us?'

'You bet your ass it does. It's the first definite link in the chain. It was a fixed, identifiable location. We need to get down to Sixth Avenue and figure out where it was. Someone might have seen him there. Someone might even know who he is.'

TWENTY-NINE

Reacher and Pauling caught a cab on Second Avenue and it took them all the way south to Houston Street and then west to Sixth. They got out on the southeast corner and glanced back at the empty sky where the Twin Towers used to be and then they turned north together into a warm breeze full of trash and grit.

'So show me the famous fireplug,' Pauling said.

They walked north until they came to it, right there on the right-hand sidewalk in the middle of the block. Fat, short, squat, upright, chipped dull paint, flanked by two protective metal posts four feet apart. The kerb next to it was empty. Every other legal parking spot on the block was taken. Pauling stood near the hydrant and pirouetted a slow circle. Looked east, north, west, south.

'Where would a military mind want to be?' she asked.

Reacher recited, 'A soldier knows that a satisfactory observation point provides an unobstructed view to the front and adequate security to the flanks and the rear. He knows it provides protection from the elements and concealment of

189

the observers. He knows it offers a reasonable likelihood of undisturbed occupation for the full duration of the operation.'

'What would the duration be?'

'Say an hour maximum, each time.'

'How did it work, the first two times?'

'He watched Gregory park, and then he followed him down to Spring Street.'

'So he wasn't waiting inside the derelict building?'

'Not if he was working alone.'

'But he still used the back door.'

'On the second occasion, at least.'

'Why not the front door?'

'I don't know.'

'Have we definitely decided he was working alone?'

'Only one of them came back alive.'

Pauling turned the same slow circle. 'So where was his observation point?'

'West of here,' Reacher said. 'He will have wanted a full-on view.'

'Across the street?'

Reacher nodded. 'Middle of the block, or not too far north or south of it. Nothing too oblique. Range, maybe up to a hundred feet. Not more.'

'He could have used binoculars. Like Patti Joseph does.'

'He would still need a good angle. Like Patti has. She's more or less directly across the street.'

'So set some limits.'

'A maximum forty-five degree arc. That's twenty-some degrees north to twenty-some degrees south. Maximum radius, about a hundred feet.'

Pauling turned to face the kerb square on. She spread her arms out straight and forty-five degrees apart and held her hands flat and upright like mimed karate chops. Scoped out the view. A forty-five degree bite out of a circle with a radius of a hundred feet gave her an arc of about seventy-eight feet to look at. More than three standard twenty-foot Greenwich Village store-fronts, less than four. A total of five establishments to consider. The centre three were possibilities. The one to the north and the one to the south were marginal. Reacher stood directly behind her and looked over her head. Her left hand was pointing at a flower store. Then came his new favourite café. Then came a picture framer. Then a double-fronted wine store, wider than the others. Her right hand was pointing at a vitamin shop.

'A flower store would be no good,' she said. 'It offers a wall behind him and a window in front of him but it wouldn't be open at eleven forty at night.'

Reacher said nothing.

'The wine store was probably open,' she said. 'But it wouldn't have been at seven in the morning.'

Reacher said, 'Can't hang around in a flower store or a wine store for an hour at a time. Neither one of them offers a reasonable likelihood of undisturbed occupation for the full duration of the operation.'

'Same with all of them, then,' she said. 'Except

the café. The café would have been open all three times. And you can sit for an hour in a café.'

'The café would have been pretty risky. Three separate lengthy spells, someone would have remembered him. They remembered me after one cup of coffee.'

'Were the sidewalks crowded when you were here?'

'Fairly.'

'So maybe he *was* just out on the street. Or in a doorway. In the shadows. He might have risked it. He was on the other side from where the cars were parking.'

'No protection from the elements and no concealment. It would have been an uncomfortable hour, three times in a row.'

'He was a Recon Marine. He was in prison in Africa for five years. He's used to discomfort.'

'I meant tactically. This part of town, he would have been afraid of getting busted for a drug dealer. Or a terrorist. South of 23rd Street they don't like you to hang around at all any more.'

'So where was he?'

Reacher looked left, looked right.

Then he looked up.

'You mentioned Patti Joseph's place,' he said. 'You called it an eyrie.'

'So?'

'What's an eyrie?'

'It's an eagle's nest.'

'Exactly. From the old French for lair. The point is that Patti is reasonably high up. Seven pre-war floors, that's a little above treetop height. An unobstructed view. A Recon Marine wants an

192

unobstructed view. And he can't guarantee that at street level. A panel truck could park right in front of him at the wrong moment.'

Lauren Pauling turned back to face the kerb and spread her arms again, this time raised at an angle. She mimed the same karate chops with her hands. They bracketed the upper floors of the same five buildings.

'Where did he come from, the first time?' she asked.

'From south of me,' Reacher said. 'From my right. I was facing a little north and east, at the end table. But he was coming back from Spring Street then. No way of knowing where he had started out from. I sat down, ordered coffee, and he was in the car before they even brought it to me.'

'But the second time, after Burke switched the bag, he must have been coming straight from the observation point, right?'

'He was almost at the car when I saw him.'

'Still moving?'

'Final two paces.'

'From what direction?'

Reacher moved up the sidewalk to where he had been after strolling around the corner from Bleecker. In his mind he put a green Jaguar beyond Pauling on the kerb and pictured the guy's last two fluid strides towards it. Then he lined up the apparent vector and checked the likely point of origin. Kept his eyes on it as he stepped back to Pauling.

'Actually very similar to the first time,' he said to her. 'North and east through the traffic. From the south of where I was sitting.'

Pauling adjusted the position of her right arm. Brought her hand south and chopped the air a fraction to the left of the café's most northerly table. That cut the view to just a slim section of the streetscape. Half of the building with the flower store in it, and most of the building with the café in it. Above the flower store were three storeys of windows with vertical blinds behind them and printers and spider plants and stacks of paper on their sills. Fluorescent tubes on the ceilings.

'Office suites,' Pauling said.

Above the café were three storeys of windows filled variously with faded drapes made of red Indian cloth, or macramé hangings, or suspended discs of stained glass. One had nothing at all. One was papered over with newsprint. One had a Che Guevara poster taped face-out on the inside of the glass.

'Apartments,' Pauling said.

Jammed between the flower store and the café was a blue recessed door. To its left was a dull silver box, with buttons and nameplates and a speaker grille. Reacher said, 'A person who came out that door heading for the fireplug would have to cross north and east through the traffic, right?'

Pauling said, 'We found him.'

THIRTY

The silver box to the left of the blue door had six black call buttons in a vertical array. The top nameplate had *Kublinski* written very neatly in pale faded ink. The bottom had *Super* scrawled with a black marker pen. The middle four were blank.

'Low rent,' Pauling said. 'Short leases. Transients. Except for Mr or Ms Kublinski. Judging by that handwriting style they've been here forever.'

'They probably moved to Florida fifty years ago,' Reacher said. 'Or died. And nobody changed the tag.'

'Shall we try the super?'

'Use one of your business cards. Put your finger over the *Ex*-part. Make out like you're still with the Bureau.'

'Think that'll be necessary?'

'We need all the help we can get. This is a radical building. We've got Che Guevara watching over us. And macramé.'

Pauling put an elegant nail on the super's call button and pressed. She was answered a long minute later by a distorted burst of sound from the speaker. It might have been the word *yes*, or *who*, or *what*. Or just a blast of static.

'Federal agents,' Pauling called. Which was remotely true. Both she and Reacher had once worked for Uncle Sam. She slipped a business card out of her purse. There was another burst of noise from the speaker.

'He's coming,' Reacher said. He had seen plenty of buildings like this one, back in the day, when his job had been chasing AWOL soldiers. They liked cash rents and short leases. And in his experience building superintendents usually co-operated. They liked their free accommodations well enough not to jeopardize them. Better that someone else should go to jail, and they should stay where they were.

Unless the super was the bad guy, of course.

But this one seemed to have nothing to hide. The blue door opened inward and revealed a tall gaunt man in a stained wife-beater. He had a black knit cap on his head and a flat Slavic face like a length of two-by-four.

'Yes?' he said. Strong Russian accent. Almost *Da?*

Pauling waved her card long enough for some of the words to register.

'Tell us about your most recent tenant,' she said.

'Most recent?' the guy repeated. No hostility. He sounded like a fairly smart guy struggling with the nuance of a foreign language, that was all.

Reacher asked, 'Did someone sign on within the last couple of weeks?'

196

'Number five,' the guy said. 'One week ago. He responded to a newspaper advertisement I was asked to place by the management.'

'We need to see his apartment,' Pauling said.

'I'm not sure I should let you,' the guy said. 'There are rules in America.'

'Homeland Security,' Reacher said. 'The Patriot Act. There are no rules in America any more.'

The guy just shrugged and turned his tall thin frame around in the narrow space. Headed for the stairs. Reacher and Pauling followed him in. Reacher could smell coffee coming through the walls from the café. There was no apartment number one or number two. Number four was the first door they came to, at the head of the stairs at the back of the building. Then number three was on the same floor, along a hallway at the front of the building. Which meant that number five was going to be directly above it, third floor, looking east across the street. Pauling glanced at Reacher, and Reacher nodded.

'The one with nothing in the window,' he said to her.

On the third floor they passed number six at the back of the building and walked forward towards number five. The smell of coffee had faded and been replaced by the universal hallway smell of boiled vegetables.

'Is he in?' Reacher asked.

The super shook his head. 'I only ever saw him twice. He's out now for sure. I was just all over the building fixing pipes.' He used a master key from a ring on his belt and unlocked the door. Pushed it open and stood back.

The apartment was what a real estate broker would have called an alcove studio. All one room, with a crooked L that was theoretically large enough for a bed if the bed was small. A kitchen corner and a tiny bathroom with an open door. But mostly what was on show was dust and floor-boards.

Because the apartment was completely empty.

Except for a single upright dining chair. The chair was not old, but it was well used. It was the kind of thing you see for sale on the Bowery sidewalks where the bankrupt restaurant dealers hawk seized inventory. It was set in front of the window and turned slightly north and east. It was about twenty feet above and three feet behind the exact spot that Reacher had chosen for coffee, two nights running.

Reacher stepped over and sat down on the chair, feet planted, relaxed but alert. The way his body settled naturally put the fireplug across Sixth directly in front of him. A shallow down-ward angle, easily enough to clear a parked panel truck. Enough to clear a parked semi. A ninety-foot range. No problem for anyone who wasn't clinically blind. He stood up again and turned a full circle. Saw a door that locked. Saw three solid walls. Saw a window free of drapes. *A soldier knows that a satisfactory observation point provides an unobstructed view to the front and adequate security to the flanks and the rear, provides protection from the elements and concealment of the observers, and offers a reasonable likelihood of undisturbed occupation for the full duration of the operation.*

'Feels just like Patti Joseph's place,' Pauling said.

'You been there?'

'Brewer described it.'

'Eight million stories,' Reacher said.

Then he turned to the super and said, 'Tell us about this guy.'

'He can't talk,' the super said.

'What do you mean?'

'He can't speak.'

'What, like he's a mute?'

'Not by birth. Because of a trauma.'

'Like something struck him dumb?'

'Not emotional,' the super said. 'Physical. He communicated with me by writing on a pad of yellow paper. Full sentences, quite patiently. He wrote that he had been injured in the service. Like a war wound. But I noticed that he had no visible scarring. And I noticed that he kept his mouth tight shut all the time. Like he was embarrassed about me seeing something. And it reminded me very strongly of something I saw once before, more than twenty years ago.'

'Which was?'

'I am Russian. For my sins I served with the Red Army in Afghanistan. Once we had a prisoner returned to us by the tribesmen as a warning. His tongue had been cut out.'

THIRTY-ONE

The super took Reacher and Pauling down to
his own apartment, which was a squared-away
semi-basement space in the back of the building.
He opened a file cabinet and took out the current
lease papers for apartment five. They had been
signed exactly a week previously by a guy calling
himself Leroy Clarkson. Which as expected was a
blatantly phoney name. Clarkson and Leroy were
the first two streets coming off the West Side
Highway north of Houston, just a few blocks
away. At the far end of Clarkson was a topless
bar. At the far end of Leroy was a car wash. In
between was a tiny aluminium coach diner that
Reacher had once eaten in.

'You don't see ID?' Pauling asked.

'Not unless they want to pay by cheque,' the
super said. 'This guy paid cash.'

The signature was illegible. The social security
number was neatly written but was no doubt just
a random sequence of nine meaningless digits.

The super gave a decent physical description,
but it didn't help much because it did nothing
more than match what Reacher himself had seen

on two separate occasions. Late thirties, maybe forty, white, medium height and weight, clean and trim, no facial hair. Blue jeans, blue shirt, ball cap, sneakers, all of them worn and comfortable.

'How was his health?' Reacher asked.

'Apart from the fact that he couldn't speak?' the super said. 'He seemed OK.'

'Did he say if he'd been out of town for a while?'

'He didn't *say* anything.'

'How long did he pay for?'

'A month. It's the minimum. Renewable.'

'This guy's not coming back,' Reacher said. 'You should go ahead and call the *Village Voice* now. Get them to run your ad again.'

'What happened to your pal from the Red Army?' Pauling asked.

'He lived,' the super said. 'Not happily, but he lived.'

Reacher and Pauling came out of the blue door and took three paces north and stopped in for espresso. They took the end table on the sidewalk and Reacher took the same seat he had used twice before.

Pauling said, 'So he wasn't working alone.'

Reacher said nothing.

Pauling said, 'Because he couldn't have made the phone calls.'

Reacher didn't reply.

Pauling said, 'Tell me about the voice you heard.'

'American,' Reacher said. 'The machine couldn't disguise the words or the cadence or the

201

rhythm. And he was patient. Intelligent, in command, in control, not worried. Familiar with the geography of New York City. Possibly military, from a couple of phrases. He wanted to know Burke's name, which suggests he's familiar with Lane's crew or he was calibrating a lie detector. Apart from that, I'm just guessing. The distortion was huge. But I felt he wasn't old. There was a lightness there. A kind of nimbleness in his voice. Maybe he was a small guy.'

'Like a Special Forces veteran.'

'Possibly.'

'Unworried and in command makes him sound like the prime mover here. Not like a sidekick.'

Reacher nodded. 'Good point. I felt that way, listening to him. It was like he was calling the shots. Like an equal partner, at the very least.'

'So who the hell is he?'

'If your Pentagon guy hadn't told us different I'd say it was both of Hobart and Knight, both still alive, back here together, working together.'

'But it isn't,' Pauling said. 'My Pentagon guy wouldn't get that kind of thing wrong.'

'So whichever one came back alive picked up a new partner.'

'One that he trusts,' Pauling said. 'And he did it real fast.'

Reacher gazed over at the hydrant. Traffic obscured his view in waves, held back and then released by the light at Houston.

'Would a remote clicker work at this distance?' he asked.

'For a car?' Pauling said. 'Maybe. I guess it would depend on the car. Why?'

202

'After Burke switched the bag I heard a sound like car doors locking. I guess the guy did it from up there in his room. He was watching. He didn't want to leave the money in an unlocked car for a second longer than he had to.'

'Sensible.'

Reacher paused a beat. 'But you know what isn't sensible? Why was he up there in the room at all?'

'We know why he was up there.'

'No, why was *he* up there and not the other guy? We've got two guys here, one can talk and the other can't. Why would the guy who can't talk go rent the apartment? Anyone who comes into contact with him isn't going to forget him in a hurry. And what's an observation point for, anyway? It's for command and control. As the visible situation develops the observer is supposed to issue a stream of orders and adjustments. But this guy couldn't even get on a cell phone. What do we suppose happened exactly, the first two times with Gregory? The guy is upstairs, he sees Gregory park, what can he do? He can't even get on the phone and tell his partner to stand by down at Spring Street.'

'Text messaging,' Pauling said.

'What's that?'

'You can send written words by cell phone.'

'When did *that* start?'

'Years ago.'

'OK,' Reacher said. 'Live and learn.' Then he said, 'But I still don't see why they sent the guy who couldn't talk to meet with the building super.'

203

'Neither do I,' Pauling said.

'Or to run the OP. It would make more sense if he had been on the other end of the phone. He can't talk, but he can listen.'

Silence for a moment.

'What next?' Pauling asked.

'Hard work,' Reacher said. 'You up for it?'

'Are you hiring me?'

'No, you're putting whatever else you're doing on hold and you're volunteering. Because if we do this right you'll find out what happened to Anne Lane five years ago. No more sleepless nights.'

'Unless I find out five years ago was for real. Then I might never sleep again.'

'Life's a gamble,' Reacher said. 'It wouldn't be so much fun otherwise.'

Pauling was quiet for a long moment.

'OK,' she said. 'I'm volunteering.'

Reacher said, 'So go hassle our Soviet pal again. Get the chair. They bought it within the last week. We'll walk it over to the Bowery and find out where it came from. Maybe the new buddy picked it out. Maybe someone will remember him.'

THIRTY-TWO

Reacher carried the chair in his hand like a bag and he and Pauling walked together east. South of Houston the Bowery had organized itself into a sequence of distinct retail areas. Like a string of unofficial malls. There were electrical supplies, and lighting fixtures, and used office gear, and industrial kitchen equipment, and restaurant front-of-house outlets. Reacher liked the Bowery. It was his kind of a street.

The chair in his hand was fairly generic, but it had a certain number of distinguishing characteristics. Impossible to describe it a moment after closing the door on it, but with it right there for direct comparison a match might be found. They started with the northernmost of six separate chaotic establishments. Less than a hundred yards of real estate, but if someone buys a used dining chair in Manhattan, chances are he buys it somewhere in that hundred yards.

Put the good stuff in the store window was the usual retail mantra. But on the Bowery the actual store windows were secondary to the sidewalk displays. And the chair in Reacher's hand wasn't the good stuff, in the sense that it couldn't have been part of a large matched set, or it wouldn't have been sold separately. Nobody with a set of twenty-four chairs leaves himself with twenty-three. So Reacher and Pauling pushed past the stuff on the sidewalk and squeezed through the narrow doors and looked at the dusty items inside. Looked at the sad leftovers, the part-sets, the singletons. They saw a lot of chairs. All the same, all different. Four legs, seats, backs, but the range of shapes and details was tremendous. None looked very comfortable. Reacher had read somewhere that there was a science to building a restaurant chair. It had to be durable, obviously, and good value for money, and it had to look reasonably inviting, but it couldn't in reality *be* too comfortable or the patrons would sit all night and a potential three-sitting evening would turn into an actual two sittings and the restaurant would lose money. Portion control and table turnover were the important factors in the restaurant trade, and Reacher figured chair manufacturers were totally on board with the turnover part.

In the first three stores they found no visual matches and nobody admitted selling the chair that Reacher was carrying.

The fourth store was where they found what they wanted.

It was a double-wide place that had chrome diner furniture out front and a bunch of Chinese owners in back. Behind the gaudy padded stools on the sidewalk were piles of old tables and sets of chairs stacked six high. Behind the piles and the stacks was a jumble of oddments. Including two chairs hung high on a wall that were exact matches for the specimen in Reacher's hand. Same style, same construction, same colour, same age.

'We shoot, we score,' Pauling said.

Reacher checked again, to be certain. But there was no doubt about it. The chairs were identical. Even the grime and the dust on them matched precisely. Same grey, same texture, same consistency.

'Let's get some help,' he said.

He carried the Sixth Avenue chair to the back of the store where a Chinese guy was sitting behind a rickety table with a closed cash box on it. The guy was old and impassive. The owner, probably. Certainly all transactions would have to pass through his hands. He had the cash box.

'You sold this chair.' Reacher held it up, and nodded back towards the wall where its siblings hung. 'About a week ago.'

'Five dollars,' the old guy said.

'I don't want to buy it,' Reacher said. 'And it isn't yours to sell. You already sold it once. I want to know who you sold it to. That's all.'

'Five dollars,' the guy said again.

'You're not understanding me.'

The old guy smiled. 'No, I think I'm understanding you very well. You want information about the purchaser of that chair. And I'm telling you that information always has a price. In this case, the price is five dollars.'

'How about you get the chair back? Then you can sell it twice.'

'I already sold it many more times than twice. Places open, places close, assets circulate. The world goes round.'

'Who bought it, a week ago?'

'Five dollars.'

'You sure you've got five dollars' worth of information?'

'I have what I have.'

'Two-fifty plus the chair.'

'You'll leave the chair anyway. You're sick of carrying it around.'

'I could leave it next door.'

For the first time the old guy's eyes moved. He glanced up at the wall. Reacher saw him think: *A set of three is better than a pair.*

'Four bucks and the chair,' he said.

'Three and the chair,' Reacher said.

'Three and a half and the chair.'

'Three and a quarter and the chair.'

No response.

'Guys, please,' Pauling said.

She stepped up to the rickety desk and opened her purse. Took out a fat black wallet and snapped off a crisp ten from a wad as thick as a paperback book. Placed it on the scarred wood and spun it around and left it there.

'Ten dollars,' she said. 'And the damn chair. So make it good.'

The old Chinese man nodded.

'Women,' he said. 'Always ready to focus.'

'Tell us who bought the chair,' Pauling said.

'He couldn't talk,' the old man said.

THIRTY-THREE

The old man said, 'At first I thought nothing of it. An American comes in, he hears us speaking our own language, very often he assumes we can't speak English, and he conducts the transaction with a combination of gestures and signs. It's a little rude in that it assumes ignorance on our part, but we're used to it. Generally I let such a customer flounder and then I pitch in with a perfectly coherent sentence as a kind of reproach.'

'Like you did with me,' Reacher said.

'Indeed. And as I did with the man you're evidently seeking. But he was completely unable to reply in any way at all. He just kept his mouth closed and gulped like a fish. I concluded that he had a deformity which prevented speech.'

'Description?' Reacher asked.

The old guy paused a beat to gather his thoughts and then launched into the same run-down that the Sixth Avenue super had given. A white man, late thirties, maybe forty, medium height and weight, clean and neat, no beard, no moustache. Blue jeans, blue shirt, ball cap, sneakers, all of them worn and comfortable. Nothing remarkable or memorable about him except for the fact that he was mute.

'How much did he pay for the chair?' Reacher asked.

'Five dollars.'

'Wasn't it unusual that a guy would want a single chair?'

'You think I should automatically call the police if someone who isn't a restaurant owner shops here?'

'Who buys chairs one at a time?'

'Plenty of people,' the old man said. 'People who are recently divorced, or down on their luck, or starting a lonely new life in a small East Village apartment. Some of those places are so tiny a single chair is all they want. At a desk, maybe, that does double duty as a dining table.'

'OK,' Reacher said. 'I can see that.'

The old man turned to Pauling and asked, 'Was my information helpful?'

'Maybe,' Pauling said. 'But it didn't add anything.'

'You already knew about the man who couldn't talk?'

Pauling nodded.

'Then I'm sorry,' the old man said. 'You may keep the chair.'

'I'm sick of carrying it around,' Reacher said.

The old man inclined his head. 'As I thought. In which case, feel free to leave it here.'

Pauling led Reacher out to the Bowery sidewalk and the last he saw of the chair was a young guy who could have been a grandson hoisting it up on a pole and hanging it back on the wall next to its two fellows.

'The hard way,' Pauling said.

'Makes no sense,' Reacher said. 'Why are they sending the guy that can't speak to meet with everyone?'

'There must be something even more distinctive about the other one.'

'I hate to think what *that* might be.'

'Lane abandoned those two guys. So why are you helping him?'

'I'm not helping him. This is for Kate and the kid now.'

'They're dead. You said so yourself.'

'Then they need a story. An explanation. The who, the where, the why. Everyone ought to know what happened to them. They shouldn't be allowed to just *go*, quietly. Someone needs to stand up for them.'

'And that's you?'

'I play the hand I'm dealt. No use whining about it.'

'And?'

'And they need to be avenged, Pauling. Because it wasn't their fight. It wasn't even remotely Jade's fight, was it? If Hobart or Knight or whichever it was had come after Lane directly, maybe I'd have been on the sidelines cheering him on. But he didn't. He came after Kate and Jade. And two wrongs don't make a right.'

'Neither do three wrongs.'

'In this case they do,' Reacher said.

'You never even saw Kate or Jade.'

'I saw their pictures. That was enough.'

'I wouldn't want you mad at me,' Pauling said.

'No,' Reacher said back. 'You wouldn't.'

They walked north towards Houston Street without any clear idea of where they were going next and on the way Pauling's cell phone must have vibrated because she pulled it out of her pocket before Reacher heard it ring. Silent cell phones made Reacher nervous. He came from a world where a sudden dive for a pocket was more likely to mean a gun than a phone. Every time it happened he had to endure a little burst of unrequited adrenalin.

Pauling stopped on the sidewalk and said her name loudly over the traffic noise and then listened for a minute. Said thanks and snapped the phone shut. Turned to Reacher and smiled.

'My Pentagon buddy,' she said. 'Some solid information. Maybe he busted into someone's file cabinet after all.'

'Did he get a name for us?' Reacher asked.

'Not yet. But he has a location. It was Burkina Faso. You ever been there?'

'I've never been anywhere in Africa.'

'It used to be called Upper Volta. It's a former French colony. About the size of Colorado, population thirteen million, with a GDP about a quarter of what Bill Gates is worth.'

'But with enough spare cash to hire Lane's crew.'

'Not according to my guy,' Pauling said. 'That's the weird thing. It's where Knight and

Hobart were captured, but there's no record of their government contracting with Lane.'

'Would your guy expect there to be a record?'

'He says there's always a record somewhere.'

'We need a name,' Reacher said. 'That's all. We don't need the history of the world.'

'He's working on it.'

'But not fast enough. And we can't wait. We need to try something on our own.'

'Like what?'

'Our guy called himself Leroy Clarkson. Maybe it was a private joke or maybe it was something in his subconscious because he lives over there.'

'Near Clarkson or Leroy?'

'Maybe on Hudson or Greenwich.'

'That's all gentrified now. A guy just back from five years in an African jail couldn't afford a closet over there.'

'But a guy who was making good money before the five-year hiatus might already own a place over there.'

Pauling nodded. 'We should stop by my office. Start with the phone book.'

There were a few Hobarts and half a page of Knights in the Manhattan White Pages but none of them were in the part of the West Village that would have made Leroy Clarkson an obvious pseudonym. Conceivably one of the Knights might have picked Horatio Gansevoort, and one of the Hobarts might have gone by Christopher Perry, but apart from those two the others lived where the streets were numbered or so far east that their subliminal choices would have been

Henry Madison or Allen Eldridge. Or Stanton Rivington.

'Too much like daytime TV,' Pauling said.

She had other databases, the kinds of things a conscientious PI with old friends in law enforcement and an internet connection can accumulate. But no unexplained Knights or Hobarts cropped up anywhere.

'He's been away five years,' Pauling said. 'Effectively he'll have dropped out of sight, won't he? Disconnected phone, unpaid utilities, like that?'

'Probably,' Reacher said. 'But not necessarily. These guys are used to sudden travel. They always were, even back in the day. They usually set up automatic payments.'

'His bank account would have emptied out.'

'Depends how much was in it to start with. If he was earning then what the others are earning now he could have paid for plenty of electric bills especially when he's not even home to turn on the lights.'

'Lane was a much smaller deal five years ago. They all were, before the terrorism gravy train left the station. Real or phoney, Anne's ransom was only a hundred grand, not ten and a half million. Wages will have been in proportion. This guy won't have been rich.'

Reacher nodded. 'He probably rented anyway. Landlord probably threw all his stuff on the sidewalk years ago.'

'So what do we do?'

'I guess we wait,' Reacher said. 'For your bureaucratic buddy. Unless we grow old and die first.'

But a minute later Pauling's phone went off again. This time it was on her desk, out in full view, and its vibration set up a soft mechanical buzz against the wood. She answered it with her name and listened for a minute. Then she closed it slowly and put it back in place.

'We're not much older,' she said.

'What's he got?' Reacher asked.

'Hobart,' she said. 'It was Hobart who came back alive.'

THIRTY-FOUR

Reacher asked, 'First name?'

Pauling said, 'Clay. Clay James Hobart.'

Reacher asked, 'Address?'

Pauling said, 'We're waiting on an answer from the VA.'

'So let's hit the phone books again.'

'I recycle my old phone books. I don't keep an archive. I certainly don't have anything from five years ago.'

'He might have family here. Who better to come back to?'

There were seven Hobarts in the book, but one of them was a duplicate. A dentist, home and office, different places, different numbers, same guy.

'Call them all,' Reacher said. 'Make like a VA administrator with a paperwork glitch.'

Pauling put her desk phone on the speaker and got two answering machines with the first two calls and a false alarm on the third. Some old guy with his own VA benefits got all excited in case they were about to disappear. Pauling calmed him down and he said he had never heard of anyone called Clay James Hobart. The fourth and fifth calls were fruitless too. The sixth call was to the dentist's office number. He was on vacation in Antigua. His receptionist said he had no relatives called Clay James. The absolute confidence in her answer made Reacher wonder if she was more than just a receptionist. Although she wasn't in Antigua with him. Maybe she had just worked for him a long time.

'So what now?' Pauling said.

'We'll try the first two again later,' Reacher said. 'Apart from that, it's back to growing old together.'

But Pauling's Pentagon buddy was on some kind of a roll because eleven minutes later her cell buzzed again and the guy came through with more information. Reacher saw Pauling put it all down on a yellow pad in fast scrawled handwriting that he couldn't read upside down and from a distance. Two pages of notes. It was a long call. So long that when it was over Pauling checked the battery icon on her phone and plugged it into a charger.

'Hobart's address?' Reacher asked her.

'Not yet,' Pauling said. 'The VA is baulking. There are confidentiality issues.'

'Where he lives isn't a medical diagnosis.'

'That's the point my friend is making.'

'So what did he have for us?'

Pauling flipped back to the first page of her notes.

'Lane is on an official Pentagon shit list,' she said.

217

'Why?'

'You know what Operation Just Cause was?'

'Panama,' Reacher said. 'Against Manuel Noriega. More than fifteen years ago. I was there, briefly.'

'Lane was there, too. He was still in uniform back then. He did very well there. That's where he made full colonel. Then he went to the Gulf the first time around and then he quit under a bit of a cloud. But not enough of a cloud to stop the Pentagon hiring him on as a private contractor afterwards. They sent him to Colombia, because he had a reputation as a Central and South America expert, because of his performance during Just Cause. He took the beginnings of his present crew with him to fight one of the cocaine cartels. He took our government's money to do it but when he got there he also took the target cartel's money to go wipe out one of their rival cartels instead. The Pentagon wasn't all that upset because one cartel is as bad as another to them, but they never really trusted Lane after- wards and never hired him again.'

'His guys said they'd been to Iraq and Afghanistan.'

Pauling nodded. 'After the Twin Towers all kinds of people went all kinds of places. Including Lane's crew. But only as subcontractors. In other words the Pentagon hired someone they trusted and that someone laid off some of the work to Lane.'

'And that was acceptable?'

'Honour was observed. The Pentagon never wrote another cheque with Lane's name on it after that first time in Colombia. But later on they needed all the warm bodies they could get, so they looked the other way.'

'He's been getting steady work,' Reacher said. 'Plenty of income. He lives like a king and most of the African money is still in its original wrappers.'

'That just shows you how big this whole racket has gotten. My guy says since Colombia, Lane has been living off the crumbs from other men's tables. That's been his only option. Big crumbs at first, but they're getting smaller. There's a lot of competition now. Apparently he got rich that one time in Africa, but whatever is left from that payment is basically all the capital he's got.'

'He makes out like he's the big dog. He told me he had no rivals or partners.'

'Then he was lying. Or maybe in a sense he was telling the truth. Because he's at the bottom of the pile. Strictly speaking he has no equals. Only superiors.'

'Was he subcontracting in Burkina Faso too?' Reacher asked.

'He must have been,' Pauling said. 'Otherwise why isn't he in the records as a principal?'

'Was our government involved there?'

'It's possible. Certainly my official friend seems a little tense.'

Reacher nodded. 'That's why he's helping, isn't it? This is not one MP to another. This is a bureaucracy trying to control the situation. Trying to manage the flow of information. This is someone deciding to feed us stuff privately so we don't go blundering about and making a lot of noise in public.'

Pauling said nothing. Then her phone went off again. She tried to pick it up with the charger attached but the wire was too short. She unclipped it and answered. Listened for fifteen seconds and turned to a new page in her pad and wrote a dollar sign, and then two numbers, and then six zeros. She clicked off the phone and spun the pad around so that Reacher could see what she had written.

'Twenty-one million dollars,' she said. 'In cash. That's how rich Lane got in Africa.'

'You were right,' Reacher said. 'Big crumbs. Not too shabby for a subcontractor.'

Pauling nodded. 'The whole deal was worth a hundred and five million. US dollars in cash from their government's central reserve. Lane got twenty per cent in exchange for supplying half the manpower and agreeing to do most of the work.'

'Beggars can't be choosers,' Reacher said.

Then he said: 'OK.'

'OK what?'

'What's half of twenty-one?'

'Ten and a half.'

'Exactly. Kate's ransom was exactly half of the Burkina Faso payment.'

Silence in the room.

'Ten and a half million dollars,' Reacher said. 'It always was a weird amount. But now it makes some kind of sense. Lane probably skimmed fifty per cent as his profit. So Hobart got home and figured he was entitled to Lane's share for his suffering.'

'Reasonable,' Pauling said.

'I would have wanted more,' Reacher said. 'I would have wanted all of it.'

Pauling slid her fingernail down the fine print on the *H* page of the phone book and used the speaker to try the first two Hobart numbers again. She got the same two answering machines. She hung up. Her little office went quiet. Then her cell buzzed again. This time she unclipped the charger first and flipped the phone open. Said her name and listened for a moment and then turned to another fresh page in her yellow pad and wrote just three lines.

Then she closed her phone.

'We have his address,' she said.

THIRTY-FIVE

Pauling said, 'Hobart moved in with his sister. To a building on Hudson Street that I'm betting is on the block between Clarkson and Leroy.'

'A married sister,' Reacher said. 'Otherwise we would have found her name in the phone book.'

'Widowed,' Pauling said. 'I guess she kept her married name, but she lives alone now. Or at least she did, until her brother came home from Africa.'

The widowed sister was called Dee Marie Graziano and she was right there in the phone book at an address on Hudson. Pauling dialled up a city tax database and confirmed her domicile.

'Rent-stabilized,' she said. 'Been there ten years. Even with the cheap lease it's going to be a small place.' She copied Dee Marie's social security number and pasted it into a box in a different database. 'Thirty-eight years old. Marginal income. Doesn't work much. Doesn't even get close to paying federal income taxes. Her late husband was a Marine too. Lance Corporal Vincent Peter Graziano. He died three years ago.'

'In Iraq?'

'I can't tell.' Pauling closed the databases and opened Google and typed *Dee Marie Graziano*. Hit the return key. Glanced at the results and something about them made her click off Google and open Lexis-Nexis. The screen rolled down and came up with a whole page of citations.

'Well, look at this,' she said.

'Tell me,' Reacher said.

'She sued the government. State and the DoD.'

'For what?'

'For news about her brother.'

Pauling hit the print button and fed Reacher the pages one by one as they came off the machine. He read the hard copy and she read the screen. Dee Marie Graziano had waged a five-year campaign to find out what had happened to her brother Clay James Hobart. It had been a long, hard, bitter campaign. That was for sure. At the outset Hobart's employer Edward Lane of Operational Security Consultants had signed an affidavit swearing that Hobart had been a subcontractor for the United States Government at the relevant time. So Dee Marie had gone ahead and petitioned her congressman and both her senators. She had called out of state to the chairmen of the Armed Services Committees in both the House and the Senate. She had written to newspapers and talked to journalists. She had been prepped for the *Larry King Show* but had been cancelled prior to the recording. She had hired an investigator, briefly. Finally she had found a pro bono lawyer and sued the Department of Defense. The Pentagon had denied any knowledge of Clay James Hobart's activities subsequent to his last day in a USMC uniform. Then Dee Marie had sued the Department of State. Some fifth-rung State lawyer had come back and promised that Hobart would be put on file as a tourist missing in West Africa. So Dee Marie had gone back to pestering journalists and had filed a string of Freedom of Information Act petitions. More than half of them had already been denied and the others were still choked in red tape.

'She was really going at it,' Pauling said. 'Wasn't she? Metaphorically she was lighting a candle for her brother every single day for five years.'

'Like Patti Joseph,' Reacher said. 'This is a tale of two sisters.'

'The Pentagon knew Hobart was alive after twelve months. And they knew where he was. But they kept quiet for four years. They let this poor woman suffer.'

'What was she going to do anyway? Lock and load and go to Africa and rescue him single-handed? Bring him back to stand trial for Anne Lane's homicide?'

'There was never any evidence against him.'

'Whatever, keeping her in the dark was probably the best policy.'

'Spoken like a true military man.'

'Like the FBI is a fount of free information?'

'She could have gone over there and petitioned the new government in Burkina Faso personally.'

'That only works in the movies.'

'You're very cynical, you know that?'

'I don't have a cynical bone in my body. I'm realistic, is all. Shit happens.'

Pauling went quiet.

'What?' Reacher said.

'You said lock and load. You said Dee Marie could lock and load and go to Africa.'

'No, I said she couldn't.'

'But we agree that Hobart picked up a new partner, right?' she said. 'As soon as he got back? One that he trusts, and real fast?'

'Clearly,' Reacher said.

'Could it be the sister?'

Reacher said nothing.

'The trust would be there,' Pauling said. 'Wouldn't it? Automatically? And *she* was there, which would explain the speed. And the commitment would have been there, on her part. Commitment, and a lot of anger. So is it possible that the voice you heard on the car phone was a woman?'

Reacher was quiet for a beat.

'It's possible,' he said. 'I guess. I mean, it never struck me that way. But that could just be a preconception on my part. An unconscious bias. Because those machines are tough. They could make Minnie Mouse sound like Darth Vader.'

'You said there was a lightness to the voice. Like a small man.'

Reacher nodded. 'Yes, I did.'

'Therefore like a woman. With the pitch altered an octave, it's plausible.'

'It could be,' Reacher said. 'Certainly whoever it was knew the West Village streets pretty well.'

'Like a ten-year resident would. Plus military

jargon, from having had a husband and a brother in the Marine Corps.'

'Maybe,' Reacher said. 'Gregory told me a woman showed up in the Hamptons. A fat woman.'

'Fat?'

'Gregory said heavyset.'

'Surveillance?'

'No, she and Kate talked. They went walking on the beach.'

'Maybe it was Dee Marie. Maybe she's fat. Maybe she was asking for money. Maybe Kate blew her off and that was the last straw.'

'This is about more than money.'

'But that doesn't mean this isn't at least partly about money,' Pauling said. 'And judging by where she's living Dee Marie needs money. Her share would be more than five million dollars. She might think of it like compensation. For five years of stonewalling. A million dollars a year.'

'Maybe,' Reacher said again.

'It's a hypothesis,' Pauling said. 'We shouldn't rule it out.'

'No,' Reacher said. 'We shouldn't.'

Pauling pulled a city directory off her shelf and checked the Hudson Street address.

'They're south of Houston,' she said. 'Between Vandam and Charlton. Not between Clarkson and Leroy. We were wrong.'

'Maybe they like a bar a few blocks north,' Reacher said. 'He couldn't have called himself Charlton Vandam, anyway. That's way too phoney.'

'Whatever, they're only fifteen minutes from here.'

'Don't get your hopes up. This is another brick in the wall, that's all. One or both of them, whichever, they must be long gone already. They'd be crazy to stick around.'

'You think?'

'They've got blood on their hands and money in their pockets, Pauling. They'll be in the Caymans by now. Or Bermuda, or Venezuela, or wherever the hell people go these days.'

'So what do we do?'

'We head over to Hudson Street, and we hope like crazy that the trail is still a little bit warm.'

THIRTY-SIX

Between them in their previous lives and afterwards Reacher and Pauling had approached probably a thousand buildings that may or may not have contained hostile suspects. They knew exactly how to do it. There was efficient back-and-forth tactical discussion. They were coming from a position of weakness, in that neither of them was armed and Hobart had met Pauling twice before. She had interviewed Lane's whole crew at length after Anne Lane's disappearance. Chances were Hobart would remember her even after the traumatic five-year interval. Balancing those disadvantages was Reacher's strong conviction that the Hudson Street apartment would be empty. He expected to find nothing there except hastily tossed closets and one last can of rotting trash.

There was no doorman. It wasn't that kind of a building. It was a boxy five-storey tenement faced with dull red brick and a black iron fire escape. It was the last hold-out on a block full of design offices and bank branches. It had a chipped black door with an aluminium squawk box chiselled sideways into the frame. Ten black buttons. Ten nametags. *Graziano* was written neatly against 4L.

'Walk-up,' Pauling said. 'Central staircase. Long thin front-to-back apartments, two to a floor, one on the left, one on the right. Four-L will be on the fourth floor, on the left.'

Reacher tried the door. It was locked and solid.

'What's at the back?' he asked.

'Probably an air shaft between this and the back of the building on Greenwich.'

'We could rappel off the roof and come in through her kitchen window.'

'I trained for that at Quantico,' Pauling said. 'But I never did it for real.'

'Neither did I,' Reacher said. 'Not a kitchen. I did a bathroom window once.'

'Was that fun?'

'Not really.'

'So what shall we do?'

Normally Reacher would have hit a random button and claimed to be a UPS or FedEx guy. But he wasn't sure whether that would work with this particular building. Courier deliveries probably weren't regular occurrences there. And he figured it was almost four o'clock in the afternoon. Not a plausible time for pizza or Chinese food. Too late for lunch, too early for dinner. So he just hit every button except 4L's and said in a loud slurred voice, 'Can't find my key.' And at least two households must have had an errant member missing because the door buzzed twice and Pauling pushed it open.

Inside was a dim centre hallway with a narrow

staircase on the right. The staircase ran up one floor and then doubled back and started over again at the front of the building. It was covered in cracked linoleum. It was illuminated with low wattage bulbs. It looked like a death trap.

'Now what?' Pauling asked.

'Now we wait,' Reacher said. 'At least two people are going to be sticking their heads out looking for whoever lost their key.'

So they waited. One minute. Two. Way above them in the gloom a door opened. Then closed again. Then another door opened. Closer. Second floor, maybe. Thirty seconds later it slammed shut.

'OK,' Reacher said. 'Now we're good to go.'

He put his weight on the bottom tread of the staircase and it creaked loudly. The second tread was the same. And the third. As he stepped onto the fourth Pauling started up behind him. By the time he was halfway up the whole structure was creaking and cracking like small arms fire.

They made it to the second floor hallway with no reaction from anywhere.

In front of them at the top of the stairs were two paired doors, one on the left and one on the right. 2L and 2R. Clearly these were railroad flats with front-to-back corridors that dog-legged halfway along their lengths to accommodate the entrances. Probably there were wall-mounted coat hooks just inside the doors. Straight ahead to the living rooms. Kitchens in the back. Turn back on yourself at the door, you would find the bathroom, and then the bedroom at the front of the building, overlooking the street.

'Not so bad,' Reacher said quietly.

Pauling said, 'I wouldn't want to carry my groceries up to five.'

Since childhood Reacher had never carried groceries into a home. He said, 'You could throw a rope off the fire escape. Haul them up through the bedroom.'

Pauling said nothing to that. They turned one-eighty together and walked the length of the hallway to the foot of the next flight of stairs. Stepped noisily up to three. 3L and 3R were right there in front of them, identical to the situation one floor below and presumably identical to the situation one floor above.

'Let's do it,' Reacher said.

They walked through the hallway and turned and glanced up into the fourth-floor gloom. They could see 4R's door. Not 4L's. Reacher went first. He took the stairs two at a time to cut the number of creaks and cracks by half. Pauling followed, putting her feet near the edges of the treads where any staircase is quieter. They made it to the top. Stood there. The building hummed with the kind of subliminal background noises you find in any packed dwelling in a big city. Muted traffic sounds from the street. The blare of car horns and the wail of sirens, dulled by the thickness of walls. Ten refrigerators running, window air conditioners, room fans, TV, radio, electricity buzzing through faulty fluorescent ballasts, water flowing through pipes.

4L's door had been painted a dull institutional green many years previously. Old, but there was nothing wrong with the job. Probably a union

231

painter, well trained by a long and painstaking apprenticeship. The careful sheen was overlaid with years of grime. Soot from buses, grease from kitchens, rail dust from the subways. There was a clouded spy lens about level with Reacher's chest. The *4* and the *L* were separate cast-brass items attached straight and true with brass screws.

Reacher turned sideways and bent forward from the waist. Put his ear on the crack where the door met the jamb. Listened for a moment.

Then he straightened up.

'There's someone in there,' he whispered.

THIRTY-SEVEN

Reacher bent forward and listened again. 'Straight ahead. A woman, talking.' Then he straightened up and stepped back. 'What's the layout going to be?'

'A short hallway,' Pauling whispered. 'Narrow for six feet, until it clears the bathroom. Then maybe it opens out to the living room. The living room will be maybe twelve feet long. The back wall will have a window on the left into the light well. Kitchen door on the right. The kitchen will be bumped out to the back. Maybe six or seven feet deep.'

Reacher nodded. Worst case, the woman was in the kitchen, a maximum twenty-five feet away down a straight and direct line of sight to the door. Worse than worst case, she had a loaded gun next to her on the countertop and she knew how to shoot.

Pauling asked, 'Who's she talking to?'

Reacher whispered, 'I don't know.'

'It's them, isn't it?'

'They'd be nuts to still be here.'

'Who else can it be?'

Reacher said nothing.

Pauling asked, 'What do you want to do?'

'What would you do?'

'Get a warrant. Call a SWAT team. Full body armour and a battering ram.'

'Those days are gone.'

'Tell me about it.'

Reacher took another step back. Pointed at 4R's door.

'Wait there,' he said. 'If you hear shooting, call an ambulance. If you don't, follow me in six feet behind.'

'You're just going to knock?'

'No,' Reacher said. 'Not exactly.'

He took another step back. He was six feet five inches tall and weighed about two hundred and fifty pounds. His shoes were bench-made by a company called Cheaney, from Northampton in England. Smarter buys than Church's, which were basically the same shoes but with a premium tag for the name. The style Reacher had chosen was called Tenterden, which was a brown semi-brogue made of heavy pebbled leather. Size twelve. The soles were heavy composite items bought in from a company called Dainite. Reacher hated leather soles. They wore out too fast and stayed wet too long after rain. Dainites were better. Their heels were a five-layer stack an inch and a quarter thick. The Cheaney leather welt, the Dainite welt, two slabs of hard Cheaney leather, and a thick Dainite cap.

Each shoe on its own weighed more than two pounds.

4L's door had three keyholes. Three locks.

Probably good ones. Maybe a chain inside. But door furniture is only as good as the wood it is set into. The door itself was probably hundred-year-old Douglas fir. Same for the frame. Cheap to start with, damp and swelled all through a hundred summers, dry and shrunken all through a hundred winters. A little eaten-out and wormy.

'Stand by now,' Reacher whispered.

He put his weight on his back foot and stared at the door and bounced like a high jumper going for a record. Then he launched. One pace, two. He smashed his right heel into the door just above the knob and wood splintered and dust filled the air and the door smashed open and he continued running without breaking stride. Two paces put him in the centre of the living room. He stopped dead there. Just stood still and stared. Lauren Pauling crowded in behind him and stopped at his shoulder.

Just stared.

The apartment was laid out exactly as Pauling had predicted. A dilapidated kitchen dead ahead, a twelve-foot living room on the left with a worn-out sofa and a dim window onto a light well. The air was hot and still and foul. In the kitchen doorway stood a heavyset woman in a shapeless cotton shift. She had long brown hair parted in the centre of her head. In one hand she held an open can of soup and in the other she held a wooden spoon. Her eyes and her mouth were open wide in bewilderment and surprise. She was trying to scream, but shock had punched all the air out of her lungs.

In the living room, horizontal on the worn-out sofa, was a man.

Not a man Reacher had ever seen before.

This man was sick. Prematurely old. He was savagely emaciated. He had no teeth. His skin was yellow and glittered with fever. All that was left of his hair were long wisps of grey.

He had no hands.

He had no feet.

Pauling said, '*Hobart?*'

There was nothing left that could surprise the man on the sofa. Not any more. With a lot of effort he just moved his head and said, 'Special Agent Pauling. It's a pleasure to see you again.'

He had a tongue. But with nothing else but gums in his mouth his speech was mumbled and indistinct. And weak. And faint. But he could talk. He could talk just fine.

Pauling looked at the woman and said, 'Dee Marie Graziano?'

'Yes,' the woman said.

'My sister,' Hobart said.

Pauling turned back to him. 'What the hell happened to you?'

'Africa,' Hobart said. 'Africa happened to me.'

He was wearing stiff new denims, dark blue. Jeans, and a shirt. The sleeves and legs were rolled to clear the stumps of his wrists and his shins, which were all smeared with a clear salve of some kind. The amputations were crude and brutal. Reacher could see the end of a yellow forearm bone protruding like a broken piano key. There was no stitching of the severed flesh.

No reconstruction. Mostly just a thick mass of scarring. Like burns.

'What happened?' Pauling asked again.

'Long story,' Hobart said.

'We need to hear it,' Reacher said.

'Why? The FBI is here to help me now? After kicking down my sister's door?'

'I'm not FBI,' Reacher said.

'Me either,' Pauling said. 'Not any more.'

'So what are you now?'

'A private investigator.'

Hobart's eyes moved to Reacher's face. 'And you?'

'The same,' Reacher said. 'More or less. Freelance. I don't have a licence. I used to be an MP.'

Nobody spoke for a minute.

'I was making soup,' Dee Marie Graziano said.

Pauling said, 'Go ahead. Please. Don't let us hold you up.'

Reacher stepped back through the hallway and pushed the shattered door as far shut as it would go. When he got back to the living room Dee Marie was in the kitchen with a flame under a saucepan. She was pouring the soup from the can into it. Stirring the soup with the spoon as it flowed. Pauling was still staring at the broken abbreviated man on the sofa.

'What happened to you?' she asked him for the third time.

'First he eats,' Dee Marie called.

THIRTY-EIGHT

His sister sat on the sofa next to him and cradled his head and fed him the soup slowly and carefully with a spoon. Hobart licked his lips after every mouthful and from time to time started to raise one or other of his missing hands to wipe a dribble off his chin. He would look at first perplexed for a fleeting second and then rueful, as if he were amazed at how long the memory of simple physical routines endured even after they were no longer possible. Each time it happened his sister would wait patiently for his handless wrist to return to his lap and then she would wipe his chin with a cloth, tenderly, lovingly, as if he were her child and not her brother. The soup was thick and made from some kind of a light green vegetable, maybe celery or asparagus, and by the time the bowl was empty the cloth was badly stained.

Pauling said, 'We need to talk.'

'About what?' Hobart asked.

'About you.'

'I'm not much to talk about. What you see is what you get.'

'And Edward Lane,' Pauling said. 'We need to talk about Edward Lane.'

'Where is he?'

'When was the last time you saw him?'

'Five years ago,' Hobart said. 'In Africa.'

'What happened there?'

'I was taken alive. Not smart.'

'And Knight too?'

Hobart nodded.

'Knight too,' he said.

'How?' Reacher asked.

'You ever been to Burkina Faso?'

'I've never been anywhere in Africa.'

Hobart paused for a long moment. He seemed to decide to clam up, and then he seemed to change his mind and decide to talk.

'There was a civil war,' he said. 'There usually is. We had a city to defend. We usually do. This time it was the capital. We couldn't even say its name. I learned it later. It's called Ouagadougou. But back then we called it O-Town. You were an MP. You know how that goes. The military deploys overseas and changes names. We think we're doing it for intelligibility, but really we're depersonalizing the place, psychologically. Making it ours, so we don't feel so bad when we destroy it.'

'What happened there?' Pauling asked.

'O-Town was about the size of Kansas City, Missouri. All the action was to the northeast. The tree line was about a mile outside the city limit. Two roads in, radial, like spokes in a wheel. One was north of northeast and the other was east of northeast. We called them the One O'clock Road

and the Two O'clock Road. Like the face of
a wristwatch? If twelve o'clock was due north,
there were roads at the one o'clock position and
the two o'clock position. The One O'clock Road
was the one we had to worry about. That's the
one the rebels were going to be using. Except
they wouldn't exactly be using it. They would
be flanking it in the jungle. They would be twenty
feet off the shoulder and we'd never see them.
They were nothing but infantry, with nothing
that wasn't man-portable. They were going to be
creeping along in the weeds, and we wouldn't see
them until they passed the tree line and came out
in the open.'

'Tree line was a mile away?' Reacher said.

'Exactly,' Hobart said. 'Not a problem. They
had a mile of open ground to cross and we had
heavy machine guns.'

'So where was the problem?'

'If you were them, what would you have done?'

'I would have moved to my left and outflanked
you to the east. With at least half my force,
maybe more. I would have stayed in the weeds
and moved around and come out at you maybe
from the four o'clock position. Co-ordinated
attacks. Two directions. You wouldn't have
known which was your front and which was your
flank.'

Hobart nodded. A small painful motion
that brought out all the tendons in his scrawny
neck.

'We anticipated exactly that,' he said. 'We
figured they'd be tracking the One O'clock Road
with half their force on the right shoulder and the

other half on the left shoulder. We figured about two miles out the half that was on the right shoulder as we were looking at it would wheel ninety degrees to its left and attempt an out-flanking manoeuvre. But that meant that maybe five thousand guys would have to cross the Two O'clock Road. Spokes in a wheel, right? We'd see them. The Two O'clock Road was dead straight. Narrow, but a clear cut through the trees for fifty miles. We could see all the way to the horizon. It was going to be like watching a crosswalk in Times Square.'

'So what happened?' Pauling asked.

'Knight and I had been together forever. And we had been Recon Marines. So we volunteered to set up forward OPs. We crawled out about three hundred yards and found a couple of good depressions. Old shell holes, from back in the day. Those places are always fighting. Knight set up with a good view of the One O'clock Road and I set up with a good view of the Two O'clock Road. Plan was if they didn't attempt to outflank us we'd take them head-on and if we were making good progress with that our main force would come out to join us. If their attack was heavy Knight and I would fall back to the city limit and we'd set up a secondary line of defence there. And if I saw the outflanking manoeuvre in progress we'd fall back immediately and reorganize on two fronts.'

Reacher asked, 'So where did it all go wrong?'

'I made two mistakes,' Hobart said. Just four words, but the effort of getting them out seemed to suddenly exhaust him. He closed his eyes and his lips tightened against his toothless gums and he started wheezing from the chest.

'He has malaria and tuberculosis,' his sister said. 'You're tiring him out.'

'Is he getting care?' Pauling asked.

'We have no benefits. The VA does a little. Apart from that I take him to the St Vincent's ER.'

'How? How do you get him up and down the stairs?'

'I carry him,' Dee Marie said. 'On my back.'

Hobart coughed hard and dribbled blood-flecked spittle down his chin. He raised his severed wrist high and wiped himself with what was left of his bicep. Then he opened his eyes.

Reacher asked him, 'What two mistakes?'

'There was an early feint,' Hobart said. 'About ten point men came out of the trees a mile ahead of Knight. They were going for death or glory, you know, running and firing unaimed. Knight let them run for about fifteen hundred yards and then he dropped them all with his rifle. I couldn't see him. He was about a hundred yards away but the terrain was uneven. I crawled over to check he was OK.'

'And was he?'

'He was fine.'

'Neither of you had been wounded?'

'Wounded? Not even close.'

'But there had been small arms fire?'

'Some.'

'Go on.'

'When I got to Knight's position I realized I could see the Two O'clock Road even better from

242

his hole than from mine. Plus I figured when the shooting starts it's always better to be paired up. We could cover each other for jams and reloads. So that was my first mistake. I put myself in the same foxhole as Knight.'

'And the second mistake?'

'I believed what Edward Lane told me.'

THIRTY-NINE

Reacher asked, 'What did Edward Lane tell you?'

But Hobart couldn't answer for a minute. He was consumed with another bout of coughing. His caved chest heaved. His truncated limbs flailed uselessly. Blood and thick yellow mucus rimed his lips. Dee Marie ducked back to the kitchen and rinsed her cloth and filled a glass with water. Wiped Hobart's face very carefully and let him sip from the glass. Then she took him under the arms and hauled him into an upright position. He coughed twice more and then stopped as the fluid settled lower in his lungs.

'It's a balance,' Dee Marie said, to nobody in particular. 'We need to keep his chest clear but coughing too much wears him out.'

Reacher asked, 'Hobart? What did Lane tell you?'

Hobart panted for a moment and fixed his eyes on Reacher's in a mute appeal for patience. Then he said, 'About thirty minutes after that first feint Lane showed up in Knight's foxhole.

He seemed surprised to see me there too. He checked that Knight was OK and told him to stay with the mission. Then he turned to me and told me he had definitive new intelligence that we *were* going to see men crossing the Two O'clock Road but that they would be government troops coming in from the bush and circling around to reinforce us through the rear. He said they had been on a night march and were taking it slow and stealthy because they were so close to the rebels. Both sides were incoming on parallel tracks less than forty yards apart. No danger of visual contact because of how thick the vegetation was, but they were worried about noise. So Lane told me to sit tight and watch the road and just count them across it, and the higher the number was the better I should feel about it, because they were all on our side.'

'And you saw them?'

'Thousands and thousands of them. Your basic ragtag army, all on foot, no transport, decent firepower, plenty of Browning automatic rifles, some M60s, some light mortars. They crossed two abreast and it took hours.'

'And then?'

'We sat tight. All day, and into the night. Then all hell broke loose. We had night scopes and we could see what was happening. About five thousand guys just stepped out of the trees and assembled on the One O'clock Road and started marching straight towards us. At the same time another five thousand stepped out of the brush just south of the four o'clock position and came straight at us. They were the same guys I had counted earlier. They weren't government troops. They were rebels. Lane's new intelligence had been wrong. At least that's what I thought at first. Later I realized he had lied to me.'

'What happened?' Pauling said.

'At first nothing computed. The rebels started firing from way too far away. Africa's a big continent but most of them probably missed it. At that point Knight and I were kind of relaxed. Plans are always bullshit. Everything in war is improvisation. So we expected some suppressing fire from behind us to allow us to fall back. But it never came. I was turned around staring at the city behind me. It was just three hundred yards away. But it was all dark and silent. Then I turned back and saw these ten thousand guys coming at me. Two different directions ninety degrees apart. Dead of night. Suddenly I had the feeling Knight and I were the only two Westerners left in the country. Turns out I was probably right. The way I pieced it together afterwards, Lane and all the other crews had pulled out twelve hours before. He must have gotten back from his little visit with us and just hopped straight into his jeep. Mounted everyone up and headed due south for the border with Ghana. Then to the airport at Tamale, which was where we came in.'

Reacher said, 'What we need to know is why he did that.'

'That's easy,' Hobart said. 'I had plenty of time to figure it out afterwards, believe me. Lane

246

abandoned us because he wanted Knight dead. I just happened to be in the wrong foxhole, that's all. I was collateral damage.'

'Why did Lane want Knight dead?'

'Because Knight killed Lane's wife.'

FORTY

Pauling asked, 'Did Knight confess that to you directly?'

Hobart didn't answer. Just waved the stump of his right wrist, weakly, vaguely, a dismissive little gesture.

'Did Knight confess to killing Anne Lane?'

Hobart said, 'He confessed to about a hundred thousand different things.' Then he smiled ruefully. 'You had to be there. You had to know how it was. Knight was raving for four years. He was completely out of his mind for three. Me too, probably.'

'So how was it?' Pauling asked. 'Tell us.'

Dee Marie Graziano said, 'I don't want to hear this again. I *can't* hear this again. I'm going out.'

Pauling opened her purse and took out her wallet. Peeled off part of her wad. Didn't count it. Just handed the sheaf of bills straight to Dee Marie.

'Get stuff,' she said. 'Food, medicine, whatever you need.'

Dee Marie said, 'You can't buy his testimony.'

'I'm not trying to,' Pauling said. 'I'm trying to help, that's all.'

'I don't like charity.'

'Then get over it,' Reacher said. 'Your brother needs everything he can get.'

'Take it, Dee,' Hobart said. 'Be sure to get something for yourself.'

Dee Marie shrugged, then took the money. Jammed it in the pocket of her shift and collected her keys and walked out. Reacher heard the front door open. The hinges squealed where he had damaged them. He stepped into the hallway.

'We should call a carpenter,' Pauling said, from behind him.

'Call that Soviet super from Sixth Avenue,' Reacher said. 'He looked competent and I'm sure he moonlights.'

'You think?'

Reacher whispered, 'He was with the Red Army in Afghanistan. He won't freak when he sees a guy with no hands and no feet.'

'You talking about me?' Hobart called.

Reacher followed Pauling back to the living room and said, 'You're lucky to have a sister like that.'

Hobart nodded. The same slow, painful movement.

'But it's hard on her,' he said. 'You know, with the bathroom and all. She has to see things a sister shouldn't see.'

'Tell us about Knight. Tell us about the whole damn thing.'

Hobart laid his head back on the sofa cushion. Stared up at the ceiling. With his sister gone, he

249

seemed to relax. His ruined body settled and quieted.

'It was one of those unique moments,' he said. 'Suddenly we were sure we were alone, outnumbered ten thousand to two, dead of night, in no man's land, in the middle of a country we had no right to be in. I mean, you think you've been in deep shit before, and then you realize you have absolutely no conception of how deep shit can really be. At first we didn't do anything. Then we just looked at each other. That was the last moment of true peace I ever felt. We looked at each other and I guess we just took an unspoken decision to go down fighting. Better to die, we figured. We all have to die sometime, and that looked like as good an occasion as any. So we started firing. I guess we figured they'd lay some mortar rounds on us and that would be that. But they didn't. They just kept on coming, tens and twenties, and we just kept on firing, putting them down. Hundreds of them. But they kept on coming. Now I guess it was a tactic. We started to have equipment problems, like they knew we would. Our M60 barrels overheated. We started to run short of ammunition. We only had what we had been able to carry. When they sensed it, they all charged. OK, I thought, bring it on. I figured bullets or bayonets right there in the hole would be as good as mortar rounds from a distance.'

He closed his eyes and the little room went quiet.

'But?' Reacher said.

Hobart opened his eyes. 'But it didn't happen that way. They got to the lip of the hole and

250

stopped and just stood there. Waited in the moonlight. Watched us floundering around looking for fresh clips. We didn't have any. Then the crowd parted and some kind of an officer walked through. He looked down at us and smiled. Black face, white teeth, in the moonlight. It hit us then. We thought we'd been in deep shit *before*, but that was nothing. *This* was deep shit. We'd just killed hundreds of their guys and we were about to be captured.'

'How did it go down?'

'Surprisingly well, at the beginning. They stole everything of any value immediately. Then they slapped us around a little bit for a minute, but it was really nothing. I had worse from the NCOs in boot camp. We had these little Stars and Stripes patches on our BDUs, and I thought maybe they counted for something. The first few days were chaos. We were chained all the time, but that was more out of necessity than cruelty. They had no jail facilities. They had nothing, really. They'd been living in the bush for years. No infrastructure. But they fed us. Appalling food, but it was the same as they were eating, and it's the thought that counts. Then after a week it was clear the coup had succeeded, so they all moved into O-Town proper and took us with them and put us in the city prison. We were in a separate wing for about four weeks. We figured they were maybe negotiating with Washington. They fed us and left us alone. We could hear bad stuff elsewhere in the building, but we figured we were special. So altogether the first month was a day at the beach compared to what came later.'

'What came later?'

'Evidently they gave up on Washington or stopped thinking we were special because they took us out of the separate wing and tossed us in with some of the others. And that was bad. Real bad. Incredible overcrowding, filth, disease, no clean water, almost no food. We were skeletons inside a month. Savages after two. I went six months without even lying down, the first cell was so crowded. We were ankle deep in shit, literally. There were worms. At night the place crawled with them. People were dying from disease and starvation. Then they put us on trial.'

'You had a trial?'

'I guess it was a trial. War crimes, probably. I had no idea what they were saying.'

'Weren't they speaking French?'

'That's for government and diplomacy. The rest of them speak tribal languages. It was just two hours of noise to me, and then they found us guilty. They took us back to the big house and we found out that the part we'd already been in was the VIP accommodations. Now we were headed for general population, which was a whole lot worse. Two months later I figured I was about as low as I could go. But I was wrong. Because then I had a birthday.'

'What happened on your birthday?'

'They gave me a present.'

'Which was?'

'A choice.'

'Of what?'

'They hauled out about a dozen guys. I guess we all shared the same birthday. They took us to a courtyard. First thing I noticed was a big bucket of tar on a propane burner. It was bubbling away. Real hot. I remembered the smell from when I was a kid, from when they were blacktopping roads where I lived. My mother believed some old superstition that said if a kid sniffed the tar smell it would protect him from getting coughs and colds. She would send us out to chase the trucks. So I knew the smell real well. Then I saw next to the bucket was a big stone block, all black with blood. Then some big guard grabbed a machete and started screaming at the first guy in line. I had no idea what he was saying. The guy next to me spoke a little English and translated for me. He said we had a choice. Three choices, actually. To celebrate our birthdays we were going to lose a foot. First choice, left or right. Second choice, short pants or long pants. That was a kind of joke. It meant we could be cut above the knee or below. Our choice. Third choice, we could use the bucket or not. Our choice. You plunge the stump in there, the boiling tar seals the arteries and cauterizes the wound. Choose not to, and you bleed out and die. Our choice. But the guard said we had to choose fast. We weren't allowed to mess around and hold up the queue behind us.'

Silence in the tiny room. Nobody spoke. There was no sound at all, except faint incongruous New York City sirens in the far distance.

Hobart said, 'I chose left, long pants, and yes to the bucket.'

FORTY-ONE

For a long time the small room stayed quiet as a tomb. Hobart rolled his head from side to side to ease his neck. Reacher sat down in a small chair near the window.

Hobart said, 'Twelve months later on my next birthday I chose right, long pants, and yes to the bucket.'

Reacher said, 'They did this to Knight too?'

Hobart nodded. 'We thought we had been close before. But some things really bring you together.'

Pauling was leaning up in the kitchen doorway, white as a sheet. 'Knight told you about Anne Lane?'

'He told me about a lot of things. But remember, we were doing seriously hard time. We were sick and starving. We had infections. We had malaria and dysentery. We were out of our heads for weeks at a time with fevers.'

'What did he tell you?'

'He told me he shot Anne Lane in New Jersey.'

'Did he tell you why?'

'He gave me a whole bunch of different

254

reasons. Different day, different reason. Some-times it was that he had been having an affair with her, and she broke it off, and he got mad. Other times it was that Lane was mad at her and asked him to do it. Other times he said he was working for the CIA. Once he said she was an alien from another planet.'

'Did he kidnap her?'

Hobart nodded, slowly, painfully. 'Drove her to the store, but didn't stop there. Just pulled a gun and kept on going, all the way to New Jersey. Killed her there.'

'Immediately?' Pauling asked.

Hobart said, 'Yes, immediately. She was dead a day before you ever even heard of her. There was nothing wrong with your procedures. He killed her that first morning and drove back and waited outside the store until it was time to sound the alarms.'

'Not possible,' Pauling said. 'His EZ-Pass records showed he hadn't used a bridge or a tunnel that day.'

'Give me a break,' Hobart said. 'You pull the tag off the windshield and put it in the foil packet they mailed it in. Then you use a cash lane.'

'Were you really in Philadelphia?' Reacher asked.

'Yes, I really was,' Hobart said.

'Did you know what Knight was doing that day?'

'No, I really didn't.'

'Who faked Anne's voice on the phone?' Pauling asked. 'Who set up the ransom drop?'

'Sometimes Knight would say it was a couple of

his buddies. Sometimes he would say Lane took care of all of that.'

'Which version did you believe?'

Hobart's head dropped to his chest and canted left. He stared towards the floor. Reacher asked, 'Can I get you something?'

'I'm just looking at your shoes,' Hobart said. 'I like nice shoes too. Or at least I did.'

'You'll get prosthetics. You can wear shoes with them.'

'Can't afford them. Prosthetics, or shoes.'

Pauling said, 'What was the truth about Anne Lane?'

Hobart pulled his head back to the cushion so he could look straight up at Pauling. He smiled, sadly.

'The truth about Anne Lane?' he said. 'I thought about that a lot. Believe me, I obsessed over it. It became the central question of my life, because basically it was responsible for what was happening to me. The third birthday I spent in there, they took me back to the courtyard. The second choice was phrased slightly different. Long sleeves or short? Stupid question, really. Nobody ever chose short sleeves. I mean, who the hell would? I saw a thousand amputees in there and nobody ever took it above the elbow.'

Silence in the room.

'The things you remember,' Hobart said. 'I remember the stink of the blood and the tar bucket and the pile of severed hands behind that big stone block. A bunch of black ones and one little white one.'

Pauling asked, 'What was the truth about Anne?'

'The waiting was the hardest part. I spent a year looking at my right hand. Doing things with it. Making a fist, spreading my fingers, scratching myself with my nails.'

'Why did Knight kill Anne Lane?'

'They weren't having an affair. Not possible. Knight wasn't that type of a guy. I'm not saying he had scruples. He was just a little timid around women, that's all. He did OK with trash in bars or with hookers, but Anne Lane was way out of his league. She was classy, she had personality, she had energy, she knew who she was. She was intelligent. She wouldn't have responded to the kind of thing that Knight had to offer. Not in a million years. And Knight wouldn't have offered anything anyway, because Anne was the CO's wife. That's the biggest no-no of all time for an American fighting man. In the movies they show it maybe, but not in real life. Just wouldn't happen, and if it did, Knight would have been the last Marine on earth to try it.'

'You sure?'

'I knew him very well. And he didn't have the kind of buddies that could have faked the voices. Certainly not a woman's voice. He had no women friends. He didn't have *any* friends outside of me and the unit. Not really. Not close enough for work like that. What Marine does? That's when I knew he was bullshitting. There was nobody he knew where he could just walk up to them and say, hey, help me out with this phoney kidnap thing, why don't you?'

'So why did he even try bullshitting you?'

'Because he understood better than me that reality was over for us. There was really no difference between truth and fantasy for us at that point. They were of absolutely equal value. He was just amusing himself. Maybe he was trying to amuse me too. But I was still analysing stuff. He gave me a whole rainbow of reasons and details and facts and scenarios and I checked them over very carefully in my mind for five long years and the only story I really believed was that Lane set the whole thing up because Anne wanted out of the marriage. She wanted a divorce and she wanted alimony and Lane's ego couldn't take it. So he had her killed.'

'Why would Lane want Knight dead if all he had done was act on Lane's own orders?'

'Lane was covering his ass. Tying up the loose ends. And he was avoiding being in someone else's debt. That was the main thing, really. Ultimately that was the true reason. A guy like Lane, his ego couldn't take that, either. Being grateful to someone.'

Silence in the room.

'What happened to Knight in the end?' Reacher asked.

'His fourth birthday,' Hobart said. 'He didn't go for the bucket. He didn't want to go on. The pussy just quit on me. Some damn jarhead he was.'

FORTY-TWO

Ten minutes later Dee Marie Graziano got home. The squawk box in the hallway sounded and she asked for help carrying packages up the stairs. Reacher went down four flights and hauled four grocery bags back up to the apartment. Dee Marie unpacked them in the kitchen. She had bought a lot of soup, and Jell-O, and painkillers, and antiseptic creams.

Reacher said, 'We heard that Kate Lane had a visitor in the Hamptons.'

Dee Marie said nothing.

'Was it you?' Reacher asked.

'I went to the Dakota first,' she said. 'But the doorman told me they were away.'

'So then you went.'

'Two days later. We decided that I should. It was a long day. Very expensive.'

'You went there to warn Anne Lane's successor.'

'We thought she should be told what her husband was capable of doing.'

'How did she react?'

'She listened. We walked on the sand and she listened to what I had to say.'

'That was all?'

'She took it all in. Didn't react much.'

'How definite were you?'

'I said we had no proof. Equally I said we had no doubt.'

'And she didn't react?'

'She just took it all in. Gave it a fair hearing.'

'Did you tell her about your brother?'

'It's a part of the story. She listened to it. Didn't say much. She's beautiful and she's rich. People like that are different. If it's not happening to them, it's not happening at all.'

'What happened to your husband?'

'Vinnie? Iraq happened to Vinnie. Fallujah. A roadside booby-trap.'

'I'm sorry.'

'They told me he was killed instantly. But they always say that.'

'Sometimes it's true.'

'I hope it was. Just that one time.'

'The Corps or private?'

'Vinnie? The Corps. Vinnie hated private contractors.'

Reacher left Dee Marie in the kitchen and stepped back into the living room. Hobart's head was laid back and his lips were stretched in a grimace. His neck was thin and bulging with ligaments. His torso was painfully wasted and looked bizarrely long in proportion to the stumps of his limbs.

'You need anything?' Reacher asked him.

Hobart said, 'Silly question.'

'What would the three of clubs mean to you?'

'Knight.'

'How so?'

'Three was his lucky number. Club was his nickname in the Corps. Because of how he liked to party, and because of the pun on his name. Knight Club, nightclub, like that. They called him Club, back in the day.'

'He left a playing card on Anne Lane's body. The three of clubs.'

'He did? He told me that. I didn't believe him. I thought it was embellishment. Like a book or a movie.'

Reacher said nothing.

'I need the bathroom,' Hobart said. 'Tell Dee.'

'I'll do it,' Reacher said. 'Let's give Dee a break.'

He stepped over and bunched the front of Hobart's shirt and hauled him upright. Slipped an arm behind his shoulders. Ducked down and caught him under the knees and lifted him up off the sofa. He was incredibly light. Probably close to a hundred pounds. Not much of him left.

Reacher carried Hobart to the bathroom and grabbed the front of his shirt again one-handed and held him vertical in the air like a rag doll. Undid his pants and eased them down.

'You've done this before,' Hobart said.

'I was an MP,' Reacher said. 'I've done every-thing before.'

*   *   *

Reacher put Hobart back on the sofa and Dee Marie fed him more soup. Used the same damp cloth to clean his chin.

Reacher said, 'I need to ask you both one important question. I need to know where you've been and what you've been doing for the last four days.'

Dee Marie answered. No guile, no hesitation, nothing phoney or over-rehearsed. Just a slightly incoherent and therefore completely convincing pieced-together narrative account of four random days from an ongoing nightmare. The four days had started with Hobart in St Vincent's hospital. Dee Marie had taken him to the ER the night before with a severe malaria relapse. The ER doctor had admitted him for forty-eight hours of IV medication. Dee Marie had stayed with him most of the time. Then she had brought him home in a taxi and carried him on her back up the four flights of stairs. They had been alone in the apartment since then, eating what was in the kitchen cupboards, doing nothing, seeing nobody, until their door had smashed open and Reacher had ended up in the middle of their living room.

'Why are you asking?' Hobart said.

'The new Mrs Lane was kidnapped. And her kid.'

'You thought I did it?'

'For a spell.'

'Think again.'

'I already have.'

'Why would I?'

'For revenge. For money. The ransom was exactly half the Burkina Faso payment.'

262

'I would have wanted all of it.'

'Me too.'

'But I wouldn't have gone after a woman and a kid.'

'Me either.'

'So why pick me out?'

'We got a basic report on you and Knight. We heard about mutilations. No specific details. Then we heard about a guy with no tongue. We put two and two together and made three. We thought it was you.'

'No tongue?' Hobart said. 'I wish. I'd take that deal.' Then he said, 'But no tongue is a South American thing. Brazil, Colombia, Peru. Maybe Sicily in Europe. Not Africa. You can't get a machete in somebody's mouth. Lips, maybe. I saw that, sometimes. Or ears. But not the tongue.'

'We apologize,' Pauling said.

'No harm, no foul,' Hobart said.

'We'll have the door fixed.'

'I'd appreciate that.'

'And we'll help you if we can.'

'I'd appreciate that too. But see to the woman and the child first.'

'We think we're already too late.'

'Don't say that. It depends who took them. Where there's hope, there's life. Hope kept me going, five hard years.'

Reacher and Pauling left Hobart and Dee Marie right there, together on their battered sofa, the bowl of soup half gone. They walked down four flights to the street and stepped out into the afternoon shadows of a fabulous late-summer day. Traffic ground past on the street, slow and angry. Horns blared and sirens barked. Fast pedestrians swerved by on the sidewalk.

Reacher said, 'Eight million stories in the naked city.'

Pauling said, 'We're nowhere.'

FORTY-THREE

Reacher led Pauling north on Hudson, across Houston, to the block between Clarkson and Leroy. He said, 'I think the man with no tongue lives near this spot.'

'Twenty thousand people live near this spot,' Pauling said.

Reacher didn't reply.

'What now?' Pauling said.

'Back to the hard way. We wasted some time, that's all. Wasted some energy. My fault entirely. I was stupid.'

'How?'

'Did you see how Hobart was dressed?'

'Cheap new denims.'

'The guy I saw driving the cars away was wearing old denims. Both times. Old, soft, washed, worn, faded, comfortable denims. The Soviet super said the same thing. And the old Chinese man. No way was the guy I saw just back from Africa. Or back from anywhere. It takes ages to get jeans and a shirt looking like that. The guy I saw has been safe at home for five years doing his laundry, not jammed up in some hellhole jail.'

Pauling said nothing.

'You can split now,' Reacher said. 'You got what you wanted. Anne Lane wasn't your fault. She was dead before you ever even heard of her. You can sleep at night.'

'But not well. Because I can't touch Edward Lane. Hobart's testimony is meaningless.'

'Because it's hearsay?'

'Hearsay is sometimes OK. Knight's dying declaration would be admissible, because the court would assume he had no motive to lie from his deathbed.'

'So what's the problem?'

'There was no dying declaration. There were dozens of random fantasies spun over a four-year period. Hobart chose to back one of them, that's all. And he freely admits that both he and Knight were as good as insane most of the time. I'd be laughed out of court, literally.'

'But you believed him.'

Pauling nodded. 'No question.'

'So you can settle for half a loaf. Patti Joseph, too. I'll drop by and tell her.'

'Would you be happy with half a loaf?'

'I said you can split. Not me. I'm not quitting yet. My agenda is getting longer and longer by the minute.'

'I'll stick with it too.'

'Your choice.'

'I know. You want me to?'

Reacher looked at her. Answered honestly. 'Yes, I do.'

'Then I will.'

'Just don't get all scrupulous on me. This thing

266

isn't going to be settled in any court of law with any dying declarations.'

'How is it going to be settled?'

'The first colonel I really fell out with, I shot him in the head. And so far I like Lane a lot less than that guy. That guy was practically a saint compared to Lane.'

'I'll come with you to Patti Joseph's.'

'No, I'll meet you there,' Reacher said. 'Two hours from now. We should travel separately.'

'Why?'

'I'm going to try to get killed.'

Pauling said she would be in the Majestic's lobby in two hours and headed for the subway. Reacher started walking north on Hudson, not fast, not slow, centre of the left-hand sidewalk. Twelve storeys above him and ten yards behind his left shoulder was a north-facing window. It had heavy black cloth taped behind it. The cloth had been peeled back across a quarter of its width to make a tall narrow slit, as if a person in the room had wanted at least a partial view of the city.

Reacher crossed Morton, and Barrow, and Christopher. On West 10th he started zigzagging through the narrow tree-lined Village streets, east for a block, then north, then west, then north again. He made it to the bottom of Eighth Avenue and walked north for a spell and then started zigzagging again where the Chelsea side streets were quiet. He stopped in the lee of a brownstone's front steps and bent down and retied his shoes. Walked on and stopped again behind a big square plastic trash bin and studied something on the ground. At West 23rd Street he turned east and then north again on Eighth. Stuck to the centre of the left-hand sidewalk and slow-marched onward. Patti Joseph and the Majestic lay a little more than two miles ahead in a dead straight line, and he had a whole hour to get there.

Thirty minutes later at Columbus Circle, Reacher entered Central Park. Daylight was fading. Shadows had been long, but now they were indistinct. The air was still warm. Reacher stuck to the paths for a spell and then he stepped off and walked a haphazard and unofficial route through the trees. He stopped and leaned against one trunk, facing north. Then another, facing east. He got back on the path and found an empty bench and sat down with his back to the stream of people walking past. He waited there until the clock in his head told him it was time to move.

Reacher found Lauren Pauling waiting in one of a group of armchairs in the Majestic's lobby. She had freshened up. She looked good. She had qualities. Reacher found himself thinking that Kate Lane might have ended up looking like that, twenty years down the road.

'I stopped by and asked that Russian super,' she said. 'He'll go over later tonight to fix the door.'

'Good,' Reacher said.

'You didn't get killed,' she said.

He sat down beside her.

'Something else I got wrong,' he said. 'I've been assuming there was inside help from one of Lane's crew. But now I don't think there can have been. Yesterday morning Lane offered me a million bucks. This morning when he lost hope he told me to find the bad guys. Seek and destroy. He was about as serious as a man can get. Anyone watching from the inside would have to assume I was pretty well motivated. And I've shown them that I'm at least partially competent. But nobody has tried to stop me. And they would try, wouldn't they? Any kind of an inside ally would be expected to. But they haven't. I just spent two hours strolling through Manhattan. Side streets, quiet places, Central Park. I kept stopping and turning my back. I gave whoever it might be a dozen chances to take me out. But nobody tried.'

'Would they have been on your tail?'

'That's why I wanted to start between Clarkson and Leroy. That's got to be some kind of a base camp. They could have picked me up there.'

'How could they have done this whole thing without inside help?'

'I have absolutely no idea.'

'You'll figure it out.'

'Say that again.'

'Why? You need inspiration?'

'I just like the sound of your voice.'

'You'll figure it out,' Pauling said, low and husky, like she had been getting over laryngitis for the last thirty years.

*   *   *

They checked in at the desk and then rode up to seven in the elevator. Patti Joseph was out in the corridor, waiting for them. There was a little awkwardness when she and Pauling met. Patti had spent five years thinking Pauling had failed her sister, and Pauling had spent the same five years thinking pretty much the same thing. So there was ice to break. But the implied promise of news helped Patti thaw. And Reacher figured Pauling had plenty of experience with grieving relatives. Any investigator does.

'Coffee?' Patti said, before they were even in through the door.

'I thought you'd never ask,' Reacher said.

Patti went to the kitchen to set up the machine and Pauling walked straight to the window. Looked at the stuff on the sill, and then checked the view. Raised her eyebrows in Reacher's direction and gave a small shrug that said: *Weird, but I've seen weirder*.

'So what's up?' Patti called through.

Reacher said, 'Let's wait until we're all sitting down.' And ten minutes later they all were, with Patti Joseph in tears. Tears of grief, tears of relief, tears of closure.

Tears of anger.

'Where is Knight now?' she asked.

'Knight died,' Reacher said. 'And he died hard.'

'Good. I'm glad.'

'No argument from me.'

'What are we going to do about Lane?'

'That remains to be seen.'

'I should call Brewer.'

'Brewer can't do anything. There's truth here, but there's no evidence. Not the kind that a cop or a prosecutor needs.'

'You should tell the other guys about Hobart. Tell them what Lane did to their buddy. Send them down there to see for themselves.'

'Might not work. They might not care. Guys that were likely to care wouldn't have obeyed the order in Africa in the first place. And now, even if they did care, the best way to deal with their own guilt would be to stay in denial. They've had five years' practice.'

'But it might be worth it. To see with their own eyes.'

'We can't risk it. Not unless we know for sure ahead of time what their reactions would be. Because Lane will assume Knight spilled the beans in prison. Therefore Lane will see Hobart as a loose end now. And a threat. Therefore Lane will want Hobart dead now. And Lane's guys will do whatever the hell Lane tells them to. So we can't risk it. Hobart's a sitting duck, literally. A puff of wind would blow him away. And his sister would get caught in the crossfire.'

'Why are you here?'

'To give you the news.'

'Not *here*. In New York, in and out of the Dakota.'

Reacher said nothing.

'I'm not a fool,' Patti said. 'I know what goes on. Who knows more than me? Who possibly could? And I know that the day after I stop seeing Kate Lane and Jade any more, you show up and people put bags in cars and you hide in the back seat and you come here to interrogate Brewer about the last time one of Edward Lane's wives disappeared.'

Reacher asked, 'Why do you think I'm here?'

'I think he's done it again.'

Reacher looked at Pauling and Pauling shrugged like maybe she agreed Patti deserved to hear the story. Like somehow she had earned the right through five long years of fidelity to her sister's memory. So Reacher told her everything he knew. Told her all the facts, all the guesses, all the assumptions, all the conclusions. When he finished she just stared at him.

She said: 'You think it's real this time because of how good an *actor* he is?'

'No, I think nobody's that good of an actor.'

'Hello? Adolf Hitler? He could work himself into all kinds of phoney rages.'

Patti stood up and stepped over to an armoire drawer and pulled out a packet of photographs. Checked the contents and tossed the packet into Reacher's lap. A fresh new envelope. A one-hour service. Thirty-six exposures. He thumbed through the stack. Top picture was of himself, face on, coming out of the Dakota's lobby, preparing to turn towards the subway on Central Park West. *Early this morning*, he thought. *The B train to Pauling's office*.

'So?'

'Keep going.'

He thumbed backward and close to the end of the stack he saw Dee Marie Graziano, face on, coming out of the Dakota's lobby. The sun in the west. Afternoon. The picture behind it showed her from the back, going in.

'That's Hobart's sister, am I right?' Patti said. 'It has to be, according to your story. She's in my notebook, too. Close to forty, overweight, not rich. Previously unexplained. But now I know. That's when the Dakota doorman told her the family was in the Hamptons. Then she went out there.'

'So?'

'Isn't it obvious? Kate Lane takes this weird woman walking on the beach, and she hears a weird and fantastical story, but there's something about it and something about her husband that stops her from just dismissing it out of hand. Enough of a grain of truth there to make her think for a moment. Maybe enough to make her ask her husband for an explanation.'

Reacher said nothing.

Patti said, 'In which case all hell would break loose. Don't you see? Suddenly Kate is no longer a loyal and obedient wife. Suddenly she's as bad as Anne was. And suddenly she's a loose end, too. Maybe even a serious threat.'

'Lane would have gone after Hobart and Dee Marie, too. Not just Kate.'

'If he could find them. You only found them because of the Pentagon.'

'And the Pentagon hates Lane,' Pauling said. 'They wouldn't give him the time of day.'

'Two questions,' Reacher said. 'If this is history repeating itself, Anne all over again, why is Lane pushing me to help?'

'He's gambling,' Patti said. 'He's gambling because he's arrogant. He's putting on a show for his men, and he's betting that he's smarter than you are.'

'Second question,' Reacher said. 'Who could be playing Knight's part this time around?'

'Does that matter?'

'Yes, it matters. It's an important detail, don't you think?'

Patti paused. Looked away.

'It's an inconvenient detail,' she said. 'Because there's nobody missing.' Then she said, 'OK, I apologize. Maybe you're right. Just because it was fake for Anne doesn't mean it's fake for Kate.' Then she said, 'Just remember one thing, while you're spending your time helping him. You're not looking for a woman he loves. You're looking for a prize possession. This is like somebody stole a gold watch from him, and he's angry about it.'

Then out of what Reacher guessed was sheer habit Patti moved to the window and stood with her hands linked behind her back, staring out and down.

'It's not over for me,' she said. 'It won't be over for me until Lane gets what he deserves.'

FORTY-FOUR

Reacher and Pauling rode down to the Majestic's lobby in silence. They stepped out to the sidewalk. Early evening. Four lanes of traffic, and lovers in the park. Dogs on leashes, tour groups, the bass bark of fire truck horns.

Pauling asked, 'Where now?'

'Take the night off,' Reacher said. 'I'm going back to the lions' den.'

Pauling headed for the subway and Reacher headed for the Dakota. The doorman sent him up without making a call. Either Lane had put him on some kind of an approved list or the doorman had grown accustomed to his face. Either way it didn't feel good. Poor security, and Reacher didn't want to be recognized as part of Lane's crew. Not that he expected to be around the Dakota ever again. It was way above his pay grade.

There was nobody waiting for him in the corridor on five. Lane's door was closed. Reacher knocked and then found a bell button and pushed it. A minute later Kowalski opened up. The biggest of Lane's guys, but no giant. Maybe six

275

feet, maybe two hundred pounds. He seemed to be alone. There was nothing but stillness and silence behind him. He stepped back and held the door and Reacher stepped inside.

'Where is everybody?' Reacher asked.

'Out shaking the trees,' Kowalski said.

'What trees?'

'Burke has a theory. He thinks we're being visited by ghosts from the past.'

'What ghosts?'

'You know what ghosts,' Kowalski said. 'Because Burke told you first.'

'Knight and Hobart,' Reacher said.

'The very same.'

'Waste of time,' Reacher said. 'They died in Africa.'

'Not true,' Kowalski said. 'A friend of a friend of a friend called a VA clerk. Only one of them died in Africa.'

'Which one?'

'We don't know yet. But we'll find out. You know what a VA clerk makes?'

'Not very much, I guess.'

'Everyone has a price. And a VA clerk's is pretty low.'

They moved through the foyer to the deserted living room. Kate Lane's picture still had pride of place on the table. There was a recessed light fixture in the ceiling that put a subtle glow on it.

'Did you know them?' Reacher asked. 'Knight and Hobart?'

'Sure,' Kowalski said.

'Did you go to Africa?'

'Sure.'

'So whose side are you on? Theirs or Lane's?'

'Lane pays me. They don't.'

'So you have a price too.'

'Only a bullshitter doesn't.'

'What were you, back in the day?'

'Navy SEAL.'

'So you can swim.'

Reacher stepped into the interior hallway and headed for the master bedroom. Kowalski kept close behind him.

'You going to follow me everywhere?' Reacher asked.

'Probably,' Kowalski said. 'Where are you going anyway?'

'To count the money.'

'Is that OK with Lane?'

'He wouldn't have given me the combination if it wasn't.'

'He gave you the combination?'

I hope so, Reacher thought. *Left hand. Index finger, curled. Ring finger, straight. Middle finger, straight. Middle finger, curled. 3785. I hope.*

He pulled the closet door and entered 3785 on the security keypad. There was an agonizing second's wait and then it beeped and the inner door's latch clicked.

'He never gave me the combination,' Kowalski said.

'But I bet he lets you be the lifeguard out in the Hamptons.'

Reacher opened the inner door and pulled the chain for the light. The closet was about six feet deep and three wide. A narrow walk space on the left, money on the right. Bales of it. All of them

277

intact except for one that was opened and half empty. That was the one Lane had thrown around the room and then repacked. Reacher dragged it out. Carried it to the bed and dumped it down. Kowalski stayed at his shoulder.

'You know how to count?' Reacher asked.

'Funny man,' Kowalski said.

'So count that.'

Reacher stepped back to the closet and eased in sideways and crouched. Hefted an intact plastic bale off the top of the pile and turned it over and over in his hands and checked all six sides. On one face under the legend *Banque Centrale* there was smaller print that said *Gouvernement National, Ouagadougou, Burkina Faso*. Under that was printed: *USD 1,000,000*. The plastic was old and thick and grimy. Reacher licked the ball of his thumb and rubbed a small circle and saw Ben Franklin's face. Hundred-dollar bills. Ten thousand of them in the bale. The shrink wrap was original and untouched. A million bucks, unless the gentlemen bankers of Burkina Faso's national government in O-Town had been cheating, which they probably hadn't.

A million bucks, in a package about as heavy as a loaded carry-on suitcase.

Altogether there were ten intact bales. And ten empty wrappers.

A total of twenty million dollars, once upon a time.

'Fifty packets,' Kowalski called from the bed. 'Ten thousand dollars each.'

'So how much is that?' Reacher called back.

Silence.

'What, you were out sick the day they taught multiplication?'

'It's a lot of money.'

You got that right, Reacher thought. *It's five hundred grand. Half a million. Total of ten and a half million still here, total of ten and a half million gone*.

Original grand total, back in the day, twenty-one million dollars.

The whole of the Burkina Faso payment, Lane's capital, untouched for five years.

Untouched until three days ago.

Kowalski appeared in the closet doorway with the torn wrapper. He had repacked the remaining money neatly into two equal stacks with one extra brick sideways across the top. Then he had bundled and folded the heavy plastic into a tidy package that was about half the original size and almost opaque.

Reacher said, 'Were you out sick the day they taught numbers too?'

Kowalski said nothing.

'Because I wasn't,' Reacher said. 'I showed up that day.'

Silence.

'See, there are even numbers and there are odd numbers. An even number would make two stacks the same size. I guess that's why they call them even. But with an odd number, you'd have to lay the extra one sideways across the top.'

Kowalski said nothing.

'Fifty is an even number,' Reacher said. 'Whereas, for instance, forty-nine is an odd number.'

'So what?'

'So take the ten grand you stole out of your pocket and give it to me.'

Kowalski stood still.

'Make a choice,' Reacher said. 'You want to keep that ten grand, you'll have to beat me in a fistfight. If you do, then you'll want to take more, and you will take more, and then you'll run. And then you'll be on the outside, and Lane and his guys will come and shake the trees for you. You want it to be that way?'

Kowalski said nothing.

'You wouldn't beat me anyway,' Reacher said.

'You think?'

'Demi Moore could kick your ass.'

'I'm a trained man.'

'Trained to do what? Swim? You see any water here?'

Kowalski said nothing.

'The first punch will decide it,' Reacher said. 'It always does. So who are you going to back? The runt or the big guy?'

'You don't want me for an enemy,' Kowalski said.

'I wouldn't want you for a friend,' Reacher said. 'That's for damn sure. I wouldn't want to go with you to Africa. I wouldn't want to crawl up to a forward OP with you watching my back. I wouldn't want to turn around and see you driving off into the sunset.'

'You don't know how it was.'

'I know exactly how it was. You left two men three hundred yards up the line. You're disgusting.'

'You weren't there.'

'You're a disgrace to the uniform you once wore.'

Kowalski said nothing.

'But you know which side your bread is buttered,' Reacher said. 'Don't you? And you don't want to get caught biting the hand that feeds you. Do you?'

Kowalski held still for a long moment and then dropped the bundled package and reached behind him to his hip pocket and came back with a banded sheaf of hundred-dollar bills. It was folded in half. He dropped it on the floor and it resumed its former flat shape like a flower opening its petals. Reacher tucked it back in the open bale and heaved the bale onto the top of the stack. Pulled the chain and killed the light and closed the door. The electronic lock clicked and beeped.

'OK?' Kowalski said. 'No harm, no foul, right?'

'Whatever,' Reacher said.

He led Kowalski back to the living room and then detoured to the kitchen and glanced in at the office. At the computer. At the file drawers. Something about them nagged at him. He stood in the empty silence for a second. Then a new thought struck him. Like an ice cube dropped down the back of his neck.

'What trees are they shaking?' he asked.

'Hospitals,' Kowalski said. 'We figure whoever is back has got to be sick.'

'Which hospitals?'

'I don't know,' Kowalski said. 'All of them, presumably.'

'Hospitals don't tell anyone anything.'

'You think? You know what an ER nurse makes?'

Silence for a moment.

'I'm going out again,' Reacher said. 'You stay here.'

Three minutes later he was at the pay phone, dialling Pauling's cell.

FORTY-FIVE

Pauling answered on the second ring. Or the second vibration, Reacher thought. She said her name and Reacher asked, 'You got a car?'

She said, 'No.'

'Then jump in a cab and get over to Dee Marie's place. Lane and his guys are out scouting hospitals, looking for either Knight or Hobart. They don't know which one came back yet. But it's only a matter of time before they hit St Vincent's and get a match on Hobart's name and buy his address. So I'll meet you there. We're going to have to move them.'

Then he hung up and flagged a cab of his own on Ninth Avenue. The driver was fast but the traffic was slow. It got a little better after they crossed Broadway. But not much. Reacher sprawled sideways on the seat and rested his head on the window. Breathed slow and easy. He thought: *No use fretting about what you can't control.* And he couldn't control Manhattan's traffic. Red lights controlled Manhattan's traffic. Approximately seventy-two of them between the Dakota Building and Hobart's current billet.

*   *   *

Hudson Street runs one way south to north below West 14th so the cab took Bleecker and Seventh Avenue and Varick. Then it made the right into Charlton. Reacher stopped it halfway down the block and made the final approach on foot. There were three parked cars near Dee Marie's place. But none of them was an expensive sedan with OSC plates. He glanced south at the oncoming traffic and hit 4L's button. Pauling answered and Reacher said his name and the street door buzzed.

Up on the fourth floor the apartment door still hung open. Burst hinges, splintered frame. Beyond it were voices in the living room. Dee Marie's and Pauling's. Reacher stepped inside and they stopped talking. They just glanced beyond him at the door. He knew what they were thinking. It was no kind of a secure barrier against the outside world. Dee Marie was still in her cotton shift but Pauling had changed. She was wearing jeans and a T-shirt. She looked good. Hobart himself was where Reacher had last seen him, propped up on the sofa. He looked bad. Pale and sick. But his eyes were blazing. He was angry.

'Lane's coming here?' he asked.

'Maybe,' Reacher said. 'Can't discount the possibility.'

'So what are we going to do?'

'We're going to be smart. We're going to make sure he finds an empty apartment.'

Hobart said nothing. Then he nodded, a little reluctantly.

284

'Where should you be?' Reacher asked him. 'Medically?'

'Medically?' Hobart said. 'I have no idea. I guess Dee Marie did some checking.'

Dee Marie said, 'Birmingham, Alabama, or Nashville, Tennessee. One of the big university hospitals down there. I got brochures. They're good.'

'Not Walter Reed?' Reacher said.

'Walter Reed is good when they get them fresh from the battlefield. But his left foot happened nearly five years ago. And even his right wrist is completely healed. Healed all wrong, but healed all the same. So he needs a whole lot of preliminary stuff first. Bone work, and reconstruction. And that's after the malaria and the tuberculosis are taken care of. And the malnutrition and the parasites.'

'We can't get him to Birmingham or Nashville tonight.'

'We can't get him there ever. The surgery alone could be over two hundred thousand dollars. The prosthetics could be even more than that.' She picked up two brochures from a small table and handed them over. There were expensive graphics and glossy photographs on the fronts. Blue skies, green lawns, warm brick buildings. Inside were details of surgical programmes and prosthetics designers. There were more photographs. Kindly men with white hair and white coats cradled mechanical limbs like babies. One-legged people in athletic vests braced themselves on sleek titanium struts at marathon start lines. The captions under the pictures were full of optimism.

'Looks good,' Reacher said. He handed the brochures back. Dee Marie put them exactly where they had been before, on the table.

'Pie in the sky,' she said.

'A motel tonight,' Pauling said. 'Somewhere close. Maybe we could rent you a car. Can you drive?'

Dee Marie said nothing.

'Take the offer, Dee,' Hobart said. 'Easier on you.'

'I have a licence,' Dee Marie said.

'Maybe we could even rent a wheelchair.'

'That would be good,' Hobart said. 'A ground floor room, and a wheelchair. Easier for you, Dee.'

'Maybe an efficiency,' Pauling said. 'With a little kitchen. For the cooking.'

'I can't afford it,' Dee Marie said.

The room went quiet and Reacher stepped out the front door and checked the hallway. Checked the stairwell. Nothing was happening. He came back inside and pulled the door as far closed as it would go. Turned left in the entry and walked past the bathroom to the bedroom. It was a small space nearly filled by a queen bed. He guessed Hobart slept there, because the night table was piled with tubes of antiseptic creams and bottles of over-the-counter painkillers. The bed was high. He pictured Dee Marie hoisting her brother on her back, turning around, reversing towards the bed, dumping him down on the mattress. He pictured her straightening him out, tucking him in. Then he pictured her heading for another night on the sofa.

The bedroom window had a wood frame and the glass was streaked with soot. There were faded drapes, three-quarters open. Ornaments on the sill, and a colour photograph of a Marine Lance Corporal. Vinnie, Reacher guessed. The dead husband. Blown to bits on a Fallujah roadside. Killed instantly, or not. He had the bill of his dress cap low on his brow and the colours in the picture were vivid and smoothed and airbrushed. An off-post photographer, Reacher guessed. Two prints for about a day's pay, two cardboard mailers included, one for the mother and one for the wife or the girlfriend. There were similar pictures of Reacher somewhere in the world. For a spell every time he got promoted he would have a picture taken and send it to his mother. She never displayed them, because he wasn't smiling. Reacher never smiled for the camera.

He stepped close to the window and glanced north. Traffic flowed away from him like a river. He glanced south. Watched the traffic coming towards him.

And saw a black Range Rover slowing and pulling in to the kerb.

Licence plate: OSC 19.

Reacher spun around and was out of the bedroom in three long strides. Back in the living room after three more.

'They're here,' he said. 'Now.'

Silence for a split second.

Then Pauling said, 'Shit.'

'What do we do?' Dee Marie said.

'Bathroom,' Reacher said. 'All of you. Now.'

He stepped over to the sofa and grabbed the

front of Hobart's denim shirt and lifted him into the air. Carried him to the bathroom and laid him gently in the tub. Dee Marie and Pauling crowded in after him. Reacher pushed his way past them and back out to the hallway.

'You can't be out there,' Pauling said.

'I have to be,' Reacher said. 'Or they'll search the whole place.'

'They shouldn't find you here.'

'Lock the door,' Reacher said. 'Sit tight and keep quiet.'

He stood in the hallway and heard a click from the bathroom door and a second later the intercom buzzed from the street. He waited a beat and hit the button and said, 'Yes?' Heard amplified traffic noise and then a voice. Impossible to tell whose it was.

It said: 'VA visiting nurse service.'

Reacher smiled. *Nice*, he thought.

He hit the button again and said, 'Come on up.'

Then he walked back to the living room and sat down on the sofa to wait.

FORTY-SIX

Reacher heard loud creaking from the staircase. *Three people*, he guessed. He heard them make the turn and start up towards four. Heard them stop at the head of the stairs, surprised by the broken door. Then he heard the door open. There was a quiet metallic groan from a damaged hinge and after that there was nothing but the sound of footsteps in the foyer.

First into the living room was Perez, the tiny Spanish guy.

Then Addison, with the knife scar above his eye.

Then Edward Lane himself.

Perez stepped left and stopped dead and Addison stepped right and stopped dead and Lane moved into the centre of the small static arc and stood still and stared.

'The hell are you doing here?' he asked.

'I beat you to it,' Reacher said.

'How?'

'Like I told you. I used to do this for a living. I could give you guys a mirror on a stick and I'd still be hours ahead of you.'

'So where is Hobart?'

'Not here.'

'It was you who broke down the door?'

'I didn't have a key.'

'Where is he?'

'In the hospital.'

'Bullshit. We just checked.'

'Not here. In Birmingham, Alabama, or Nashville, Tennessee.'

'How do you figure that?'

'He needs specialized care. St Vincent's recommended one of those big university hospitals down south. They gave him literature.'

Reacher pointed at the small table and Edward Lane broke ranks with his men and stepped over to pick up the shiny brochures. He flipped through both of them and asked, 'Which one?'

Reacher said, 'It doesn't matter which one.'

'The hell it doesn't,' Lane said.

'Hobart didn't kidnap Kate.'

'You think?'

'No, I know.'

'How?'

'You should have bought more information than just his address. You should have asked why he was at St Vincent's in the first place.'

'We did. They said malaria. He was admitted for IV chloroquine.'

'And?'

'And nothing. A guy just home from Africa can expect to have malaria.'

'You should have gotten the whole story.'

'Which is?'

Reacher said, 'First, he was strapped down to a

bed getting that IV chloroquine at the exact time that Kate was taken. And second, he has a pre-existing condition.'

'What condition?'

Reacher shifted his gaze and looked straight at Perez and Addison.

'He's a quadruple amputee,' he said. 'No hands, no feet, can't walk, can't drive, can't hold a gun or dial a telephone.'

Nobody spoke.

'It happened in prison,' Reacher said. 'Back in Burkina Faso. The new regime had a little fun. Once a year. On his birthday. Left foot, right foot, left hand, right hand. With a machete. Chop, chop, chop, chop.'

Nobody spoke.

'After you all ran away and left him behind,' Reacher said.

No reaction. No guilt, no remorse.

No anger.

Just nothing.

'You weren't there,' Lane said. 'You don't know how it was.'

'But I know how it is now,' Reacher said. 'Hobart's not the guy you're looking for. He's not physically capable.'

'You sure?'

'Beyond certain.'

'I still want to find him,' Lane said.

'Why?'

No answer. *Checkmate*. Lane couldn't say why without going all the way back and admitting what he had asked Knight to do for him five years previously, and he couldn't do that without

291

blowing his cover in front of his men.

'So we're back at square one,' he said. 'You know who it wasn't. Great job, major. You're making real progress here.'

'Not quite square one,' Reacher said.

'How?'

'I'm close,' Reacher said. 'I'll give you the guy.'

'When?'

'When you give me the money.'

'What money?'

'You offered me a million bucks.'

'To find my wife. It's too late now.'

'OK,' Reacher said. 'So I won't give you the guy. I'll give you a mirror on a stick instead.'

Lane said, 'Give me the guy.'

'Then meet my price.'

'You're that kind of a man?'

'Only a bullshitter doesn't have a price.'

'High price.'

'I'm worth it.'

'I could have it beaten out of you.'

'You couldn't,' Reacher said. He hadn't moved at all. He was sitting back on the sofa, relaxed, sprawled, arms resting easy along the back cushions, legs spread, six-five, two-fifty, a picture of supreme physical self-confidence. 'You try that shit and I'll bend you over and I'll use Addison's head to hammer Perez up your ass like a nail.'

'I don't like threats.'

'This from the guy who said he'd have me blinded?'

'I was upset.'

'I was broke. I still am.'

Silence in the room.

'OK,' Lane said.

'OK what?' Reacher said.

'OK, a million bucks. When do I get the name?'

'Tomorrow,' Reacher said.

Lane nodded. Turned away. Said to his men, 'Let's go.'

Addison said, 'I need the bathroom.'

FORTY-SEVEN

The air in the room was hot and still. Addison asked, 'Where's the bathroom?'

Reacher stood up, slowly. Said, 'What am I, the architect?' But he glanced over his left shoulder, at the kitchen door. Addison followed his gaze and moved a step in that direction and Reacher moved a step the other way. Just a subtle piece of psychological choreography, but due to the small size of the living room their relative positions were reversed. Now Reacher was nearer the bathroom.

Addison said, 'I think that's the kitchen.'

'Maybe,' Reacher said. 'Check it out.'

He moved into position in the mouth of the hallway and watched Addison open the kitchen door. Addison glanced inside just long enough to make sure what room it was and then he backed out. Then he stopped, in a slow-motion double-take. Checked again.

'When did Hobart go south?' he asked.

'Don't know,' Reacher said. 'Today, I guess.'

'He sure left in a hurry. There's soup on the stove.'

'You think he should have washed the dishes?'

'Most people do.'

'Most people with no hands?'

'So how was he cooking soup at all?'

'With help,' Reacher said. 'Don't you think? Some welfare person, probably. The ambulance comes for Hobart, loads him up, you think some minimum-wage government housekeeper is going to stick around afterwards and clean up? Because I don't.'

Addison shrugged and closed the kitchen door. 'So where's the bathroom?' he said.

Reacher said, 'Go home and use yours.'

'What?'

'One day Hobart's going to come back here with the kind of metal hands that can unzip his fly and he's not going to want to think about you pissing in the same bowl as him.'

'Why?'

'Because you're not fit to piss in the same bowl as him. You left him behind.'

'You weren't there.'

'For which you can thank your lucky stars. I'd have kicked your ass and dragged you up the line by your ears.'

Edward Lane took a step forward. 'The sacrifice was necessary to save the unit.'

Reacher looked straight at him. 'Sacrificing and saving are two different things.'

'Don't question my orders.'

'Don't question mine,' Reacher said. 'Get these runts out of here. Let them piss in the gutter.'

Silence for a long moment. Nothing in Perez's

face, a scowl on Addison's, shrewd judgement in Lane's eyes.

'The name,' Lane said. 'Tomorrow.'

'I'll be there,' Reacher said.

Lane nodded to his men and they trooped out in the same order they had come in. First Perez, then Addison, with Lane bringing up the rear. Reacher listened to their feet on the stairs and waited for the street door to bang and then he stepped back to the bedroom. Watched them climb into the black Range Rover and take off north. He let a minute pass and when he judged they were through the light at Houston he walked back to the foyer and knocked on the bathroom door.

'They're gone,' he said.

Reacher carried Hobart back to the sofa and sat him up like a rag doll. Dee Marie stepped into the kitchen and Pauling looked down at the floor and said, 'We heard everything.'

Dee Marie said, 'The soup is still warm. Lucky that guy didn't get any closer.'

'Lucky for him,' Reacher said.

Hobart shifted his position on the sofa and said, 'Don't kid yourself. These are not pussycats. You were minutes away from getting hurt bad. Lane doesn't hire nice people.'

'He hired you.'

'Yes, he did.'

'So?'

'I'm not a nice person,' Hobart said. 'I fit right in.'

'You seem OK.'

296

'That's just the sympathy vote.'

'So how bad are you?'

'I was dishonourably discharged. Kicked out of the Corps.'

'Why?'

'I refused an order. Then I beat the shit out of the guy who gave it to me.'

'What was the order?'

'To fire on a civilian vehicle. In Bosnia.'

'Sounds like an illegal order.'

Hobart shook his head. 'No, my lieutenant was right. The car was full of bad guys. They wounded two of our own later that day. I screwed up.'

Reacher asked, 'Suppose it had been Perez and Addison in those forward OPs in Africa? Would you have left them there?'

'A Marine's job is to obey orders,' Hobart said. 'And I had learned the hard way that sometimes officers know better.'

'Bottom line? No bullshit?'

Hobart stared into space. 'I wouldn't have left them there. No way on earth. I don't see how anyone could. I sure as hell don't see how they could have left me there. And I wish to God they hadn't.'

'Soup,' Dee Marie said. 'Time to stop talking and start eating.'

Pauling said, 'We should move you first.'

'No need now,' Dee Marie said. 'They won't come back. Right now this is the safest place in the city.'

'It would be easier on you.'

'I'm not looking for easy. I'm looking for right.'

Then the buzzer from the street sounded and

297

they heard a Russian accent on the intercom. The super from Sixth Avenue, come to fix the broken door. Reacher met him in the hallway. He was carrying a bag of tools and a length of spare lumber.

'Now we're definitely OK,' Dee Marie said.

So Pauling just paid the Russian and she and Reacher walked down the stairs to the street.

Pauling was quiet and faintly hostile as they walked. She kept her distance and looked straight ahead. Avoided looking even close to Reacher's direction.

'What?' he asked.

'We heard everything from the bathroom,' she said.

'And?'

'You signed on with Lane. You sold out. You're working for him now.'

'I'm working for Kate and Jade.'

'You could do that for free.'

'I wanted to test him,' Reacher said. 'I still need proof it's for real this time. If it wasn't, he'd have backed off. He'd have said the money was off the table because I was too late. But he didn't. He wants the guy. Therefore there is a guy.'

'I don't believe you. It's a meaningless test. Like Patti Joseph said, Lane's gambling. He's putting on a show for his men and gambling that he's smarter than you are.'

'But he had just found out that he's not smarter than I am. I found Hobart before he did.'

'Whatever, this is about the money, isn't it?'

'Yes,' Reacher said. 'It is.'

'At least you might try to deny it.'

Reacher smiled and kept on walking.

'You ever seen a million dollars in cash?' he asked. 'Ever held a million dollars in your hands? I did, today. It's a hell of a feeling. The weight, the density. The *power*. It felt warm. Like a little atom bomb.'

'I'm sure it was very impressive.'

'I wanted it, Pauling. I really did. And I can get it. I'm going to find the guy anyway. For Kate and Jade. I might as well sell his name to Lane. Doesn't change the basic proposition.'

'It does. It makes you a mercenary. Just like them.'

'Money is a great enabler.'

'What are you going to do with a million dollars anyway? Buy a house? A car? A new shirt? I just don't see it.'

'I'm often misunderstood,' he said.

'The misunderstanding was all mine. I liked you. I thought you were better than this.'

'You work for money.'

'But I choose who I work for, very carefully.'

'It's a lot of money.'

'It's dirty money.'

'It'll spend just the same.'

'Well, enjoy it.'

'I will.'

She said nothing.

He said, 'Pauling, give me a break.'

'Why would I?'

'Because first I'm going to pay you for your time and your services and your expenses, and then I'm going to send Hobart down to Birmingham or

299

Nashville and get him fixed up right. I'm going to buy him a lifetime's supply of spare parts and I'm going to rent him a place to live and I'm going to give him some walking-around money because my guess is he's not very employable right now. At least not in his old trade. And then if there's anything left, then sure, I'll buy myself a new shirt.'

'Seriously?'

'Of course. I need a new shirt.'

'No, about Hobart?'

'Dead serious. He needs it. He deserves it. That's for damn sure. And it's only right that Lane should pay for it.'

Pauling stopped walking. Grabbed Reacher's arm and stopped him too.

'I'm sorry,' she said. 'I apologize.'

'Then make it up to me.'

'How?'

'Work with me. We've got a lot to do.'

'You told Lane you'd give him a name tomorrow.'

'I had to say something. I had to get him out of there.'

'Can we do it by tomorrow?'

'I don't see why not.'

'Where are we going to start?'

'I have absolutely no idea.'

FORTY-EIGHT

They started in Lauren Pauling's apartment. She lived in a small co-op on Barrow Street, near West 4th. The building had once been a factory and had vaulted brick ceilings and walls two feet thick. Her apartment was painted mostly yellow and felt warm and friendly. There was an alcove bedroom with no window, and a bathroom, and a kitchen, and a room with a sofa and a chair and a television set and a lot of books. There were muted rugs and soft textures and dark woods. It was a single woman's place. That was clear. One mind had conceived it and decorated it. There were small framed photographs of children, but Reacher knew without asking that they were nephews and nieces.

He sat on the sofa and rested his head back on the cushion and stared up at the vaulted brick above. He believed that anything could be reverse-engineered. If one human or group of humans put something together then another human or group of humans could take it apart again. It was a basic principle. All that was required was empathy and thought and

imagination. And he liked pressure. He liked
deadlines. He liked a short and finite time to
crack a problem. He liked a quiet space to work
in. And he liked a similar mind to work with.
He started out with no doubt at all that he and
Pauling could get the whole thing figured before
morning.

That feeling lasted about thirty minutes.

Pauling dimmed the lights and lit a candle and
called out for Indian food. The clock in Reacher's
head crawled around to nine thirty. The sky
outside the window turned from navy blue to
black and the city lights burned bright. Barrow
Street itself was quiet but the cabs on West 4th
used their horns a lot. Occasionally an ambulance
would scream by a couple of blocks over, heading
up to St Vincent's. The room felt like part of the
city but a little detached, too. A little insulated. A
partial sanctuary.

'Do that thing again,' Reacher said.

'What thing?'

'The brainstorming thing. Ask me questions.'

'OK, what have we got?'

'We've got an impossible takedown and a guy
that can't speak.'

'And the tongue thing is culturally unrelated to
Africa.'

'But the money is related to Africa, because it's
exactly half.'

Silence in the room. Nothing but a faraway
siren burning past, going south on Seventh
Avenue.

'Start at the very beginning,' Pauling said.
'What was the very first false note? The first

302

red flag? Anything at all, however trivial or random.'

So Reacher closed his eyes and recalled the beginning: the granular feel of the foam espresso cup in his hand, textured, temperature-neutral, neither warm nor cold. He recalled Gregory's walk in from the kerb, alert, economical. His manner while questioning the waiter, watchful, aware, like the elite veteran he was. His direct approach to the sidewalk table.

Reacher said, 'Gregory asked me about the car I had seen the night before and I told him it drove away before eleven forty-five, and he said no, it must have been closer to midnight.'

'A dispute about timing?'

'Not really a dispute. Just a trivial thing, like you said.'

'What would it mean?'

'That I was wrong or he was.'

Pauling said, 'You don't wear a watch.'

'I used to. I broke it. I threw it away.'

'So he was more likely to be right.'

'Except I'm usually pretty sure what time it is.'

'Keep your eyes closed, OK?'

'OK.'

'What time is it now?'

'Nine thirty-six.'

'Not bad,' Pauling said. 'My watch says nine thirty-eight.'

'Your watch is fast.'

'Are you serious?'

Reacher opened his eyes. 'Absolutely.'

Pauling rooted around on her coffee table and came up with the TV remote. Turned on the weather channel. The time was displayed in the corner of the screen, piped in from some official meteorological source, accurate to the second. Pauling checked her watch again.

'You're right,' she said. 'I'm two minutes fast.'

Reacher said nothing.

'How do you *do* that?'

'I don't know.'

'But it was twenty-four hours after the event that Gregory asked you about it. How precise could you have been?'

'I'm not sure.'

'What would it mean if Gregory was wrong and you were right?'

'Something,' Reacher said. 'But I'm not sure what exactly.'

'What was the next thing?'

Right now more likely death than life, Gregory had said. That had been the next thing. Reacher had checked his cup again and seen less than a lukewarm eighth-inch of espresso left, all thick and scummy. He had put it down and said *OK, so let's go*.

He said, 'Something about getting into Gregory's car. The blue BMW. Something rang a bell. Not right then, but afterwards. In retrospect.'

'You don't know what?'

'No.'

'Then what?'

'Then we arrived at the Dakota and it was off to the races.' *The photograph*, Reacher thought. *After that, everything was about the photograph*.

Pauling said, 'We need to take a break. We can't force these things.'

304

'You got beer in the refrigerator?'

'I've got white wine. You want some?'

'I'm being selfish. You didn't blow it five years ago. You did everything right. We should take a minute to celebrate that.'

Pauling was quiet for a moment. Then she smiled.

'We should,' she said. 'Because to be honest it feels really good.'

Reacher went with her to the kitchen and she took a bottle out of the refrigerator and he opened it with a corkscrew from a drawer. She took two glasses from a cupboard and set them side by side on the counter. He filled them. They picked them up and clinked them together.

'Living well is the best revenge,' he said.

They each took a sip and moved back to the sofa. Sat close together. He asked, 'Did you quit because of Anne Lane?'

She said, 'Not directly. I mean, not right away. But ultimately, yes. You know how these things are. It's like a naval convoy where one of the battleships gets holed below the waterline. No visible damage, but it falls a little behind, and then a little more, and it drifts a little off course, and then when the next big engagement comes along it's completely out of sight. That was me.'

He said nothing.

She said, 'But maybe I was maxed out anyway. I love the city and I didn't want to move, and head of the New York office is an Assistant Director's job. It was always a long shot.'

She took another sip of wine and pulled her legs up under her and turned a little sideways so she could see him better. He turned a little too, until they were more or less facing each other from a foot away.

'Why did you quit?' she asked him.

He said, 'Because they told me I could.'

'You were looking to get out?'

'No, I was looking to stay in. But as soon as they said that leaving was an option it kind of broke the spell. Made me realize I wasn't personally essential to their plans. I guess they'd have been happy enough if I stayed, but clearly it wasn't going to break their hearts if I went.'

'You need to be needed?'

'Not really. It just broke the spell, is all. I can't really explain it.' He stopped talking and watched her, silent. She looked great in the candlelight. Liquid eyes, soft skin. Reacher liked women as much as any guy and more than most but he was always ready to find something wrong with them. The shape of an ear, the thickness of an ankle, height, size, weight. Any random thing could ruin it for him. But there was nothing wrong with Lauren Pauling. Nothing at all. That was for sure.

'Anyway, congratulations,' he said. 'Sleep well tonight.'

'Maybe I will,' she said.

Then she said, 'Maybe I won't get the chance.'

He could smell her fragrance. Subtle perfume, soap, clean skin, clean cotton. Her hair fell to her collarbones. The shoulder seams on her T-shirt stood up a little and made enticing shadowy tunnels. She was slim and toned, except where she shouldn't be.

He said, 'Won't get the chance why?'

She said, 'Maybe we'll be working all night.'

He said, 'All work and no play makes Jack a dull boy.'

'You're not a dull boy,' she said.

'Thank you,' he said, and leaned forward and kissed her, just lightly, on the lips.

Her mouth was open a little and was cool and sweet from the wine. He slid his free hand under her hair to the back of her neck. Pulled her closer and kissed her harder. She did the same thing with her free hand. They held the clinch for a whole minute, kissing, two wine glasses held approximately level in mid-air. Then they parted and put their glasses down on the table and Pauling asked, 'What time is it?'

'Nine fifty-one.'

'How do you do that?'

'I don't know.'

She held the pause for another beat and then leaned in and kissed him again. Used both her hands, one behind his head, the other behind his back. He did the same thing, symmetrically. Her tongue was cool and quick. Her back was narrow. Her skin was warm. He slid his hand under her shirt. Felt her hand bunching into a tiny fist and dragging his shirt out of his waistband. Felt her nails against his skin.

'I don't usually do this,' she said, her mouth hard against his. 'Not to people I work with.'

'We're not working,' he said. 'We're taking a break.'

'We're celebrating.'

'That's for sure.'

She said, 'We're celebrating the fact that we're not Hobart, aren't we? Or Kate Lane.'

'I'm celebrating the fact that you're you.'

She raised her arms over her head and held the pose and he pulled her shirt off. She was wearing a tiny black bra. He raised his arms in turn and she knelt up on the sofa and hauled his shirt up over his head. Then his T-shirt. She spread her hands like small starfish on the broad slab of his chest. Ran them south to his waist. Undid his belt. He unclipped her bra. Lifted her up and laid her down flat on the sofa and kissed her breasts. By the time the clock in his head was showing five past ten they were in her bed, naked under the sheet, locked together, making love with a kind of patience and tenderness he had never experienced before.

'Older woman,' she said. 'We're worth it.'

He didn't answer. Just smiled and ducked his head and kissed her neck below her ear, where her skin was damp and tasted of saltwater.

Afterward they showered together and finished their wine and went back to bed. Reacher was too tired to think and too relaxed to care. He just floated, warm, spent, happy. Pauling snuggled against him and they fell asleep like that.

Much later Reacher felt Pauling stir and woke up to find her hands over his eyes. She asked him in a whisper, 'What time is it?'

'Eighteen minutes to seven,' he said. 'In the morning.'

'You're unbelievable.'

'It's not a very useful talent. Saves me the price of a new watch, maybe.'

'What happened to the old one?'

'I stepped on it. I put it by the bed and I stood on it when I got up.'

'And that broke it?'

'I was wearing shoes.'

'In bed?'

'Saves time getting dressed.'

'You *are* unbelievable.'

'I don't do it all the time. It depends on the bed.'

'What would it mean if Gregory was wrong about the time and you were right?'

He took a breath and opened his mouth to say *I don't know*.

But then he stopped.

Because suddenly he saw what it would mean.

'Wait,' he said.

He lay back on the pillow and stared up at the darkened ceiling.

'Do you like chocolate?' he asked.

'I guess.'

'You got a flashlight?'

'There's a small Maglite in my purse.'

'Put it in your pocket,' he said. 'Leave the purse home. And wear pants. The skirt is no good.'

FORTY-NINE

They walked, because it was a beautiful city morning and Reacher was too restless to ride the subway or take a cab. Barrow, to Bleecker, then south on Sixth Avenue. It was already warm. They took it slow, to time it right. They turned east on Spring Street at seven thirty exactly. Crossed Sullivan, crossed Thompson.

'We're going to the abandoned building?' Pauling asked.

'Eventually,' Reacher said.

He stopped outside the chocolate shop. Cupped his hands against the glass and peered in. There was a light in the kitchen. He could see the owner moving about, small, dark, tired, her back to him. *Sixteen-hour days*, she had said. *Regular as clockwork, seven days a week, small business, we never rest.*

He knocked on the glass, loud, and the owner stopped and turned and looked exasperated until she recognized him. Then she shrugged and admitted defeat and walked through the front of the store to the door. Undid the locks and opened the door a crack and said, 'Hello.'

Air bitter with chocolate flooded out at him.

He asked, 'Can we come through to the alley again?'

'Who's your friend this time?'

Pauling stepped forward and said her name.

The owner asked, 'Are you really exterminators?'

'Investigators,' Pauling said. She had a business card ready.

'What are you investigating?'

'A woman disappeared,' Reacher said. 'And her child.'

Silence for a moment.

The owner asked, 'You think they're next door?'

'No,' Reacher said. 'Nobody's next door.'

'That's good.'

'This is just routine.'

'Would you like a chocolate?'

'Not for breakfast,' Reacher said.

'I would love one,' Pauling said.

The owner held the door wide and Pauling and Reacher stepped inside. Pauling took a moment choosing a chocolate. She settled on a raspberry fondant as big as a golf ball. Took a little bite and made a noise that sounded like appreciation. Then she followed Reacher through the kitchen and down the short tiled hallway. Out through the back door to the alley.

The rear of the abandoned building was exactly as Reacher had last seen it. The dull red door, the corroded black knob, the filthy ground-floor window. He turned the knob and pushed, just in case, but the door was locked, as expected. He bent down and unlaced his shoe. Took it off and held the toe in his hand and used the heel like a two-pound hammer. Used it to break the window glass, low down and on the left, close to the door lock.

He tapped a little more and widened the hole and then put his shoe back on. Put his arm through the hole in the glass up to his shoulder and hugged the wall and groped around until he found the inside door handle. He unlocked it and withdrew his arm very carefully.

'OK,' he said.

He opened the door and stood aside to let Pauling get a good look.

'Just like you told me,' Pauling said. 'Uninhabitable. No floors.'

'You up for a trip down the ladder?'

'Why me?'

'Because if I'm wrong I might just give up and stay down there forever.'

Pauling craned in and took a look at the ladder. It was right there where it had been before, propped to the right, steeply angled, leaning on the narrow piece of wall that separated the window and the door.

'I did worse at Quantico,' she said. 'But that was a long time ago.'

Reacher said, 'It's only ten feet if you fall.'

'Thanks.' She turned around and backed up to the void. Reacher took her right hand in his and she sidled left and swung her left foot and left hand onto the ladder. Got steady and let Reacher's hand go and paused a beat and climbed down into the dark. The ladder bounced and rattled a little and then he heard the crunch and rustle of trash as she hit bottom and stepped off.

'It's filthy down here,' she called.

'Sorry,' he said.

'There could be rats.'

'Use the flashlight.'

'Will that scare them off?'

'No, but you'll see them coming.'

'Thanks a lot.'

He leaned in over the pit and saw her flashlight beam stab the gloom. She called, 'Where am I going?'

'Head for the front of the building. Directly underneath the door.'

The flashlight beam levelled out and established a direction and jerked forward. The basement walls had been whitewashed years before with some kind of lime compound and they reflected a little light. Reacher could see deep drifts of garbage everywhere. Paper, cartons, piles of unidentifiable rotted matter.

Pauling reached the front wall. The flashlight beam stabbed upward and she located the door above her. She moved left a little and lined herself up directly beneath it.

'Look down now,' Reacher called. 'What do you see?'

The beam stabbed downward. Short range, very bright.

'I see trash,' Pauling called.

Reacher called, 'Look closer. They might have bounced.'

'What might have bounced?'

'Dig around and you'll see. I hope.'

The flashlight beam traced a small random circle. Then a wider one. Then it stopped dead and held steady.

'OK,' Pauling called. 'Now I see. But how the hell did you know?'

Reacher said nothing. Pauling held still for a second longer and then bent down. Stood up again with her hands held high. In her right hand was the flashlight. In her left hand were two sets of car keys, one for a Mercedes Benz and one for a BMW.

FIFTY

Pauling waded through the garbage back to the base of the ladder and tossed the keys up to Reacher. He caught them one-handed, left and then right. Both sets were on chrome split rings and both had black leather fobs decorated with enamel car badges. The three-pointed Mercedes star, the blue and white BMW propeller. Both had a single large car key and a remote clicker. He blew dust and fragments of trash off them and put them in his pocket. Then he leaned in over the void and caught Pauling's arm and hauled her off the ladder to the safety of the alley. She brushed herself down and kicked the air hard to get trash off her shoes.

'So?' she said.

'We're one for one,' he said.

He closed the dull red door and put his arm back through the hole in the window glass and hugged the wall again and clicked the lock from the inside. Extricated himself carefully and tested the knob. It was solid. Safe.

'This whole thing with the mail slot was a pure decoy,' he said. 'Just a piece of nonsense designed to distract attention. The guy already had keys. He had spares from the file cabinet in Lane's office. There was a whole bunch of car stuff in there. Some of the valet keys were filed away and some of them were missing.'

'So you were right about the time.'

Reacher nodded. 'The guy was in the apartment above the café. Sitting on the chair, looking out the window. He watched Gregory park at eleven forty and watched him walk away but he didn't follow him down here to Spring Street. He didn't need to. He didn't give a damn about Spring Street. He just came out his door and crossed Sixth Avenue and used the valet key from his pocket. Immediately, much closer to eleven forty than midnight.'

'Same thing with the blue BMW the second morning.'

'Exactly the same thing,' Reacher said. 'I watched the damn door for twenty minutes and he never came anywhere near it. He never even came south of Houston Street. He was in the BMW about two minutes after Gregory got out of it.'

'And that's why he specified the cars so exactly. He needed to match them with the stolen keys.'

'And that's why it bugged me when Gregory let me into his car that first night. Gregory used the remote thing from ten feet away, like anyone would. But the night before the other guy didn't do that with the Mercedes. He walked right up to it and stuck the key in the door. Who does that any more? But he did, because he had to, because he didn't have the remote. All he had was the valet key. Which also explains why he used the Jaguar for the final instalment. He wanted to be able to lock it from the other side of the street, as soon as Burke put the money in it. For safety's sake. He could do that with the Jaguar only, because the only remote he had was for the Jaguar. He inherited it at the initial takedown.'

Pauling said nothing.

Reacher said, 'I told Lane the guy used the Jaguar as a taunt. As a reminder. But the real reason was practical, not psychological.'

Pauling was quiet for a second more. 'But you're back to saying there was inside help. Aren't you? And there must have been, right? To steal the valet keys? But you already discounted inside help. You already decided there wasn't any.'

'I think I've got that figured.'

'Who?'

'The guy with no tongue. He's the key to the whole ballgame.'

FIFTY-ONE

Pauling and Reacher trooped back through the chocolate shop and were back on the street before eight thirty in the morning. They were back in Pauling's office on West 4th before nine.

'We need Brewer now,' Reacher said. 'And Patti Joseph.'

'Brewer's still asleep,' Pauling said. 'He works late.'

'Today he's going to work early. He's going to get his ass in gear. Because we need a definitive ID on that body from the Hudson River.'

'Taylor?'

'We need to know for certain it's Taylor. I'm sure Patti has got a photograph of him. I bet she's got a photograph of everyone who ever went in or out of the Dakota. If she gave a good clear shot to Brewer he could head for the morgue and make the ID for us.'

'Patti's not our best buddy here. She wants to take Lane down, not help him.'

'We're not helping him. You know that.'

'I'm not sure Patti sees the difference.'

'All we want is one lousy photograph. She can go that far.'

So Pauling called Patti Joseph. Patti confirmed that she had a file of photographs of all Lane's men stretching back through the four years that she had occupied the Majestic apartment. At first she was reluctant to grant access to it. But then she saw that a positive ID of Taylor's body would put some kind of pressure on Lane, either directly or indirectly. So she agreed to pick out the best full-frontal and put it aside for Brewer to collect. Then Pauling called Brewer and woke him up. He was bad-tempered about it but he agreed to pick up the picture. There was an element of self-interest there, too. ID on an as-yet-unexplained DOA would net him some NYPD Brownie points.

'Now what?' Pauling asked.

'Breakfast,' Reacher said.

'Do we have time? Lane is expecting a name today.'

'Today lasts until midnight.'

'What after breakfast?'

'Maybe you'll want to take a shower.'

'I'm OK. That basement wasn't too bad.'

'I wasn't thinking about the basement. I figured we might take coffee and croissants back to your place. Last time we were there we both ended up taking showers.'

Pauling said, 'I see.'

'Only if you want to.'

'I know a great croissant shop.'

*   *   *

319

Two hours later Reacher was drying his hair on a borrowed towel and trying to decide whether or not to back a hunch. In general he wasn't a big fan of hunches. Too often they were just wild-assed guesses that wasted time and led nowhere. But in the absence of news from Brewer he had time to waste and nowhere to go anyway. Pauling came out of the bedroom looking spectacular. Shoes, stockings, tight skirt, silk blouse, all in black. Brushed hair, light make-up. Great eyes, open, frank, intelligent.

'What time is it?' she asked.

'Eleven thirteen,' he said. 'Give or take.'

'Sometime you're going to have to explain how you do that.'

'If I ever figure it out you'll be the first to know.'

'Long breakfast,' she said. 'But fun.'

'For me too.'

'What next?'

'We could do lunch.'

'I'm not hungry yet.'

'We could skip the eating part.'

She smiled.

'Seriously,' she said. 'We have things to do.'

'Can we go back to your office? There's something I want to check.'

Barrow Street was quiet but West 4th was busy with the front end of the city's lunch break envelope. The sidewalks were packed. Reacher and Pauling had to go with the flow, slower than they would have liked. But there was no alternative. Pedestrian traffic gridlocks just the same as automotive traffic. A five-minute walk took ten. The street door below Pauling's office was already unlocked. Other tenants were open for business and had been for hours. Reacher followed Pauling up the stairs and she used her keys and they stepped into her waiting room. He walked ahead of her into the back office where the bookshelves and the computer were.

'What do you want to check?' she asked.

'The phone book first,' he said. 'T for Taylor.'

She hauled the white pages off the shelf and opened it on the desk. There were plenty of Taylors listed. It was a reasonably common name.

She asked, 'Initial?'

'No idea,' he said. 'Work off the street addresses. Look for private individuals in the West Village.'

Pauling used an optimistic realtor's definition of the target area and made pencil check marks in the phone book's margins. She ended up with seven possibilities. West 8th Street, Bank, Perry, Sullivan, West 12th, Hudson, and Waverly Place.

Reacher said, 'Start with Hudson Street. Check the city directory and find out what block that address is on.'

Pauling laid the directory over the phone book and slid it down until the top edge of the directory's jacket underlined the Taylor on Hudson Street. Then she flipped pages and traced the street number to a specific location on a specific block.

She looked up.

'It's exactly halfway between Clarkson and Leroy,' she said.

Reacher said nothing.

'What's going on here?'

'Your best guess?'

'The guy with no tongue knew Taylor? Lived with him? Was working with him? Killed him?'

Reacher said nothing.

'Wait,' Pauling said. 'Taylor was the inside man, wasn't he? He stole the valet keys. He stopped the car outside Bloomingdale's exactly where the other guy wanted him to. You were always worried about the initial takedown. That's the only way it could have worked.'

Reacher said nothing.

Pauling asked, 'Was it really Taylor in the river?'

'We'll know that as soon as Brewer calls.'

'The boat basin is a long way north of downtown. And downtown is where all the action seems to be.'

'The Hudson is tidal all the way to the Tappan Zee. Technically it's an estuary, not a river. A floater could drift north as much as south.'

'What exactly is going on here?'

'We're sweating the details and we're working the clues. That's what's going on here. We're doing it the hard way. One step at a time. Next step, we go visit the Taylor residence.'

'Now?'

'It's as good a time as any.'

'Will we get in?'

'Do bears shit in the woods?'

Pauling took a sheet of paper and copied *G. Taylor* and the address from the phone book. Said, 'I wonder what the G stands for.'

'He was British, don't forget,' Reacher said. 'Could be Geoffrey with a G. Or Gerald. Or Gareth or Glynn. Or Gervaise or Godfrey or Galahad.'

They walked. The noon heat raised sour smells from the milk in dumped lattes in trash cans and gutters. Panel trucks and taxis jammed the streets. Drivers hit their horns in anticipation of potential fractional delays. Second-storey air conditioners dripped condensation like fat raindrops. Vendors hawked fake watches and umbrellas and cell phone accessories. The city, in full tumult. Reacher liked New York more than most places. He liked the casual indifference of it all and the frantic hustle and the total anonymity.

Hudson Street between Clarkson and Leroy had buildings on the west side and James J. Walker Park on the east. Taylor's number matched a brick cube sixteen storeys high. It had a plain entrance but a decent lobby. Reacher could see one lone guy behind a long desk. No separate doorman out on the sidewalk. Which made it easier. One guy was always easier than two. No witnesses.

'Approach?' Pauling asked.

'The easy way,' Reacher said. 'The direct approach.'

They pulled the street door and stepped inside. The lobby had dark burr veneers and brushed metal accents. A granite floor. Up to the minute décor, a lot of minutes ago. Reacher walked straight to the desk and the guy behind it looked up and Reacher pointed to Pauling.

'Here's the deal,' he said. 'This lady will give you four hundred bucks if you let us into Mr G. Taylor's apartment.'

The easy way. The direct approach. Concierges are human. And it was a well-chosen sum. Four hundred was a slightly unusual number. It wasn't glib or run of the mill. It didn't go in one ear and out the other. It commanded attention. It was big enough to feel like serious cash. And in Reacher's experience it created an irresistible temptation to bargain upward towards five hundred. And in Reacher's experience once that temptation had taken hold the battle was won. Like prostitution. Once the principle was established, all that was left was the price.

The desk guy glanced left, glanced right. Saw nobody.

No witnesses. Easier.

'Alone?' the desk guy asked.

'I don't mind,' Reacher said. 'Come with us. Send a handyman.'

The guy paused. Said, 'OK, I'll send a handyman.'

But you'll keep the cash for yourself, Reacher thought.

'Five hundred,' the guy said.

Reacher said, 'Deal.'

Pauling opened her purse and her wallet and licked her thumb and counted off five hundred-dollar bills. Folded them around her index finger and slipped them across the desk.

'Twelfth floor,' the concierge said. 'Turn left, go to the door at the end on the right. The handyman will meet you there.' He pointed

324

towards the elevator bank and picked up a
walkie-talkie to summon the guy. Reacher and
Pauling stepped over and pressed the up arrow.
An elevator door slid open like it had been waiting for them.

'You owe me a lot of money,' Pauling said.

'I'm good for it,' Reacher said. 'I'll be rich
tonight.'

'I hope the staff in my building are better than
that.'

'Dream on. I was in and out of a lot of buildings, back in the day.'

'You had a bribery budget?'

'Huge. Before the peace dividend. That dropped
a rock on a lot of budgets.'

The elevator car stopped on twelve and the
door slid back. The corridor was part exposed
brick and part white paint and the only lighting
was supplied by television screens set waist-high
behind glass. They were all glowing dim purple.

'Nice,' Pauling said.

Reacher said, 'I like your place better.'

They turned left and found the end door on
the right. It had an integrated box mounted eye-
high with a peephole lens and an apartment
number and a slot with a black tape sign that
said *Taylor*. Northeast corner of the building. The
corridor was still and quiet and smelled faintly of
air freshener or carpet cleaner.

Reacher asked, 'What is he paying for a place
like this?'

'Rental?' Pauling said. She glanced at the
distance between doors to judge the size of the
apartments and said, 'Small two-bedroom, maybe

four grand a month. Maybe four and a quarter in a building like this.'

'That's a lot.'

'Not when you make twenty-five.'

To their right the elevator bell dinged and a man in a green uniform and a tan tool belt stepped off. The handyman. He walked up and pulled a key ring from his pocket. Asked no questions. Just unlocked Taylor's door and pushed it open and stood back.

Reacher went in first. The apartment felt empty. The air inside was hot and still. There was a foyer the size of a phone booth and then a stainless steel kitchen on the left and a coat closet on the right. Living room dead ahead, two bedrooms side by side away to the left, one of them larger than the other. The kitchen and the living room were spotlessly clean and immaculately tidy. The décor was mid-century modern, restrained, tasteful, masculine. Dark wood floors, pale walls, thick wool rugs. There was a maple desk. An Eames lounge chair and an ottoman opposite a Florence Knoll sofa. A Le Corbusier chaise and a Noguchi coffee table. Stylish. Not cheap. Classic pieces. Reacher recognized them from pictures in magazines he had read. There was an original painting on the wall. An urban scene, busy, bright, vibrant, acrylic on canvas. There were lots of books, shelved neatly and alphabetically. A small television set. Lots of CDs and a quality music system dedicated to headphones only. No loudspeakers. A considerate guy. A good neighbour.

'Very elegant,' Pauling said.

'An Englishman in New York,' Reacher said. 'Probably drank tea.'

The bigger bedroom was spare, almost monastic. White walls, a king bed, grey linens, an Italian desk light on a night table, more books, another painting by the same artist. The closet had a hanging rail and a wall of open shelves. The rail was full of suits and jackets and shirts and pants grouped precisely by season and colour. Each garment was clean and pressed and ironed. Each hanger was exactly one inch from the next. The shelves were stacked with piles of T-shirts and underwear and socks. Each stack was exactly vertical and the same height as all the others. The bottom shelf held shoes. They were all solid English items like Reacher's own, black and brown, shined like mirrors. They all had cedar shoe trees in them.

'This is amazing,' Pauling said. 'I want to marry this guy.'

Reacher said nothing and moved on to the second bedroom. The second bedroom was where the money or the will or the enthusiasm had run out. It was a small plain undecorated space. It felt unused. It was dark and hot and damp. There was no light bulb in the ceiling fixture. The room held nothing but two narrow iron beds. They had been pushed together. There were used sheets on them. Dented pillows. The window was covered with a width of black fabric. It had been duct-taped to the walls, across the top, across the bottom, down both sides. But the tape had been picked away on one side and a narrow rectangle of cloth had been folded back to provide a sliver of a view, or air, or ventilation.

'This is it,' Reacher said. 'This is where Kate and Jade were hidden.'

'By who? The man who can't talk?'

'Yes,' Reacher said. 'The man who can't talk hid them here.'

FIFTY-TWO

Pauling stepped over next to the twin beds and bent to examine the pillows. 'Long dark hairs,' she said. 'A woman's and a girl's. They were tossing and turning all night.'

'I bet they were,' Reacher said.

'Maybe two nights.'

Reacher walked back to the living room and checked the desk. The handyman watched him from the doorway. The desk was as neatly organized as the closet, but there wasn't much in it. Some personal papers, some financial papers, some lease papers for the apartment. Taylor's first name was Graham. He was a UK citizen and a resident alien. He had a social security number. And a life insurance policy, and a retirement plan. There was a console telephone on the desk. A stylish thing, made by Siemens. It looked brand new and recently installed. It had ten speed dial buttons with paper strips next to them under plastic. The paper strips were marked with initials only. At the top was L. For Lane, Reacher guessed. He hit the corresponding button and a 212 number lit up in neat alphanumeric script in a grey LCD window. Manhattan. The Dakota, presumably. He hit the other nine buttons one after the other. The grey window showed three 212 numbers, three 917 numbers, two 718s, and a long number with 01144 at the beginning. The 212s would all be Manhattan. Buddies, probably, maybe including Gregory, because there was a G on the paper strip. The 917s would be cell phones. Maybe for the same set of guys, for when they were on the road, or for people who didn't have land lines. The 718s would be for Brooklyn. Probably buddies who weren't up for Manhattan rents. The long 01144 number would be for Great Britain. Family, maybe. The corresponding initial was S. A mom or a dad, possibly.

Reacher kept on pressing buttons on the phone for a while and then he finished up at the desk and went back to the second bedroom. Pauling was standing at the window, half turned away, looking through the narrow slot.

'Weird,' she said. 'Isn't it? They were right here in this room. This view was maybe the last thing they ever saw.'

'They weren't killed here. Too difficult to get the bodies out.'

'Not literally the last view. Just the last normal thing from their old lives.'

Reacher said nothing.

'Can you feel them in here?'

Reacher said, 'No.'

He tapped the wall with his knuckles and then knelt and tapped the floor. The walls felt thick and solid and the floor felt like concrete under hardwood. An apartment building was an odd place to keep people prisoner but this one felt safe enough. Terrorize your captives into silence and adjacent residents wouldn't know much. If anything. Ever. Like Patti Joseph had said: *This city is incredibly anonymous. You can go years without ever laying eyes on your neighbour*.

Or his guests, Reacher thought.

'You think there are doormen here twenty-four hours?' he asked.

'I doubt it,' Pauling said. 'Not this far down-town. Mine aren't. They're probably part-time here. Maybe until eight.'

'Then that might explain the delays. He couldn't bring them in past a doorman. Not kicking and struggling. The first day, he would have had to wait hours. Then he kept the intervals going for consistency.'

'And to create an impression of distance.'

'That was Gregory's guess. He was right and I was wrong. I said the Catskills.'

'It was a reasonable assumption.'

Reacher said nothing.

Pauling asked, 'What next?'

'I'd like to meet with your Pentagon buddy again.'

'I'm not sure if he'll agree to. I don't think he likes you.'

'I'm not crazy about him either. But this is business. Make him an offer.'

'What can we offer him?'

'Tell him we'll take Lane's crew off the board if he helps us out with one small piece of infor-mation. He'll take that deal. Ten minutes with us in a coffee shop will get him more than ten years of talking at the UN. One whole band of real live mercenaries out of action forever.'

'Can we deliver that?'

'We'll have to anyway. Sooner or later it's going to be them or us.'

They walked back to Pauling's office by their previous route in reverse. St Luke's Place, Seventh Avenue, Cornelia Street, West 4th. Then Reacher lounged in one of Pauling's visitor chairs while she played phone tag around the UN building, looking for her friend. She got him after about an hour of trying. He was reluctant but he agreed to meet in the same coffee shop as before, at three o'clock in the afternoon.

'Time is moving on,' Pauling said.

'It always does. Try Brewer again. We need to hear from him.'

But Brewer wasn't back at his desk and his cell was switched off. Reacher leaned back and closed his eyes. *No use fretting about what you can't control.*

At two o'clock they went out to find a cab, well ahead of time, just in case. But they got one right away and were in the Second Avenue coffee shop forty minutes early. Pauling tried Brewer again. Still no answer. She closed her phone and put it on the table and spun it like a top. It came to rest with its antenna pointing straight at Reacher's chest.

'You've got a theory,' she said to him. 'Haven't you? Like a physicist. A unified theory of every-thing.'

332

'No,' Reacher said. 'Not everything. Not even close. It's only partial. I'm missing a big component. But I've got a name for Lane.'

'What name?'

'Let's wait for Brewer,' Reacher said. He waved to the waitress. The same one as before. He ordered coffee. Same brown mugs, same Bunn flask. Same hot, strong, generic taste.

Pauling's phone buzzed with thirty minutes to go before the Pentagon guy was due to show. She answered it and said her name and listened for a spell and then she gave their current location. *A coffee shop, east side of Second between 44th and 45th, booth in the back.* Then she hung up.

'Brewer,' she said. 'Finally. He's meeting us here. Wants to talk face to face.'

'Why?'

'He didn't say.'

'Where is he now?'

'He's leaving the morgue.'

'It's going to be crowded in here. He's going to arrive at the same time as your guy.'

'My guy's not going to like that. I don't think he likes crowds.'

'If I see him baulking I'll talk to him outside.'

But Pauling's Pentagon friend showed up a little early. Presumably to scope out the situation ahead of the rendezvous. Reacher saw him out on the sidewalk, looking in, checking the clientele one face at a time. He was patient about it. Thorough. But eventually he was satisfied and he pulled the door. Walked quickly through the room and slid into the booth. He was wearing the

333

same blue suit. Same tie. Probably a fresh shirt, although there was no real way of telling. One white button-down Oxford looks pretty much the same as another.

'I'm concerned about your offer,' he said. 'I can't condone illegality.'

Take the poker out of your ass, Reacher thought. *Be grateful for once in your miserable life. You might be a general now but you know how things are.* But he said, 'I understand your concern, sir. Completely. And you have my word that no cop or prosecutor anywhere in America will think twice about anything that I do.'

'I have your word?'

'As an officer.'

The guy smiled. 'And as a gentleman?'

Reacher didn't smile back. 'I can't claim that distinction.'

'No cop or prosecutor anywhere in America?'

'I guarantee it.'

'You can do that, realistically?'

'I can do that absolutely.'

The guy paused. 'So what do you want me to do?'

'Get me confirmation of something so I don't waste my time or money.'

'Confirmation of what?'

'I need you to check a passenger name against flight manifests out of this area during the last forty-eight hours.'

'Military?'

'No, commercial.'

'That's a Homeland Security issue.'

Reacher nodded. 'Which is why I need you to

334

do it for me. I don't know who to call. Not any more. But I'm guessing you do.'

'Which airport? What flight?'

'I'm not sure. You'll have to go fishing. I'd start with JFK. British Airways, United, or American to London, England. I'd start with late evening the day before yesterday. Failing that, try flights out of Newark. No hits, try JFK again yesterday morning.'

'Definitely transatlantic?'

'That's my assumption right now.'

'OK,' the guy said, slowly, like he was taking mental notes. Then he asked, 'Who am I looking for? One of Edward Lane's crew?'

Reacher nodded. 'A recent ex-member.'

'Name?'

Reacher said, 'Taylor. Graham Taylor. He's a UK citizen.'

FIFTY-THREE

The Pentagon guy left with a promise to liaise in due course via Lauren Pauling's cell phone. Reacher got a coffee refill and Pauling said, 'You didn't find Taylor's passport in his apartment.'

Reacher said, 'No, I didn't.'

'So either he's still alive or you think someone's impersonating him.'

Reacher said nothing.

Pauling said, 'Let's say Taylor was working with the guy with no tongue. Let's say they fell out over something, either what they did to Kate and Jade in the end, or the money, or both. Then let's say one of them killed the other and ran, on Taylor's passport, with all the money.'

'If it's the guy with no tongue, why would he use Taylor's passport?'

'Maybe he doesn't have one of his own. Plenty of Americans don't. Or maybe he's on a watch list. Maybe he couldn't get through an airport with his own name.'

'Passports have photographs.'

'They're often old and generic. Do you look like your passport photograph?'

'A little.'

Pauling said, 'A little is sometimes all you need. Going out, they don't care as much as when you're coming in.'

Reacher nodded and looked up and saw Brewer coming in the door. Big, fast, energetic. Something in his face, maybe frustration, maybe concern, Reacher couldn't tell. Or perhaps the guy was just tired. He had been woken up early. He hurried through the room and slid into the booth and sat in the same spot the Pentagon guy had just vacated.

He said, 'The body in the river was not the guy in Patti's photograph.'

'You sure?' Reacher asked.

'As sure as I've ever been about anything. Patti's guy is about five-nine and athletic and the floater was six-three and wasted. Those are fairly basic differences, wouldn't you say?'

Reacher nodded. 'Fairly basic.'

Pauling asked, 'Did he have a tongue?'

'A what?' Brewer said.

'A tongue. Did the floater have a tongue?'

'Doesn't everybody? What kind of question is that?'

'We're looking for a guy who had his tongue cut out.'

Brewer looked straight at her. 'Then the floater ain't yours. I was just at the morgue. He's got everything except a heartbeat.'

'You sure?'

'Medical examiners tend to notice things like that.'

'OK,' Reacher said. 'Thanks for your help.'

'Not so fast,' Brewer said. 'Talk to me.'

'About what?'

'About why you're interested in this guy.'

Something in his face.

Reacher asked, 'Did you get an ID?'

Brewer nodded. 'From his fingerprints. They were mushy, but we made them work. He was an NYPD snitch. Relatively valuable. I've got buddies uptown who are relatively unhappy.'

'What kind of a snitch?'

'Methamphetamine out of Long Island. He was due to testify.'

'Where had he been?'

'He just got out of Rikers. They swept him up along with a bunch of others to keep his cover intact. Held him a few days, then turned him loose.'

'When?'

'He just got out. The ME figures he was dead about three hours after walking through the gates.'

'Then we don't know anything about him,' Reacher said. 'He's completely unrelated.'

This time it was Brewer who said: 'You sure?'

Reacher nodded. 'I promise.'

Brewer gave him a long hard look, cop to cop. Then he just shrugged and said, 'OK.'

Reacher said, 'Sorry we can't help.'

'Shit happens.'

'You still got Patti's photograph?'

'Photographs,' Brewer said. 'She gave me two. Couldn't decide which one was better.'

'You still got them?'

'In my pocket.'

'Want to leave them with me?'

Brewer smiled, man to man. 'You planning on returning them personally?'

'I could,' Reacher said. 'But first I want to look at them.'

They were in a standard white letter-size envelope. Brewer pulled it from his inside pocket and laid it on the table. Reacher saw the name *Taylor* and the words *For Brewer* written on the front in blue ink and neat handwriting. Then Brewer left. Just stood up and walked back out to the street with the same kind of speed and energy and hustle he had used on the way in. Reacher watched him go and then he turned the envelope face down and squared it on the table in front of him. Looked at it hard but left it unopened.

'What have we got?' he asked.

'We've got the same as we always had,' Pauling said. 'We've got Taylor and the guy who can't talk.'

Reacher shook his head. 'Taylor *is* the guy who can't talk.'

FIFTY-FOUR

Pauling said, 'That's absurd. Lane wouldn't employ anyone who can't talk. Why would he? And nobody mentioned it. You asked about Taylor several times. They said he was a good soldier. They didn't say he was a good soldier except he can't talk. They'd have mentioned that little detail, don't you think?'

'Two words,' Reacher said. 'All we need to do is add two words and the whole thing makes perfect sense.'

'What two words?'

'We've been saying the guy can't talk. Truth is, he can't *afford to* talk.'

Pauling paused a long moment.

Then she said: 'Because of his accent.'

Reacher nodded. 'Exactly. All along we've been saying nobody was missing, but by definition Taylor was missing from the start. And Taylor was behind this whole damn thing. He planned it, and he set it up, and he executed it. He rented the apartment and he bought the chair. He probably did other stuff we didn't catch up with yet. And everywhere he went, he couldn't

340

risk opening his mouth. Not even once. Because he's English. Because of his accent. He was realistic. He knew he had to be leaving a trail. And if whoever was tracking him came along later and heard all about an average-looking forty-year-old man with an English accent, they would have made him in a second. It would have been a total no-brainer. Who else would anyone have thought of? Because he was the last one to see Kate and Jade alive.'

'He did the same thing as Knight, five years ago. That's how the takedown worked.'

'Exactly,' Reacher said again. 'It's the only way to explain it. Possibly he drove them to Bloomingdale's but certainly he didn't stop there. He just pulled a gun and kept on going. Maybe threatened to shoot Kate in front of the kid. That would have kept her quiet. Then he just dropped off the radar and started relying on a kind of double alibi he had created for himself. First, he was presumed dead. And second, all anyone would ever remember of him was a guy that couldn't speak. A guy with no tongue. It was a perfect piece of misdirection. Weird, exotic, absolutely guaranteed to get us chasing off in the wrong direction.'

Pauling nodded. 'Brilliant, in a way.'

'It was all anyone remembered,' Reacher said. 'Like that old Chinese man? All he really recalled was the way the guy gulped like a fish. And the super on Sixth Avenue? We said, tell us about the guy, and he said he keeps his mouth tight shut all the time because he's embarrassed that he can't talk. That was the beginning and the end of his description. The obvious thing and the only thing. Everything else was trivial by comparison.'

'Open the envelope,' Pauling said. 'Confirm it.'

So Reacher lifted the envelope's flap and slid the two photographs out, face down. He tapped the back of the top picture like a card sharp looking for luck.

Then he flipped it over.

It was the guy he had seen twice before.

No question about it.

Taylor.

White, a little sunburned, lean, chiselled, clean-shaven, jaw clamped, not smiling, maybe forty years old. Blue jeans, blue shirt, blue ball cap, white sneakers. All the clothing worn and comfortable. It was clearly a very recent shot. Patti Joseph had caught him coming out of the Dakota one late-summer morning. It looked like he had paused on the sidewalk and lifted his gaze to check the weather. By doing so he had met the angle of Patti's long Nikon lens perfectly.

'No doubt about it,' Reacher said. 'That's the guy I saw getting into the Mercedes and the Jaguar.'

He turned the second picture over. It was a closer shot. Maximum zoom, and therefore not quite as clear. There was a little camera shake. The focus wasn't perfect. But it was a viable photograph. Same location, same angle, different day. Same guy. But this time his mouth was open. His lips were drawn back. He wasn't smiling. Maybe he was just grimacing against the sudden glare of the sun after stepping out of the dark

Dakota lobby. He had terrible teeth. Some were missing. The rest were gappy and uneven.

'There you go,' Reacher said. 'There's another reason. No wonder everyone told us he kept his mouth clamped shut all the time. He's not dumb. He was concealing two pieces of evidence at the same time, not just one. His English accent, and his British dentistry. Because that's *really* a no-brainer. Someone from Lane's crew hears about a Brit with bad teeth? It would have been like wearing a name tag around his neck.'

'Where is he now? England?'

'That's my guess. He flew home, where he feels safe.'

'With the money?'

'Checked luggage. Three bags.'

'Could he do that? With all the X-rays?'

'I don't see why not. I once had a lesson about paper money from an expert. Right here in New York City, as a matter of fact. At Columbia University. The paper isn't really paper, as such. It's mostly linen and cotton fibres. More in common with the shirt on your back than a newspaper. I think it would show up like clothing on an X-ray machine.'

Pauling slid the photographs across the table and butted them together side by side in front of her. Looked at one, looked at the other. Reacher sensed her running through an explanation in her head. An analysis. A narrative.

'He's tan from the Hamptons,' she said. 'He was there all summer with the family. And then he was worried about someone checking his apartment from the street, afterwards. That's why

343

he took the light bulb out of the guest room and covered the window. The place had to look empty, if anyone ever checked.'

'He was very thorough.'

'And very unsentimental. He walked away from that great apartment.'

'He can rent ten apartments now.'

'That's for sure.'

'It's a shame,' Reacher said. 'I liked him when I thought he was dead. Everyone spoke well of him.'

'Who was doing the speaking? I wouldn't take recommendations from those guys.'

'I guess not. But I usually like Brits. Gregory seems OK.'

Pauling said, 'He's probably as bad as the rest of them.'

Then she stacked the photographs and slid them back.

'Well, you've got the name to give to Lane,' she said.

Reacher didn't reply.

'A unified theory of everything,' she said. 'Like a physicist. I don't see why you say it's only partial. Taylor did it all.'

'He didn't,' Reacher said. 'He didn't make the phone calls. An American made the phone calls.'

FIFTY-FIVE

'Taylor had a partner,' Reacher said. 'Obviously. He had to, because of the accent thing again. At first I thought it might be the guy in the river. Like you said, I thought maybe they fell out afterwards. Or that Taylor got greedy and wanted the whole nine yards for himself. But that won't work now. The guy in the river was just a regular New York corpse. An unrelated homicide. He was in Rikers at the relevant time. So, I don't know who made the phone calls. That's why it's only a partial theory.'

'Lane will want to know who the partner was. He won't settle for half a loaf.'

'You bet your ass he won't.'

'He's not going to pay.'

'He'll pay part. We'll get the rest later. When we tell him who the partner was.'

'How do we find out who the partner was?'

'The only sure way is to find Taylor and ask him.'

'*Ask* him?'

'Make him tell us.'

'In England?'

345

'If that's where your Pentagon buddy says he went. I guess he could check for us who Taylor was sitting next to on the flight. There's a slim chance they flew together.'

'Unlikely.'

'Very. But it's maybe worth a try.'

So Pauling went through ten more minutes of phone tag at the UN and then gave up and left a voice mail message asking the guy to check whether Taylor had had a travelling companion.

'What now?' she said.

'Wait for your guy to get back to you,' Reacher said. 'Then book us a car to the airport and flights to London, if that's where Taylor went, which it probably is. Tonight's red-eye, I guess. I'm betting Lane will ask me to go over there. He'll want me to do the advance work. Then he'll bring his whole crew over for the kill. And we'll deal with them there.'

Pauling looked up. 'That's why you promised no cop or prosecutor in America is going to think twice.'

Reacher nodded. 'But their opposite numbers in England are going to get pretty uptight. That's for damn sure.'

Reacher put Patti Joseph's photographs back in their envelope and jammed it in the front pocket of his shirt. Kissed Pauling on the sidewalk and headed for the subway. He was outside the Dakota before five in the afternoon.

The name. Tomorrow.

Mission accomplished.

But he didn't go inside. Instead he walked

straight ahead and crossed Central Park West and went in through the gate to Strawberry Field. The John Lennon memorial, in the park. Near where Lennon was killed. Like most guys his age Reacher felt that the Beatles were part of his life. They were its soundtrack, its background. Maybe that was why he liked English people.

Maybe that was why he didn't want to do what he was about to do.

He patted his shirt pocket and felt the photographs and ran through the narrative one more time the same way Pauling had. But there was no doubt about it. Taylor was the bad guy. No question. Reacher himself was an actual eyewitness. First the Mercedes, then the Jaguar.

No doubt about it.

Maybe there was just no joy in giving one bad guy to another.

But this is for Kate, Reacher thought. *For Jade. For Hobart's money.*

Not for Lane.

He took a deep breath and stood for a second with his face tilted up to catch the last of the sun before it fell away behind the buildings to the west. Then he turned around and walked back out of the park.

Edward Lane fanned the two photographs of Taylor quite delicately between his finger and his thumb and asked one simple question: 'Why?'

'Greed,' Reacher said. 'Or malice, or jealousy, or all of the above.'

'Where is he now?'

'My guess is England. I'll know soon.'

'How?'

'Sources.'

'You're good.'

'The best you ever saw.' *Or they'd have nailed you in the army*.

Lane handed back the photographs and said, 'He must have had a partner.'

'Obviously.'

'For the phone calls. Someone with an American accent. Who was it?'

'You'll have to ask Taylor that.'

'In England?'

'I don't suppose he'll be coming back here anytime soon.'

'I want you to find him for me.'

'I want my money.'

Lane nodded. 'You'll get it.'

'I want it now.'

'Ten per cent now. The rest when I'm face to face with Taylor.'

'Twenty per cent now.'

Lane didn't answer.

Reacher said, 'Or I'll cut my losses and walk away. And you can stroll down to Barnes and Noble and buy a UK map and a pin. Or a mirror and a stick.'

Lane said, 'Fifteen per cent now.'

Reacher said, 'Twenty.'

'Seventeen and a half.'

'Twenty. Or I'm out of here.'

'Jesus Christ,' Lane said. 'OK, twenty per cent now. But you'll leave now, too. Right now, tonight. You can have one day's start. That should be enough for a smart boy like you. Then we'll

348

follow you twenty-four hours later. The seven of us. Me, Gregory, Groom, Burke, Kowalski, Addison, and Perez. That should be enough. You know London?'

'I've been there before.'

'We'll be at the Park Lane Hilton.'

'With the rest of the money?'

'Every penny of it,' Lane said. 'I'll show it to you when you meet us at the hotel and you tell us where Taylor is. I'll give it to you when I've got actual visual contact with him.'

'OK,' Reacher said. 'Deal.' And ten minutes later he was back in the subway, heading south, with two hundred thousand US dollars in cash wrapped in a plastic Whole Foods shopping bag.

Reacher met Pauling at her apartment and gave her the bag and said, 'Take out what I owe you and hide the rest. It's enough to get Hobart started with the preliminaries at least.'

Pauling took the bag and held it away from her body like it was contagious. 'Is this the African money?'

Reacher nodded. 'Direct from Ouagadougou. Via Edward Lane's closet.'

'It's dirty.'

'Show me money that isn't.'

Pauling paused a beat and then opened the bag and peeled off some bills and put them on the kitchen counter. Then she refolded the bag and put it in the oven.

'I don't have a safe here,' she said.

'The oven will do,' Reacher said. 'Just don't forget and start to cook something.'

She took four bills from the stack on the counter and handed them to him.

'For clothes,' she said. 'You're going to need them. We leave for England tonight.'

'Your guy got back to you?'

She nodded. 'Taylor was on British Airways to London less than four hours after Burke put the money in the Jaguar.'

'Alone?'

'Apparently. As far as we can tell. He was seated next to some British woman. Doesn't mean he didn't have a partner who checked in separately and sat somewhere else. That would have been a fairly basic precaution. There were sixty-seven unaccompanied adult American males on the flight.'

'Your guy is very thorough.'

'Yes, he is. He got the whole manifest. By fax. Including the baggage manifest. Taylor checked three bags.'

'Overweight charge?'

'No. He was in business class. They might have let it slide.'

Reacher said, 'I don't need four hundred dollars for clothes.'

Pauling said, 'You do if you're travelling with me.'

I was an MP, Reacher had said to Hobart. *I've done everything before.* But he hadn't. Thirty minutes later he was doing something he had never done in his life. He was buying clothes in a department store. He was in Macy's on Herald Square, in the men's department, in front

350

of a cash register, holding a pair of grey pants, a grey jacket, a black T-shirt, a black V-neck sweater, a pair of black socks and a pair of white boxer shorts. His choices had been limited by the availability of suitable sizes. Inseam, arm length, and chest. He was worried that his brown shoes would be a colour clash. Pauling told him to buy new shoes too. He vetoed that idea. He couldn't afford them. So she said brown shoes would be just fine with grey pants. He shuffled to the head of the line and paid, three hundred and ninety-six dollars and change, with tax. He showered and dressed back at Pauling's apartment and took his creased and battered passport and Patti Joseph's envelope of photographs out of his old pants and shoved them in his new pants. Took his folding toothbrush out of his old shirt pocket and put it in his new jacket pocket. Carried his old clothes down the corridor to the compactor room and dropped them in the garbage chute. Then he waited with Pauling downstairs in the lobby, neither of them saying much, until the car service showed up to take them to the airport.

FIFTY-SIX

Pauling had booked them business class on the same flight that Taylor had taken forty-eight hours previously. It was maybe even the same plane, assuming it flew a round trip every day. But neither one of them could have been in Taylor's actual seat. They were in a window-and-aisle pair, and the Homeland Security manifest had shown that Taylor had been in the first of a block of four in the centre.

The seats themselves were strange bathtub-shaped cocoons that faced alternating directions. Reacher's window seat faced aft and next to him Pauling faced forward. The seats were advertised as reclining into fully flat beds, which might have been true for her but was about twelve inches shy of being true for him. But the seats had compensations. The face-to-face thing meant that he was going to spend seven hours looking directly at her, which was no kind of a hardship.

'What's the strategy?' she asked.

'We'll find Taylor, Lane will take care of him, and then I'll take care of Lane.'

'How?'

'I'll think of something. Like Hobart said, everything in war is improvisation.'

'What about the others?'

'That will be a snap decision. If I think the crew will fall apart with Lane gone, then I'll leave the rest alone and let it. But if one of them wants to step up to the officer class and take over, I'll do him too. And so on and so forth, until the crew really does fall apart.'

'Brutal.'

'Compared to what?'

'Taylor won't be easy to find,' she said.

'England's a small country,' he said.

'Not that small.'

'We found Hobart.'

'With help. We were given his address.'

'We'll get by.'

'How?'

'I've got a plan.'

'Tell me.'

'You know any British private investigators? Is there an international brotherhood?'

'There might be a sisterhood. I've got some numbers.'

'OK, then.'

'Is that your plan? Hire a London PI?'

'Local knowledge,' Reacher said. 'It's always the key.'

'We could have done that by phone.'

'We didn't have time.'

'London alone is eight million people,' Pauling said. 'Then there's Birmingham, Manchester, Sheffield, Leeds. And a whole lot of countryside. The Cotswolds. Stratford-upon-Avon. And

Scotland and Wales. Taylor stepped out the door at Heathrow two days ago. He could be anywhere by now. We don't even know where he's from.'

'We'll get by,' Reacher said again.

Pauling took a pillow and a blanket from a stewardess and reclined her seat. Reacher watched her sleep for a while and then he lay down too, with his knees up and his head jammed against the bathtub wall. The cabin lighting was soft and blue and the hiss of the engines was restful. Reacher liked flying. Going to sleep in New York and waking up in London was a fantasy that could have been designed expressly for him.

The stewardess woke him to give him breakfast. *Like being in the hospital*, he thought. *They wake you up to feed you.* But the breakfast was good. Mugs of hot coffee and bacon rolls. He drank six and ate six. Pauling watched him, fascinated.

'What time is it?' she asked.

'Five to five,' he said. 'In the morning. Which is five to ten in the morning in this time zone.'

Then all kinds of muted bells went off and signs went on to announce the start of their approach into Heathrow Airport. London's northerly latitude meant that at ten in the morning in late summer the sun was high. The landscape below was lit up bright. There were small clouds in the sky that cast shadows on the fields. Reacher's sense of direction wasn't as good as his sense of time but he figured they had looped past the city and were approaching the airport from the east.

Then the plane turned sharply and he realized they were in a holding pattern. Heathrow was notoriously busy. They were going to circle London at least once. Maybe twice.

He put his forehead against the window and stared down. Saw the Thames, glittering in the sun like polished lead. Saw Tower Bridge, white stone, recently cleaned, detailed with fresh paint on the ironwork. Then a grey warship moored in the river, some kind of a permanent exhibit. Then London Bridge. He craned his neck and looked for St Paul's Cathedral, north and west. Saw the big dome, crowded by ancient winding streets. London was a low-built city. Densely and chaotically packed near the dramatic curves of the Thames, spreading infinitely into the grey distance beyond.

He saw railroad tracks fanning out into Waterloo Station. Saw the Houses of Parliament. Saw Big Ben, the tower shorter and stumpier than he remembered it. And Westminster Abbey, white, bulky, a thousand years old. There was some kind of a giant Ferris wheel on the opposite bank of the river. A tourist thing, maybe. Green trees everywhere. He saw Buckingham Palace and Hyde Park. He glanced north of where the palace gardens ended and found the Park Lane Hilton. A round tower, bristling with balconies. From above it looked like a squat wedding cake. Then he glanced a little farther north and found the American Embassy. Grosvenor Square. He had once used an office there, in a windowless basement. Four weeks, for some big-deal army investigation he could barely recall. But he remembered the neighbourhood. He remembered it pretty well. Too rich for his blood, until you escaped east into Soho.

He asked Pauling, 'Have you been here before?'

'We did exchange training with Scotland Yard,' she said.

'That could be useful.'

'It was a million years ago.'

'Where did you stay?'

'They put us up in a college dormitory.'

'You know any hotels?'

'Do you?'

'Not the sort where they let you in wearing four hundred dollars' worth of clothes. Mostly the sort where you wear your shoes in bed.'

'We can't stay anywhere close to Lane and his guys. We can't be associated with him. Not if we're going to do something to him.'

'That's for sure.'

'What about somewhere really great? Like the Ritz?'

'That's the opposite problem. Four hundred dollars is too shabby for them. And we need to stay low-profile. We need the kind of place where they don't look at your passport and they let you pay cash. Bayswater, maybe. West of downtown, a clear run back to the airport afterwards.'

Reacher turned to the window again and saw a wide six-lane east–west highway with slow traffic driving on the left. Then suburbs, two-family houses, curving roads, tiny green backyards, garden sheds, and then acres of airport parking full of small cars, many of them red. Then the airport fence. Then the chevrons at the start of the runway. Close to the ground the plane seemed huge again after feeling cramped for seven hours. From being a narrow tube it became a two-hundred-ton monster doing two hundred miles an hour. It landed hard and roared and braked and then suddenly it was quiet and docile again, rolling slowly towards the terminal. The steward welcomed the passengers to London over the public address system and Reacher turned and looked across the cabin at the exit door. Taylor's first few steps would be easy enough to follow. After baggage claim and the taxi rank the job would get a whole lot harder. Harder, but maybe not impossible.

'We'll get by,' he said, even though Pauling hadn't spoken to him.

FIFTY-SEVEN

They filled in landing cards and had their passports stamped by an official in a grey suit. *My name on a piece of English paper*, Reacher thought. *Not good*. But there was no alternative. And his name was already on the airline passenger manifest, which could apparently get faxed all over the place at the drop of a hat. They waited at the carousel for Pauling's bag and then Reacher got stopped in Customs not because he had suspicious luggage but because he had none at all. Which made the guy stopping him a Special Branch cop or an MI5 agent in disguise, Reacher thought, not a real Customs guy. Travelling light was clearly a red flag. The detention was brief and the questions were casual, but the guy got a good look at his face and was all over his passport. *Not good*.

Pauling changed a wad of the O-Town dollars at a Travelex booth and they found the fast train to Paddington station. Paddington was a good first stop, Reacher figured. His kind of an area. Convenient for the Bayswater hotels, full of trash and hookers. Not that he expected to find Taylor there. Or anywhere close. But it would make a good anonymous base camp. The railway company promised the ride into town would be fifteen minutes, but it turned out to be closer to twenty. They came out to the street in central London just before twelve noon. West 4th Street to Eastbourne Terrace in ten short hours. Planes, trains and automobiles.

At street level that part of London was bright and fresh and cold and to a stranger's eyes it seemed full of trees. The buildings were low and had old cores and sagging roofs but most of them had new frontages tacked on to disguise age and disrepair. Most things were chains or franchises except for the ethnic take-out food stores and the town car services which still seemed to be mom-and-pop operations. Or cousin-and-cousin. The roads had good smooth blacktop heavily printed with instructions for drivers and pedestrians. The pedestrians were warned to *Look Left* or *Look Right* at every possible kerb and the drivers were guided by elaborate lines and arrows and cross-hatching and *Slow* signs anywhere the direction deviated from absolutely straight, which was just about everywhere. In some places there was more white on the road than black. *The welfare state*, Reacher thought. *It sure as hell takes care of you.*

He carried Pauling's bag for her and they walked south and east towards Sussex Gardens. From previous trips he recalled groups of row houses joined together into cheap hotels, on Westbourne Terrace, Gloucester Terrace, Lancaster Gate. The kinds of places that had thick crusted carpet in the hallways and thick scarred paint on the millwork and four meaningless symbols lit up above the front doors as if some responsible standards agency had evaluated the offered services and found them to be pleasing. Pauling rejected the first two places he found before understanding that there wasn't going to be anything better just around the next corner. So she gave up and agreed to the third, which was four neighbouring townhouses knocked through to make a single long sloping not-quite-aligned building with a name seemingly picked at random from a selection of London tourist-trade hot-button buzzwords: Buckingham Suites. The desk guy was from Eastern Europe and was happy to take cash. The rate was cheap for London, if expensive for anywhere else in the world. There was no register. The *Suites* part of the name seemed to be justified by the presence of a small bathroom and a small table in each room. The bed was a queen with a green nylon counterpane. Beyond the bed and the bathroom and the table there wasn't a whole lot of space left.

'We won't be here long,' Reacher said.

'It's fine,' Pauling said.

She didn't unpack. Just propped her suitcase open on the floor and looked like she planned to live out of it. Reacher kept his toothbrush in his pocket. He sat on the bed while Pauling washed. Then she came out of the bathroom and moved to the window and stood with her head tilted up, looking out over the rooftops and the chimneys opposite.

'Nearly ninety-five thousand square miles,' she said. 'That's what's out there.'

'Smaller than Oregon,' he said.

'Oregon has three and a half million people. The UK has sixty million.'

'Harder to hide here, then. You've always got a nosy neighbour.'

'Where do we start?'

'With a nap.'

'You want to sleep?'

'Well, afterwards.'

She smiled. It was like the sun coming out.

'We'll always have Bayswater,' she said.

Sex and jet lag kept them asleep until four. Their one day's start, mostly gone.

'Let's get going,' Reacher said. 'Let's call on the sisterhood.'

So Pauling got up and fetched her purse and took out a small device that Reacher hadn't seen her use before. An electronic organizer. A Palm Pilot. She called up a directory and scrolled down a screen and found a name and an address.

'Gray's Inn Road,' she said. 'Is that near here?'

'I don't think so,' Reacher said. 'I think it's east of here. Nearer the business district. Maybe where the lawyers are.'

'That would make sense.'

'Anyone closer?'

'These people are supposed to be good.'

'We can get there on the subway, I guess. The Central Line, I think. To Chancery Lane. I should have bought a derby and an umbrella. I would have fit right in.'

'I don't think you would have. Those City people are very civilized.' She rolled over on the bed and dialled the phone on the night table. Reacher heard the foreign ring tone from the earpiece, a double purr instead of a single. Then he heard someone pick up and he listened to Pauling's end of the conversation. She explained who she was, temporarily in town, a New York private investigator, ex-FBI, a member of some kind of an international organization, and she gave a contact name, and she asked for a courtesy appointment. The person on the other end must have agreed readily enough because she asked 'How does six o'clock suit you?' and then said nothing more than 'OK, thank you, six o'clock it is,' and hung up.

Reacher said, 'The sisterhood comes through.'

'Brotherhood,' Pauling said. 'The woman whose name I had seems to have sold the business. But they were always going to agree. Like that ten-sixty-two thing you tried with the General. What if they have to come to New York? If we don't help each other, who will?'

Reacher said, 'I hope Edward Lane doesn't have a Palm Pilot full of London numbers.'

They showered and dressed again and walked down to the subway stop at Lancaster Gate. Or, in London English, to the tube station. It had a dirty tiled lobby that looked like a ballpark toilet, except for a flower seller. But the platform was clean and the train itself was new. And futuristic. Somehow, like its name, it was more tubular than its New York counterparts. The tunnels

362

were rounded, like they had been sucked down to an exact fit for the cars. Like the whole system could be powered by compressed air, not electricity.

It was a crowded six-stop ride through stations with famous and romantic names. Marble Arch, Bond Street, Oxford Circus, Tottenham Court Road, Holborn. The names reminded Reacher of the cards in a British Monopoly set he had found abandoned on a NATO base as a kid. Mayfair and Park Lane had been the prize properties. Where the Park Lane Hilton was. Where Lane and his six guys were due in about eighteen hours.

They came up out of the Chancery Lane station at a quarter to six into full daylight and narrow streets that were choked with traffic. Black cabs, red buses, white vans, diesel fumes, small five-door sedans that Reacher didn't recognize. Motorbikes, pedal bikes, sidewalks thick with people. Boldly striped pedestrian crossings, blinking lights, beeping signals. It was fairly cold but people were walking in shirtsleeves with jackets folded over their arms as if it was warm to them. There were no horns and no sirens. It was like the oldest parts of downtown Manhattan lopped off at the fifth floor and compressed in size and therefore heated up in speed but also somehow cooled down in temper and made more polite. Reacher smiled. Certainly he loved the open road and miles to go but he loved the crush of the world's great cities just as much. New York yesterday, London today. Life was good.

So far.

They walked north on Gray's Inn Road, which

looked like being longer than they had anticipated. There were old buildings left and right, modernized on the ground floors, ancient above. A sign said that the house where Charles Dickens had lived was ahead and on the left. But for all that London was a historic city Dickens wouldn't have recognized the place. No way. Not close. Even Reacher felt that things had changed a lot in the ten or so years since he had last been in town. He remembered red phone boxes and polite unarmed coppers in pointed hats. Now most of the phone boxes he saw were plain glass cabins and everyone was using cell phones anyway. And the cops he saw were patrolling in pairs, blank-faced, dressed in flak jackets and carrying Uzi machine pistols in the ready position. There were surveillance cameras on poles everywhere.

Pauling said, 'Big brother is watching you.'

'I see that,' Reacher said. 'We're going to have to take Lane out of town. Can't do anything to him here.'

Pauling didn't answer. She was checking doors for numbers. She spotted the one she wanted across the street on the right. It was a narrow maroon door with a glass fanlight. Through it Reacher could see a staircase that led to suites of rooms upstairs. Not dissimilar from Pauling's own place three thousand miles away. They crossed the street between standing traffic and checked the brass plates on the stonework. One was engraved: *Investigative Services plc*. Plain script, plain message. Reacher pulled the door and thought it was locked until he remembered that British doors worked the other way around. So he pushed and found that it was open. The staircase was old but it was covered in new linoleum. They walked up two flights until they found the right door. It was standing open onto a small square room with a desk set at a forty-five degree angle so that its occupant could see out the door and the window at the same time. The occupant was a small man with thin hair. He was maybe fifty years old. He was wearing a sleeveless sweater over a shirt and a tie.

'You must be the Americans,' he said. For a second Reacher wondered how exactly he had known. Clothes? Teeth? Smell? A deduction, like Sherlock Holmes? But then the guy said, 'I stayed open especially for you. I would have been on my way home by now if you hadn't telephoned. I didn't have any other appointments.'

Pauling said, 'Sorry to hold you up.'

'Not a problem,' the guy said. 'Always happy to help a fellow professional.'

'We're looking for someone,' Pauling said. 'He arrived from New York two days ago. He's English, and his name is Taylor.'

The guy glanced up.

'Twice in one day,' he said. 'Your Mr Taylor is a popular person.'

'What do you mean?'

'A man telephoned directly from New York with the same enquiry. Wouldn't give his name. I imagined he was trying all the London agencies one by one.'

'Was he American?'

'Absolutely.'

Pauling turned to Reacher and mouthed, 'Lane.'

Reacher nodded. 'Trying to go it alone. Trying to bilk me out of my fee.'

Pauling turned back to the desk. 'What did you tell the guy on the phone?'

'That there are sixty million people in Great Britain and that possibly several hundred thousand of them are called Taylor. It's a fairly common name. I told him that without better information I couldn't really help him.'

'Can you help us?'

'That depends on what extra information you have.'

'We have photographs.'

'They might help eventually. But not at the outset. How long was Mr Taylor in America?'

'Many years, I think.'

'So he has no base here? No home?'

'I'm sure he doesn't.'

'Then it's hopeless,' the guy said. 'Don't you see? I work with databases. Surely you do the same in New York? Bills, electoral registers, council tax, court records, credit reports, insurance policies, things like that. If your Mr Taylor hasn't lived here for many years he simply won't show up anywhere.'

Pauling said nothing.

'I'm very sorry,' the guy said. 'But surely you understand?'

Pauling shot Reacher a look that said: *Great plan*.

Reacher said, 'I've got a phone number for his closest relative.'

FIFTY-EIGHT

Reacher said, 'We searched Taylor's apartment in New York and we found a desk phone that had ten speed dials programmed. The only British number was labelled with the letter S. I'm guessing it's for his mother or father or his brother or sister. More likely a brother or sister because I think a guy like him would have used M or D for his mom or his dad. It'll be Sam, Sally, Sarah, Sean, something like that. And the sibling relationship will probably be fairly close, or else why bother to program a speed dial? And if the relationship is fairly close, then Taylor won't have come back to Britain without at least letting them know. Because they've probably got him on speed dial too, and they would worry if he wasn't answering his phone at home. So I'm guessing they'll have the information we need.'

'What was the number?' the guy asked.

Reacher closed his eyes and recited the 01144 number he had memorized back on Hudson Street. The guy at the desk wrote it down on a pad of paper with a blunt pencil.

'OK,' he said. 'We delete the international

367

prefix, and we add a zero in its place.' He did exactly that, manually, with his pencil. 'Then we fire up the old computer and we look in the reverse directory.' He spun his chair one-eighty to a computer table behind him and tapped the space bar and unlocked the screen with a password Reacher didn't catch. Then he pointed and clicked his way to a dialog box where he entered the number. 'This will give us the address only, you understand. We'll have to go elsewhere to discover the exact identity of the person who lives there.' He hit *Submit* and a second later the screen redrew and came up with an address.

'Grange Farm,' he said. 'In Bishops Pargeter. Sounds rural.'

Reacher asked, 'How rural?'

'Not far from Norwich, judging by the post-code.'

'Bishops Pargeter is the name of a town?'

The guy nodded. 'It'll be a small village, probably. Or a hamlet, possibly. Perhaps a dozen buildings and a thirteenth-century Norman church. That would be typical. In the county of Norfolk, in East Anglia. Farming country, very flat, windy, the Fens, that kind of thing, north and east of here, about a hundred and twenty miles away.'

'Find the name.'

'Hang on, hang on, I'm getting there.' The guy dragged and dropped the address to a temporary location elsewhere on the screen and opened up a different database. 'The electoral register,' he said. 'That's always my preference. It's in the public domain, quite legal, and it's usually fairly comprehensive and reliable. If people take the trouble to vote, that is, which they don't always do, of course.' He dragged the address back to a new dialog box and hit another *Submit* command. There was a long, long wait. Then the screen changed. 'Here we are,' the guy said. 'Two voters at that address. Jackson. That's the name. Mr Anthony Jackson, and let's see, yes, Mrs Susan Jackson. So there's your S. S for Susan.'

'A sister,' Pauling said. 'Married. This is like Hobart all over again.'

'Now then,' the guy said. 'Let's do a little something else. Not quite legal this time, but since I'm among friends and colleagues, I might as well push the boat out.' He opened a new database that came up in old-fashioned plain DOS script. 'Hacked, basically,' he said. 'That's why we don't get the fancy graphics. But we get the information. The Department of Work and Pensions. The nanny state at work.' He entered Anthony Jackson's name and address and then added a complex keyboard command and the screen rolled down and came back with three separate names and a mass of figures. 'Anthony Jackson is thirty-nine years old and his wife Susan is thirty-eight. Her maiden name was indeed Taylor. They have one child, a daughter, age eight, and they seem to have saddled her with the unfortunate name of Melody.'

'That's a nice name,' Pauling said.

'Not for Norfolk. I don't suppose she's happy at school.'

Reacher asked, 'Have they been in Norfolk

369

long? Is that where the Taylors are from? As a family?'

The guy scrolled up the screen. 'The unfortunate Melody seems to have been born in London, which would suggest not.' He exited the plain DOS site and opened another. 'The Land Registry,' he said. He entered the address. Hit another *Submit* command. The screen redrew. 'No, they bought the place in Bishops Pargeter just over a year ago. Sold a place in south London at the same time. Which would suggest they're city folk heading back to the land. It's a common fantasy. I give them another twelve months or so before they get tired of it.'

'Thank you,' Reacher said. 'We appreciate your help.'

He picked up the guy's blunt pencil from the desk and took Patti Joseph's envelope out of his pocket and wrote *Anthony, Susan, Melody Jackson, Grange Farm, Bishops Pargeter, Norfolk* on it. Then he said, 'Maybe you could forget all about this if the guy from New York calls again.'

'Money at stake?'

'Lots of it.'

'First come, first served,' the guy said. 'The early bird catches the worm. And so on and so forth. My lips are sealed.'

'Thank you,' Reacher said again. 'What do we owe you?'

'Oh, nothing at all,' the guy said. 'It was my pleasure entirely. Always happy to help a fellow professional.'

*   *   *

Back on the street Pauling said, 'All Lane has to do is check Taylor's apartment and find the phone and he's level with us. He could get back to a different guy in London. Or call someone in New York. Those reverse directories are available on-line.'

'He won't find the phone,' Reacher said. 'And if he did, he wouldn't make the connection. Different skill set. Mirror on a stick.'

'Are you sure?'

'Not entirely. So I took the precaution of erasing the number.'

'That's called taking an unfair advantage.'

'I want to make sure I get the money.'

'Should we just go ahead and call Susan Jackson?'

'I was going to,' Reacher said. 'But then you mentioned Hobart and his sister and now I'm not so sure. Suppose Susan is as protective as Dee Marie? She'd just lie to us about anything she knows.'

'We could say we were buddies passing through.'

'She'd check with Taylor before she told us anything.'

'So what next?'

'We're going to have to go up there ourselves. To Bishops Pargeter, wherever the hell that is.'

FIFTY-NINE

Obviously their hotel didn't even come close to offering concierge service so Reacher and Pauling had to walk down to Marble Arch to find a car rental office. Reacher had neither a driver's licence nor a credit card so he left Pauling to fill in the forms and kept on going down Oxford Street to look for a bookstore. He found a big place that had a travel section in back with a whole shelf of motoring atlases of Britain. But the first three he checked didn't show Bishops Pargeter at all. No sign of it anywhere. It wasn't in the index. *Too small*, he figured. *Not even a dot on the map*. He found London and Norfolk and Norwich. No problem with those places. He found market towns and large villages. But nothing smaller. Then he saw a cache of Ordnance Survey maps. Four shelves, low down, against a wall. A whole series. Big folded sheets, meticulously drawn, government sponsored. For hikers, he guessed. Or for serious geography freaks. There was a choice of scales. Best was a huge thing that showed detail all the way down to some individual buildings. He pulled all the

Norfolk sheets off the shelf and tried them one by one. He found Bishops Pargeter on the fourth attempt. It was a crossroads hamlet about thirty miles south and west of the Norwich outskirts. Two minor roads met. Not even the roads themselves showed up on the motoring atlases.

He bought the map for detail and the cheapest atlas for basic orientation. Then he hiked back to the rental office and found Pauling waiting with the key to a Mini Cooper.

'A red one,' she said. 'With a white roof. Very cool.'

He said, 'I think Taylor might be right there. With his sister.'

'Why?'

'His instinct would be to go hide somewhere lonely. Somewhere isolated. And he was a soldier, so deep down he'd want somewhere defensible. It's flat as a pool table there. I just read the map. He'd see someone coming from five miles away. If he's got a rifle he's impregnable. And if he's got four-wheel-drive he's got a three-sixty escape route. He could just take off across the fields in any direction.'

'You can't murder two people and steal more than ten million dollars and just go home to your sister.'

'He wouldn't have to give her chapter and verse. He wouldn't really have to tell her anything at all. And it might only be temporary. He might need a break. He's been under a lot of stress.'

'You sound sorry for him.'

'I'm trying to think like him. He's been planning

373

for a long time and the last week must have been hell. He must be exhausted. He needs to hole up and sleep.'

'His sister's place would be too risky, surely. Family is the first thing anyone thinks of. We did, with Hobart. We tried every Hobart in the book.'

'His sister is a Jackson, not a Taylor. Like Graziano wasn't a Hobart. And Grange Farm is not an ancestral pile. The sister only just moved there. Anyone tracking his family would get bogged down in London.'

'There's a kid up there. His niece. Would he put innocent people in physical danger?'

'He just killed two innocent people. He's a little underdeveloped in the conscience department.'

Pauling swung the car key on her finger. Back and forth, thinking.

'It's possible,' she said. 'I guess. So what's our play?'

'Taylor was with Lane three years,' Reacher said. 'So he never met you and he sure as hell never met me. So it doesn't really make much difference. He's not going to shoot every stranger who comes to the house. He can't really afford to. It's something we should bear in mind, is all.'

'We're going right to the house?'

Reacher nodded. 'At least close enough to scope it out. If Taylor's there, we back off and wait for Lane. If he isn't, we go all the way in and talk to Susan.'

'When?'

'Now.'

* * *

The rental guy brought the Mini Cooper out from a garage space in back and Reacher shoved the passenger seat hard up against the rear bench and slid inside. Pauling got in the driver's seat and started the engine. It was a cute car. It looked great in red. But it was a handful to drive. Stick shift, wrong side of the road, wheel on the right, early evening traffic in one of the world's most congested cities. But they made it back to the hotel OK. They double parked and Pauling ran in to get her bag. Reacher stayed in the car. His toothbrush was already in his pocket. Pauling got back after five minutes and said, 'We're on the west side here. Convenient for the airport. But now we need to exit the city from the east.'

'Northeast,' Reacher said. 'On a highway called the M11.'

'So I have to drive all the way through the centre of London in rush hour.'

'No worse than Paris or Rome.'

'I've never been to Paris or Rome.'

'Well, now you'll know what to expect if you ever get there.'

Heading east and north was a simple enough proposition but like any major city London was full of one-way systems and complex junctions. And it was full of lines of stalled traffic at every light. They made halting progress as far as a district called Shoreditch and then they found a wide road labelled A10 that speared due north. Too early, but they took it anyway. They figured they would make the lateral adjustment later, away from the congestion. Then they found the M25, which was a kind of beltway. They hit it clockwise and two exits later they were on the M11, heading north and east for Cambridge, Newmarket, and ultimately Norfolk. Nine o'clock in the evening, and getting dark.

Pauling asked, 'You know this area we're going to?'

'Not really,' Reacher said. 'It was air force country, not army. Bomber bases all over the place. Flat, spacious, close to Europe. Ideal.'

England was a lit-up country. That was for damn sure. Every inch of the highway was bathed in bright vapour glow. And people drove fast. The limit was posted at seventy miles an hour, but it was widely ignored. High eighties, low nineties seemed to be the norm. Lane discipline was good. Nobody passed on the inside. The highway exits all followed the same coherent grammar. Clear signs, plenty of warning, long deceleration lanes. Reacher had read that highway fatalities were low in Britain. Safety through infrastructure.

Pauling asked, 'What's Grange Farm going to be like?'

'I don't know,' Reacher said. 'Technically in Old English a grange was a large barn for grain storage. Then later it became a word for the main building in a gentleman's arable farm. So I guess we're going to see a big house and a bunch of smaller outbuildings. Fields all around. Maybe a hundred acres. Kind of feudal.'

'You know a lot.'

'A lot of useless information,' Reacher said. 'Supposed to fire my imagination.'

'But you can't get no satisfaction?'

'None at all. I don't like anything about this whole situation. It feels wrong.'

'Because there are no good guys. Just bad guys and worse guys.'

'They're all equally terrible.'

'The hard way,' Pauling said. 'Sometimes things aren't black and white.'

Reacher said, 'I can't get past the feeling that I'm making a bad mistake.'

England is a small country but East Anglia was a large empty part of it. In some ways it was like driving across the prairie states. Endless forward motion without much visible result. The little red Mini Cooper hummed along. The clock in Reacher's head crawled around to ten in the evening. The last of the twilight disappeared. Beyond the bright ribbon of road was nothing but full darkness.

They bypassed Cambridge and blew through a town called Fenchurch St Mary. The road narrowed and the street lights disappeared. They saw a sign that said *Norwich 40 miles*. So Reacher switched maps and they started hunting the turn down to Bishops Pargeter. The road signs were clear and helpful. But they were all written with the same size lettering and there seemed to be a maximum permitted length for a fingerpost. Which meant that the longer names were abbreviated. Reacher saw a sign to *B'sh'ps P'ter* flash by and they were two hundred yards past it before he figured out what it meant. So Pauling jammed to a stop in the lonely darkness and U-turned and went back. Paused a second and then turned off the main drag onto a much smaller road. It was narrow and winding and the surface was bad. Pitch dark beyond the headlight beams.

'How far?' Pauling asked.

Reacher spanned his finger and thumb on the map.

'Maybe nine miles,' he said. The motoring atlas had showed nothing but a blank white triangle between two roads that fanned out south of the city of Norwich. The Ordnance Survey sheet showed the triangle to be filled with a tracery of minor tracks and speckled here and there with small settlements. He put his finger on the Bishops Pargeter crossroads. Then he looked out the car window.

'This is pointless,' he said. 'It's too dark. We're not even going to see the house, let alone who's living in it.' He looked back at the map. It showed buildings about four miles ahead. One was labelled *PH*. He checked the legend in the corner of the sheet.

'Public house,' he said. 'A pub. Maybe an inn. We should get a room. Go out again at first light.'

Pauling said, 'Suits me, boss.'

He realized she was tired. Travel, jet lag, unfamiliar roads, driving stress. 'I'm sorry,' he said. 'We overdid it. I should have planned better.'

'No, this works,' she said. 'We're right on the spot for the morning. But how much further?'

'Four miles to the pub now, and then five more to Bishops Pargeter tomorrow.'

'What time is it?'

He smiled. 'Ten forty-seven.'

'So you can do it in multiple time zones.'

'There's a clock on the dashboard. I can see it from here. I'm practically sitting in your lap.'

Eight minutes later they saw a glow in the distance that turned out to be the pub's spotlit sign. It was swinging in a gentle night breeze on a high gallows. *The Bishop's Arms*. There was a blacktopped parking lot with five cars in it and then a row of lit windows. They looked warm and inviting. Beyond the dark outline of the building there was absolutely nothing at all. Just endless flatness under a vast night sky.

'Maybe it was a coaching inn,' Pauling said.

'Can't have been,' Reacher said. 'It's not on the way to anywhere. It was for farm labourers.'

She turned in at the entrance of the parking lot and slotted the tiny car between a dirty Land Rover and a battered sedan of indeterminate make and age. Turned the motor off and dropped her hands off the wheel with a sigh. Silence rolled in, and with it came the smell of moist earth. The night air was cold. A little damp. Reacher carried Pauling's bag to the pub's door. There was a foyer inside, with a swaybacked staircase on the right and a low beamed ceiling and a patterned carpet and about ten thousand brass ornaments. Dead ahead was a hotel reception counter made from dark old wood varnished to an amazing shine. It was unattended. To the left was a doorway marked *Saloon Bar*. It led to a room that seemed to be empty. To the right beyond the stairs was a doorway marked *Public Bar*. Through it Reacher could see a bartender at work and the backs of four drinkers hunched on stools. In the far corner he could see the back of a man sitting alone at a table. All five customers were drinking from pint pots of ale.

Reacher stepped up to the empty reception counter and dinged the bell. A long moment later the bartender came in through a door behind the counter. He was about sixty, large and florid. Tired. He was wiping his hands on a towel.

'We need a room,' Reacher said to him.

'Tonight?' he said back.

'Yes, tonight.'

'It'll cost you forty pound. But that's with breakfast included.'

'Sounds like a bargain.'

'Which room would you like?'

'Which would you recommend?'

'You want one with a bath?'

Pauling said, 'Yes, a bath. That would be nice.'

'OK, then. That's what you can have.'

She gave him four ten-pound notes and he gave her a brass key on a tasselled fob. Then he handed Reacher a ballpoint pen and squared a register in front of him. Reacher wrote *J. & L. Bayswater* on the *Name* line. Then he checked a box for *Place of Business* rather than *Place of Residence* and wrote Yankee Stadium's street address on the next line. *East 161st Street, Bronx, New York, USA*. He wished that was his place of business. He always had. In a space labelled *Make of Vehicle* he scrawled *Rolls Royce*. He guessed *Registration Number* meant licence plate and he wrote R34CHR. Then he asked the bartender, 'Can we get a meal?'

'You're a little too late for a meal, I'm afraid,'

the bartender said. 'But you could have sandwiches, if you like.'

'That would be fine,' Reacher said.

'You're Americans, aren't you? We get a lot of them here. They come to see the old airfields. Where they were stationed.'

'Before my time,' Reacher said.

The bartender nodded sagely and said, 'Go on in and have a drink. Your sandwiches will be ready soon.'

Reacher left Pauling's bag at the foot of the stairs and stepped in through the door to the public bar. Five heads turned. The four guys at the bar looked like farmers. Red weathered faces, thick hands, blank uninterested expressions.

The guy alone at the table in the corner was Taylor.

SIXTY

Like the good soldier he was Taylor kept his eyes on Reacher long enough to assess the threat level. Pauling's arrival behind Reacher's shoulder seemed to reassure him. *A well-dressed man, a refined woman, a couple, tourists.* He looked away. Turned back to his beer. Beginning to end he had stared only a fraction of a second longer than any man would in a barroom situation. And actually shorter than the farmers. They were slow and ponderous and full of the kind of entitlement a regular patron shows to a stranger.

Reacher led Pauling to a table on the other side of the room from Taylor and sat with his back to the wall and watched the farmers turn back to the bar. They did it one by one, slowly. Then the last one picked up his glass again and the atmosphere in the room settled back to what it had been before. A moment later the bartender reappeared. He picked up a towel and started wiping glasses.

Reacher said, 'We should act normally. We should buy a drink.'

Pauling said, 'I guess I'll try the local beer. You know, when in Rome.'

So Reacher got up again and stepped over to the bar and tried to think back ten years to when he had last been in a similar situation. It was important to get the dialect right. He leaned between two of the farmers and put his knuckles on the bar and said, 'A pint of best, please, and a half for the lady.' It was important to get the manners right too, so he turned left and right to the four farmers and added: 'And will you gentlemen join us?' Then he glanced at the bartender and said: 'And can I get yours?' Then the whole dynamic in the room funnelled towards Taylor as the only patron as yet uninvited. Taylor turned and looked up from his table as if compelled to and Reacher mimed a drinking action and called, 'What can I get you?'

Taylor looked back at him and said, 'Thanks, but I've got to go.' A flat British accent, a little like Gregory's. Calculation in his eyes. But nothing in his face. No suspicion. Maybe a little awkwardness. Maybe even a hint of dour amiability. A guileless half-smile, a flash of the bad teeth. Then he drained his glass and set it back on the table and got up and headed for the door.

'Goodnight,' he said, as he passed by.

The bartender pulled six and a half pints of best bitter and lined them up like sentries. Reacher paid for them and pushed them around a little as a gesture towards distribution. Then he picked his own up and said, 'Cheers,' and took a sip. He carried Pauling's half-size glass over to

383

her and the four farmers and the bartender all turned towards their table and toasted them. Reacher thought: *Instant social acceptance for less than thirty bucks. Cheap at twice the price.* But he said, 'I hope I didn't offend that other fellow somehow.'

'Don't know him,' one of the farmers said. 'Never saw him before.'

'He's at Grange Farm,' another farmer said. 'Must be, because he was in Grange Farm's Land Rover. I saw him drive up in it.'

'Is he a farmer?' Reacher asked.

'He don't look like one,' the first farmer said. 'I never saw him before.'

'Where's Grange Farm?'

'Down the road apiece. There's a family there now.'

'Ask Dave Kemp,' the third farmer said. 'He'll tell you.'

Reacher said, 'Who's Dave Kemp?'

'Dave Kemp in the shop,' the third farmer said, impatiently, like Reacher was an idiot. 'In Bishops Pargeter. He'll know. Dave Kemp knows everything, on account of the post office. Nosy bugger.'

'Is there a pub there? Why would someone from there drink here?'

'This is the only pub for miles, lad. Why else do you think it's so crowded?'

Reacher didn't answer that.

'They're offcomers at Grange Farm,' the first farmer said, finally completing his earlier thought. 'That family. Recent. From London, I reckon. Don't know them. Organic, they are. Don't hold with chemicals.'

And that information seemed to conclude what the farmers felt they owed in exchange for a pint of beer because they fell to talking among themselves about the advantages and disadvantages of organic farming. It felt like a well-worn argument. According to what Reacher overheard there was absolutely nothing in its favour except for the inexplicable willingness of townsfolk to pay over the odds for the resulting produce.

'You were right,' Pauling said. 'Taylor's at the farm.'

'But will he stay there now?' Reacher said.

'I don't see why not. Your big dumb generous American act was pretty convincing. You weren't threatening. Maybe he thought we're just tourists looking at where our dads were based. They get them all the time here. That guy said so.'

Reacher said nothing.

Pauling said, 'I parked right next to him, didn't I? That farmer said he was in a Land Rover and there was only one Land Rover in the lot.'

Reacher said, 'I wish he hadn't been in here.'

'This is probably one of the reasons he chose to come back. English beer.'

'You like it?'

'No, but I believe Englishmen do.'

Their sandwiches were surprisingly good. Fresh crusty home-made bread, butter, rare roast beef, creamy horseradish sauce, farmhouse cheese on the side, with thin potato chips as a garnish. They ate them and finished their beers. Then they headed upstairs to their room. It was better than their suite in Bayswater. More spacious, partly due to the fact that the bed was a double, not a queen. Four feet six, not five feet. *Not really a hardship*, Reacher thought. *Not in the circumstances*. He set the alarm in his head for six in the morning. First light. *Taylor will stay or Taylor will run, and either way we'll watch him do it.*

SIXTY-ONE

The view out the window at six the next morning was one of infinite misty flatness. The land was level and grey-green all the way to the far horizon, interrupted only by straight ditches and occasional stands of trees. The trees had long thin supple trunks and round compact crowns to withstand the winds. Reacher could see them bending and tossing in the distance.

Outside it was very cold and their car was all misted over with dew. Reacher cleared the windows with the sleeve of his jacket. They climbed inside without saying much. Pauling backed out of the parking space and crunched into first gear and took off through the lot. Braked briefly and then joined the road, due east towards the morning sky. Five miles to Bishops Pargeter. Five miles to Grange Farm.

They found the farm before they found the village. It filled the upper left-hand square of the quadrant formed by the crossroads. They saw it first from the southwest. It was bounded by ditches, not fences. They were dug straight and crisp and deep. Then came flat fields, neatly ploughed, dusted pale green with late crops recently planted. Then closer to the centre were small stands of trees, almost decorative, like they had been artfully planted for effect. Then a large grey stone house. Larger than Reacher had imagined. Not a castle, not a stately home, but more impressive than a mere farmhouse had any right to be. Then in the distance to the north and the east of the house were five outbuildings. Barns, long, low, and tidy. Three of them made a three-sided square around some kind of a yard. Two stood alone.

The road they were driving on was flanked by the ditch that formed the farm's southern boundary. With every yard they drove their perspective rotated and changed, like the farm was an exhibit on a turntable, on display. It was a big handsome establishment. The driveway crossed the boundary ditch on a small flat bridge and then ran north into the distance, beaten earth, neatly cambered. The house itself was end-on to the road, a half-mile in. The front door faced west and the back door faced east. The Land Rover was parked between the back of the house and one of the stand-alone barns, tiny in the distance, cold, inert, misted over.

'He's still there,' Reacher said.

'Unless he has a car of his own.'

'If he had a car of his own he would have used it last night.'

Pauling slowed to a walk. There was no sign of activity around the house. None at all. There was thin smoke from a chimney, blown horizontal by the wind. A banked fire for a water heater, maybe. No lights in the windows.

Pauling said, 'I thought farmers got up early.'

'I guess livestock farmers do,' Reacher said. 'To milk the cows or whatever. But this place is all crops. Between ploughing and harvesting I don't see what they have to do. I guess they just sit back and let the stuff grow.'

'They need to spray it, don't they? They should be out on tractors.'

'Not organic people. They don't hold with chemicals. A little irrigation, maybe.'

'This is England. It rains all the time.'

'It hasn't rained since we got here.'

'Eighteen hours,' Pauling said. 'A new record. It rained all the time I was at Scotland Yard.'

She coasted to a halt and put the stick in neutral and buzzed her window down. Reacher did the same thing and cold damp air blew through the car. Outside was all silence and stillness. Just the hiss of wind in distant trees and the faint suggestion of morning shadows in the mist.

Pauling said, 'I guess all the world looked like this once.'

'These were the north folk,' Reacher said. 'Norfolk and Suffolk, the north folk and the south folk. Two ancient Celtic kingdoms, I think.'

Then the silence was shattered by a shotgun. A distant blast that rolled over the fields like an explosion. Enormously loud in the quiet. Reacher and Pauling both ducked instinctively. Then they scanned the horizon, looking for smoke. Looking for incoming fire.

Pauling said, 'Taylor?'

Reacher said, 'I don't see him.'

'Who else would it be?'

'He was too far away to be effective.'

'Hunters?'

'Turn the motor off,' Reacher said. He listened hard. Heard nothing more. No movement, no reload.

'I think it was a bird scarer,' he said. 'They just planted a winter crop. They don't want the crows to eat the seeds. I think they have machines that fire blanks all day at random.'

'I hope that's all it was.'

'We'll come back,' Reacher said. 'Let's go find Dave Kemp in the shop.'

Pauling fired the engine up and took off again and Reacher twisted in his seat and watched the eastern half of the farm go by. It looked exactly the same as the western half. But in reverse. Trees near the house, then wide flat fields, then a ditch on the boundary. Then came the northern leg of the Bishops Pargeter crossroads. Then the hamlet itself, which was little more than an ancient stone church standing alone in the upper right-hand quadrant and a fifty-yard string of buildings along the shoulder of the road opposite. Most of the buildings seemed to be residential cottages but one of them was a long low multi-purpose store. It was a newspaper shop, and a grocery, and a post office. Because it sold newspapers and breakfast requisites it was already open.

'The direct approach?' Pauling asked.

'A variant,' Reacher said.

She parked opposite the store where the

shoulder was gravelled near the entrance to the churchyard. They got out of the car into a stiff wind that blew strong and steady out of the east. Reacher said, 'Guys I knew who served here swore it blew all the way from Siberia without anything getting in its way.' The village store felt warm and snug by comparison. There was some kind of a gas heater going that put warm moisture into the air. There was a shuttered post office window and a central section that sold food and a newspaper counter at the far end. There was an old guy behind the counter. He was wearing a cardigan and a scarf. He was sorting newspapers, and his fingers were grey with ink.

'Are you Dave Kemp?' Reacher asked.

'That's my name,' the old guy said.

'We were told you're the man to ask.'

'About what?'

'We're here on a mission,' Reacher said.

'You're certainly here early.'

'First come first served,' Reacher said, because the London guy had, and therefore it might sound authentic.

'What do you want?'

'We're here to buy farms.'

'You're Americans, aren't you?'

'We represent a large agricultural corporation in the United States, yes. We're looking to make investments. And we can offer very generous finders' fees.'

The direct approach. A variant.

'How much?' Kemp asked.

'It's usually a percentage.'

'What farms?' Kemp asked.

391

'You tell us. Generally we look for tidy well-run places that might have issues with ownership stability.'

'What the hell does that mean?'

'It means we want good places that were recently bought up by amateurs. But we want them quick, before they're ruined.'

'Grange Farm,' Kemp said. 'They're bloody amateurs. They've gone organic.'

'We heard that name.'

'It should be top of your list. It's exactly what you said. They've bitten off more than they can chew there. And that's when they're both at home. Which they aren't always. Just now the chap was left alone there for a few days. It's far too much for one man to run. Especially a bloody amateur. And they've got too many trees. You can't make money growing trees.'

'Grange Farm sounds like a good prospect,' Reacher said. 'But we heard that someone else is snooping around there too. He's been seen, recently. On the property. A rival, maybe.'

'Really?' Kemp said, excited, conflict in the offing. Then his face fell, deflated. 'No, I know who you mean. That's not a bloody rival. That's the woman's brother. He's moved in with them.'

'Are you sure about that? Because it makes a difference to us, how many people we have to relocate.'

Kemp nodded. 'The chap came in here and introduced himself. Said he was back from somewhere or other and his wandering days were over. He was posting a packet to America. Airmail. We don't get much of that here. We had quite a nice chat.'

'So you're sure he's going to be a long-term resident? Because it makes a difference.'

'That's what he said.'

Pauling asked, 'What did he post to America?'

'He didn't tell me what it was. It was going to a hotel in New York. Addressed to a room, not a person, which I thought was strange.'

Reacher asked, 'Did you guess what it was?'

Dave Kemp, the farmer in the bar had said. *Nosy bugger.*

'It felt like a thin book,' Kemp said. 'Not many pages. A rubber band around it. Maybe he had borrowed it. Not that I squeezed it or anything.'

'Didn't he fill out a customs declaration?'

'We put it down as printed papers. Don't need a form for that.'

'Thanks, Mr Kemp,' Reacher said. 'You've been very helpful.'

'What about the fee?'

'If we buy the farm, you'll get it,' Reacher said. *If we buy the farm*, he thought. *Unfortunate turn of phrase*. He felt suddenly cold.

Dave Kemp had no take-out coffee so they bought Coke and candy bars and stopped to eat them on the side of the road a mile west where they could watch the front of the farmhouse. The place was still quiet. No lights, the same thin trickle of smoke catching the wind and dispersing sideways.

Reacher said, 'Why did you ask about the air-mail to the States?'

393

'An old habit,' Pauling said. 'Ask about every-thing, especially when you're not sure about what's important and what isn't. And it was kind of weird. Taylor just got out, and the first thing he does is mail something back? What could it have been?'

'Maybe something for his partner,' Reacher said. 'Maybe he's still in the city.'

'We should have gotten the address. But we did pretty well, overall. You were very plausible. It fit very well with last night. All that false bonhomie in the bar? Assuming Kemp spreads the word Taylor's going to put you down as a conman looking to make a fast buck buying farms for fifty cents on the dollar.'

'I can lie with the best of them,' Reacher said. 'Sadly.'

Then he shut up fast because he caught a glimpse of movement a half-mile away. The farm-house door was opening. There was morning mist and the sun was on the other side of the house and the distance was at the outer limit of visibility but he made out four figures emerging into the light. Two big, one slightly smaller, one very small. Probably two men, a woman, and a little child. Possibly a girl.

'They're up,' he said.

Pauling said, 'I see them, but only just. Four people. The bird scarer probably woke them. Louder than a rooster. It's the Jackson family and Taylor, right? Mommy, daddy, Melody, and her loving uncle.'

'Must be.'

They all had things on their shoulders. Long

straight poles. Comfortable for the adults, way too big for the girl.

'What are they doing?' Pauling asked.

'Those are hoes,' Reacher said. 'They're going out to the fields.'

'To dig weeds?'

'Organic farming. They can't use herbicides.'

The tiny figures grouped together and moved north, away from the road. They dwindled to nothingness, just faint remote blurs in the mist that were more ghostly illusion than reality.

'He's staying,' Pauling said. 'Isn't he? He must be staying. You don't go out to hoe weeds for your sister if you're thinking about running.'

Reacher nodded. 'We've seen enough. The job is done. Let's get back to London and wait for Lane.'

SIXTY-TWO

They hit commuter traffic on the road to London. Lots of it. It seemed like for hundreds of miles England was one of two things: either London or a dormitory serving London. The city was like a gigantic sprawling magnet sucking inward. According to Reacher's atlas the M11 was just one of twenty or so radial arteries that fed the capital. He guessed they were all just as busy, all full of tiny flowing corpuscles that would get spat back out at the end of the day. *The daily grind*. He had never worked nine to five, never commuted. At times he felt profoundly grateful for that fact. This was one of them.

The stick shift was hard work in the congestion. Two hours into the ride they pulled off and got gas and he changed places with Pauling, even though he wasn't on the paperwork and wasn't insured to drive. It seemed like a minor transgression compared to what they were contemplating for later. He had driven in Britain before, years earlier, in a large British sedan owned by the US Army. But now the roads were busier. Much busier. It seemed to him like the whole island was packed to capacity. Until he thought back to Norfolk. That county was empty. The island was unevenly packed, he thought. That was the real problem. Either full or empty. No middle ground. Which was unusual for Brits, in his experience. Normally Brits fudged and muddled like champions. The middle ground was where they lived.

They came to the M25 beltway and decided that discretion was the better part of valour. Decided to hit it for a quarter-circle counter-clockwise and then head down to the West End on an easier route. But the M25 itself was pretty much a parking lot.

'How do people stand this every day?' Pauling said.

'Houston and LA are as bad,' Reacher said.

'But it kind of explains why the Jacksons escaped.'

'I guess it does.'

And the traffic moved on slowly, circulating like water around a bathtub drain, before yielding to the inexorable pull of the city.

They came in through St John's Wood, where the Abbey Road studios were, past Regent's Park, through Marylebone, past Baker Street, where Sherlock Holmes had lived, through Marble Arch again, and onto Park Lane. The Hilton hotel was at the south end, near the truly world-class automotive insanity that was Hyde Park Corner. They parked in a commercial garage underground at a quarter to eleven in the morning. Maybe an hour before Lane and his guys were due to check in.

'Want lunch?' Pauling said.

'Can't eat,' Reacher said. 'I'm too knotted up.'

'So you're human after all.'

'I feel like I'm delivering Taylor to an executioner.'

'He deserves to die.'

'I'd rather do it myself.'

'So make the offer.'

'Wouldn't be good enough. Lane wants the partner's name. I'm not up for torturing it out of the guy personally.'

'So walk away.'

'I can't. I want retribution for Kate and Jade and I want the money for Hobart. No other way of getting either. And we have a deal with your Pentagon buddy. He delivered, so now I have to deliver. But all things considered I think I'll skip lunch.'

Pauling asked, 'Where do you want me?'

'In the lobby. Watching. Then go get yourself a room somewhere else. Leave me a note at the Hilton's desk. Use the name Bayswater. I'll take Lane to Norfolk, Lane will deal with Taylor, I'll deal with Lane. Then I'll come back and get you, whenever. Then we'll go somewhere together. Bath, maybe. To the Roman spas. We'll try to get clean again.'

They walked past an automobile showroom that was displaying brand-new examples of the Mini Cooper they had been driving. They walked past discreet set-back entrances to blocks of mansion flats. They went up a short flight of concrete steps to the Park Lane Hilton's lobby. Pauling detoured to a distant group of armchairs and Reacher walked to the desk. He stood in line. Watched the clerks. They were busy with their phones and their computers. There were printers and Xerox machines behind them on credenzas. Above the Xerox machines was a brass plaque that said: *By statute some documents may not be photocopied. Like banknotes*, Reacher thought. They needed a law, because modern Xerox machines were just too good. Above the credenzas was a line of clocks set to world time, from Tokyo to Los Angeles. He checked New York's against the time in his head. Spot on. Then the person in front of him finished up. He moved to the head of the line.

'Edward Lane's party,' he said. 'Have they checked in yet?'

The clerk tapped his keyboard. 'Not yet, sir.'

'I'm waiting for them. When they get here, tell them I'm across the lobby.'

'Your name, sir?'

'Taylor,' Reacher said. He walked away, clear of the busiest areas, and found a quiet spot. He was going to be counting eight hundred thousand dollars in cash and he didn't want an audience. He dumped himself down in one of a group of four armchairs. He knew from long experience that nobody would try to join him. Nobody ever did. He radiated subliminal *stay away* signals and sane people obeyed them. Already a nearby family was watching him warily. Two kids and a mother, camped out in the next group of chairs, presumably off an early flight and waiting for their room to be ready. The mother looked tired and the kids looked fractious. She had unpacked half their stuff, trying to keep them amused. Toys, colouring books, battered teddy bears, a doll missing an arm, battery-driven video games. He could hear the mother's half-hearted suggestions of how to fill the time: *Why don't you do this? Why don't you do that? Why don't you draw a picture of something you're going to see?* Like therapy.

He turned away and watched the door. People came in, a constant stream. Some weary and travel-stained, some busy and bustling. Some with mountains of luggage, some with briefcases only. All kinds of nationalities. In the next group of chairs one kid threw a bear at the other kid's head. It missed and skidded across the tile and hit Reacher's foot. He leaned down and picked it up. All the stuffing was out of it. He tossed it back. Heard the mother suggesting some other pointless activity: *Why don't you do this?* He thought: *Why don't you shut the hell up and sit still like normal human beings?*

He looked back at the door and saw Perez walk in. Then Kowalski. Then Edward Lane himself, third in line. Then Gregory, and Groom, and Addison, and Burke. Roll-on bags, duffels, suit carriers. Jeans and sport coats, black nylon warm-up jackets, ball caps, sneakers. Some shades, some earphones trailing thin wires. Tired from the overnight flight. A little creased and crumpled. But awake and alert and aware. They looked exactly like what they were: a group of Special Forces soldiers trying to travel incognito.

He watched them line up at the desk. Watched

them wait. Watched them shuffle up one place at a time. Watched them check in. Watched the clerk give Lane the message. Saw Lane turn around, searching. Lane's gaze moved over everybody in the lobby. Over Pauling, without stopping. Over the fractious family. Onto Reacher's own face. It stopped there. Lane nodded. Reacher nodded back. Gregory took a stack of key cards from the clerk and all seven men hoisted their luggage again and started through the lobby. They eased their way through the crowds shoulders first and stopped in a group outside the ring of armchairs. Lane dropped one bag and kept hold of another and sat down opposite Reacher. Gregory sat down too and Carter Groom took the last chair. Kowalski and Perez and Addison and Burke were left standing, making a perimeter, with Burke and Perez facing outward. Awake and alert and aware, thorough and cautious.

'Show me the money,' Reacher said.

'Tell me where Taylor is,' Lane said.

'You first.'

'Do you know where he is?'

Reacher nodded. 'I know where he is. I made visual contact twice. Last night, and then again this morning. Just a few hours ago.'

'You're good.'

'I know.'

'So tell me where he is.'

'Show me the money first.'

Lane said nothing. In the silence Reacher heard the harassed mother say: *Draw a picture of Buckingham Palace*. He said, 'You called a bunch

401

of London private eyes. Behind my back. You tried to get ahead of me.'

Lane said, 'A man's entitled to save himself an unnecessary expense.'

'Did you get ahead of me?'

'No.'

'Therefore the expense isn't unnecessary.'

'I guess not.'

'So show me the money.'

'OK,' Lane said. 'I'll show you the money.' He slid the duffel off his knees and placed it on the floor and unzipped it. Reacher glanced right. Glanced left. Saw the kid about to throw the tattered bear again. Saw him catch the expression on Lane's face and saw him shrink back towards his mother. Reacher shuffled forward on his chair and leaned down. The duffel was full of money. One of the O-Town bales, newly opened, part depleted.

'No trouble on the flight?' he asked.

Lane said, 'It was X-rayed. Nobody got their panties in a wad. You'll get it home OK. Assuming you earn it first.'

Reacher pulled back the torn plastic and put a fingernail under one of the paper bands. It was tight. Therefore full. There were four equal stacks of twenty bricks each. Total of eighty bricks, an even number. A hundred hundreds in each brick. Eighty times a hundred times a hundred was eight hundred thousand.

So far, so good.

He lifted the edge of a bill and rubbed it between his finger and thumb. Glanced across the lobby to the brass sign at the Xerox station: *By*

statute some documents may not be photocopied.
But these hadn't been. They were real. He could
feel the engraving. He could smell the paper and
the ink. Unmistakable.

'OK,' he said, and sat back.

Lane leaned down and zipped the duffel. 'So
where is he?'

Reacher said, 'First we have to talk.'

'You better be kidding me.'

'There are civilians there. Innocent people.
Non-combatants. A family.'

'So?'

'So I can't have you charging in there like
maniacs. I can't allow collateral damage.'

'There won't be any.'

'I need to be sure of that.'

'You have my word.'

Reacher said, 'Your word ain't worth shit.'

'We won't be shooting,' Lane said. 'Let's be
clear on that. A bullet is too good for Taylor.
We'll go in and we'll get him and we'll bring
him out without harming a hair on his or anyone
else's head. Because that's the way I want it. I
want him all in one piece. I want him alive and
well and conscious and feeling everything. He'll
tell us about his partner and then he'll die, long,
slow, and hard. Over a week or two. So a gun-
fight is no good to me. Not because I care about
non-combatants, true. But because I don't want
any accidents with Taylor. I would hate to give it
to him easy. You can take my word on *that*.'

'OK,' Reacher said.

'So where is he?'

Reacher paused. Thought about Hobart, and

403

Birmingham, Alabama, and Nashville, Tennessee, and kindly white-haired doctors in lab coats holding artificial limbs.

'He's in Norfolk,' he said.

'Where's that?'

'It's a county, north and east of here. About a hundred and twenty miles.'

'Where in Norfolk?'

'A place called Grange Farm.'

'He's on a farm?'

'Flat country,' Reacher said. 'Like a pool table. With ditches. Easy to defend.'

'Nearest big city?'

'It's about thirty miles south and west of Norwich.'

'Nearest town?'

Reacher didn't reply.

'Nearest town?' Lane asked again.

Reacher glanced back at the reception desk. *By statute some documents may not be photocopied.* He watched a Xerox machine at work, a ghostly stripe of green light cycling horizontally back and forth beneath a lid. He glanced at the harassed mother and heard her voice in his head: *Why don't you draw a picture of something you're going to see?* He looked at the kid's doll, missing an arm. Heard Dave Kemp's voice, in the country store: *It felt like a thin book. Not many pages. A rubber band around it.* Recalled the tiny imperceptible impact of the kid's tattered bear skidding on the tile and landing against his shoe.

Lane said, 'Reacher?'

Reacher heard Lauren Pauling's voice in his mind: *A little is sometimes all you need. Going*

404

*out, they don't care as much as when you're com-
ing in.*

Lane said, 'Reacher? Hello? What's the nearest town?'

Reacher dragged his focus back from the middle distance, slowly, carefully, painfully, and he looked directly into Lane's eyes. He said, 'The nearest town is called Fenchurch St Mary. I'll show you exactly where it is. Be ready to leave in one hour. I'll come back for you.'

Then he stood up and concentrated hard on walking infinitely slowly across the lobby floor. One foot in front of the other. Left, then right. He caught Pauling's eye. Walked out the door. Down the concrete steps. He made it to the sidewalk.

Then he ran like hell for the parking garage.

SIXTY-THREE

Reacher had parked the car, so he still had the keys. He blipped the door from thirty feet away and wrenched it open and threw himself inside. Jammed the key in the ignition and started the motor and shoved the stick in reverse. Stamped on the gas and hurled the tiny car out of the parking space and braked hard and spun the wheel and took off again forward with the front tyres howling and smoking. He threw a ten-pound note at the barrier guy and didn't wait for the change. Just hit the gas as soon as the pole was raised forty-five degrees. He blasted up the ramp and shot straight across two lanes of oncoming traffic and jammed to a stop on the opposite kerb because he saw Pauling hurrying towards him. He threw open her door and she slid inside and he took off again and he was twenty yards down the road before she got the door closed behind her.

'North,' he said. 'Which way is north?'

'North? North is behind us,' she said. 'Go around the traffic circle.'

Hyde Park Corner. He blew through two red lights and swerved the car like a dodgem from one lane to another. Came all the way around and back onto Park Lane in the other direction doing more than sixty miles an hour. Practically on two wheels.

'Where now?' he said.

'What the hell is going on?'

'Just get me out of town.'

'I don't know how.'

'Use the atlas. There's a city plan.'

Reacher dodged buses and taxis. Pauling turned pages frantically.

'Go straight,' she said.

'Is that north?'

'It'll get us there.'

They made it through Marble Arch with the engine screaming. They got green lights all the way past the Marylebone Road. They made it into Maida Vale. Then Reacher slowed a little. Breathed out for what felt like the first time in half an hour.

'Where next?'

'Reacher, what happened?'

'Just give me directions.'

'Make a right onto St John's Wood Road,' Pauling said. 'That will take us back to Regent's Park. Then make a left and go out the same way we came in. And please tell me exactly what the hell is going on.'

'I made a mistake,' Reacher said. 'Remember I told you I couldn't shake the feeling I was making a bad mistake? Well, I was wrong. It wasn't a bad mistake. It was a catastrophic mistake. It was the biggest single mistake ever made in the history of the cosmos.'

'What mistake?'

'Tell me about the photographs in your apartment.'

'What about them?'

'Nieces and nephews, right?'

'Lots of them,' Pauling said.

'You know them well?'

'Well enough.'

'Spend time with them?'

'Plenty.'

'Tell me about their favourite toys.'

'Their toys? I don't really know about their toys. I can't keep up. X-boxes, video games, whatever. There's always something new.'

'Not the new stuff. Their old favourites. Tell me about their favourite old toys. What would they have run into a fire to save? When they were eight years old?'

'When they were eight years old? I guess a teddy bear or a doll. Something they'd had since they were tiny.'

'Exactly,' Reacher said. 'Something comforting and familiar. Something they loved. The kind of thing they would want to take on a journey. Like the family next to me in the lobby just now. The mother got them all out of the suitcase to quiet them down.'

'So?'

'What did those things look like?'

'Like bears and dolls, I guess.'

'No, later. When the kids were eight years old.'

'When they were eight? They'd had them forever by then. They looked like crap.'

Reacher nodded at the wheel. 'The bears all

worn, with the stuffing out? The dolls all chipped, with the arms off?'

'Yes, like that. All kids have toys like that.'

'Jade didn't. That's precisely what was missing from her room. There were new bears and new dolls. Recent things she hadn't taken to. But there were no old favourites there.'

'What are you saying?'

'I'm saying that if Jade had been kidnapped on the way to Bloomingdale's on a normal everyday morning I would have found all her favourite old toys still in her room afterwards. But I didn't.'

'But what does that mean?'

'It means Jade knew she was leaving. It means she packed.'

Reacher made the left at Regent's Park and headed north, towards the M1, which would carry them all the way back to the M25 beltway. After the turn he drove on a little more sedately. He didn't want to get arrested by any English traffic cops. He didn't have time for that. He figured he was right then about two hours ahead of Edward Lane. It would take an hour for Lane to realize he had been ditched, and then it would take at least another hour for him to get hold of a car and organize a pursuit. So, two hours. Reacher would have liked more, but he figured two hours might be enough.

Might be.

Pauling said, 'Jade packed?'

'Kate packed too,' Reacher said.

'What did Kate pack?'

'Just one thing. But her most precious thing. Her best memory. The photograph with her daughter. From the bedroom. One of the most beautiful photographs I've ever seen.'

Pauling paused a beat.

'But you saw it,' she said. 'She didn't take it.'

Reacher shook his head. 'I saw a photocopy. From Staples, colour digital, laser, two bucks a sheet. Brought home and slipped into the frame. It was very good, but not quite good enough. A little vivid in the colours, a little plastic in the contours.'

'But who packs for a kidnap? I mean, who the hell gets the chance?'

'They weren't kidnapped,' Reacher said. 'That's the thing. They were rescued. They were liberated. They were set free. They're alive somewhere. Alive and well and happy. A little tense, maybe. But free as birds.'

They drove on, slow and steady, through the northern reaches of London, through Swiss Cottage and up the Finchley Road towards Hendon.

'Kate believed Dee Marie,' Reacher said. 'That's what happened. Out there in the Hamptons. Dee Marie told her about Anne, and warned her, and Kate believed her. Like Patti Joseph said, there was something about the story and something about her husband that made Kate believe. Maybe she was already feeling the same kinds of things that Anne had felt five years before. Maybe she was already planning to go down the same road.'

Pauling said, 'You know what this means?'

'Of course I do.'

'Taylor helped them.'

'Of course he did.'

'He rescued them, and he hid them, and he sheltered them, and he risked his life for them. He's the good guy, not the bad guy.'

Reacher nodded. 'And I just told Lane where he is.'

They made it through Hendon and negotiated their last London traffic circle and joined the M1 motorway at its southern tip. Reacher hit the gas and forced the little Mini up to ninety-five miles an hour.

Pauling said, 'What about the money?'

'Alimony,' Reacher said. 'It was the only way Kate was ever going to get any. We thought it was half of the Burkina Faso payment, and it was, but in Kate's eyes it was also half of their community property. Half of Lane's capital. She was entitled to it. She probably put money in, way back. That's what Lane seems to want his wives for. Apart from their trophy status.'

'Hell of a plan,' Pauling said.

'They probably thought it was the only way. And they were probably right.'

'But they made mistakes.'

'They sure did. If you really want to disappear, you take nothing with you. Absolutely nothing at all. It's fatal.'

'Who helped Taylor?'

'Nobody.'

'He had an American partner. On the phone.'

411

'That was Kate herself. You were half right, days ago. It was a woman using that machine. But not Dee Marie. It was Kate herself. It must have been. They were a team. They collaborated. She did all the talking, because Taylor couldn't. Not easy for her. Every time Lane wanted to hear her voice for a proof of life she had to pull the machine off the mouthpiece and then put it back on again.'

'Did you really tell Lane where Taylor is?'

'As good as. I didn't say Bishops Pargeter. I stopped myself just in time. I said Fenchurch St Mary instead. But that's close. And I had already said Norfolk. I had already said thirty miles from Norwich. And I had already said Grange Farm. He'll be able to work it out. Two minutes, with the right map.'

'He's way behind us.'

'At least two hours.'

Pauling was quiet for a second.

Reacher said, 'What?'

'He's two hours behind us right now. But he won't always be. We're taking the long way around because we don't know the English roads.'

'Neither does he.'

'But Gregory does.'

Reacher drove seven exits on the M1, acutely aware that the road was taking him west of north, not east of north. Then he drove six clockwise exits on the M25 beltway before finding the M11. All completely dead time. If Gregory drove Lane straight through the centre of London directly to the southern tip of the M11 he would cut the two-hour deficit by an exactly corresponding amount.

Pauling said, 'We should stop and call ahead. You know the number.'

'That's a big gamble,' Reacher said. 'At highway speeds it costs time to slow down, turn off, park, find a phone that works, call, and get back on the road. A lot of time, at British speeds. And suppose there's no answer? Suppose they're still out there hoeing the weeds? We'd end up doing it again and again.'

'We have to try to warn them. There's the sister to think about. And Melody.'

'Susan and Melody are perfectly safe.'

'How can you say that?'

'Ask yourself where Kate and Jade are.'

'I have no idea where they are.'

'You do,' Reacher said. 'You know exactly where they are. You saw them this morning.'

SIXTY-FOUR

They turned off the motorway south of
Cambridge and set out cross-country towards
Norwich. This time the road was familiar, but that
didn't make it any faster. Forward motion, without any visible result. A big sky, whipped clean by
wind.

'Think about the dynamic here,' Reacher said.
'Why would Kate ask Taylor for help? How could
she ask any of them for help? They're all insanely
loyal to Lane. Did Knight help Anne? Kate had
just heard that story. Why would she walk up cold
to another of Lane's killers and say, hey, want to
help me get out of here? Want to double-cross
your boss? Help me steal his money?'

Pauling said, 'They already had a thing going.'

Reacher nodded at the wheel. 'That's the only
way to explain it. They had already started an
affair. Maybe long ago.'

'The CO's wife? Hobart said no fighting man
would do that.'

'He said no American fighting man would
do that. Maybe the British do things differently.
And there were signs. Carter Groom is about as

414

emotional as a fence post but he said that Kate liked Taylor and that Taylor got on well with the kid.'

'Dee Marie showing up must have acted like a kind of tipping point.'

Reacher nodded again. 'Kate and Taylor made a plan and put it in action. But first they explained it to Jade. Maybe they thought it would be too much of a sudden trauma not to. They swore her to secrecy, as much as they could with an eight-year-old. And the kid did pretty well.'

'What did they tell her?'

'That she already had one replacement daddy, now she was getting another. That she already lived in one new place, now she was moving on.'

'Big secret for a kid to keep.'

'She didn't exactly keep it,' Reacher said. 'She was worried about it. She straightened it out in her head by drawing it. Maybe it was an old habit. Maybe mothers always say draw a picture of something you're going to see.'

'What picture?'

'There were four in her room. On her desk. Kate didn't sanitize well enough. Or maybe she just mistook them for regular clutter. There was a big grey building with trees in front. At first I thought it was the Dakota from Central Park. Now I think it was the Grange Farm farmhouse. They must have shown her photographs, to prepare her. She got the trees just right. Thin straight trunks, round crowns. To withstand the wind. Like light green lollipops on brown sticks. And then there was a picture of a family group. I

415

thought the guy was Lane, obviously. But there was something weird about his mouth. Like half his teeth had been punched out. So it wasn't Lane. It was Taylor, clearly. The dentistry. Jade was probably fascinated by it. She drew her new family. Taylor, Kate, and her. To internalize the idea.'

'And you think Taylor brought them here to England?'

'I think Kate wanted him to. Maybe even begged him to. They needed a safe haven. Somewhere very distant. Out of Lane's reach. And they were having an affair. They didn't want to be apart. So if Taylor's here, then Kate's here too. Jade did a picture of three people in an airplane. That was the journey she was going to take. Then she did one of two families together. Like double vision. I had no idea what it meant. But now my guess is that was Jackson and Taylor, and Susan and Kate, and Melody and herself. Her new situation. Her new extended family. Happy ever after on Grange Farm.'

'Doesn't work,' Pauling said. 'Their passports were still in the drawer.'

'That was crude,' Reacher said. 'Wasn't it? You must have searched a thousand desks. Did you ever see passports all alone in a drawer? Kind of ostentatiously displayed like that? I never did. They were always buried under other junk. Leaving them on show like that was a message. It said, hey, we're still in the country. Which meant actually they weren't.'

'How do you get out without a passport?'

'You don't. But you once said they don't look

as closely on the way out. You said sometimes a little resemblance is all you need.'

Pauling paused a beat. 'Someone else's passport?'

'Who do we know that fits the bill? A woman in her thirties and an eight-year-old girl?'

Pauling said, 'Susan and Melody.'

'Dave Kemp told us Jackson had been alone at the farm,' Reacher said. 'That was because Susan and Melody had flown to the States. They got all the correct entry stamps. Then they gave their passports to Kate and Jade. Maybe in Taylor's apartment. Maybe over dinner. Like a little ceremony. Then Taylor booked on British Airways. He was sitting next to a British woman on the plane. We know that for sure. A buck gets ten she's on the passenger manifest as Mrs Susan Jackson. And another buck gets ten that next to her was a little British kid called Ms Melody Jackson. But they were really Kate and Jade Lane.'

'But that leaves Susan and Melody stuck in the States.'

'Temporarily,' Reacher said. 'What did Taylor mail back?'

'A thin book. Not many pages. With a rubber band around it.'

'Who puts a rubber band around a thin book? It was actually two *very* thin books. Two passports, bundled together. Mailed to Susan's New York City hotel room, where she and Melody are right now sitting and waiting to get them back.'

'But the stamps will be out of sequence now.

When they leave they'll be exiting without having entered.'

Reacher nodded. 'It's an irregularity. But what are the people at JFK going to do about it? Deport them? That's exactly what they want. So they'll get home OK.'

'Sisters,' Pauling said. 'This whole thing has been about the loyalty of sisters. Patti Joseph, Dee Marie Graziano, Susan Jackson.'

Reacher drove on. Said nothing.

'Unbelievable,' Pauling said. 'We saw Kate and Jade this morning.'

'Setting out with their hoes,' Reacher said. 'Starting out on their new lives.'

Then he accelerated a little, because the road was widening and straightening for the bypass around a town called Thetford.

John Gregory was hitting the gas, too. He was at the wheel of a rented dark green seven-seat Toyota Land Cruiser sports utility vehicle. Edward Lane was next to him in the front passenger seat. Kowalski and Addison and Carter Groom were shoulder to shoulder on the rear bench. Burke and Perez were on the jump seats way in back. They were joining the M11 at its southern tip, having blasted straight through central London to the northeast corner of the inner city.

418

SIXTY-FIVE

This time in full daylight Reacher saw the sign to *B'sh'ps P'ter* a hundred yards away and slowed well in advance and made the turn like he had been driving the back roads of Norfolk all his life. It was close to two o'clock in the afternoon. The sun was high and the wind was dropping. Blue skies, small white clouds, green fields. A perfect English late-summer day. Almost.

Pauling said, 'What are you going to tell them?'

'That I'm sorry,' Reacher said. 'I think that might be the best place to start.'

'Then what?'

'Then I'll probably say it again.'

'They can't stay there.'

'It's a farm. Someone's got to stay there.'

'Are you volunteering?'

'I might have to.'

'Do you know anything about farming?'

'Only what I've seen in the movies. Usually they get locusts. Or a fire.'

'Not here. Floods, maybe.'

'And idiots like me.'

'Don't beat yourself up. They faked a kidnap.

Don't blame yourself for taking it seriously.'

'I should have seen it,' Reacher said. 'It was weird from the start.'

They passed the Bishop's Arms. The pub. The end of the lunch hour. Five cars in the lot. The Grange Farm Land Rover was not one of them. They drove on, roughly east, and in the distance they saw the Bishops Pargeter church tower, grey, square, and squat. Only forty-some feet tall, but it dominated the flat landscape like the Empire State Building. They drove on. They passed the ditch that marked Grange Farm's western boundary. Heard the bird scarer again, a loud booming shotgun blast.

'I hate that thing,' Pauling said.

Reacher said, 'You might end up loving it. Camouflage like that could be our best friend.'

'Could be Taylor's best friend too. In about sixty seconds from now. He's going to think he's under attack.'

Reacher nodded.

'Take a deep breath,' he said.

He slowed the car well before the small flat bridge. Turned in wide and deliberate. Left it in second gear. Small vehicle, low speed. Unthreatening. He hoped.

The driveway was long and it looped through two curves. Around unseen softness in the dirt, maybe. The beaten earth was muddy and less even than it had looked from a distance. The tiny car rocked and bounced. The farmhouse's gable wall was blank. No windows. The smoke from the chimney was thicker now and straighter. Less wind. Reacher opened his window and heard nothing at all except the noise of his engine and the slow rolling crunch of his tyres on gravel and small stones.

'Where is everybody?' Pauling said. 'Still out hoeing?'

'You can't hoe for seven hours straight,' Reacher said. 'You'd break your back.'

The driveway split thirty yards in front of the house. A fork in the road. West, the formal approach to the front door. East, a shabbier track towards the spot where the Land Rover had been parked, and the barns beyond. Reacher went east. The Land Rover wasn't there any more. All the barn doors were closed. The whole place was quiet. Nothing was moving.

Reacher braked gently and backed up. Took the wider path west. There was a gravel circle with a stunted ash tree planted at its centre. Around the tree was a circular wooden bench way too big for the thin trunk. Either the tree was a replacement or the carpenter had been thinking a hundred years ahead. Reacher drove around the circle clockwise, the British way. Stopped ten feet from the front door. It was closed. Nothing was moving anywhere, except the column of slow smoke rising from the chimney.

'What now?' Pauling asked.

'We knock,' Reacher said. 'We move slow and we keep our hands visible.'

'You think they're watching us?'

'Someone is. For sure. I can feel it.'

He killed the motor and sat for a moment. Then he opened his door. Unwound his huge frame slow and easy and stood still next to the car with his hands held away from his sides. Pauling did the same thing six feet away. Then they walked together to the front door. It was a large slab of ancient oak, as black as coal. There were iron bands and hinges, newly painted over pits of old rust and corrosion. There was a twisted ring hinged in the mouth of a lion and positioned to strike down on a nail head as big as an apple. Reacher used it, twice, putting heavy thumps into the oak slab. It resonated like a bass drum.

It brought no response.

'Hello?' Reacher called.

No response.

He called, 'Taylor? Graham Taylor?'

No response.

'Taylor? Are you there?'

No answer.

He tried the knocker again, twice more.

Still no response.

No sound at all.

Except for the shuffle of a tiny foot, thirty feet away. The backward scrape of a thin sole on a stone. Reacher turned fast and glanced to his left. Saw a small bare knee pull back around the far corner of the house. Back into hiding.

'I saw you,' Reacher called.

No reply.

'Come on out now,' he called. 'It's OK.'

No response.

'Look at our car,' Reacher called. 'Cutest thing you ever saw.'

Nothing happened.

'It's red,' Reacher called. 'Like a fire engine.'

No response.

'There's a lady here with me,' Reacher called. 'She's cute too.'

He stood still next to Pauling and a long moment later he saw a small dark head peer out from around the corner. A small face, pale skin, big green eyes. A serious mouth. A little girl, about eight years old.

'Hello,' Pauling called. 'What's your name?'

'Melody Jackson,' Jade Lane said.

SIXTY-SIX

The kid was instantly recognizable from the imperfect Xerox Reacher had seen on the desk in the Dakota bedroom. She was about a year older than she had been in the picture but she had the same long dark hair, slightly wavy, as fine as silk, the same green eyes, and the same porcelain skin. It had been a striking photograph, but the reality was way better. Jade Lane was a truly beautiful child.

'My name is Lauren,' Pauling said. 'This man is called Reacher.'

Jade nodded her head. Grave and serious. She said nothing. Didn't come closer. She was wearing a summer dress, sleeveless, green seersucker stripes. Maybe from Bloomingdale's on Lexington Avenue. Maybe one of her favourite garments. Maybe part of her hasty and unwise packing. She had white socks on, and thin summer sandals. They were dusty.

Pauling said, 'We're here to talk to the grown-ups. Do you know where they are?'

Thirty feet away Jade nodded her head again. Said nothing.

Pauling asked, 'Where are they?'

A voice thirty feet away in the other direction said, 'One of them is right here, lady,' and Kate Lane stepped out from around the other corner of the house. She was pretty much unchanged from her photograph, too. Dark hair, green eyes, high cheekbones, a bud of a mouth. Extremely, impossibly beautiful. Maybe a little more tired than she had been in the photographer's studio. Maybe a little more stressed. But definitively the same woman. Outside of what the portrait had shown she was maybe five feet nine inches tall, not much more than a hundred and fifteen pounds, slim and willowy. Exactly what an ex-model should look like, Reacher figured. She was wearing a man's flannel shirt, big and clearly borrowed. She looked great in it. But then, she would have looked great in a garbage bag with holes torn for her arms and legs and head.

'I'm Susan Jackson,' she said.

Reacher shook his head. 'You're not, but I'm very glad to meet you anyway. And Jade, too. You'll never know how glad I am.'

'I'm Susan Jackson,' she said again. 'That's Melody.'

'We don't have time for that, Kate. And your accent isn't real convincing anyway.'

'Who are you?'

'My name is Reacher.'

'What do you want?'

'Where's Taylor?'

'Who?'

Reacher glanced back at Jade and then took a

step towards Kate. 'Can we talk? Maybe a little ways down the track?'

'Why?'

'For privacy.'

'What happened?'

'I don't want to upset your daughter.'

'She knows what's going on.'

'OK,' Reacher said. 'We're here to warn you.'

'About what?'

'Edward Lane is an hour behind us. Maybe less.'

'Edward is here?' Kate said. For the first time, real fear in her face. 'Edward is here in England? Already?'

Reacher nodded. 'Heading this way.'

'Who are you?'

'He paid me to find Taylor.'

'So why warn us?'

'Because I just figured out it wasn't for real.'

Kate said nothing.

'Where's Taylor?' Reacher asked again.

'He's out,' Kate said. 'With Tony.'

'Anthony Jackson? The brother-in-law?'

Kate nodded. 'This is his farm.'

'Where did they go?'

'To Norwich. For a part for the backhoe. They said we need to dredge some ditches.'

'When did they leave?'

'About two hours ago.'

Reacher nodded again. Norwich. The big city. Thirty miles there, thirty miles back. About a two-hour trip. He glanced south at the road. Nothing moving on it.

'Let's all go inside,' he said.

426

'I don't even know who you are.'

'You do,' Reacher said. 'Right now I'm your best friend.'

Kate stared at Pauling for a moment and seemed reassured by the presence of another woman. She blinked once and opened the front door. Led them all in. The farmhouse itself was dark and cold inside. It had low beamed ceilings and irregular stone floors. Thick walls and flowered wallpaper and small leaded windows. The kitchen was the hub of the home. That was clear. It was a large rectangular room. There were bright copper pans hanging from hooks, and sofas and armchairs and a fireplace big enough to live in and a huge old-fashioned range. There was a massive oak dining table with twelve chairs around it and a separate pine desk with a phone and stacks of papers and envelopes and jars of pens and pencils and postage stamps and rubber bands. All the furniture was old and worn and comfortable and smelled of dogs, even though there were no dogs in the house. They had belonged to the previous owners, maybe. Maybe the furniture had been included in the sale. Maybe there had been bankruptcy problems.

Reacher said, 'I think you should get out, Kate. Right now. You and Jade. Until we see what happens.'

'How?' Kate asked. 'The truck isn't here.'

'Take our car.'

'I've never driven here before. I've never even been here before.'

Pauling said, 'I'll drive you.'

'Where to?'

'Anywhere you want to go. Until we see what happens.'

'Is he really here already?'

Pauling nodded. 'He left London at least an hour ago.'

'Does he know?'

'That it was all a sham? Not yet.'

'OK,' Kate said. 'Take us somewhere. Anywhere. Now. Please.'

She stood up and grabbed Jade's hand. No purse, no coat. She was ready to go, right there and then. No pause, no hesitation. Just panic. Reacher tossed Pauling the Mini's keys and followed them all outside again. Jade climbed through to the tiny car's rear bench and Kate got in next to Pauling. Pauling adjusted the seat and the mirror and clipped her belt and started the engine.

'Wait,' Reacher said.

On the road a mile to the west he could see a dark green shape moving fast behind a stand of trees. Green paint. Glinting in the watery sun. Clean and polished and shiny, not filthy like the farm truck.

A mile away. Ninety seconds. No time.

'Everybody back in the house,' he said. 'Right now.'

SIXTY-SEVEN

Kate and Jade and Pauling ran straight upstairs and Reacher headed for the southeast corner of the house. Flattened himself against the wall and crept around to where he could get a look at the bridge over the ditch. He got there just in time to see a truck turn in. It was an old-style Land Rover Defender, bluff and square, an appliance more than a car, mud-and-snow tyres, a brown canvas back. Two guys in it, rocking and bouncing behind the sparkling windshield. One of them was the vague shape Reacher had seen early that morning. Tony Jackson. The farmer. The other was Taylor. The truck was the Grange Farm Land Rover, newly cleaned and polished. Unrecognizable from the night before. Clearly the Norwich itinerary had included a stop at the car wash as well as the backhoe dealership.

Reacher ducked into the kitchen and shouted an all clear up the stairs. Then he went back outside to wait. The Land Rover pulled left and right through the driveway curves and paused a second as Jackson and Taylor took a long hard look at the Mini from fifty yards away.

Then it speeded up again and skidded to a halt in its parking spot between the back of the house and the barns. The doors opened and Jackson and Taylor climbed out. Reacher stayed where he was and Jackson walked right up to him and said, 'You're trespassing. Dave Kemp told me what you want. You talked to him this morning. In the shop? And the answer is no. I'm not selling.'

'I'm not buying,' Reacher said.

'So why are you here?'

Jackson was a lean and compact guy, not unlike Taylor himself. Same kind of height, same kind of weight. Same kind of generic English features. Similar accent. Better teeth, and lighter hair worn a little longer. But overall they could have been brothers, not just brothers-in-law.

Reacher said, 'I'm here to see Taylor.'

Taylor stepped up and said, 'What for?'

'To apologize to you,' Reacher said. 'And to warn you.'

Taylor paused a beat. Blinked once. Then his eyes flicked left, flicked right, full of intelligence and calculation.

'Lane?' he asked.

'He's less than an hour away.'

'OK,' Taylor said. He sounded calm. Composed. Not surprised. But Reacher didn't expect him to be surprised. Surprise was for amateurs. And Taylor was a professional. A Special Forces veteran, and a smart and a capable one. Precious seconds spent being surprised were precious seconds wasted, and Taylor was spending the precious seconds exactly like he had been trained to: thinking, planning, revising tactics, reviewing options.

'My fault,' Reacher said. 'I'm sorry.'

'I saw you on Sixth Avenue,' Taylor said. 'When I was getting in the Jaguar. Didn't think much of it, but I saw you again last night. In the pub. So then I knew. I thought you'd be heading up to your room to call Lane. But it looks like he mobilized himself faster than I thought he would.'

'He was already en route.'

'Good of you to stop by and let me know.'

'Least I could do. In the circumstances.'

'Does he have this precise location?'

'More or less. I said Grange Farm. I stopped myself saying Bishops Pargeter. I said Fenchurch St Mary instead.'

'He'll find us in the phone book. There's no Grange Farm in Fenchurch. We're the nearest.'

'I'm sorry,' Reacher said again.

'When did you figure it all out?'

'Just a little bit too late.'

'What tipped you off?'

'Toys. Jade packed her best toys.'

'Did you meet her yet?'

'Five minutes ago.'

Taylor smiled. Bad teeth, but a lot of warmth there. 'She's a great kid, isn't she?'

'Seems to be.'

'What are you, a private cop?'

'I was a US Army MP.'

'What's your name?'

'Reacher.'

'How much did Lane pay you?'

'A million bucks.'

Taylor smiled again. 'I'm flattered. And you're good. But it was always only a matter of time. The longer nobody found my body, the more people would get to thinking. But this is a little quicker than I thought it would be. I thought I might have a couple of weeks.'

'You've got about sixty minutes.'

They gathered in the farmhouse kitchen for a council of war, all six of them, Taylor and Kate and Jade, and Jackson, and Pauling and Reacher. Jade was neither specifically included nor excluded. She just sat at the table and drew, crayons and butcher paper, the same bold colourful strokes Reacher had seen in her bedroom in the Dakota, and listened to the grown-ups talk. First thing Taylor said was, 'Let's light the fire again. It's cold in here. And let's have a cup of tea.'

Pauling asked, 'Do we have time for that?'

'The British army,' Reacher said. 'They always have time for a cup of tea.'

There was a wicker basket of kindling sticks near the hearth. Taylor stacked a bunch of them over a pyramid of crumpled newspaper and struck a match. When the flame had taken he added bigger logs. Meanwhile Jackson was at the stove, heating a kettle of water and stuffing tea bags into a pot. He didn't seem very worried, either. Just calm and competent and unhurried.

'What were you, back in the day?' Reacher asked him.

'First Para,' Jackson replied.

Reacher nodded. The First Parachute Regiment.

The British equivalent of the US Army Rangers, roughly. Air-mobile tough guys, not quite SAS, but close. Most SAS freshmen were First Para graduates.

'Lane's got six guys with him,' Reacher said.

'The A-team?' Taylor asked. 'Used to be seven guys. Before I resigned.'

'Used to be nine guys,' Reacher said.

'Hobart and Knight,' Taylor said. 'Kate heard that story. From Hobart's sister.'

'Was that the trigger?'

'Partly. And partly something else.'

'What else?'

'Hobart isn't the only one. Not even close. He's the worst, maybe, from what his sister said, but there are others. Lane got a lot of people killed and wounded over the years.'

'I saw his Rolodex,' Reacher said.

'He doesn't do anything for them. Or their families.'

'Is that why you wanted the money?'

'The money is Kate's alimony. She's entitled to it. And how she spends it is up to her. But I'm sure she'll do the right thing.'

Tony Jackson poured the tea from the pot, hot and strong, into five chipped and unmatched mugs. Jade was working on a glass of apple juice.

'Do we have time for this?' Pauling asked again.

'Reacher?' Taylor said. 'Do we have time for this?'

'That depends,' Reacher said. 'On what exactly your aim is.'

'My aim is to live happily ever after.'

'OK,' Reacher said. 'This is England. If it was Kansas, I'd be worried. If it was Kansas, Dave Kemp's little store and a hundred others like it would be selling rifles and ammunition. But this isn't Kansas. And no way did Lane bring anything in with him on the plane. So if he shows up now, he's unarmed. He can't do anything more than pick rocks off the driveway and throw them at us. Walls this thick and windows this small, that isn't going to hurt us much.'

'He could burn us out,' Pauling said. 'Bottles filled with gasoline, flaming rags in them, or whatever.'

Reacher said nothing. Just glanced at Taylor. Taylor said, 'He wants to take me alive, Ms Pauling. I'm sure of that. Fire might be in his plan for me eventually, but he'd want to do it slow and controlled. Something quick and easy just wouldn't work for him.'

'So we're just going to sit here?'

'Like Reacher said, if he shows up now he's harmless.'

'This might be England, but there have to be weapons available somewhere.'

Taylor nodded. 'All over the place, as a matter of fact. Private armourers for the British mercenary crews, bent army quartermasters, gangs of regular bad boys. But none of them are in the Yellow Pages. It takes time to find them.'

'How much time?'

'Twelve hours minimum, I would guess, depending on your connections. So like your man said, if Lane shows up now he's harmless, and if he wants to lock and load first, he can't show up until at least tomorrow. Plus, he likes dawn raids. He always has. Zero-dark-thirty, that's what Delta taught him. Attack with the first rays of the sun.'

'Are you armed here?' Reacher asked.

'This is a farm,' Jackson answered. 'Farmers are always prepared for vermin control.'

Something in his voice. Some kind of lethal determination. Reacher looked between him and Taylor. *Same kind of height, same kind of weight, same kind of generic English features. Overall they could have been brothers. Sometimes a little resemblance is all you need.* He got up out of his chair and walked over and took a look at the phone on the pine desk. It was an old-fashioned black instrument. It had a cord and a rotary dial. No memories. No speed dials.

He turned back to Taylor.

'You wanted this,' he said.

'Did I?'

'You used the name Leroy Clarkson. To point the way to your apartment.'

Taylor said nothing.

'You could have stopped Jade from bringing her toys. You could have told Kate to leave the photograph behind. Your sister Susan could have brought Tony's passport over for you. She could have carried it in her purse. Then there would have been three Jacksons on the airplane manifest, not two Jacksons and a Taylor. Without your real name you couldn't have been followed back to England.'

Taylor said nothing.

435

'The phone in your apartment was new,' Reacher said. 'You didn't have it before, did you? You bought it so that you could leave Susan's number in it.'

'Why would I do that?' Taylor asked.

'Because you wanted Lane to find you here.'

Taylor said nothing.

'You talked to Dave Kemp in the village store,' Reacher said. 'You gave him all kinds of unnecessary details. And he's the biggest gossip in the county. Then you went and hung out in the pub with a bunch of nosy farmers. I'm sure you would have rather stayed home, in the circumstances. With your new family. But you couldn't do that. Because you wanted to lay a clear trail. Because you knew Lane would hire someone like me. And you wanted to help someone like me find you. Because you wanted to bring Lane here for a showdown.'

Silence in the room.

Reacher said, 'You wanted to be on your home turf. And you figured this is an easy place to defend.'

More silence. Reacher glanced at Kate.

'You were upset,' he said. 'Not that Lane was coming, but that he was coming *now*. Already. Too soon.'

Kate said nothing. But Taylor nodded. 'Like I said before, he was a little faster than we expected. But yes, we wanted him to come.'

'Why?'

'You just said it. We wanted a showdown. Closure. Finality.'

'Why now?'

436

'I told you.'

'Reparations for the wounded aren't urgent. Not like this.'

Kate Lane looked up from her chair by the fire. 'I'm pregnant,' she said.

SIXTY-EIGHT

In the soft light of the flames from the hearth, Kate's simple and vulnerable beauty was emphasized to the point of heartbreak. She said, 'When Edward and I first started fighting he accused me of being unfaithful. Which wasn't actually true back then. But he was in a rage. He said if he ever caught me sleeping around he would show me how much it hurt him by doing something to Jade that would hurt me even more. He went into the kind of detail I can't repeat now. Not in front of her. But it was very frightening. It was so frightening that I persuaded myself not to take it seriously. But after hearing about Anne and Knight and Hobart I knew I had to take it seriously. By which time I really did have something to hide. So we ran. And here we are.'

'With Lane right behind you.'

'He deserves whatever he gets, Mr Reacher. He's truly a monster.'

Reacher turned to Jackson. 'You're not fixing the backhoe to dredge ditches, are you? It's not raining and the ditches look fine anyway. And

438

you wouldn't take time out to do something like that. Not right now. Not in these circumstances. You're fixing the backhoe to dig graves, aren't you?'

'At least one grave,' Taylor said. 'Maybe two or three, until the whole crew goes home and leaves us alone. You got a problem with that?'

We'll find Taylor, Reacher had said, on the plane. *Lane will take care of him, and then I'll take care of Lane.* Pauling had asked him, *What about the others?* Reacher had said: *If I think the crew will fall apart with Lane gone, then I'll leave the rest alone and let it. But if one of them wants to step up and take over, I'll do him too. And so on and so forth, until the crew really does fall apart.*

Pauling had said: *Brutal.*

Reacher had asked: *Compared to what?*

He looked straight at Taylor.

'No,' he answered. 'I guess I don't have a problem with that. Not really. No problem at all, in fact. I'm just not used to finding people on the same wavelength as me.'

'You keeping your million bucks?'

Reacher shook his head. 'I was going to give it to Hobart.'

'That's good,' Kate said. 'That frees up some of our money for the others.'

Taylor said, 'Ms. Pauling? What about you? Do you have a problem?'

Pauling said, 'I ought to. I ought to have a huge problem. Once upon a time I swore an oath to uphold the law.'

'But?'

439

'I can't get to Lane any other way. So no, I don't have a problem.'

'So we're in business,' Taylor said. 'Welcome to the party.'

After they finished their tea Jackson took Reacher into a small mudroom off the back of the kitchen and opened a double-door wall cupboard above a washing machine. In it were racked four Heckler & Koch G36 automatic rifles. The G36 was a very modern design that had shown up in service just before Reacher's military career had ended. Therefore he wasn't very familiar with it. It had a nineteen-inch barrel and an open folding stock and was basically fairly conventional apart from a huge superstructure that carried a bulky optical sight integrated into an oversized carrying handle. It was chambered for the standard 5.56mm NATO round and like most German weapons it looked very expensive and beautifully engineered.

Reacher asked, 'Where did you get these from?'

'I bought them,' Jackson said. 'From a bent quartermaster in Holland. Susan went over there and picked them up.'

'For this thing with Lane?'

Jackson nodded. 'It's been a heavy few weeks. Lots of planning.'

'Are they traceable?'

'The Dutch guy's paperwork shows they were destroyed in a training accident.'

'Got ammunition?'

Jackson moved across the room and opened

another cupboard, lower down. Behind a row of muddy Wellington boots Reacher could see the glint of black metal. A lot of it.

'Seventy magazines,' Jackson said. 'Two thousand one hundred rounds.'

'That should do the trick.'

'We can't use it. Not more than three or four rounds. Too noisy.'

'How close are the cops?'

'Not very. Norwich, I suppose, unless there happens to be a patrol car out. But people here have phones. Some of them even know how to use them.'

'You can turn the bird scarer off for a day.'

'Obviously. But I shouldn't really be using that either. An organic farm doesn't need a bird scarer. No pesticides means plenty of insects for the birds to eat. They don't go after the seed. Sooner or later people are going to realize that.'

'So the bird scarer is new too?'

Jackson nodded. 'Part of the planning. Set to start firing at dawn. That's when we expect Lane to come.'

'If I had a sister and a brother-in-law I'd want them to be like you and Susan.'

'I go a long way back with Taylor. We were in Sierra Leone together. I'd do anything for him.'

'I never went to Africa.'

'Lucky you. We were fighting a bunch of rebels called the West Side Boys. I saw what they did to people. So I know what Hobart went through. Burkina Faso wasn't far away.'

'You OK with all of this? You've got roots here, literally.'

'What's the alternative?'

'Take a vacation. All of you. I'll stay.'

Jackson shook his head. 'We'll be OK. One round might do it. The G36 is a pretty accurate piece.'

Jackson stayed in the mudroom and closed and locked both cupboards. Reacher stepped back into the kitchen and sat down next to Taylor.

'Tell me about Gregory,' he said.

'What about him?'

'Is he going to stand by Lane? Or you?'

'Lane, I think.'

'Even though you served together?'

'Lane bought him. When he was in uniform Gregory always wanted an officer's commission, but he never got it. It burned him up. And then Lane made him a kind of unofficial lieutenant. Status, at last. Meaningless bullshit, of course, but it's the thought that counts. So I think Gregory will stick with him. Plus he'll be offended that I didn't share my secret. He seemed to think that two Brits abroad should share everything.'

'Does he know this area?'

Taylor shook his head. 'He's a Londoner, like me.'

'What about the others? Will any of them turn?'

'Not Kowalski,' Taylor said. 'Not Perez. Turning would require some brain activity, and those two are room-temperature IQs at best. Probably not Addison, either. But Groom and Burke aren't dumb. If they see the ship is sinking they'll get off fast enough.'

'That's not the same thing as turning.'

'None of them is going to come over to our side. You can forget about that. The best we can hope for is neutrality from Groom and Burke. And I wouldn't bet the farm on that.'

'How good are they? All of them, as a whole?'

'They're about as good as me. Which is to say they're on a slippery slope. They used to be outstanding, and now they're well on the way to average. Plenty of experience and ability, but they don't train any more. And training is important. Back in the day, training was ninety-nine per cent of what we did.'

'Why did you join them?'

'The money,' Taylor said. 'That's why I joined them. Then I stayed with them because of Kate. I loved her from the first moment I saw her.'

'Did she love you back?'

'Eventually,' Taylor said.

'Not eventually,' Kate said, from her chair by the fire. 'Truth is it was really pretty quick. One day I asked him why he had never had his teeth fixed and he told me that he had never even thought about it. I like that kind of self-respect and self-confidence in a man.'

'You see anything wrong with my teeth?' Taylor asked.

'Plenty,' Reacher said. 'I'm surprised you can eat. Maybe that's why you're so small.'

Taylor said, 'I am what I am.'

Exactly one hour after they came in and lit the fire they drew lots for the first round of look-out duty. Jackson and Pauling pulled the short straws.

Jackson sat in the Land Rover at the back of the house and Pauling sat in the Mini at the front. That way each of them could cover a little more than one hundred and eighty degrees. Across the flat land they could see a mile or more. Ninety seconds' warning if Lane came in by road, a little more if he came in across the fields, which would be a slower approach.

Reasonable security.

As long as the daylight lasted.

SIXTY-NINE

The daylight lasted until a little after eight o'clock. By then Reacher was in the Land Rover and Kate Lane was in the Mini. The sky darkened in the east and reddened in the west. Twilight rolled in fast, and with it came an evening mist that looked picturesque but cut visibility to less than a hundred yards. The bird scarer fell silent. All afternoon and into the evening it had been firing at unpredictable random intervals between a minimum of fifteen and a maximum of forty minutes. Now its sudden silence was more noticeable than its noise.

Taylor and Jackson were in one of the barns, working on the backhoe. Pauling was in the kitchen, opening cans for dinner. Jade was still at the table, drawing.

By eight thirty visibility was so marginal that Reacher slid out of the Land Rover and headed for the kitchen. He met Jackson on the way. Jackson was coming back from the barn. His hands were covered with grease and oil.

Reacher asked, 'How's it going?'

'It'll be ready,' Jackson said.

Then Taylor appeared out of the gloom.

'Ten hours to go,' he said. 'We're safe until dawn.'

'You sure?' Reacher said.

'Not really.'

'Me either.'

'So what does the US Army field manual say about night-time perimeter security?'

Reacher smiled. 'It says you put a shitload of Claymores about a hundred yards out. If you hear one go off you know you just killed an intruder.'

'What if you don't have any Claymores?'

'Then you hide.'

'That's the SAS way. But we can't hide the house.'

'We could take Kate and Jade someplace else.'

Taylor shook his head. 'Better if they stay. I don't want my focus split.'

'How do they feel about that?'

'Ask them.'

So Reacher did. He took a short cut through the house and went out to the Mini. Told Kate to take a break for dinner. Then he offered to drive her and Jade anywhere she wanted to go, a hotel, a resort, a spa, Norwich, Birmingham, London, anywhere. She refused. She said as long as Lane was alive she wanted Taylor close by with a gun. She said a farmhouse with stone walls three feet thick was the best place she could think of to be. Reacher didn't argue with her. Privately he agreed with Taylor. Split focus was a bad thing. And it was possible that Lane's guys already had covert surveillance going. Maybe even likely.

446

If so, they would have the roads covered. They would be watching cars pass by. Looking for Taylor, primarily. But if they were given the chance to see that what was supposed to be Susan and Melody Jackson was actually Kate and Jade Lane, then the whole game would change.

Dinner was a random mixture of canned stuff that Pauling had found in cupboards. She wasn't much of a cook. She was too accustomed to dialling her Barrow Street telephone and calling out for whatever she wanted. But nobody seemed to mind. Nobody was in the mood for a gourmet menu. They planned as they ate. Agreed to set up two two-person watches, sequential, five hours each. That would take them through until dawn. One person would patrol the blind gable wall to the south, and one would do the same thing to the north. Each would be armed with a loaded G36. The first watch would be Taylor and Jackson, and at half past one in the morning Reacher and Pauling would take over. Kate Lane would sit it out. The possibility that a hostile night-time reconnaissance probe might identify her was too much of a risk.

Reacher cleared the table and washed the dishes and Taylor and Jackson went outside with their G36s cocked and locked. Kate went upstairs to put Jade to bed. Pauling put logs on the fire. Watched Reacher at the sink.

'You OK?' she asked him.

'I've done KP before.'

'I didn't mean that.'

447

He said, 'We've got an SAS guy on one end of the house and a Parachute Regiment guy on the other. They've both got automatic weapons. And they're both personally motivated. They won't fall asleep.'

'I didn't mean that either. I meant with the whole thing.'

'I told you we wouldn't be putting anybody on trial.'

Pauling nodded.

'She's cute,' she said. 'Isn't she?'

'Who?'

'Kate. She makes me feel ancient.'

'Older women,' Reacher said. 'Good for something.'

'Thanks.'

'I mean it. Give me a choice, I'd go home with you, not her.'

'Why?'

'Because I'm weird like that.'

'I'm supposed to put people on trial.'

'So was I, once. But I'm not going to this time. And I'm OK with that.'

'Me too. That's what's bothering me.'

'You'll get over it. The backhoe and a plane ticket will help.'

'Distance? Six feet of earth and three thousand air miles?'

'Works every time.'

'Does it? Really?'

'We splattered a thousand bugs on our windshield yesterday. A thousand more today. One extra won't make any difference.'

'Lane isn't a bug.'

'No, he's worse.'

'What about the others?'

'They've got a choice. The purest kind of choice there is. They can stay or they can go. Entirely up to them.'

'Where do you think they are now?'

'Somewhere out there,' Reacher said.

A half-hour later Kate Lane came downstairs again. The tails of her borrowed shirt were tied at her waist and the sleeves were rolled to her elbows.

'Jade's asleep,' she said. She turned sideways to squeeze past a displaced dining chair and Reacher figured it was possible to see that she was pregnant. Just. Now that he had been told.

He asked, 'Is she doing OK?'

'Better than we could have hoped,' Kate said. 'She's not sleeping great. The jet lag has screwed her up. And she's a little nervous, I guess. And she doesn't understand why there are no animals here. She doesn't understand arable farming. She thinks we're hiding a whole bunch of cute little creatures from her.'

'Does she know about the new brother or sister or whatever it's going to be?'

Kate nodded. 'We waited until we were on the plane. We tried to make it all part of the adventure.'

'How was it at the airport?'

'No problem. The passports were fine. They looked at the names more than the pictures. To make sure they matched the tickets.'

Pauling said, 'So much for Homeland Security.'

Kate nodded again. 'We got the idea from something we read in the newspaper. Some guy left on a short-notice business trip, grabbed his passport from the drawer, and he'd been through six separate countries before he realized it was his wife's passport that he had grabbed.'

Reacher said, 'Tell me how the whole thing went down.'

'It was pretty easy, really. We did stuff in advance. Bought the voice machine, rented the room, got the chair, took the car keys.'

'Taylor did most of that, right?'

'He said people would remember me more than him.'

'He was probably right.'

'But I had to buy the voice machine. Too weird if a guy who couldn't talk wanted one.'

'I guess.'

'Then I copied the photograph at Staples. That was tough. I had to let Groom drive me. It would have been too suspicious to insist on Graham all the time. But after that it was easy. We left for Bloomingdale's that morning and went straight to Graham's apartment instead. Just holed up there and waited. We kept really quiet in case anyone checked with the neighbours. We kept the lights off and covered the window in case anyone passed by on the street. Then later we started the phone calls. Right from the apartment. I was very nervous at first.'

'You forgot to say no cops.'

'I know. I thought I'd blown it immediately. But Edward didn't seem to notice. Then it got much easier later. With practice.'

'I was in the car with Burke. You sounded great by then.'

'I thought there was someone with him. There was something in his voice. And he kept narrating where he was. He was telling you, I guess. You must have been hidden.'

'You asked for his name in case you slipped and used it anyway.'

Kate nodded. 'I knew who it was, obviously. And I thought it might sound dominating.'

'You know Greenwich Village pretty well.'

'I lived there before I married Edward.'

'Why did you split the demands into three parts?'

'Because to ask for it all at once would have been too much of a clue. We thought we better let the stress build up a little. Then maybe Edward would miss the connection.'

'I don't think he missed it. But I think he misinterpreted it. He started thinking about Hobart and the Africa connection.'

'How bad is Hobart, really?'

'About as bad as it gets.'

'That's unforgivable.'

'No argument from me.'

'Do you think I'm cold-blooded?'

'If I did it wouldn't be a criticism.'

'Edward wanted to own me. Like a chattel. And he said if I was ever unfaithful he would rupture Jade's hymen with a potato peeler. He said he would tie me up and make me watch him do it. He said that when she was five years old.'

Reacher said nothing.

Kate turned to Pauling and asked, 'Do you have children?'

Pauling shook her head.

Kate said, 'You blot a thing like that right out of your mind. You assume it was just the sick product of a temporary rage. Like he wasn't quite right in the head. But then I heard the story about Anne and I knew he was capable of really doing it. So now I want him dead.'

Reacher said, 'He's going to be. Very soon.'

'They say you should never get between a lioness and her cub. I never really understood that before. Now I do. There are no limits.'

The room went as quiet as only the countryside can. The flames in the fireplace flickered and danced. Strange shadows moved on the walls.

Reacher asked, 'Are you planning on staying here forever?'

'I hope to,' Kate said. 'Organic farming is going to be a big thing. Better for people, better for the land. We can buy some more acres from the locals. Maybe expand a little.'

'We?'

'I feel like a part of it.'

'What are you growing?'

'Right now, just grass. We're in the hay business for the next five years or so. We have to work the old chemicals out of the soil. And that takes time.'

'Hard to picture you as a farmer.'

'I think I'm going to enjoy it.'

'Even when Lane is out of the picture permanently?'

'In that case I guess we would go back to New

York occasionally. But downtown only. I won't go back to the Dakota.'

'Anne's sister lives directly opposite. In the Majestic. She's been watching Lane every day for four years.'

Kate said, 'I'd like to meet her. And I'd like to see Hobart's sister again.'

'Like a survivors' club,' Pauling said.

Reacher got out of his chair and walked to the window. Saw nothing but night-time blackness. Heard nothing but silence.

'First we have to survive,' he said.

They kept the fire going and dozed quietly in the armchairs. When the clock in Reacher's head hit one-thirty in the morning he tapped Pauling on the knee and stood up and stretched. Then they headed outside together into the dead-of-night dark and cold. Called softly and met Taylor and Jackson in a huddle outside the front door. Reacher took Taylor's weapon and headed for the south end of the house. The gun was warm from Taylor's hands. The safety was above and behind the trigger. It had tritium markings, which made them faintly luminous. Reacher selected single fire and raised the rifle to his shoulder and checked the fit. It felt pretty good. It balanced fairly well. The carrying handle was like an exaggerated version of an M16's, with a neat little oval aperture in the front slope to provide a line-of-sight back to the built-in scope, which was a plain 3× monocular, which according to the laws of optics pulled the target three times closer than the naked eye but also made it three stops darker, which rendered it functionally useless at night. Three stops darker than pitch black was no use to anyone. But overall the thing was a handsome weapon. It would be fine by dawn.

He put his back against the blind gable wall and settled in and waited. He could smell wood smoke from the kitchen chimney. After a minute his eyesight had adjusted and he saw that there was a little moonlight behind heavy cloud, maybe one shade lighter than total darkness. But still comforting. Nobody would see him from a distance. He was wearing grey pants and a grey jacket and he was leaning on a grey wall holding a black gun. In turn he would see headlights miles away and he would see men on foot about ten feet away. Close quarters. But at night vision was not the sense that counted anyway. In the darkness, hearing was primary. Sound was the best early-warning system. Reacher himself could be totally silent, because he wasn't moving. But no intruder could be. Intruders had to move.

He stepped forward two paces and stood still. Turned his head slowly left and right and scoped out a two hundred degree arc all around him, like a huge curved bubble of space from which he had to be aware of every sound. Assuming that Pauling was doing the same thing north of the house they had every angle of approach covered between them. At first he heard nothing. Just an absolute absence of sound. Like a vacuum. Like he was deaf. Then as he relaxed and concentrated he started to pick up tiny imperceptible sounds drifting in across the flat land. The thrill of faint breezes in distant trees. The hum of power lines a mile away. The soak of water turning earth to mud in ditches. Grains of dirt drying and falling into furrows. Field mice, in burrows. Things growing. He turned his head left and right like radar and knew that any human approach might as well be accompanied by a marching band. He would hear it clearly a hundred yards away, however quiet anyone tried to be.

Reacher, alone in the dark. Armed and dangerous. Invincible.

He stood in the same spot for five straight hours. It was cold, but bearable. Nobody came. By six thirty in the morning the sun was showing far away to his left. There was a bright horizontal band of pink in the sky. A thick horizontal blanket of mist on the ground. Grey visibility was spreading westward slowly, like an incoming tide.

The dawn of a new day.

The time of maximum danger.

Taylor and Jackson came out of the house carrying the third and fourth rifles. Reacher didn't speak. Just took up a new station against the rear façade of the house, his shoulder against the corner, facing south. Taylor mirrored his position against the front wall. Reacher knew without looking that sixty feet behind them Jackson and Pauling were doing the same thing. Four weapons, four pairs of eyes, all trained outward.

Reasonable security.

For as long as they could bear to stay in position.

SEVENTY

They stayed in position all day long. All through the morning and all through the afternoon and well into the evening. Fourteen straight hours.

Lane didn't come.

One at a time they took short meal breaks and shorter bathroom breaks. They rotated stations clockwise around the house for variety. Their eight-pound rifles started to feel like eight tons in their hands. Jackson slipped away for a minute and turned the bird scarer back on. Thereafter the stillness was periodically shattered by loud random shotgun blasts. Even though they knew for sure they were due each sentry jumped and ducked every time they arrived.

Lane didn't come.

Kate and Jade stayed in the house, out of sight. They made food and poured drinks and carried them on trays to the windows and the doors, tea for Taylor and Jackson, coffee for Reacher, orange juice for Pauling. The sun burned through the mist and the day grew warm, and then it grew cold again in the late afternoon.

Lane didn't come.

Jade drew pictures. Every twenty minutes or so she would bring a new one to a different window and ask for an opinion concerning its merit. When it was his turn to judge, Reacher would duck his head down and give the paper a look. Then he would turn back to the outward view and talk out of the side of his mouth. *Very good*, he would say. And generally the pictures merited the praise. The kid wasn't a bad little artist. She had switched from future predictions to straightforward reportage. She drew the red Mini Cooper, she drew Pauling with her gun, she drew Taylor with a mouth like a wrecked Buick's grille. She drew Reacher, huge, taller than the house. Then late in the day she switched from reportage to fantasy and drew farm animals in the barns, even though she had been told that the Jacksons didn't have any, not even a dog.

Lane didn't come.

Kate fixed sandwiches for an early dinner and Jade took to visiting the corner windows and asking everyone in turn if she could come outside and explore. Everyone in turn said no, she had to hide. On the third go-round Reacher heard her modify her request and ask Taylor if she could come out after dark, and he heard Taylor say maybe, like worn-down parents everywhere.

Lane didn't come.

By eight thirty in the evening visibility had died away to nothing again and Reacher had been on his feet for nineteen hours. Pauling too. Taylor and Jackson had done twenty-four, spelled only by a five-hour break. They all met in a loose huddle in the gathering gloom by the front door, shaky with fatigue, frustrated, made anxious by fruitless vigilance.

Taylor said, 'He's waiting us out.'

'Therefore he's going to win,' Jackson said. 'We can't keep this up much longer.'

'He's had twenty-seven hours,' Pauling said. 'We have to assume he's armed by now.'

'He'll come tomorrow at dawn,' Taylor said.

'You sure?' Reacher asked.

'Not really.'

'Me either. Three or four in the morning would work just as well.'

'Too dark.'

'If they've bought guns they could have bought night vision too.'

'How would you do it?'

'Three guys loop around and walk in from the north. The other four come up the driveway, maybe two in a car, lights off, high speed, with the other two flanking it on foot. Two directions, seven guys, their choice of seven windows, we couldn't stop at least three of them getting inside. They'd get you or a hostage before we could react.'

'You're a real ray of sunshine,' Taylor said.

'I'm just trying to think like them.'

'We'd get them before they got anywhere near the house.'

'Only if all four of us can stay awake and alert for the next eight hours. Or the next thirty-two hours, if he delays another day. Or the next fifty-six hours, if he delays two days. Which he might. He's in no hurry. And he's not dumb. If he's decided to wait us out, why not do it properly?'

Taylor said, 'We're not moving. This place is a stronghold.'

'Three-dimensionally it's fine,' Reacher said. 'But battles are fought in four dimensions, not three. Length, breadth and height, plus time. And time is on Lane's side, not ours. This is a siege now. We're going to run out of food, and sooner or later all four of us are going to be asleep at the same time.'

'So we'll halve the guard. One man north, one man south, the other two resting but ready.'

Reacher shook his head. 'No, it's time to get aggressive.'

'How?'

'I'm going to go find them. They've got to be holed up somewhere close. It's time to pay them a visit. They won't be expecting that.'

'Alone?' Pauling said. 'That's insane.'

'I have to anyway,' Reacher said. 'I didn't get Hobart's money yet. There's eight hundred grand out there. Can't let it go to waste.'

Taylor and Pauling stayed on guard and Reacher fetched the big Ordnance Survey map from the Mini's glove box. He took Jade's latest drawings off the kitchen table and piled them on a chair and spread out the map in their place. Then he went over it with Jackson. Jackson had a year's worth of local knowledge, which was less than Reacher would have liked, but it was better than nothing. The map clarified most of the terrain issues all by itself with its faint orange contour lines, which were very widely spaced and which curved only gently. Flat land, probably the flattest

459

in the British Isles. Like a pool table. Grange Farm and Bishops Pargeter were roughly in the centre of a wide triangle of empty space bounded to the east by the road that ran south from Norwich to Ipswich in Suffolk and to the west by the Thetford road that Reacher and Pauling had driven three times already. Elsewhere in the triangle were meandering minor tracks and isolated farm settlements. Here and there chance and history had nestled small communities in the angles of crossroads. They were shown on the map as tiny grey squares and rectangles. Some of the rectangles represented short rows of houses. Some of the larger buildings were shown individually. The only one within any kind of a reasonable distance from Bishops Pargeter and labelled *PH* was the Bishop's Arms.

This is the only pub for miles, lad, the farmer at the bar had said. *Why else do you think it's so crowded?*

'Are they there, do you think?' Reacher asked.

Jackson said, 'If they stopped in Fenchurch St Mary first and then aimed for Bishops Pargeter afterwards, then that's the only place they could have passed. But they could have gone north. Nearer Norwich there are a lot of places.'

'Can't buy guns in Norwich,' Reacher said. 'Not if you had to call Holland.'

'Shotguns up there,' Jackson said. 'Nothing heavier.'

'So they probably didn't go there,' Reacher said. He recalled the motoring atlas. The city of Norwich had been shown as a dense stain in the top-right corner of the bulge that was East

460

Anglia. The end of the line. Not on the way to anywhere else.

'I think they stayed close,' he said.

'Then the Bishop's Arms could be it,' Jackson said.

Five miles, Reacher thought. *On foot, that's a three-hour round trip. Back by midnight.*

'I'm going to check it out,' he said.

He detoured via the mudroom and collected two spare magazines for his G36. Found Pauling's purse in the kitchen and borrowed her little Maglite. Folded the map and put it in his pocket. Then he huddled with the others in the dark outside the front door and agreed a password. He didn't want to get shot at when he arrived back. Jackson suggested *Canaries*, which was the Norwich soccer team's nickname, for its yellow uniforms.

'Are they any good?' Reacher asked.

'They used to be,' Jackson said. 'Twenty-some years ago, they were great.'

Them and me both, Reacher thought.

'Take care,' Pauling said, and kissed him on the cheek.

'I'll be back,' he said.

He started by walking north behind the house. Then he turned west, staying parallel to the road, about a field's width away. There was a little leftover twilight in the sky. Just the last remnant. Torn and ragged clouds with pale stars beyond. The air was cold and a little damp. There was a knee-high blanket of thin mist clinging to the earth. The dirt was soft and heavy underfoot. He carried his G36 by its handle, left-handed, ready to swing it up into position when needed.

Reacher, alone in the dark.

The Grange Farm boundary was a trench ten feet across with a muddy bottom six feet down. Drainage, for the flat land. Not exactly canals like in Holland, but not anything easily cleared, either. Not anything to just step across. Reacher had to slide down the near bank, struggle through the mud, and then climb up the far bank again. A mile into the trip his pants were a real mess. And he was going to have to invest some serious shoeshine time on the trip home. Or else deduct the price of a new pair of Cheaneys from Hobart's compensation. Maybe he could detour to the source. The motoring atlas had shown Northampton about forty miles west of Cambridge. Maybe he could talk Pauling into a two-hour shopping expedition. He had let her insist on Macy's, after all.

Two miles into the trip he was very tired. And slow. Behind schedule. He changed course and moved slightly south and west. Came closer to the road. Found a tractor route through the next farmer's fields. Huge tyres had beaten the earth into hard ruts either side of a grassy centre hump. He wiped his shoes on the grass and speeded up a little. Found that the next ditch was crossed by an improvised trestle made of old railway ties. Strong enough for a tractor, strong enough for him. He followed the tyre tracks until they turned abruptly north. Then he struck off through the fields again on his own.

After four miles the clock in his head told him that it was ten thirty at night. Twilight had gone completely but the rags of cloud had cleared a little and the moon was bright. The stars were out. Far away to his left he could see occasional cars passing by on the road. Three had gone west and two had gone east. Bright lights, sedate speeds. Theoretically the two heading east could have been Lane's guys, but he doubted it. Ten and eleven in the evening was no kind of a time to attack. He guessed rural roads saw a minor traffic peak right around then. Pubs letting out, friends going home. Too many witnesses. If he knew it, then Lane knew it too. Certainly Gregory knew it.

He kept on going. The spare magazines in his pocket were bruising his hip. Five minutes before eleven o'clock he spotted the glow from the pub's sign. Just an electric brightness in the misty air, because the sign itself was hidden by the bulk of the building. He could smell wood smoke from a chimney. He looped around towards the light and the smell, staying well to the north of the road, just in case Lane had watchers out. He kept to the fields until he was facing the back of the building from four hundred yards away. He saw small squares of harsh white fluorescent light. Windows. Undraped and unglamorous. Therefore kitchens and bathrooms, he guessed. Therefore frosted or pebbled glass. No view out.

He headed south, straight for the squares of light.

SEVENTY-ONE

Directly behind the pub the parking lot had been closed off and turned into a service yard. It was full of crates of bottles and stacks of metal beer kegs and big commercial-size trash receptacles. There was a broken-down old car with bricks wedged under its brake drums. No wheels. Another old car, humped under a stained tarpaulin. Behind it the building had a rear door, inconspicuous among all the chaos, almost certainly unlocked during business hours to allow easy access from the kitchen to the trash pile.

Reacher ignored the door. He circled the building in the dark, clockwise, thirty feet out from the walls, well away from the spill of light from the windows.

The small bright rooms in back were clearly bathrooms. Their windows blazed with the kind of green-tinged light that comes from cheap tubes and white tile. Around the corner in the end wall to the east of the building there were no windows at all, just an unbroken expanse of brick. Around the next corner in the front wall east of the entrance there were three windows into the public bar. From a distance Reacher peered in and saw the same four farmers he had seen two nights previously. On the same stools. And the same bartender, busy as before with his beer pumps and his towel. The lighting was dim, but there was nobody else in the room. None of the tables was occupied.

Reacher moved on.

The front door was closed. The parking lot had four cars in it, haphazardly slotted side by side. None of the cars was new. None of them was the kind of thing a Park Lane rental company could have produced in a hurry. They were all old and dirty and battered. Bald tyres. Dented fenders. Streaks of mud and manure. Farmers' cars.

Reacher moved on.

West of the entrance were three more windows, into the saloon bar.

Two nights previously the saloon bar had been empty.

It wasn't empty any more.

Now a single table was occupied.

By three men: Groom, and Burke, and Kowalski.

Reacher could see them clearly. On the table in front of them he could see the long-dead remains of a meal and half a dozen empty glasses. And three half-full glasses. Pint mugs of beer, half gone. It was a rectangular table. Kowalski and Burke were shoulder to shoulder on one side and Groom was opposite them, alone. Kowalski was talking and Burke was listening to him. Groom had his chair tipped back and was staring into space. There was a log fire burning in a soot-stained grate beyond him. The room was lit up warm and bright and inviting.

Reacher moved on.

Around the next corner there was a single window in the end wall to the west and through it Reacher got a different version of the same view. Groom, Burke and Kowalski at their table. Drinking. Talking. Passing time. They were all alone in the room. The door to the foyer was closed. A private party.

Reacher backtracked four short steps and then headed for the front corner of the building on an exact forty-five degree angle. Invisible from any window. He touched the wall and dropped to his knees. He kept his right palm on the brick and shuffled north and stretched out his left arm as far as it would go and very carefully laid his rifle on the ground directly under the west-facing window. He put it tight against the base of the wall where the shadows were deep. Then he shuffled south and stood up again and backed away on the same angle and checked. He couldn't see the rifle. Nobody would find it, unless they tripped over it.

He backed away until he was clear of the light spill and looped through the lot. Headed for the front door. Opened it up and stepped into the foyer. The low beams, the patterned carpet, the ten thousand brass ornaments. The shiny reception desk.

The register.

He stepped to the desk. To his right he could hear sociable silence from the public bar. The farmers, drinking, not saying much. The bartender, working quietly. To his left he could hear Kowalski's voice, muffled by the closed door. He couldn't make out what he was saying. He couldn't hear individual words. Just a low drone. Occasional rising intonations. Short barks of contempt. Old soldier's bullshit, probably.

He turned the register through a hundred and eighty degrees. It moved easily, leather on shiny varnish. He opened it up. Leafed through the pages until he found his own entry. Two nights previously, *J. & L. Bayswater, East 161st Street, Bronx, New York, USA, Rolls Royce, R34CHR*. Then he scanned ahead. The following night three guests had registered: C. Groom, A. Burke, L. Kowalski. They had been less shy than Reacher himself about supplying personal information. Their business address had been accurately given as One 72nd Street, New York, New York, USA, which was the Dakota Building. *Make of Vehicle* had been given as Toyota Land Cruiser. There was a plate number entered, a British seven-character mix of letters and numbers that meant nothing to Reacher beyond the fact that the car had to be a rental from London.

No Toyota Land Cruiser in the lot.

And where were Lane, Gregory, Perez, and Addison?

He leafed backward through the book and saw that on any given night the Bishop's Arms had a maximum of three rooms to let. So assuming that Groom and Burke and Kowalski had been given a room each, there had been no room at the inn for the others. They had gotten back into their rented Toyota and driven somewhere else.

But where?

Reacher glanced at the saloon bar's door but went the other way. Into the public bar. The bartender looked up at him and the four farmers turned slowly on their stools and started up with their complacent who-are-you barroom stares until they recognized him. Then they nodded guarded greetings and turned back to their pint glasses. The bartender stayed poised and polite, ready for fast service. *Instant acceptance, for less than thirty bucks.*

Reacher asked, 'Where did you send the other four?'

The bartender said, 'Who?'

'Seven guys showed up yesterday. Three of them are here. Where did you send the other four?'

'We've only got three rooms,' the guy said.

'I know that,' Reacher said. 'Where's your overspill recommendation?'

'I sent them down to Maston Manor.'

'Where's that?'

'The other side of Bishops Pargeter. About six mile beyond.'

'I didn't see another inn on the map.'

'It's a country house. She takes paying guests.'

One of the farmers half turned and said, 'It's a bed and breakfast hotel. Very nice. Classier than this place. I reckon they all drew lots and the losers stayed here.'

His friends laughed, low and slow. Barroom humour, the same the world over.

'It's more expensive there,' the bartender said defensively.

'It should be,' the farmer said.

'Is it on this road?' Reacher asked.

The bartender nodded. 'Straight through Bishops Pargeter, past the church, past Dave Kemp's shop, keep on about six mile. You can't miss it. She's got a sign. Maston Manor.'

'Thanks,' Reacher said. He headed back to the foyer. Closed the door behind him. Stepped across the patterned carpet and stopped in front of the saloon bar's door. Kowalski was still talking. Reacher could hear him. He put his hand on the knob. Paused a beat and then turned it and pushed the door open.

SEVENTY-TWO

Carter Groom was facing the door on the far side of the table. He looked up just like the bartender had but Kowalski and Burke moved a lot faster than the farmers. They spun around and stared. Reacher stepped the rest of the way into the room and closed the door gently behind him. Stood completely still.

'We meet again,' he said, just to break the silence.

'You've got some nerve,' Groom said.

The room was decorated in the same style as the foyer. Low ceiling beams, dark varnished wood, ornate wall sconces, thousands of brass ornaments, a wall-to-wall carpet patterned in a riot of red and gold swirls. Reacher moved towards the fireplace. Tapped the toes of his shoes against the edge of the hearth to shed some mud. Took a heavy iron poker from a hook and used the end of it to scrape dirt off his heels. Then he hung the poker back up and flapped at the bottom of his trouser legs with his hands. Altogether he spent more than a minute cleaning up, with his back turned, but he was watching a clear convex reflection of the table in a bright copper bucket that held kindling sticks. And nobody was moving. The three guys were just sitting there, waiting. Smart enough not to start anything in a public place.

'The situation has changed,' Reacher said. He moved on, towards the west-facing window. It had open drapes and a sliding storm pane on the inside and a regular wooden frame on the outside that would open like a door. He pulled out a chair from the table nearest to it and sat down, six feet away from the three guys, four feet and two panes of glass away from his rifle.

'Changed how?' Burke said.

'There was no kidnap,' Reacher said. 'It was faked. Kate and Taylor are an item. They fell in love, they eloped. Because they wanted to be together. That was all. And they took Jade with them, obviously. But they had to dress the whole thing up, because Lane is a psychopath where his marriages are concerned. Among other things.'

'Kate's alive?' Groom said.

Reacher nodded. 'Jade, too.'

'Where?'

'Somewhere in the States, I guess.'

'So why is Taylor here?'

'He wants a showdown with Lane on his own turf.'

'He's going to get one.'

Reacher shook his head. 'I'm here to tell you that's a bad idea. He's on a farm, and it's surrounded by ditches too deep to drive through. So you'd be going in on foot. And he's got a lot of help there. He's got eight of his old SAS buddies

471

with him, and his brother-in-law was a kind of Green Beret for the Brits, and he's brought in six of his guys, too. They've got Claymores on a hundred-yard perimeter and heavy machine guns in every window. They've got night vision and grenade launchers.'

'They can't possibly use them. Not here. This is England, not the Lebanon.'

'He's prepared to use them. Believe it. But actually he won't have to. Because four of the SAS guys are snipers. They've got PSG1s. Heckler and Koch sniper rifles, from the black market in Belgium. They'll drop you all three hundred yards out. With their eyes shut. Seven rounds, game over. They're miles from anywhere. Nobody will hear. And if they do, they won't care. This is the back of beyond. Farm country. Somebody's always shooting something. Foxes, road signs, burglars, each other.'

The room went quiet. Kowalski picked up his drink and sipped. Then Burke did, and then Groom. Kowalski was left-handed. Burke and Groom were right-handed. Reacher said, 'So your best play is to just forget it and go home now. Lane is going to die. There's no doubt about that. But there's no reason why you should die with him. This isn't your fight. This is all about Lane's ego. It's between him and Kate and Taylor. Don't get yourselves killed for that kind of bullshit.'

Burke said, 'We can't just walk away.'

'You walked away in Africa,' Reacher said. 'You left Hobart and Knight behind, to save the unit. So now you should leave Lane behind, to save yourselves. You can't win here. Taylor's good. You know that. And his buddies are just as good. You're outnumbered more than two to one. Which is totally upside down. You know that, too. A situation like this, you need to outnumber the defenders. You're going to get your asses kicked.'

Nobody spoke.

'You should go home,' Reacher said again. 'Hook up somewhere else. Maybe start up on your own.'

Groom asked, 'Are you with Taylor?'

Reacher nodded. 'And I'm good with a rifle. Back in the day, I won the Marine sniper trophy. I showed up in army green and I beat all of you miserable jarheads hands down. So maybe I'll grab one of the PSGs. Maybe I'll drop you all six hundred yards out, just for the fun of it. Or eight hundred, or a thousand.'

Silence in the room. No sound at all, except the shift and crackle of logs in the fire. Reacher looked straight at Kowalski.

'Five, seven, one, three,' he lied. 'That's the combination for Lane's closet door. There's still more than nine million dollars behind it. In cash. You should go get it, right now.'

No response.

'Walk away,' Reacher said. 'Live to fight another day.'

'They stole all that money,' Burke said.

'Alimony. Easier than asking for it straight up. Asking for alimony is what got Anne Lane killed. Kate found that out.'

'That *was* a kidnap.'

Reacher shook his head. 'Knight offed her. For

473

Lane, because Anne wanted out. That's why you all abandoned Knight in Africa. Lane was covering his ass. He sacrificed Hobart too because he was in the same OP.'

'That's bullshit.'

'I found Hobart. Knight told him all about it. While they were busy getting their hands and feet cut off.'

Silence.

Reacher said, 'Don't get killed for this kind of crap.'

Burke looked at Groom. Groom looked at Burke. They both looked at Kowalski. There was a long pause. Then Burke looked up.

'OK,' he said. 'I guess we could sit this one out.'

Groom nodded. Kowalski shrugged. Reacher stood up.

'Smart decision,' he said. He moved towards the door. Stopped at the hearth and kicked his shoes against the stone again. Asked, 'Where are Lane and the others?'

Quiet for a beat. Then Groom said, 'There was no room here. They went up to Norwich. The city. Some hotel up there. The guy here recommended it.'

Reacher nodded. 'And when is he locking and loading?'

Another pause.

'Dawn the day after tomorrow.'

'What did he buy?'

'Sub-machine guns. MP5Ks, one each plus two spares. Ammunition, night vision, flashlights, various bits and pieces.'

474

'Are you going to call him? As soon as I'm gone?'

'No,' Burke said. 'He's not the kind of guy you call with this kind of news.'

'OK,' Reacher said. Then he stepped fast to his left and lifted the poker off its hook. Reversed it in his hands and spun around in one smooth movement and swung it hard and level and caught Carter Groom across the upper right arm, hard and straight and level, halfway between the elbow and the shoulder. The poker was a heavy iron bar and Reacher was a strong and angry man and Groom's humerus shattered like a piece of dropped china. Groom opened his mouth wide in sudden pain and shock but before any kind of a scream got out Reacher had sidestepped two paces to his left and broken Kowalski's left arm with a vicious backhanded blow. *Kowalski was left-handed. Burke and Groom were right-handed.* Reacher knocked Kowalski out of his way with his hip and wound up like an old newsreel of Mickey Mantle getting ready to hit one out of the park and smashed Burke across the right wrist with a line drive and pulverized every bone in there. Then he breathed out and turned away and stepped to the fireplace and put the poker back on its hook.

'Just making sure,' he said. 'You didn't entirely convince me with your answers. Especially the one about Lane's hotel.'

Then he walked out of the saloon bar and closed the door quietly behind him. It was exactly eleven thirty-one in the evening, according to the clock in his head.

*   *   *

At exactly eleven thirty-two by the platinum
Rolex on his left wrist Edward Lane closed
the Toyota's rear door on nine Heckler & Koch
MP5K sub-machine guns, sixty thirty-round
magazines of 9mm Parabellums, seven sets of
night vision goggles, ten flashlights, six rolls of
duct tape, and two long coils of rope. Then John
Gregory started the engine. Behind him on the
rear bench were Perez and Addison, quiet and
pensive. Lane climbed into the front passenger
seat and Gregory turned the truck around and
took off west. Standard Special Forces doctrine
called for dawn assaults, but it also called for the
insertion of a small advance force for a lengthy
period of lying-up and prior surveillance.

At exactly eleven thirty-three by the clock on her
night table Jade woke up, confused and hot and
feverish with time-zone confusion. She sat up in
bed for a spell, dazed and quiet. Then she swung
her feet to the floor. Crossed the room slowly and
pulled back her curtain. It was dark outside. And
she could go outside in the dark. Taylor had said
so. She could go visit the barns, and find the
animals she knew had to be there.

Reacher retrieved his G36 from under the saloon
bar window at eleven thirty-four precisely and set
out to walk back on the road, which he figured
would make the return trip faster. Five miles,
level ground, no hills, decent pace. He anticipated
about seventy-five minutes total. He was tired,
but content. Fairly satisfied. Three trigger fingers

out of action, the opposing force degraded to about 57 per cent of its original capacity, the odds evened up to an attractive four-on-four, some useful intelligence gained. Groom's ingrained loyalty had led him to lie about Lane's hotel and probably about the timing of the planned attack, too. Dawn *the day after* tomorrow was almost certainly a clumsy and hasty camouflaging of the truth, which therefore in reality would be simply dawn tomorrow. But the shopping list had probably been right. Night vision was a no-brainer for night-time surveillance and MP5Ks were pretty much what a guy like Lane would want for a subsequent fast and mobile assault. Light, accurate, reliable, familiar, available.

Forewarned is forearmed, Reacher thought. *Not bad for an evening's work.* He walked on, energy in his stride, a grim smile on his face.

Alone in the dark. Invincible.

That feeling lasted exactly an hour and a quarter. It ended just after he walked the length of the Grange Farm driveway and saw the dark and silent bulk of the house looming in front of him. He had called the password at least half a dozen separate times. At first quietly, and then louder.

Canaries, canaries, canaries.
Canaries, canaries, canaries.
He had gotten no response at all.

SEVENTY-THREE

Without conscious thought Reacher raised his rifle to the ready position. Stock nestled high against his right shoulder, safety off, right index finger inside the trigger guard, barrel just a degree or two below the horizontal. Long years of training, absorbed right down at the cellular level, permanently written in his DNA. *No point in having a weapon at all unless it's ready for instant use*, his instructors had screamed.

He stood absolutely still. Listened hard. Heard nothing at all. He moved his head left. Listened. Nothing. He moved his head right. Nothing.

He tried the password one more time, soft and low: *Canaries*.

He heard no reply.

Lane, he thought.

He wasn't surprised. Surprise was strictly for amateurs, and Reacher was a professional. He wasn't upset, either. He had learned a long time ago that the only way to keep fear and panic at bay was to concentrate ruthlessly on the job in hand. So he spent no time thinking about Lauren Pauling or Kate Lane. Or Jackson or Taylor. Or

Jade. No time at all. He just walked backward and to his left. Pre-programmed. Like a machine. Silently. Away from the house. Making himself smaller as a target and improving his angle of view. He checked the windows. They were all dark. Just a faint red glow from the kitchen. The remains of the fire. The front door was closed. Near it was the faint shape of the Mini Cooper, cold and grey in the dark. It looked odd. Canted down at the front, like it was kneeling.

He walked towards it through the dark, slow and stealthy. Knelt down on the driver's side near the front bumper and felt for the tyre. It wasn't there. There were torn shreds of rubber and a vicious curled length of bead wire. And shards of plastic from the shattered wheel well lining. That was all. He shuffled quietly around the tiny car to the other side. Same situation. The wheel had its alloy rim on the ground.

A front-wheel-drive vehicle, comprehensively disabled. Both wheels. One had not been enough. A single tyre can be changed. Two sub-machine gun bursts had been necessary. Twice the risk of detection. Although in Reacher's experience an MP5 set to fire bursts of three sounded more innocent than a rifle firing single shots. A single gunshot was unmistakable. It was a singularity. It was a precise pinpoint of noise. An MP5 was rated to fire 900 rounds a minute. Fifteen every second. Which meant that a burst of three lasted a fifth of a second. Not quite a singularity. Altogether a different sound. Like a brief blurred purr instead. Like a distant motorcycle heard waiting at a light.

Lane, he thought again.

But when?

Seventy-five minutes previously he had been five miles away. Audibility decays according to the inverse square law. Twice the distance, the sound gets four times as quiet. Four times the distance, sixteen times as quiet. He had heard nothing. He was sure of that. Across land as flat and featureless and in night air as thick and damp as Norfolk's he would have expected to hear MP5 bursts a couple of miles away. Therefore Lane had been gone at least thirty minutes. Maybe more.

He stood still and listened hard. Heard nothing. Headed for the front door. It was closed but unlocked. He dropped his left hand off the rifle and turned the handle. Pushed the door open. Raised the rifle. The house was dark. It felt empty. He checked the kitchen. It was warm. Dull red embers in the hearth. Jade's drawings were still on the kitchen chair where he had left them. Pauling's purse was still where he had dumped it after taking the Maglite. There were empty mugs of tea all over the place. Dishes in the sink. The room looked exactly like he had left it, except there were no people in it.

He switched on the flashlight and clamped it in his left palm under the rifle's barrel. Used it to check all the other ground floor rooms. A formal dining room, empty, cold, dark, unused. Nobody in it. A formal parlour, furnished like the Bishop's Arms saloon bar, still and quiet. Nobody in it. A powder room, a coat closet, the mudroom. All empty.

He crept up the stairs. The first room he came to was clearly Jade's. He saw the green seersucker sundress folded on a chair. Drawings on the floor. The battered old toys that had been missing from the Dakota were all arrayed in a line along the bed, leaning on the wall. A one-eyed bear with the fur worn down to its backing, sitting up. A doll, one eye open and one eye closed, a lipstick effect inexpertly applied with a red marker pen. The bed had been slept in. The pillow was dented and the sheets had been thrown back.

No sign of the child herself.

The next room belonged to the Jacksons. That was clear. There was a vanity table cluttered with British cosmetic brands and tortoiseshell hairbrushes and matching hand mirrors. There were framed photographs of a girl that wasn't Jade. Melody, Reacher guessed. On the back wall there was a bed with a high headboard and freestanding armoires in matching dark veneers, full of clothes, men's and women's. There was a backhoe catalogue on one of the night tables. Tony Jackson's bedtime reading.

No sign of Jackson himself.

The next room was Kate and Taylor's. An old queen bed, an oak night table. Austere, undecorated, like a guest room. The photograph was propped on a dresser. Kate and Jade, together. The original print. No frame. The two faces glowed in the Maglite's beam. Love, captured on film. There was an empty tote bag. Kate's luggage. No sign of the money. Just three empty leather duffels piled together in a corner. Reacher had carried one of them himself, down in the Dakota's elevator to the black BMW, with Burke restless at his side.

He moved on, looking for boxrooms or bathrooms. Then he stopped, halfway along the upstairs hallway.

Because there was blood on the floor.

It was a small thin stain, a foot long, curved, like flung paint. Not a puddle. Not neat. It was dynamic, suggestive of rapid movement. Reacher stepped back to the head of the stairs. Sniffed the air. There was a faint smell of gunpowder. He sighted down the hallway with the Maglite beam and saw an open bathroom door at the far end. A smashed tile on the back wall, at chest height. A neat burst, contained by a single six-inch by six-inch ceramic square. A running target, a raised gun, a squeezed trigger, three shots, a through-and-through flesh wound, probably to an upper arm. A short shooter, otherwise the downward angle would be more pronounced. The smashed tile would be lower. Perez, probably. Perez, firing maybe the first of at least seven bursts that night. This one, inside the house. Then the two Mini Cooper tyres. Then four Land Rover tyres, for sure. A four-wheel-drive vehicle would need all four tyres taken out for a cautious man to be satisfied. A desperate driver might get somewhere on two.

Seven sub-machine gun bursts in the dead of night. Maybe more. Forty or more minutes ago. *People here have phones*, Jackson had said. *Some of them even know how to use them*. But they hadn't used them. That was for sure. The

Norwich cops would have arrived in less than forty minutes. Thirty miles, empty roads, lights and sirens, they could have done it in twenty-five or less. So nobody had called. Because of the MP5's other-worldly rate of fire. Machine guns on TV or in the movies were generally old-fashioned and much slower. In order to be properly convincing. So forty or more minutes ago people wouldn't have known what they were hearing. Just a random series of inexplicable blurred purrs, like sewing machines. Like jamming your tongue on the roof of your mouth and blowing. If they had heard anything at all.

So, Reacher thought. *At least one wounded and the cavalry ain't coming.*

He eased down the stairs and back out into the night.

He circled the house, clockwise. The barns were distant and dark and quiet. The old Land Rover was collapsed on its rims, as he had been certain it would be. Four blown tyres. He walked straight past it and stopped against the south gable wall. Turned the Maglite off and stared down the driveway into the darkness.

How had it happened?

He trusted Pauling because he knew her and he trusted Taylor and Jackson even without knowing them. Three professionals. Experience, savvy, plenty of active brain cells. Tired, but functioning. A long perilous approach from the intruders' point of view. No contest. He should have been looking at four riddled bodies and a wrecked rental car. Right about then Jackson should have been firing up the backhoe. Pauling should have been cracking cans of beer and Kate should have been making toast and heating beans.

So why weren't they?

Distraction, he figured. As ever, the answer was in Jade's pictures. The animals in the barns. *She's not sleeping great*, Kate had said. *The jet lag has screwed her up*. Reacher pictured the child waking, maybe around midnight, getting out of bed, running out of the house into the imagined safety of the darkness, four adults scrambling after her, confusion, panic, a search, unseen watchers rising from the grassland and moving in. Lane, blasting up the driveway in the rented Toyota SUV. Taylor and Jackson and Pauling holding their fire in case they hit each other or Kate or Jade.

Lane, headlights on now, jamming to a stop.

Lane, headlights on now, recognizing his own stepdaughter.

His own wife.

Reacher shivered once, a violent uncontrollable spasm. He closed his eyes, and then opened them again. He clicked the Maglite on and lowered the beam to light his way and walked on down the driveway. Towards the road. Towards he knew not where.

Perez flipped his night vision goggles into the up position on his forehead and said, 'OK, Reacher's gone. He's out of here.'

Edward Lane nodded. Paused a second and then backhanded Jackson across the face with his flashlight, once, twice, three times, massive blows, until Jackson fell. Gregory hauled him upright again and Addison tore the tape off his mouth.

Lane said, 'Tell me about your diet.'

Jackson spat blood. 'My what?'

'Your diet. What you eat. What your absent wife feeds you.'

'Why?'

'I want to know if you eat potatoes.'

'Everybody eats potatoes.'

'So I'll find a peeler in the kitchen?'

SEVENTY-FOUR

Reacher kept his flashlight beam trained down about ten feet in front of him, a narrow bright oval dancing left and right a little and bouncing as he walked. The light showed him the ruts and the dips and the holes in the beaten earth. It made it easier to hurry. He walked through the first curve in the driveway. Then he fixed his eyes on the darkness ahead and started to run towards the road.

Lane turned to Perez and said, 'Go find the kitchen. Bring me what I need. And find a telephone. Call the Bishop's Arms. Tell the others to get here now.'

'We've got the truck,' Perez said.

'Tell them to walk,' Lane said.

Jackson said, 'Reacher will come back, you know.' He was the only one who could talk. He was the only one without tape on his mouth.

Lane said, 'I know he'll come back. I'm counting on it. Why do you think we didn't chase him? Worst case for us he'll walk six miles east and find nothing and walk back here again. It will take him four hours. You'll be dead by then. He can take your place. He can watch the child die, and then Ms Pauling, and then I'll kill him. Slowly.'

'You're insane. You need help.'

'I don't think so,' Lane said.

'He'll hitch a lift.'

'In the dead of night? Carrying an assault rifle? I don't think so.'

'You're nuts,' Jackson said. 'You've lost it completely.'

'I'm angry,' Lane said. 'And I think I have a right to be.'

Perez left, to find the kitchen.

Reacher ran through the second curve in the driveway. Then he slowed a little.

Then he stopped dead.

He killed the flashlight beam and closed his eyes. Stood still in the darkness and breathed hard and concentrated on the after-image of what he had just seen.

The driveway curved twice for no apparent reason. Not practical, not aesthetic. It went left and then right for some other purpose. To avoid unseen softness in the dirt, he had guessed before. To avoid a couple of badly drained sinkhole patches. And he had seen that he had been correct. All the way through the curves the track was soft and damp. Muddy, even though it hadn't rained for days.

And the mud showed tyre tracks.

Three sets.

First, Tony Jackson's old Land Rover. The farm truck. Blocky mud-and-snow treads. Chunky, worn, in and out many hundreds of times. The Land Rover's tracks were all over the place. Old, faded, eroded, new, clear, recent. Everywhere. Like background noise.

Second, the Mini Cooper's tyres. A very different look. Narrow, crisp, new, aggressive treads built for good adhesion and fast cornering on tarmac. Just one set. Reacher had turned in the day before, slow and wide and deliberate, second gear, a small car at a moderate speed, unthreatening. He had driven through the curves and parked the car outside the house. And he had left it there. It was still there. It hadn't moved. It hadn't driven out again. It probably never would. It would leave on a flatbed truck.

Hence, one set of tyre tracks only.

The third set was also a single set. One pass, one way. Wider tyres. A large heavy vehicle, open treads, new and crisp. The kind of semi-serious off-road tyres a prestige SUV would wear.

The kind of tyres a rented Toyota Land Cruiser would wear.

One set only.

One way.

The Toyota was a very capable off-road vehicle. Reacher knew that. It was one of the best in the world. But it was inconceivable that it had entered the farm overland. Not in a million years. The farm was bounded by ditches ten feet across and six feet deep. Steep sides. Impossible approach and exit angles. A Humvee couldn't do it. A Bradley couldn't do it. An Abrams couldn't do it. The Grange Farm ditches were better than tank traps. So the Toyota hadn't come in overland. It had driven in across the little flat bridge and up the length of the driveway. No other way.

And it hadn't driven out again.

One set of tyre tracks.

One way.

Lane was still on the property.

Lane hit Jackson in the head with the flashlight one more time, hard. The lens smashed and Jackson went down again.

'I need a new flashlight,' Lane said. 'This one seems to be broken.'

Addison smiled and took a new one out of a box. Lauren Pauling stared at the door. Her mouth was taped and her hands were bound behind her. The door was still closed. But it was going to open any minute. Through it would come either Perez or Reacher. Bad news or good.

Let it be Reacher, she thought. *Please. Bugs on windshields, no scruples. Please let it be Reacher.*

Lane took the new flashlight from Addison and stepped up close to Kate. Face to face, six inches from her. Eye to eye. They were about the same height. He lit up the flashlight beam and held it just under her chin, shining it directly upward, turning her exquisite face into a ghastly Halloween mask.

'Till death us do part,' he said. 'That's a phrase I take seriously.'

Kate turned her head away. Gasped behind the tape. Lane clamped her chin in his free hand and turned her head back.

'Forsaking all others,' he said. 'I took that part seriously too. I'm so sorry that you didn't.'

Kate closed her eyes.

Reacher kept on walking south. To the end of the driveway, over the bridge, east on the road, away from the farm, his flashlight on all the way. In case he was being watched. He figured he needed to let them see him go. Because the human mind loves continuity. To see a small spectral night-vision figure strolling south, and south, and then east, and east, and east sets up an irresistible temptation to believe that it's going to go east forever. *It's gone*, you say. *It's out of here.* And then you forget all about it, because you know where it's going, and you don't see it coming back because you're not watching it any more.

He walked east for two hundred yards and clicked off the Maglite beam. Then he walked east for another two hundred yards in the dark. Then he stopped. Turned ninety degrees and hiked north across the shoulder and slid down the boundary ditch's nearside slope. Floundered through the thick black mud in the bottom and clawed his way up the far side with his rifle held one-handed high in the air. Then he ran, fast, straight north, stretching his stride long to hit the top of every ploughed furrow.

Two minutes later he was a quarter-mile in, level with the cluster of barns, three hundred yards behind them to the east, and out of breath. He paused in the lee of a stand of trees to recover. Thumbed his fire selector to single shots.

Then he put the stock against his shoulder and walked forward. West. Towards the barns.

Reacher, alone in the dark. Armed and dangerous. Coming back.

Edward Lane was still face to face with Kate. He said, 'I'm assuming you've been sleeping with him for years.'

Kate said nothing.

Lane said, 'I hope you've been using condoms. You could catch a disease from a guy like that.'

Then he smiled. A new thought. A joke, to him.

'Or you could get pregnant,' he said.

Something in her terrified eyes.

He paused.

'What?' he said. 'What are you telling me?'

She shook her head.

'You're pregnant,' he said. 'You're pregnant, aren't you? You *are*. I know it. You look different. I can tell.'

He put the flat of his hand on her belly. She pulled away, backward, hard against the pole she was tied to. He shuffled forward half a step. 'Oh, man, this is unbelievable. You're going to die with another man's child inside you.'

Then he spun away. Stopped, and turned back. Shook his head.

'Can't allow that,' he said. 'Wouldn't be right. We'll have to abort it first. I should have told Perez to find a coat hanger. But I didn't. So we'll find something else instead. There's got to be something here. This is a farm, after all.'

Kate closed her eyes.

'You're going to die anyway,' Lane said, like the most reasonable man in the world.

Reacher knew they were in a barn. They had to be. That was clear. Where else could they hide their truck? He knew there were five barns in total. He had seen them in the daylight, vaguely, in the distance. Three stood around a beaten earth yard, and two stood alone. All of them had vehicle ruts heading for big doors. Storage, he had guessed, for the backhoe, and tractors, and trailers, and balers, and all kinds of other farm machinery. Now in the dark the dirt under his feet felt dry and dusty, hard and stony. It wouldn't show tyre marks. No point in risking a flash of the Maglite beam.

So which barn?

He started with the nearest, hoping to get lucky. But he didn't get lucky. The nearest barn was one of the two that stood alone. It was a wide wooden structure made of weathered boards. The whole thing had been blown slightly off kilter by two hundred years of relentless winds. It leaned to the west, beaten down. Reacher put his ear on a crack between two boards and listened hard. Heard nothing inside. He put his eye on the crack and saw nothing. Just darkness. There was a smell of cold air and damp earth and decayed sacking.

He moved on fifty yards to the second barn, hoping to get lucky. But he didn't get lucky. The second barn was just as dark and quiet as the first. Musty and cold, nothing moving inside. A sharp nitrogen smell. Old fertilizer. He moved on through the blackness, slow and stealthy, towards the three barns grouped around the yard. They were a hundred yards away. He got a quarter of the way there.

Then he stopped dead.

Because in the corner of his eye he saw light to his left and behind him. Light and movement, in the house. The kitchen window. A flashlight beam, in the room. Fast shadows jumping and leaping across the inside of the glass.

Lane turned to Gregory and said, 'Find some baling wire.'

'Before we do the kid?' Gregory asked.

'Why not? It can be like a preview for her. She's going to get the same thing anyway as soon as Perez gets back with the potato peeler. I told her mother years ago what would happen if she cheated on me. And I always try to keep my word.'

'A man ought to,' Gregory said.

'We need an operating table,' Lane said. 'Find something flat. And turn the truck's lights on. I need to be able to see what I'm doing.'

'You're sick,' Jackson said. 'You need help.'

'Help?' Lane said. 'No, I'm pretty sure not. It was always a one-person procedure, as I understand. Old women, usually, in back alleys, I believe.'

Reacher moved fast and quiet to the back door of the house. Pressed himself tight against the wall on the far side. Waited. He could feel the rough stones against his back. He could hear a voice through the door. Very faintly, one side of a two-way conversation. A slight Hispanic accent. Perez, on the phone. Reacher reversed his rifle in his hands. Gripped the forestock in front of the carrying handle and took a practice swing.

Then he waited. Alone in the dark.

Gregory found an old door, rustic, made from lapped boards and Z-braced on the back. He pulled it out from a stack of discarded lumber and stood it upright.

'That's perfect,' Lane called to him.

Perez stepped out into the night and turned to close the door behind him and Reacher swung, arms extended, hips twisting, driving forward off the back foot, wrists snapping. No good. Late. A foul ball for sure, left field, upper deck, off the façade, maybe out into the street. But Perez's head was not a baseball. And the G36 was not a bat. It was an eight-pound yard of steel. The sight block caught Perez in the temple and punched a shard of bone sideways through his left eye socket and on through the bridge of his nose and halfway through his right eye socket. Then it stopped when the top edge of the stock crushed his ear flat against the side of his skull. So, not a perfect swing. A millisecond earlier and two inches farther back a blow like that would have taken the top of the guy's head off like opening a soft-boiled egg. Late as it was, it just ploughed a deep messy lateral trench between his cheeks and his forehead.

Messy, but effective. Perez was dead long

before he hit the ground. He was too small to go down like a tree. He just melted into the beaten earth like he was a part of it.

Lane turned to Addison and said, 'Go find out what the hell Perez is up to. He should have been back by now. I'm getting bored. Nobody's bleeding yet.'

'I'm bleeding,' Jackson said.

'You don't count.'

'Taylor's bleeding. Perez shot him.'

'Wrong,' Lane said. 'Taylor's stopped bleeding. For the moment.'

'Reacher's out there,' Jackson said.

'I don't think so.'

Jackson nodded. 'He is. That's why Perez isn't back. Reacher got him.'

Lane smiled. 'So what should I do? Go out and search? With my two men? Leaving you people all alone in here to organize a pathetic escape attempt behind my back? Is that what you're trying to achieve? Not going to happen. Because right about now Reacher is walking past the Bishops Pargeter church. Or are you just trying to give your comrades a little hope in their hour of need? Is this British pluck? The famous stiff upper lip?'

Jackson said, 'He's out there. I know it.'

He was crouching outside the kitchen door, sorting through all the things that Perez had dropped. An MP5K with a thirty-round magazine and a ballistic nylon shoulder sling. A flashlight, now broken. Two black-handled kitchen knives, one long, one short, one serrated, one plain. A souvenir corkscrew from a car ferry operator.

And a potato peeler.

Its handle was a plain wooden peg. Once red, now faded. Tightly bound to it with thick wrapped string was a simple pressed-metal blade. Slightly pointed, with a raised flange and a slot. An old-fashioned design. Plain, utilitarian, well used.

Reacher stared at it for a moment. Then he put it in his pocket. He buried the longer knife to its hilt in Perez's chest. Tucked the shorter knife in his own shoe. Kicked the corkscrew and the broken flashlight into the shadows. Used his thumb to clean Perez's blood and frontal lobe off the G36's monocular lens. Picked up the MP5 sub-machine gun and slung it over his left shoulder.

Then he headed back north and east towards the barns.

Reacher, alone in the dark. Doing it the hard way.

SEVENTY-FIVE

Reacher stepped into the beaten earth yard. It was a little more than a hundred feet square, with barns barely visible in the dark on the north side, and the east, and the south. All three barns looked to be pretty much identical. Same vintage, same construction, same materials. They had tall sliding doors and tile roofs and wood wall planks, dull grey in the starlight. They were newer than the stand-alone barns, and much stronger. Straight and square and solid. Which was good news if you were Jackson the farmer, Reacher guessed. But bad news for him. No warped boards, no gaps, no cracks, no knot holes.

No immediate way of telling which one was currently occupied.

He stood still. North or east, he guessed. Easier for the truck. Either a straight path in, or a simple ninety degree right hook. Not the south, he thought. It would have needed a one-eighty U-turn to reach the doors, and it had its back to the house and the driveway anyway. Not a comfortable feeling. Psychologically the possibility of a direct line of sight out the door was important. Even in the pitch dark.

He crossed the yard, slow and silent. His ruined shoes helped. The thick layer of mud on the soles kept them quiet. Like sneakers. Like walking on carpet. He made it to the near left-hand corner of the north barn and disappeared into the blackness alongside it. Circled it, clockwise. Felt the walls. Tapped them, gently. Stout boards, maybe oak, maybe an inch thick. Nailed to a frame that might have been built from foot-thick timbers itself. Like an old sailing ship. Maybe there was an inner skin of inch-thick boards. He had lived in worse places.

He came all the way around to the right-hand front corner and paused. There was no way in except for the main front doors. They were made from four-inch timbers banded together with galvanized steel straps and hung from sliders at the top. U-shaped channels were bolted to the barn's structure, and wheels the size of the Mini Cooper's were bolted to the doors. More U-shaped channels were set in concrete at the bottom, with smaller wheels in them. Practically industrial. The doors would slide apart like theatre curtains. They would open maybe forty feet. Enough to get combine harvesters in and out, he guessed.

He crept along the front wall and put his ear on the space between the door and the wall. Heard nothing. Saw no chink of light.

Wrong one, he thought.

He turned and glanced east. *Has to be*, he thought. He set off towards it. Diagonally across the square. He was twenty feet from it when the door rolled back. The door was noisy. The wheels rumbled in their tracks. A yard-wide bar of bright blue light spilled out. Xenon beams. The Toyota SUV, parked inside, its headlights on. Addison stepped out through the bar of light. His MP5 was slung over his shoulder. He cast a monstrous moving shadow westward. He turned to roll the door shut again. Both hands, bent back, big effort. He got it to within six inches of closed and left it like that. Still open a crack. The bar of blue light narrowed to a thin blade. Addison clicked on a flashlight and as he turned forward its beam swung lazily across Reacher's face. But Addison's gaze must have lagged it by a second. Because he didn't react. He just turned half left and set off towards the house.

Reacher thought: *Decision?*

No-brainer. Take them out one at a time, and thanks for the opportunity.

He took a deep breath and stepped through the blade of light and fell in behind Addison, twenty feet back, fast and silent. Then he was fifteen feet back. Then ten. Addison knew nothing about it. He was just walking straight ahead, oblivious, the flashlight beam swinging gently in front of him.

Five feet back.

Three feet back.

Then the two figures merged in the dark. They slowed and they stopped. The flashlight hit the dirt. It rolled slowly to a halt and its yellow beam cast long grotesque shadows and made jagged boulders out of small golden stones. Addison stumbled and went down, first to his knees, then on his face, his throat ripped clean out by the knife from Reacher's shoe.

Reacher was on his way even before Addison had stopped twitching. With an automatic rifle, two sub-machine guns, and a knife. But he didn't head back to the barns. He walked on down to the house instead. Made his first port of call upstairs in the master bedroom. Then he stopped in the kitchen, at the hearth, and at the desk. Then he came back out and stepped over Perez's corpse and a little later over Addison's. *They're not necessarily better fighters than people currently enlisted*, Patti Joseph had said, days ago. *Often they're worse.* Then Taylor had said: *They used to be outstanding, and now they're well on the way to average.* You all got that right, Reacher thought.

He walked onward, north and east, towards the barns.

He stopped beside the eastern barn and considered his ordnance. Rejected the G36. It fired only single rounds or triples, and it fired the triples too slowly. Too much like the sound of a regular machine gun on the TV or in the movies. Too recognizable, in the dead of night. And it was possible that the barrel was bent. Nothing that he would be able to see with the naked eye, but he had hit Perez hard enough to do some microscopic damage. So he laid the G36 on the ground at the base of the barn's side wall and dropped the magazine out of Perez's MP5. Nine rounds left. Twenty-one expended. Seven triples fired. Perez had been the designated trigger man. Which meant that Addison's magazine should still be full. Which it was. Thirty rounds. The fat 9mm brass winked faintly in the starlight. He put Addison's magazine in Perez's gun. A magazine he knew to be full, in a gun he knew to be working. A sensible step for a man who planned to live through the next five minutes.

He piled Addison's gun and Perez's magazine on top of the discarded G36. Rolled his shoulders and eased his neck. Breathed in, breathed out.

Showtime.

He sat on the ground with his back against the partly open door. Assembled the things he had brought from the house. A kindling stick, from the basket on the hearth. Three rubber bands, from a jar on the desk. A tortoiseshell hand mirror, from Susan Jackson's vanity table.

The stick was a straight seventeen-inch length of an ash bough, as thick as a child's wrist, cut to fit the kitchen grate. The rubber bands were strong but short. The kind of thing the postman puts around bundles of letters. The hand mirror was probably an antique. It was round, with a handle, a little like a table tennis bat.

He fixed the tortoiseshell handle to the ash bough with the rubber bands. Then he lay down flat on his front and inched the bough forward. Towards the six-inch gap where the barn door stood open. Left-handed. He tilted the stick and turned it and manipulated it until he could see a perfect reflection of the view inside.

Reacher, with a mirror on a stick.

SEVENTY-SIX

The mirror showed that the barn was strong and square because it had vertical poles inside that held up the roof ridge and reinforced the timber peg rafters. The poles were foot-square baulks of lumber anchored in concrete. There were twelve in total. Five of them had people tied to them. From left to right in the mirror Reacher could see Taylor, then Jackson, then Pauling, then Kate, then Jade. Their arms were pulled behind them and their wrists were tied behind the poles. Their ankles were tied together. They had duct tape across their mouths. All except Jackson. He had no tape. But his mouth was a bloody mess. He had deep cuts above both eyebrows. He wasn't standing. He had slumped down into a semi-conscious crouch at the base of his pole.

It was Taylor who had been wounded. His shirt was torn and soaked with blood, upper right arm. Pauling looked OK. Eyes a little wild above the slash of silver tape, hair all over the place, but she was functioning. Kate was as white as a sheet and her eyes were closed. Jade had slid down her pole and was sitting on her heels, head down, motionless. Maybe she had fainted.

The Toyota had been backed in and turned so that it was hard up against the end wall on the left. Its headlights were turned full on, high beam, shining down the long axis of the building, casting twelve harsh shadows from the poles.

Gregory had his MP5 slung across his back and was wrestling with some kind of a large flat panel. An old door, maybe. Or a table top. He was walking it across the floor of the barn, left bottom corner, right bottom corner, gripping it with both hands.

Lane was standing completely still in the middle of the floor, his right fist around his MP5's pistol grip and his left fist around the fore grip. His finger was on the trigger and all ten of his knuckles were showing bone white. He was facing the door, sideways on to the Toyota. Its xenon headlight beams lit up his face in bizarre relief. His eye sockets were like black holes. *Borderline mentally ill*, people had said. *Crossed that border long ago*, Reacher thought.

Gregory got the big flat panel front and centre and Reacher heard him say, 'Where do you want this?'

Lane answered, 'We need sawhorses.' Reacher moved the mirror and followed Lane's reflection over to where Jackson was squatting. Lane kicked Jackson in the ribs and asked him, 'Do you have sawhorses here?' and Jackson said, 'In the other barn,' and Lane said, 'I'll send

Perez and Addison for them when they get back.'

They're not coming back, Reacher thought.

'They're not coming back,' Jackson said. 'Reacher's out there and he's got them.'

'You're annoying me,' Lane said. But Reacher saw him glance towards the door anyway. And he saw what Jackson was trying to do. He was trying to focus Lane's attention outside the barn. Away from the prisoners. He was trying to buy time.

Smart guy, Reacher thought.

Then he saw Lane's reflection grow large in the mirror. He pulled the ash bough back, slowly and carefully. Aimed his MP5 at a spot an inch outside the door and five feet four inches above the ground. *Put your head out*, he thought. *Take a look. Please. I'll put three bullets in one ear and out the other.*

But no such luck. Reacher heard Lane stop just inside the door and scream, 'Reacher? You out there?'

Reacher waited.

Lane called, 'Perez? Addison?'

Reacher waited.

Lane screamed, 'Reacher? You there? Listen up. Ten seconds from now, I'm going to shoot Jackson. In the thighs. He'll bleed out through his femoral arteries. Then I'll make Lauren Pauling lick it up like a dog.'

Reacher waited.

'Ten,' Lane screamed. 'Nine. Eight.' His voice faded as he stalked back to the centre of the barn. Reacher slid the mirror back into place.

504

Saw Lane stop near Jackson and heard him say, 'He isn't out there. Or if he is, he doesn't give a shit about you.' Then Lane turned again and yelled, 'Seven. Six. Five.' Gregory was standing mute with the panel held vertical in front of him. Doing nothing.

'Four,' Lane screamed.

A lot can happen in a single second. In Reacher's case he ran thoughts through his head like a card player sorting a hand. He considered taking the risk of sacrificing Jackson. Maybe Lane didn't mean it. If he did, then certainly he was crazy enough to fire full auto and empty his weapon. Gregory was handicapped. Reacher could let Jackson take thirty rounds in the legs and wait until Lane was clicking on empty and then he could step in and put three through the flat board into Gregory's centre mass and three more into Lane's head. One KIA out of five hostages wasn't excessive. Twenty per cent. Reacher had once been given a medal for an outcome worse than that.

'Three,' Lane screamed.

But Reacher liked Jackson, and there were Susan and Melody to consider. Susan, the loyal sister. Melody, the innocent child. And there was Kate Lane's dream to think about, the new extended family farming together, growing hay, leaching the old chemicals out of the Norfolk soil, planting wholesome vegetables five years in the future.

'Two,' Lane screamed.

Reacher dropped the mirror and extended his right arm like a swimmer and hooked his fingers around the edge of the door. Crawled backward, fast, hauling the door with him. Opening it wide, staying out of sight. He dragged it through the full twenty feet of its travel.

Then he waited.

Silence inside the barn. He knew Lane's eyes were on the black void outside. Knew his ears were straining to hear something in the stillness. The oldest of all atavistic human fears, buried deep in the primeval lizard brain, still alive a hundred thousand years after leaving the caves: *There's something out there.*

Reacher heard a flat cushioned thump as Gregory dropped the panel. Then it was a foot race. From Lane's perspective the door had opened right to left, driven by some unseen agency. Therefore that agency was now outside and to the left, at the end of the door's long travel. Reacher stood up and stepped backward and turned and ran, counterclockwise around the barn. Around the first corner and fifty feet along the south side. Then the next corner, and a hundred feet along the back wall. Then fifty feet along the north wall. He took it slower than maximum speed. Three hundred feet, a hundred yards, four turns, in about thirty seconds. An Olympic athlete would have done it in ten, but an Olympic athlete didn't need to be composed enough at the finish line to fire a sub-machine gun accurately.

He took the last corner. Came back down the front wall to the doorway, mouth shut, breathing hard through his nose, controlling the heaving in his chest.

Now he was outside and to the right.

Silence inside the barn. No movement. Reacher planted his feet and leaned his left shoulder on the wall, his elbow tucked in, his wrist turned, his hand on the MP5's front grip, lightly, gently. His right hand was on the pistol grip and his right index finger had already moved the trigger through its first eighth-inch of slack. His left eye was closed and his right eye had lined up both iron sights. He waited. Heard a soft footfall on the barn's concrete floor, four feet in front of him and three feet to his left. Saw a shadow in the spill of light. He waited. Saw the back of Lane's head, just a narrow arc like a crescent moon, craning out, peering left into the darkness. Saw his right shoulder. Saw his MP5's nylon strap biting deep into the bunched canvas fabric of his jacket. Reacher didn't move his gun. He wanted to fire parallel with the barn, not into it. Moving his gun would put hostages in the line of fire. Taylor specifically, from what he recalled from the tortoiseshell mirror. Maybe Jackson, too. He had to be patient. He had to let Lane come to him.

Lane came to him. He inched out, back-to, craning left, leaning forward from the waist, looking away. He moved his front foot. Inched out a little more. Reacher ignored him. Concentrated exclusively on the MP5's sights. They were dotted with tritium and implied a geometry as real to Reacher as a laser beam piercing the night. Lane inched into it. First, the right-hand edge of his skull. Then a larger sliver. Then more. Then more. Then the front sight was on the bony ridge

507

at the back of his head. Dead-on centred. Lane was so close that Reacher could count every hair in his buzz cut.

For half a second he thought about calling Lane's name. Making him turn around, hands raised. Telling him why he was about to die. Listing his many transgressions. Like the equivalent of a legal process.

Then he thought about a fight. Man to man. With knives, or fists. Closure. Something ceremonial. Maybe something fairer.

Then he thought about Hobart, and he pulled the trigger.

A strange blurred purr, like a sewing machine or a distant motorcycle at a light. A fifth of a second, three nine millimetre bullets, three ejected shell cases spitting out and arcing through the spill of bright light and jangling on the stones twenty feet to Reacher's right. Lane's head blew up in a mist cloud that was turned blue by the light. It flopped backward and followed the rest of his body straight down. The empty thump of flesh and bone hitting concrete was clearly audible, muffled only by cotton and canvas clothing.

I hope Jade didn't see that, Reacher thought.

Then he stepped into the doorway. Gregory was halfway through a fatal split second of hesitation. He had backed up and he was looking left, but the shots that had killed Lane had come from the right. It didn't compute. His brain was locked.

'Shoot him,' Jackson said.

Reacher didn't move.

'Shoot him,' Jackson said again. 'Don't make me tell you what that table was for.'

Reacher risked a glance at Taylor. Taylor nodded. Reacher glanced at Pauling. She nodded too. So Reacher put three in the centre of Gregory's chest.

SEVENTY-SEVEN

Clean-up took the rest of the night and most of the next day. Even though they were all bone-weary, by common consensus they didn't try to sleep. Except for Jade. Kate put her to bed and sat with her while she slept. The child had fainted early and had missed most of what had gone on and seemed not to have understood the rest. Except for the fact that her ex-stepfather had been cast as a bad man. But she had been told that already and so it came as nothing more than confirmation of a view she was already comfortable with. So she slept, with no apparent ill-effects. Reacher figured that if any arrived in the days to come she would work them out with crayons on butcher paper.

Kate herself looked like she had been to hell and back. And like many people she was thriving on it. Going down there had felt really bad, and therefore coming back up again felt dispro-portionately better than really good. She had stared down at Lane's body for a long moment. Seen that half his head was missing. Understood for sure that there was going to be no Hollywood moment where he reared up again, back to life. He was gone, utterly, completely, and definitively. And she had seen it happen. That kind of certainty helps a person. She walked away from the corpse with a spring in her step.

Taylor's right tricep was all torn up. Reacher cut his shirt away with the kitchen knife from his shoe and field-dressed the wound as best he could with a first-aid kit in the upstairs bathroom. But Taylor was going to need attention. That was clear. He volunteered to delay it by a couple of days. The wound was not necessarily recognizable as a gunshot and it was unlikely anyone in the neighbourhood had heard anything, but it seemed smart to distance an A&E visit from mayhem in the night.

Jackson was OK apart from cut eyebrows and some facial bruising and a split lip and a couple of loose teeth. Nothing worse than he had experienced half a dozen times before, he said, after bar fights wherever First Para had been posted and where the local boys always seemed to have something to prove.

Pauling was fine. Reacher had cut her ropes and she had torn the tape off her mouth herself and then kissed him hard. She seemed to have had total confidence that he would show up and work something out. He wasn't sure if she was telling the truth or flattering him. Either way he didn't mention exactly how close he had come to walking away on a phantom pursuit. Didn't mention how lucky it was that a stray peripheral glance at the driveway's surface had fired some random synapse in his brain.

He searched the Toyota and found Lane's leather duffel. The one he had seen before, in the Park Lane Hilton. The eight hundred thousand dollars. It was all there. Untouched. He gave it to Pauling for safe keeping. Then he sat on the floor, leaning back on the post that Kate had been tied to, six feet away from Gregory's corpse. He was calm. Just another night of business as usual in his long and spectacularly violent life. He was used to it, literally. And the remorse gene was missing from his DNA. Entirely. It just wasn't there. Where some men might have retrospectively agonized over justification, he spent his energy figuring out where best to hide the bodies.

They hid them in a ten-acre field near the northwest corner of the farm. Fallow land, hidden by trees, unploughed for a year. Jackson finished fixing the backhoe and then fired it up and drove off with headlights blazing. Started work immediately on a massive pit that needed to be thirty feet long, nine feet wide, and nine feet deep. A ninety-yard excavation, because they had decided to bury the cars as well.

Reacher asked Pauling, 'Did you tick the box for extra insurance?'

She nodded.

He said, 'Call them tomorrow. Tell them it was stolen.'

Taylor was walking wounded so he was excused from heavy work. Instead he scoured the whole area for every piece of physical evidence he could find. He came up with all that anyone could think of, including all twenty-seven shell casings from

Perez's MP5. Pauling scrubbed his blood off the upstairs hallway floor and replaced the shattered bathroom tile. Reacher piled the bodies inside the Toyota Land Cruiser.

The sun had been up for hours before the pit was finished. Jackson had left a neat graded slope at one end and Reacher drove the Toyota down it and smashed it hard against the earth wall at the other end. Jackson drove the backhoe to the house and used the front bucket to jack the Mini up and shove it backward. He manoeuvred it all the way to the pit and rolled it down the grade and jammed it hard against the Toyota's rear bumper. Taylor showed up with all the other items and threw them in the hole. Then Jackson started to fill it. Reacher just sat and watched. The sky was pale blue and the sun was watery. There were thin high clouds and a mild breeze that felt warm. He knew that in the flat land all around him Stone Age people had been buried in long mounds called barrows, and then Bronze Age people, and Iron Age people, and Celts, and Romans, and Saxons, and Angles, and Viking invaders in longships, and Normans, and then the English themselves for a thousand years. He guessed the land could take four more dead. He watched Jackson work until the dirt hid the top of the cars, and then he walked away, slowly, back to the house.

Exactly twelve months later to the hour the ten-acre field was neatly ploughed and dusted pale green with a brand new winter crop. Tony and

Susan Jackson and Graham and Kate Taylor were working the field next to it. The sun was shining. Back at the house the nine-year-old cousins and best friends Melody Jackson and Jade Taylor were watching Jade's baby brother, a healthy five-month-old boy named Jack.

Three thousand miles west of Grange Farm it was five hours earlier and Lauren Pauling was alone in her Barrow Street apartment, drinking coffee and reading the *New York Times*. She had missed a piece inside the main section that reported the deaths of three newly arrived private military contractors in Iraq. Their names were Burke, Groom and Kowalski, and they had died two days previously when a land mine exploded under their vehicle outside Baghdad. But she caught a piece in the Metro section in which it was reported that the co-operative board at the Dakota Building had foreclosed on an apartment after twelve consecutive months of unpaid monthly maintenance. On entering the apartment they had found more than nine million dollars in a locked closet.

Six thousand miles west of Grange Farm it was eight hours earlier and Patti Joseph was fast asleep in a waterfront condominium in Seattle, Washington. She was ten months into a new job as a magazine copyeditor. Her perseverance and her relentless eye for detail made her good at it. She was seeing a local journalist from time to time. She was happy.

Far from Seattle, far from New York City, far from Bishops Pargeter, down in Birmingham, Alabama, Dee Marie Graziano was up early, in a hospital gymnasium, watching her brother grasp his new metal canes and walk across the floor.

Nobody knew where Jack Reacher was. He had left Grange Farm two hours after the backhoe had shut down, and there had been no news of him since.

THE END

ONE

The man was called Calvin Franz and the helicopter was a Bell 222. Franz had two broken legs, so he had to be loaded on board strapped to a stretcher. Not a difficult manoeuvre. The Bell was a roomy aircraft, twin-engined, designed for corporate travel and police departments, with space for seven passengers. The rear doors were as big as a panel van's and they opened wide. The middle row of seats had been removed. There was plenty of room for Franz on the floor.

The helicopter was idling. Two men were carrying the stretcher. They ducked low under the rotor wash and hurried, one backward, one forward. When they reached the open door the guy who had been walking backward got one handle up on the sill and ducked away. The other guy stepped forward and shoved hard and slid the stretcher all the way inside. Franz was awake and hurting. He cried out and jerked around a little, but not much, because the straps across his chest and thighs were buckled tight. The two men climbed in after him and got in their seats behind the missing row and slammed the doors.

Then they waited.

The pilot waited.

A third man came out a grey door and walked across the concrete. He bent low under the rotor and held a hand flat on his chest to stop his necktie whipping in the wind. The gesture made him look like a guilty man proclaiming his innocence. He tracked around the Bell's long nose and got in the forward seat, next to the pilot.

'Go,' he said, and then he bent his head to concentrate on his harness buckle.

The pilot goosed the turbines and the lazy *whop-whop* of the idling blade slid up the scale to an urgent centripetal *whip-whip-whip* and then disappeared behind the treble blast of the exhaust. The Bell lifted straight off the ground, drifted left a little, rotated slightly, and then retracted its wheels and climbed a thousand feet. Then it dipped its nose and hammered north, high and fast. Below it roads and science parks and small factories and neat isolated suburban communities slid past. Brick walls and metal siding blazed red in the late sun. Tiny emerald lawns and turquoise swimming pools winked in the last of the light.

The man in the forward seat said, 'You know where we're going?'

The pilot nodded and said nothing.

The Bell clattered onward, turning east of north, climbing a little higher, heading for darkness. It crossed a highway far below, a river of white lights crawling west and red lights crawling east. A minute north of the highway the last developed acres gave way to low hills, barren and scrubby and uninhabited. They glowed orange on the slopes that faced the setting sun and showed dull tan in the valleys and the shadows. Then the low hills gave way in turn to small rounded mountains. The Bell sped on, rising and falling, following the contours below. The man in the forward seat twisted around and looked down at Franz on the floor behind him. Smiled briefly and said, 'Twenty more minutes, maybe.'

Franz didn't reply. He was in too much pain.

The Bell was rated for a 161-mph cruise, so twenty more minutes took it almost fifty-four miles, beyond the mountains, well out over the empty desert. The pilot flared the nose and slowed a little. The man in the forward seat pressed his forehead against the window and stared down into the darkness.

'Where are we?' he asked.

The pilot said, 'Where we were before.'

'Exactly?'

'Roughly.'

'What's below us now?'

'Sand.'

'Height?'

'Three thousand feet.'

'What's the air like up here?'

'Still. A few thermals, but no wind.'

'Safe?'

'Aeronautically.'

'So let's do it.'

The pilot slowed more and turned and came to a stationary hover, three thousand feet above the desert floor. The man in the forward seat twisted around again and signalled to the two guys way in back. Both unlocked their safety harnesses. One crouched forward, avoiding Franz's feet, and held his loose harness tight in one hand and unlatched the door with the other. The pilot was half turned in his own seat, watching, and he tilted the Bell a little so the door fell all the way open under its own weight. Then he brought the craft level again and put it into a slow clockwise rotation so that motion and air pressure held the door wide. The second guy from the rear crouched near Franz's head and jacked the stretcher upward to a forty-five-degree slope. The first guy jammed his shoe against the free end of the stretcher rail to stop the whole thing sliding across the floor. The second guy jerked like a weightlifter and brought the stretcher almost vertical. Franz sagged down against the straps. He was a big guy, and heavy. And determined. His legs were useless but his upper body was powerful and straining hard. His head was snapping from side to side.

The first guy took out a gravity knife and popped the blade. Used it to saw through the strap around Franz's thighs. Then he paused a beat and sliced the strap around Franz's chest. One quick motion. At the exact same time the second guy jerked the stretcher fully upright. Franz took an involuntary step forward.

522

Onto his broken right leg. He screamed once, briefly, and then took a second instinctive step. Onto his broken left leg. His arms flailed and he collapsed forward and his upper body momentum levered him over the locked pivot of his immobile hips and took him straight out through the open door, into the noisy darkness, into the gale-force rotor wash, into the night.

Three thousand feet above the desert floor.

For a moment there was silence. Even the engine noise seemed to fade. Then the pilot reversed the Bell's rotation and rocked the other way and the door slammed neatly shut. The turbines spun up again and the rotor bit the air and the nose dropped.

The two guys clambered back to their seats.

The man in front said, 'Let's go home now.'

ECHO BURNING
BY LEE CHILD

Jack Reacher – six fool five and dangerous. Adrift in the hellish heat of Texas. Moving like a shark in the water. Looking for a lift through the vast empty landscape.

A Cadillac stops. A ride, but with a hitch. A pretty young woman, alone. Her husband's in jail. When he comes out, he's going to kill her.

Her family's hostile, she can't trust the cops, and lawyers won't help. Reacher is her last option. Will this be the first time he says no - to a lady in distress?

0553 813307 • 9780553813302

WITHOUT FAIL
BY LEE CHILD

Jack Reacher walks alone. No job, no ID, no last known address. Doesn't want to be found. But he never turns down a plea for help. Especially from a woman.

Now a woman tracks him down. A woman serving at the very heart of US power. A woman who needs Reacher's native cunning, surly charm and controlled aggression to help her with her new job.

Her job? Putting herself in the line of fire. Protecting the Vice-President of the United States. Her problem? Someone wants the VP dead.

0553 813439 • 9780553813432

PERSUADER
BY LEE CHILD

Never forgive, never forget. That's Jack Reacher's standard operating procedure. And Quinn was the worst guy he had ever met. Truly unforgivable. So Reacher was glad to know he was dead. Until the day he saw him again in Boston. Alive and well.

Never apologize. Never explain. When Reacher witnesses a brutal kidnap attempt, he takes the law into his own hands. But a cop dies. Has Reacher lost his sense of right and wrong? Just because this time, it's personal?

0553 813447 • 9780553813449

THE ENEMY
BY LEE CHILD

New Year's Day, 1990. The Berlin Wall is coming down. The Cold War is ending. Soon, America won't have any enemies left. A soldier is found dead in a sleazy motel bed. Jack Reacher is the officer on duty. The soldier turns out to be a two-star general. Then Reacher finds another corpse: The general's wife.

Lee Child's stomach-churning thriller turns back the clock. We meet a younger Reacher, in dogtags, far from the no-ties, no-last-known-address drifter of the other novels. A Reacher who imposes army discipline. Even if only in his own pragmatic way.

0553 815857 • 9780553815856

TRIPWIRE
BY LEE CHILD

Digging swimming pools by hand in Key West, Florida, Jack Reacher is as tanned and as fit as he's ever been. A local girl says he looks like a condom filled with walnuts. Being invisible has become a habit. He doesn't want to be found.

So when a private detective comes nosing around and asking questions, Reacher is not pleased. Especially when he later finds the guy dead. With his fingertips sliced off. Why was he so determined to find him? What does the vicious Wall Street honcho Hook Hobie have to do with it? And what about the reappearance of a woman from Reacher's own troubled past?

0553 811851 • 9780553811858

THE VISITOR
BY LEE CHILD

Sergeant Amy Callan and Lieutenant Caroline Cook have a lot in common. Both were army high-flyers. Both were acquainted with Jack Reacher. Both were forced to resign from the service.

Now they're both dead.

Both were found in their own home, naked, in a bath full of paint. Both apparent victims of an army man. A loner, a smart guy with a score to settle, a ruthless vigilante.

A man just like Jack Reacher.

0553 811886 • 9780553811889

ONE SHOT

BY LEE CHILD

Six shots. Five dead. One heartland city thrown into terror. But within hours the cops have it solved. A slam-dunk case. Except for one thing. The accused man claims: You got the wrong guy. After that, all he'll say is: Get Reacher for me.

Jack Reacher lives off the grid. Lone righter of wrongs, irresistible to women. What could connect the ex-military cop to this obvious psychopath?

0553 815865 • 9780553815863

BAD LUCK AND TROUBLE

BY LEE CHILD

September 11th changed Reacher's drifter lifestyle in one practical way. As well as his folding toothbrush, he now carries photo ID. Yet he is still as close to untraceable as a human being in America can get. So when a member of his old Army unit finds a way to get a message to him, he knows it must be deadly serious: *I want you to put the old unit back together*.

You *do not mess* with the Special Investigators. They always watched each other's backs. Now one of them has shown up dead in the California desert. And six others can't be found at all.

You *do not mess* with Jack Reacher. His old buddies are in big trouble, and he won't let that go. Not now, not ever.

9780593057018